SCOTTISH KISS

Kenneth gently grasped Isbel by the shoulders and pulled her close, smiling faintly when he felt her trembling beneath his hands. "Isbel, did ye truly come to find your cat?"

"Do you really wish to hear the truth?" she asked in a soft, unsteady voice.

"Aye, I have always favored the truth," he murmured and touched a kiss to her forehead.

"Nay, I didnae come to find the cat."

"What did ye come to find?" He cupped her face between his hands and brushed a kiss over her faintly parted lips.

"Another kiss," she whispered.

"Isbel, my sweet child of the faeries, if I kiss you, 'twill nae end there."

"I am nay an innocent. I ken what the kiss could lead to."

"There will be no *could* about it. It will lead to a bedding. Ye pulled away from the first kiss we shared and I let you. I cannae promise I will let ye free this time. Not unless ye put up a verra loud protest."

"I willnae put up a loud one." She curled her arms around his neck. "I dinnae think I will be inclined to even whisper one."

"Before we start to play this game, honor demands that I tell ye a few rules. I cannae promise ye I will stay—" He frowned when she stopped his words by touching her soft fingertips to his lips.

"I ken that there will be no promises made. I ask for none, save for a wee taste of the passion I felt when we kissed . . ."

Books by Hannah Howell

ONLY FOR YOU * MY VALIANT KNIGHT *
UNCONQUERED * WILD ROSES *
A TASTE OF FIRE * HIGHLAND DESTINY *
HIGHLAND HONOR * HIGHLAND PROMISE *
A STOCKINGFUL OF JOY * HIGHLAND VOW *
HIGHLAND KNIGHT * HIGHLAND HEARTS *
HIGHLAND BRIDE * HIGHLAND ANGEL *
HIGHLAND GROOM * HIGHLAND WARRIOR *
RECKLESS * HIGHLAND CONQUEROR *
HIGHLAND CHAMPION * HIGHLAND LOVER *
HIGHLAND VAMPIRE * THE ETERNAL
HIGHLANDER * MY IMMORTAL HIGHLANDER *
CONQUEROR'S KISS * HIGHLAND BARBARIAN *
BEAUTY AND THE BEAST * HIGHLAND SAVAGE *
HIGHLAND THIRST * HIGHLAND WEDDING *
HIGHLAND WOLF * SILVER FLAME *
HIGHLAND FIRE * NATURE OF THE BEAST *
HIGHLAND CAPTIVE * HIGHLAND SINNER *
MY LADY CAPTOR * IF HE'S WICKED *
WILD CONQUEST * IF HE'S SINFUL *
KENTUCKY BRIDE * IF HE'S WILD *
YOURS FOR ETERNITY * COMPROMISED HEARTS *
HIGHLAND PROTECTOR * STOLEN ECSTASY *
IF HE'S DANGEROUS * HIGHLAND HERO *
HIGHLAND HUNGER * HIGHLAND AVENGER *
HIS BONNIE BRIDE * BORN TO BITE

Published by Kensington Publishing Corporation

HANNAH HOWELL

HIGHLAND HERO

ZEBRA BOOKS
KENSINGTON PUBLISHING CORP.
http://www.kensingtonbooks.com

ZEBRA BOOKS are published by

Kensington Publishing Corp.
119 West 40th Street
New York, NY 10018

All Kensington titles, imprints and distributed lines are
available at special quantity discounts for bulk purchases
for sales promotion, premiums, fund-raising, educational
or institutional use.

Special book excerpts or customized printings can also be
created to fit specific needs. For details, write or phone the
office of the Kensington Special Sales Manager: Kensington Publishing Corp., 119 West 40th Street, New York, NY
10018. Attn. Special Sales Department. Phone: 1-800-221-
2647.

Zebra and the Z logo Reg. U.S. Pat. & TM Off.

ISBN-13: 978-1-4201-3021-8
ISBN-10: 1-4201-3021-8

First Printing: July 2011

10 9 8 7 6 5 4 3

Printed in the United States of America

CONTENTS

Edina and the Baby

Chapter 1

Scottish Highlands—Summer, 1420

"Gar? Where are ye, laddie?"

Edina MacAdam cursed as the sharp leaves of a tall thistle found the small, unprotected strip of soft white skin between the top of her knee-high deer-hide boots and the hem of her tucked-up skirts. She looked around the wooded hillside as she idly scratched the irritating small bumps raised by the plant's unwelcoming touch. Her wolfhound had left her side and bounded up the hill, evidently tracking something that had excited him. He had disappeared into the thick growth of trees at the top of the hill and, now, even his barking had stopped.

After checking that her string of rabbits was firmly secured to her sword belt, she took a deep breath and plunged into the shadowed forest. It took several moments to quell the urge to run right back out, her terror of the forest almost blinding, but she had to find her dog. Gar was the only companion she had. Forcing back the dark memories of how her lovely but heartless mother had left her in the dark forest to run off with her lover, Edina concentrated on finding her dog. The day that had bred her fears had occurred fifteen years earlier, when she was barely five. It was time to shake free of such childish terrors. Her heart pounding in her ears and the cold sweat of fear trickling down her back, Edina stepped deeper into the forest.

"Gar! Curse ye for a witless beast! Where are ye?"

A sharp yelp answered her. Edina turned toward the sound. Calling repeatedly to her pet, she followed his sharp answering barks, softly cursing the forest for trying to mislead her with its echoes and the way it concealed the true direction of a sound. When she finally saw Gar sitting beneath a tree, she was torn between the urge to hug the dog in relief and soundly scold him. Then she saw the bundle of rags he sat next to. Even as she cautiously approached, one tiny, pale, dimpled arm appeared and a little hand grabbed a clump of Gar's thick fur in a way Edina knew had to be painful. Gar just glanced at the small hand, then looked at Edina and yelped.

"A bairn," she whispered as she crouched on the other side of the child.

She reached out to touch the cooing child, saw the dirt on her hands, and grimaced. Edina trickled water onto her hands from the goatskin she carried, then rubbed them clean with the skirts of her soft gray gown. After gently detaching the baby's hand from Gar's mottled gray fur, she picked the child up in her arms and found it impossible to silence her dark memories.

As clearly as if it were happening before her eyes, Edina could see her mother riding away with her lover, laughing at her cries. She had stood where she had been left for hours, unable to believe that her mother was not going to return. The sounds of the forest had changed from enchanting to threatening with each passing moment. In her terrified child's eyes the trees had become grotesque, dangerous shapes trapping her, alone, within their shadowed home. Her dour uncle had not found her until the next day and, by then, her fear had deepened until it had scarred her very soul. It did not help her to conquer her fears when every time she looked into a mirror she saw her mother. Edina was not sure how exactly she matched the woman's looks, but she knew she had the same thick, unruly raven hair and the same faintly slanted, clear green eyes. That was more than enough to revive the painful memories. The lack of love and attention she got at her uncle's home ensured that she had nothing with which to soften those harsh memories.

"Did your mother toss ye aside?" she whispered as she undid the child's swaddling and carefully looked him over before covering him back up again, relieved to find no injuries. "At least ye are too young to ken what has happened to you and where ye are. Ye willnae be scarred by the painful memories or the fear. Why do they do this to their bairns, laddie? Mothers arenae supposed to cast aside their bairns likes the bones of a finished meal."

She held him close, carefully stood up, and began to examine the area closely, looking for any sign that might tell her why a child of six months or so had been left to fend for itself in the forest. "Mayhap I blacken your mother's name unfairly," she said as she crouched and frowned down at the clear sign of hoofprints on the moist forest floor. "There may be an even darker reason for ye to be left here to die."

Just as she was trying to figure out how many horses

had been there, she heard a sound that chilled her blood. Someone was riding toward them. She could hear the sound of horses crushing the leaves and undergrowth beneath their hooves. Even as she set the baby down, stood protectively in front of him, and drew her small sword, she heard men's voices. She patted Gar's big head as he stood beside her. She straightened her shoulders and waited, determined that no one would touch the child until she was sure he would be safe—and loved.

Lucais MacRae raised his gaze from the ground where he had been searching for tracks and reined his horse in so sharply, it startled the horses of his two companions into rearing slightly. As his cousins Ian and Andrew struggled to calm their mounts, Lucais studied the vision before him. He had spent three grueling days searching for his nephew, and the last thing he had expected to find was a belligerent little woman and a massive dog standing between him and what he had been seeking.

She was a tiny woman in both stature and height, made to look even tinier by the trees towering all around her. Thick, raven black hair tumbled around her slim shoulders in a wild, silken tangle. Her soft gray gown fitted snugly over full breasts, and her thick hair brushed against a tiny waist. The way her skirts were kilted up revealed slender, well-shaped legs. Her small, heart-shaped face was dominated by wide, heavily lashed eyes of a green so true and rich, he could see the color even from where he stood. He knew that they would be breathtaking up close. It would be easy to dismiss her for some pretty little lass, no more and certainly no threat, except for the small sword in her delicate white hands. She not only held the weapon as if she knew how to use it, but the expression on her pretty face told him that she was fully prepared to do so.

He dropped his gaze to the rag-wrapped child on the ground just behind her small, booted feet. Lucais could not see the baby's face, but the thick chestnut curls spilling out of the top of the wrappings told him that it was his nephew Malcolm. When he looked back at the girl, he felt suspicion and anger push aside his attraction and surprise.

"I have come to take my nephew home, wench," he said, and pointed at the baby.

"And what proof do ye have to tell me that he truly is your blood kin?" she demanded.

Edina fought the urge to take a step back when he glared at her, the strength of his anger frightening her. He was a big man, tall and lean yet strongly built. Thick chestnut hair that gleamed red whenever the sun touched it hung past his broad shoulders. The dark plaid draping his hard body was pinned with a brooch that identified him as a MacRae of Dunmor. The lean lines of his handsome face were taut with emotion. The clenching of his strong jaw, the light flush upon his high, wide cheekbones, and the tight line of his well-shaped mouth clearly identified that emotion as a dangerous fury. She glanced briefly at the way his long-fingered hand gripped the hilt of his sword, found herself a little too interested in the shape of his long legs, and quickly returned her gaze to his face. It was a poor time to find a man disturbingly attractive, she decided, especially since that man looked as if he would like to take her head from her shoulders.

"Look at the bairn's hair," he snapped.

"I have. He has a fine crop of curls, but brown isnae such a rare color that it alone marks him as your kin." Edina was surprised that she could look him in the eye and so sweetly dismiss his rich hair color as common. "Ye cannae expect me to just hand ye a helpless bairn because ye tell me to or because ye both have brown hair."

"And just what concern is it of yours?" he demanded as he dismounted in one graceful move. When he stepped toward her, however, the dog bristled and bared his large teeth in a low, threatening snarl, and Lucais stopped moving. "I might ask ye what ye are doing here, deep in the forest, with only an ugly dog and a bairn."

"That handsome beast is Gar, and I found this wee bairn whilst hunting." She lightly touched the rabbits hanging from her sword belt to strengthen her claim.

"A few rabbits dangling from your belt doesnae mean ye are innocent of any crime. It could just mean that ye paused now and again in the committing of the crime to do a wee bit of hunting."

Edina briefly feared that he knew she was hunting on another clan's lands, then shook that fear aside. He did not know who she was, for she wore no identifying brooch, badge, or plaid, so he could not know that she was poaching. "What crime? I have committed no crime."

"I have searched for my nephew Malcolm for three long days, and, when I finally find him, ye are here standing over him. I would not be amiss in suspecting that ye might have had something to do with his kidnapping."

"Nay? Ye would be an idiot. Ye are MacRaes from Dunmor. That is o'er a day's ride from here. Look about, fool. Do ye see a horse?"

It annoyed Lucais that he could find her low, husky voice attractive when she was so sharply insulting him. "Ye could be the one who was given the bairn after the kidnapping and ye brought him here to this desolate place intending to leave him here to die. Now ye try to keep us from saving him." He took an instinctive step back from the fury that whitened her pale skin and hardened her delicate features.

"I should kill ye for that insult," she hissed, fighting to tame her anger, for she knew she needed a clear head if she was to be an adequate protector for the child. "I would ne'er leave a bairn alone."

"Then why do ye hesitate to return him to the arms of his own kinsmen?"

"I am nae so sure that ye are his kin, and I certainly have no proof that those arms are safe ones."

Edina was beginning to doubt that this man was a threat to the child, but she feared that his handsome face might be influencing her opinion. She could not believe she could be so quickly and fiercely attracted to a man who could hurt a child. That child's life was at stake, however, and she had to be sure. The fact that he and his two companions had made no move to simply take the baby away from her, something she was sure they could do without too much danger of injury to themselves, was in their favor, but even that was not enough.

"Lucais," said the redheaded Andrew, drawing his angry cousin's attention his way. "We go nowhere with this trading of accusations and the day speeds by. Mayhap ye and the lass can come to some agreement so that we can take poor wee Malcolm to a warmer, safer place. We must spend at least one night sleeping upon the ground. If we linger here much longer, that could become two, and that willnae help poor Malcolm."

The wisdom of Andrew's words could not be ignored, and Lucais took a deep breath to calm himself before again looking at the belligerent young woman keeping him from Malcolm. "Can we agree that the child must be kept safe?"

There was still a hint of anger in his deep, rich voice, and that made his attempt to be reasonable all the more admirable in Edina's eyes, so she nodded. "Aye. That is what we both claim to want."

"And the trouble lies in the fact that I dinnae believe you and ye dinnae believe me. Ye dinnae wish to give the child to me and I dinnae wish to give the child to you, a woman I have ne'er met and dinnae even ken the name of."

"I am Edina MacAdam, niece to Ronald MacAdam of Glenfair. And, aye, ye have the right of it."

Lucais gave her a mocking bow. "And I am Lucais MacRae, Laird of Dunmor. So, we are at an impasse."

"Do I have your word that ye willnae kill me if I sheath my sword?"

"Aye. I swear it. Are ye willing to believe in my word?"

She shrugged as she sheathed her sword. "I cannae be certain that I do, but, if ye break your word, I will have the pleasure of kenning that ye will go to hell for giving an empty oath. And your name will be weel blackened, if it hasnae been already."

"Ye watch your tongue, lass," snapped young Ian, his thin face tight with anger. "The name of Lucais MacRae is an honored one. There isnae a mon in all of Scotland who wouldnae be proud to have Lucais stand at his side."

"Thank you, cousin," Lucais murmured to the youth,

who, at barely nineteen years of age, was not as skilled as he was eager to be a knight. He caught Edina rolling her eyes at the boy's effusive praise and was surprised to have to swallow a laugh. "We need an answer to our problem, mistress," he told her. "As my cousin Andrew so wisely indicated, the day wanes and we must be on our way or chance two nights on the road. 'Tis summer, but the weather isnae always this fair and warm. A night caught out in a storm could harm the child."

Keeping a close watch on the three men, Edina picked up little Malcolm. "I can keep the bairn with me until ye have ended the danger he is in."

"Nay. I dinnae ken ye or your people. He is my sister's child. I will protect him."

"Aye, and ye have done such a fine job of it thus far." She ignored his anger and thought for a moment, finally reaching a decision that both satisfied and terrified her. "I willnae leave this bairn until I am sure he is safe and ye willnae let me keep him with me. That leaves but one other answer. I must come with you."

Chapter 2

Edina grimaced and tried to stretch without disturbing the child sleeping at her side. She did not think she had ever slept on harder or colder ground. Just as she was cursing herself for riding off to a strange place with men she did not know, little Malcolm opened his big gray eyes and smiled at her. Edina sighed and knew she would make the same choice no matter how often she was presented with the problem.

As she sat up, trying not to reveal how stiff and sore she was, she looked at the three men crouched around the fire. They were roasting the last of her rabbits, she noticed with a scowl. She also noticed that she felt no fear of them. After riding behind Lucais for several hours, little Malcolm in a sling on her back, she had begun to believe that he spoke the truth. He had been neither friendly nor trusting, but he had not even tried to hurt her or shake free of her. Although he had been lacking in courtesy, he had been gentle each time he had helped her mount or dismount or put Malcolm in his sling and secure it. He had also been kind to the child and to Gar. He had even brought supplies of clothing, clean changing rags, and goat's milk for the boy. Everything indicated that he was a concerned uncle, but Edina was not ready to give Malcolm into his full care yet. Someone had left the child out in the forest to die, there was a real threat to the life of the child, and she could not turn her back on him yet.

After rolling up the bedding Lucais had grudgingly given her, she left Gar to watch over Malcolm as she slipped into the cover of the forest to relieve herself. When she returned she found that Lucais had cleaned and dressed the baby and was preparing to feed him. She stood in front of him, her hands on her hips, and scowled at the tender scene. Her attraction to the man was increasing, rapidly growing too strong to push aside. She wished he did not act so sweet around the child, for it only enhanced his attractiveness, and she did not want to want him. Even if he proved to be a very good man, she could never have him. Not only was she poor and landless, but she had certainly not endeared herself to him by thrusting herself into the midst of his troubles.

"Your dog neither snarls nor bristles," Lucais said as he looked at her. "He trusts me."

"Ye think so?" she drawled. "Try to walk away with the bairn."

She smiled as Lucais picked Malcolm up, stood up, and started to walk away. He had barely taken two steps before he was confronted by a snarling, threatening Gar. After a moment of trying to stare down the dog, he whispered a curse and handed Malcolm to her.

"How did ye get him to do that?" he asked, frowning when Gar immediately relaxed.

"He is a clever dog," she replied, patting Gar on the head. "He will help me keep this bairn safe."

"I can protect my own kin." He cursed when she just looked at him, one delicately arched brow lifted. "My sister Elspeth was unwise," he said even as he wondered why he was bothering to explain anything to her. "She took a lover when she was young and heedless, a mon she could never wed, for he had a wife already. Finally, she turned to a mon who had courted her for a long time and they were married. I ne'er learned what turned her, whether her lover had done something wrong or if she had just grown older and wiser and realized that she did not wish to spend the rest of her days as that mon's leman. She and her young mon Walter were happy and Malcolm was soon born, her lover troubling them only now and again." He shook his head, puzzled and still fighting his raw grief. "Elspeth and Walter were not afraid of her old lover, seeing him as no more than a nuisance, and I soon did the same."

Edina fed Malcolm as she listened to the sad tale, hearing Lucais's pain and struggling against the strong urge to try to comfort him. "But her lover was a danger to her, wasnae he?"

"Aye. I dinna ken what finally changed him from a nuisance to a threat, but 'tis clear that jealousy and rage finally overwhelmed him. He killed Walter and Elspeth and took Malcolm. There must have been a hint of sanity remaining, and he could not put a child to the sword."

"Nay. He just tossed the poor wee bairn into the forest so that he could feed the animals or die on his own slowly." She believed him and, as she settled Malcolm against her shoulder and rubbed his back, she scolded herself for trusting too quickly. "Do ye ken who the mon is?"

"Aye. Simon Kenney, a mon who would be poor and landless save that he made a rich marriage."

"And why havenae ye killed him yet?" Edina was a little surprised at her bloodthirst, but then Malcolm patted her cheek with one damp little hand, and she understood.

"I cannae find the mon," Lucais reluctantly admitted.

"Ye arenae having verra good luck at finding things, are ye?" she drawled. "Mayhap ye should make use of Gar."

Lucais decided to ignore that insult and glanced at her dog. "Where did ye get a name like Gar?"

"From Maida, my uncle's cook. When I brought my wee puppy to the kitchens to show him to her, she said he was so ugly, *he gars me grew*—makes me tremble. So I called him Garsmegrew, but 'tis a mouthful, so it soon became just Gar. He grew into a fine, handsome beast," she said as she patted the dog's head.

There was a distinct gleam of laughter in her beautiful eyes. Lucais was not sure he was pleased to discover that he was right, that her eyes were breathtaking when seen up close. There was a faint slant to their shape, her lashes were long, thick, and as glossy a black as her hair, and the green was the color of ivy.

Afraid he was in danger of revealing his ill-timed attraction to her, he turned his attention to her dog, and nearly smiled. Gar was big, his shaggy coat was a mottled gray, and he was indeed a very ugly dog. When the animal was snarling and baring his impressive teeth, he was threatening enough to make any grown man hesitate. Although the animal was nothing much to look at, he was well trained and a good protector for his mistress. That alone made him a worthy animal. Lucais idly wondered how easy it would be to win the dog's trust. He suspected he could never pull the animal from Edina's side, but he might be able to woo the animal just enough to get him to stop threatening him. He allowed Gar to sniff his hand, then cautiously patted the animal, inwardly pleased with that small sign of progress.

"Ye had best break your fast," he told Edina, ignoring her look of suspicion and the way she pulled her dog a little closer to her side. "There is some rabbit left. We must ride for Dunmor soon."

Edina frowned as he walked away, his two young cousins following him as he strode into the surrounding forest. For a moment she was surprised to be left alone with their horses and goods, then shook her head and went to eat some food. She might not be able to see Lucais and his cousins, but she was certain at least one of them was watching her closely. Instinct told her that Lucais was beginning to trust her, to believe that she sought only to protect the baby, but he did not trust her enough to leave her completely unguarded.

As she struggled to eat and keep Malcolm's little fingers away from the fire, her food, and the wineskin, she tried to plan what she would do when she reached Dunmor. If she could not yet trust Lucais, she certainly could not trust any of his people. That meant that she would have to keep Malcolm with her at all times. She tried not to think about the possibility that Lucais was Malcolm's true enemy, that she was blinded by her own attraction to the man. If Lucais was the enemy, she was riding into the very heart of his camp, and there was little chance that she would be able to save Malcolm.

Edina blinked and shook her head, only faintly aware of Lucais's soft laughter tickling her ear. He had insisted that she and Malcolm sit in front of him when she had started to grow sleepy. Such closeness had distracted her only briefly, for she had been too tired to dwell on it for long. Now, however, as she woke up, she was acutely aware of how she was tucked up between his long, strong legs, her back warmed by his broad chest, and how his muscular arms encircled her as if in an embrace. She rubbed her hand over Malcolm's back, trying to cleanse her mind of disturbing thoughts about Lucais's embraces with thoughts of tending to Malcolm.

"There lies Dunmor," Lucais announced, giving in to the urge to touch his lips to her soft hair, finding it as silky as he had imagined it would be.

A small chill of alarm slipped down Edina's spine as she looked at his keep. It was set upon a stony rise, giving it a clear view of the surrounding lands. To the north was a tiny village, and hearty Highland cattle grazed contentedly in the fields surrounding the castle's thick walls. It was a strong keep and, she thought with an inner sigh as they rode through the big, ironstudded gates, a rich one. It was one thing to think that a man was out of her reach, it was quite another to see the proof of that in one huge pile of stone.

The way the people of Dunmor boisterously welcomed Lucais and his cousins, and their elation over Malcolm's good health, made Edina further question her suspicions about Lucais. The people would do what their laird told them to, but she knew he could never make them all pretend to be happy. As they dismounted in the heart of the crowd, Edina clung to Malcolm and struggled to regain some sense of belonging with the child, some sense of her right to be there. Her eyes told her that Malcolm would have all she had lacked as a child—love, ready ears for his questions, stories, and even his complaints, and ready arms to hold him close and soothe his hurts and fears. He might not be completely safe, however, she told herself, and soon felt a little more confident.

A small, thin young woman named Mary, who was all brown hair and brown eyes, was selected to show her to a room and see to her needs. Lucais made only one attempt to extract Malcolm from her arms, accepted failure with an apparent calm, and sent her on her way. As she followed Mary into the keep and up the narrow stone steps that led to the bedchambers, Edina looked around at the rich tapestries and fine weaponry hanging on the thick stone walls. She followed Mary into a bedchamber, looked at the big, curtained bed, the fireplace, and the sheepskin rugs, and shivered. She had never seen such wealth, and she felt intimidated.

After meekly asking for a bath, Edina sat down on the high soft bed and waited for Mary to fulfill that request. She took several deep breaths and fought to subdue her feelings of being small and unimportant. Edina knew she had just been overwhelmed by Dunmor, its wealth, and its air of contentment. This was the sort of place she had often dreamed of, and Edina decided that it was very unsettling to see one's dreams come to life. The cynical part of her began to revive, and she also decided that such perfection was worthy of suspicion. Just because everyone and everything at Dunmor seemed perfect did not mean there could never be a snake in the garden. Edina was sure that Malcolm could have a very good life at Dunmor, but there could easily be someone behind one of the smiling faces she saw who wanted Malcolm's life to be very short or who was willing to help the man who sought that. Until she was sure that Malcolm was completely safe at Dunmor she would stay with him.

"Are ye sure ye should have let her take the bairn with her?" Andrew asked as he, Ian, and Lucais washed in Lucais's bedchamber.

"She willnae hurt the bairn," Lucais said as he dried himself, surprised and a little alarmed at how confident he felt about that, for that confidence was not based upon any facts.

"So, do ye trust her now? Ye dinnae think she has anything to do with Simon?" Andrew donned his braies and poured himself and the half-dressed Ian some wine from a decanter on a table next to the huge bed.

"All I trust in is the fact that she willnae kill Malcolm, not whilst she is so completely surrounded by MacRaes."

"Are ye sure? I think ye are beguiled by a verra bonnie pair of green eyes."

Lucais wondered about ignoring that as he donned his braies and helped himself to some of the wine his cousins were drinking so heartily. As he sipped his drink and studied his cousins, who were sprawled so comfortably on his bed, he decided that the full truth would serve better. His strong attraction to Edina was a weakness. It might be a good idea to have someone watching him and Edina to ensure that he did not give in to that weakness and that Edina did not try to use it against him.

"She does indeed have the most beautiful pair of green eyes I have ever looked into. I find most everything about the lass verra intriguing and alluring. My instincts tell me that she has naught to do with Simon, but I am not sure I should completely trust my instincts concerning her. Those instincts are also telling me that I want to lay her down in the heather and not rise from her slender arms for days."

"Oh," Ian said in a small, hoarse voice, causing both of his older cousins to laugh.

"Do ye think your loins could overwhelm your wits?" asked Andrew. "Do ye think that is why ye believe that she willnae hurt Malcolm whilst she has him alone with her?"

"Nay. She could have struck the child down back in the forest ere we could have stopped her. She did not. That could mean that she is honestly trying to protect the child, or she knew we would immediately kill her and has no wish to die. That holds true here as weel. To survive she must get away from here or continue this game."

"And so we watch her closely to see if she does try to leave with the child or if someone tries to come to her."

"Exactly. We watch her every minute. She is never to be without a guard. Ye need not be too secretive about it, as I am sure she expects it, but a little subtlety would be good. Then she might think she can elude us and we will finally see with our own eyes if she can be trusted."

"A good plan, but there is one little flaw. There is one place where we cannae watch her, certainly not with any subtlety—her bedchamber."

"We will have eyes there, too. I will ask Mary to bed in there with her. It was my mother's bedchamber, and there is a place for a maid to sleep close at hand. It is not something that will raise any great suspicion on Edina's part."

"And what will you do if she is in league with Simon?"

"If she is in league with Simon, I fear we will be given little choice about her fate. It will eventually come to the point where we must choose between her life and Malcolm's. I may lust after her far more than I have ever lusted after a woman before, but ye need not fear that I will hesitate in making that choice, and making the right one. The moment she sides with Simon, she will be the enemy."

Chapter 3

It was not easy, but Edina smiled at Mary, set a sleepy Malcolm in the woman's arms, and walked out of the bedchamber she had shared with the woman and child for a week. Her mind told her that she was foolish to worry, that she could at least trust Mary not to hurt the baby, but her heart was not ready to agree. The one who sought to harm Malcolm did not appear to be within the walls of Dunmor, but he was out there somewhere she was sure of it. The watchful attitude of everyone at Dunmor confirmed that feeling. She was not the only one who scented the danger to the child. It was past time for her to step away from the child a little, however. If nothing else, she needed to take the risk to see if anyone tried to take advantage of it. Keeping a constant watch on Malcolm while the people of Dunmor kept a constant watch on her was not getting anyone anywhere, not even in deciding who could be trusted.

As she stepped out into the sunlit bailey and took a deep breath of the clear summer air, Gar trotted up to her and she patted his head. The dog still allowed no one to go very far with Malcolm, but he showed no other signs of wariness. The animal had, in truth, settled in quite well at Dunmor. He saw no threat and that made Edina relax a little. She really needed a little rest from her self-appointed post as Malcolm's guardian. To ease the final pangs of guilt she felt about leaving the child alone, however, she ordered Gar to go to her room and watch the baby.

Enjoying the warmth of the sun, she walked around the bailey. Lucais had graciously sent word to her uncle to let him know why she was at Dunmor and assuring the man that she was safe. Her uncle was not a loving man, but he did have a strong sense of duty and she knew he would be concerned about her. She no longer had to worry about him, and could put all of her attention on the matter of Malcolm's continued safety.

After a thorough examination of the bailey, all the assorted buildings, and even venturing onto the walls to survey the surrounding lands, Edina found a shaded, secluded place near the walls of the keep and sat down. It was pleasant to be outside alone—if she ignored the way Ian shadowed her every step—and she wanted to enjoy it for just a little while longer. A cool breeze snaked its way around the walls, and she closed her eyes, savoring the way it took the summer heat from her skin. She was feeling drowsy and content, when she suddenly sensed someone was staring at her.

Cautiously, Edina opened her eyes and looked up. Lucais towered over her. There was a look of curiosity mixed with amusement on his face as she staggered to her feet. She frowned when he suddenly stepped closer, pressing her against the wall.

"What do ye want?" she asked, inwardly cursing the

huskiness in her voice as his long body lightly brushed against hers.

"Ye have taken a rest from being Malcolm's constant guard?" he murmured as he closely studied her flushed face.

"I feel I can trust Mary and I have set Gar at his door."

"Ah, aye, the ever-faithful Gar."

"Howbeit, I believe I have been idle long enough."

He just smiled when she shifted slightly, silently asking him to move so that she could leave. Lucais was pleased to catch her alone, unguarded, and out of sight of the others. He had watched her for a week, whenever he and his cousins were not hunting Simon. Her voice, her eyes, even the way she moved, stirred him. She had begun to invade his dreams, dreams that had him waking up in a sweat, hungry for her. No matter how often he had told himself it would be a big mistake to give in to the attraction he felt for her, he had not been able to put her out of his mind. He had caught her watching him enough to make him think she felt the same interest. Now, Lucais decided, was the perfect time to test that theory.

"Malcolm is probably still asleep."

Edina gasped when he leaned forward and touched his mouth to hers. "What are ye doing?"

"Something I have thought about since the day ye first marched into my life."

That was a flattering thought, and it made her relax a little. A moment later she realized that had been his intention. She tensed when he put his lips against hers again. She knew she ought to hit him or kick him, and sternly remind him of the respect owed a lady. The problem was, with a disturbing and increasing frequency since arriving at Dunmor, she had thought about kissing him. Here was her chance to know if her idle dreams matched or exceeded the real thing. In a moment of what even she saw as pure recklessness, she decided to let him play his little game with her for a while. As he pressed his lips harder against hers, she curled her arms around his neck.

Her heart raced as he pulled her into his arms, lifting and pressing her body more fully against his. When he nudged at her lips with his, she opened her mouth, groaning with delight when he began to stroke the inside of her mouth with his tongue. The way he moved his big hands over her body, nearing but not overstepping the line to real intimacy, fired her blood. Her senses swimming, she clung to him and returned his kiss.

When his heated kisses slipped to her throat and he shifted so that her body was caught in a suggestive position between his body and the wall, Edina finally grasped at a thread of common sense. She pushed him away, and her sigh of relief when he immediately obeyed held a hint of regret. The kiss had been far more stirring than she had ever imagined, blinding her with the depths of the passion it roused within her. There was a flushed, taut expression on his face that told her he had felt much the same. That was dangerous, and, realizing that, she found the strength to step out of his reach.

"I believe that was enough of that," she muttered, taking a few deep breaths to completely steady herself.

"Oh, aye?" Lucais leaned against the wall of his keep and smiled at her. "To me it tasted like just the beginning."

"I came here to protect Malcolm, not to become—" She hesitated, not sure how to word what she wanted to say.

"Not to become my lover?"

"Of course not."

"That kiss we just shared told me elsewise."

It probably had, but Edina had no intention of admitting to what she had felt, and his arrogance in thinking he knew annoyed her. "That kiss was but idle and reckless curiosity. It was also the only one ye will get."

She turned and walked back to the front of the keep, trying not to look as if she were retreating, but eager to get back inside its thick walls as quickly as she could. Lucais's soft laughter followed her, and she resisted the urge to return and kick him. His kiss was still warm upon her lips, still alive and heating her blood. Edina knew it would be very unwise to get within his reach until she had overcome that.

Lucais smiled, straightened up from the wall, and frowned when he was suddenly confronted by a grinning Andrew. "How long have ye been here?"

"Only long enough to catch a few words and see the lass hurry off," Andrew replied, his blue eyes alight with laughter but his expression serious.

"No harm in stealing a wee kiss."

"Nay, although I think it was more than that. Ye were both flushed and unsteady. Aye, it may have been only a kiss ye stole, but I think it has left ye verra hungry for more."

"And what if it has?"

Andrew grimaced and threaded his fingers through his curly red hair. "If the lass is as innocent and earnest as she appears to be, then ye are attempting to seduce a weelborn maid. That could bring ye a great deal of trouble. If she is helping Simon, then ye are showing her a weakness she could use. Just be wary, cousin. Either way ye step, there looms a problem."

Lucais had no answer for that, as it was the truth. He did not think it would deter him, however. That one sweet kiss had fired his blood, and he knew he could not simply push that aside. He wanted to taste the fullness of her passion, hungered to know if the promise in her kiss could be met. Edina was certainly trouble whether she was innocent or guilty, but Lucais knew that if the chance arose to make love to her, he would not hesitate to grab it.

Edina shut the door behind her after she entered her bedchamber and sagged against it. The last few steps to her room had been hard ones to take. A large part of her had wanted her to turn around, run back to Lucais, and savor more of his kisses. Only the certainty that it would go far beyond kisses had kept her going. She needed time to think, and that kiss had shown her that she could do little of that held in Lucais MacRae's arms.

"How is Malcolm?" she asked Mary when she saw the girl frowning at her in curiosity.

"Still asleep," Mary replied, watching Edina closely as she walked to the bed and sprawled on top of it. "Are ye all right? Ye look as if ye got too much of the sun. Ye are verra flushed."

"I met with your laird. He has a true skill at making me get flushed."

"At times ye talk as if ye dinnae like him. He is a good

mon. This trouble with Simon has sorely grieved him. He loved his sister and was most fond of her husband. When he realized the wee bairn was gone, he ne'er rested, searching everywhere."

"Aye, so I have been told." Edina had to admit that everyone at Dunmor seemed honestly fond of their laird, which would imply that he was indeed a good man.

"Some men wouldnae have tried so hard. After all, the laddie now claims a large holding that borders us on the west. Some men would want to keep that for themselves."

"Aye," Edina said as she slowly sat up and frowned at Mary. "They would indeed."

"Wee Malcolm is fortunate to have a kinsmon who will tend it, and him, most carefully until the lad is of an age to claim it."

"It wouldnae fall into Simon's hands?"

"Nay. Why should it? Simon is no kin to Malcolm. Why should ye think he would gain?"

"It would explain why he killed Elspeth and Walter and left the wee bairn to die."

Mary nodded as she walked to the door. "It would, but that is not why he now has their blood on his hands, nor why he will probably try to kill the bairn once he kens that Malcolm has survived. Simon is mad, insane with jealousy and hate. There is no explaining such things."

There was not, Edina thought after Mary left. Greed for land explained such murders far more clearly. Before, there had been no reason for either Simon or Lucais to kill Elspeth or Walter or the baby. Now she saw a reason for Lucais to commit such murders.

She cursed and fell back onto the bed. It helped to

have a reason, but she heartily wished it was one that pointed the finger of blame squarely at Simon. She was torn, part of her horrified that she would even think Lucais was capable of such crimes and another telling her not to be a fool, that it was something she could not ignore. Edina rubbed her forehead as she struggled to decide what, if anything, she should do. It was hard to decide when she did not even want to believe it.

Slowly, she sat up, then stood up. What she needed was more knowledge, knowledge about Lucais and about Dunmor and its people. Edina knew the people of Dunmor would never say anything bad about the laird, but what they said could still help her. She could learn about Lucais's past, about his likes and dislikes, and even about his character by weeding through the things his own people said about him. It was time to stop just standing guard over Malcolm and take an active part in finding out exactly who wanted the child dead. The moment Mary returned, Edina was determined to go and search out a few truths.

It was late before Edina returned to her bedchamber. For the first time since she had arrived at Dunmor she had taken her evening meal in the great hall. Her intention had been to study further the laird and his people. Instead, she had spent most of the meal torn between desire and annoyance over Lucais's blatant attempts to seduce her. She had wavered between saying yes and wanting to scream at him to stop tormenting her.

Mary helped her undress, don one of Lucais's late mother's nightgowns, and wash. After kissing little Malcolm good night, Edina crawled into bed feeling utterly exhausted even though she had done little more than talk to people. As she listened to Mary settle down to sleep in the little alcove near the fireplace, Edina tried to sort out her confused thoughts.

She had learned nothing bad about Lucais, which did not really surprise her, but it promised to make it more difficult to come to any decision. Simon was loathed by everyone, but that was not really enough to condemn him either. Everyone at Dunmor thought the man guilty of murder, although no one had mentioned any real proof that the man had actually done the killings. If there was some clue that had set Lucais on the man's trail, most of the people of Dunmor did not know what it was.

It all left her very confused. She was not sure what part of her she should listen to—her heart, her mind, or her instincts. The fact that she desired Lucais made her unwilling to fully trust anything except her mind, and it did not hold enough facts to make a decision.

There were a few things in Lucais's favor, although they were not hard, cold facts. Gar trusted the man. She simply could not bring herself to fear him. If Lucais was the murderer, then why had he done nothing to hurt her? Why had he even allowed her to come to Dunmor and keep Malcolm by her side? If there was something suspicious about all of that, she could not think what it was.

What she needed, she mused as she snuggled down beneath the covers, pausing only to pat Gar on the head before he lay down on the floor by the bed, was one strong piece of proof. She needed some act, some word, or some fact that would clear her mind of all doubt about Lucais. It had to come soon too, for instinct told her that this peace could not last much longer. No one questioned that Malcolm's life was in danger and whoever wanted to kill the child would try again. Edina desperately hoped that she would know exactly who that person was before the next attack came.

Chapter 4

Malcolm giggled as she stood over him and shook the water from her hair. Edina could not believe she had been allowed outside the walls of Dunmor with the child, but she was not about to question her good fortune too loudly or it could disappear. It was always possible that after staying at Dunmor for two weeks, people had begun to trust her.

"Gar, get back here," she called, and sighed as the dog disappeared into the trees on the far side of the brook she had been splashing in.

As she dressed she decided she needed to have a stern talk with her pet. Gar had become so comfortable at Dunmor, so pampered by the MacRaes, that he was not doing a very good job of guarding her or Malcolm anymore. Gar saw no threat and, although she found some comfort in that, for it implied that she was not sitting in the midst of the enemy, she had to strengthen her commands. There could yet come a time when she would need his aid.

She was rubbing her hair with a drying cloth when a faint sound made her tense. Immediately kneeling by the child and pulling her sword from its sheath, she carefully looked around. It could be just someone from Dunmor keeping a guard on her, but she needed to be sure. Still watching, she finished dressing and picked up Malcolm. The joy of her moment of freedom was gone now.

Knowing that Gar would find his own way back to Dunmor she decided that it was past time she and Malcolm returned to the safety of its high walls. She had barely taken three steps toward the keep when she knew she had waited too long. Six mounted and well-armed men rode out of the trees bordering the brook. Edina carefully set Malcolm down by her feet and faced the men squarely, her sword in her hands. She knew she did not have any chance of defeating six men, but she was determined to make them pay dearly for Malcolm's life.

"And where did Lucais find you?" demanded a tall, bone-thin man who rode to the fore of the others. "I dinnae ken who ye are."

"And I dinnae ken who ye are either, but I hadnae realized this was a courtesy visit."

"Ye are no MacRae."

"Nay. If it troubles ye so, I am Edina MacAdam of Glenfair. Does it help to ken who is about to kill you?"

The man laughed. "Ye have more spirit than wit, wench." He gave her a mocking bow. " 'Tis a great pity we couldnae have met at a better time and place. We could be lovers instead of enemies. I am Sir Simon Kenney."

"Lovers? I think not, Sir Simon. I ken what happens to the lovers ye grow weary of or who displease you."

The way his expression turned cold made Edina nervous. The man was obviously quick to anger. If she faced only him, that could have worked to her advantage. Now making him angry would make her death arrive all the sooner. She inwardly cursed and wondered where her dog and her guards were when she really needed them.

Lucais looked at the men slowly encircling Edina and softly cursed. "Ian, how could ye have let her come this far from Dunmor alone?"

Ian flushed with guilt. "Ye said we didnae need to guard her too closely."

"That didnae mean ye could let her wander about as if all is weel and there isnae a madmon lurking about."

"That madmon isnae lurking anymore," Andrew drawled, putting a stop to the argument. "We have three men behind Simon and his men, and we are in front of him. Ye are the one who must decide when we attack, Lucais."

"At least everyone will not think me some fool for the way I ordered so many men to arms just because one tiny woman and a bairn were out walking," Lucais muttered, dragging his fingers through his hair. "An attack could get Edina and Malcolm killed."

"There is no question that they will also die if we dinnae do something soon."

"If only we had something to briefly distract Simon and his men." Lucais looked around one last time before he gave the order to attack, an order he feared would be a death sentence for Edina, and his gaze settled on a familiar mottled-gray shape creeping toward Simon and his men. "Look, 'tis that cursed dog."

"Is he going to attack?"

"Aye, Andrew," Lucais replied, finding it hard to keep his voice low as excitement and anticipation rushed through his veins. "That ugly dog has ne'er looked more bonnie. He is about to give us the diversion we need."

"He could get hurt," Ian murmured even as he readied himself for the attack he knew would come at any moment.

"I pray that doesnae happen, for 'twill sorely grieve Edina," said Lucais, never taking his eyes from the dog, tensed for the moment when the animal would spring, for that would be when he would order the attack. "Howbeit, better a dog than a woman and a child. Now, ready, lads, for the moment that beast lunges I will give the battle cry. All eyes will turn to the dog and whatever hapless soul he chooses to sink those teeth into, and that is when we will attack."

Edina felt the sweat soak her back as Simon just studied her. There was a chance that he was trying to put her off her guard and then he would attack. She decided she had a better chance if she tried to grasp some control, if she could somehow choose the time he charged her. The easiest way to do that, she decided, was to anger him. He had already shown her how easy that could be. It was a weakness she could have used well at some other time, but now it could at least serve to ensure that she was not cut down too easily. If she could make him attack, she could at least take a few of Simon's men with her, perhaps even Simon himself.

"Why do ye hesitate? Do ye fear a wee bairn and a woman?" she asked.

"I but wonder what ye are doing here and why ye are ready to die for that child," Simon said in a tight voice, revealing that her words had already stirred his anger.

"Not everyone can kill a bairn or leave them to rot in the wood."

"Ah, so that is how he has returned to Dunmor. Ye had the misfortune to find the bastard."

" 'Tis your misfortune. Come, let us dance. I grow weary of waiting for you. I cannae understand why any mon would be so cowardly as to slay a child, but, mayhap, 'tis that verra cowardice that causes ye to hesitate now."

Simon edged closer, his thin face white with fury. "Ye sorely beg to die, wench. Mayhap I but do the lad a kindness. A bairn should be with its parents, should it not? I mean to take him there."

Just as Edina was sure he was about to lunge at her, a gray shape hurled itself at the man on Simon's right. She gaped along with Simon and his men as Gar's attack sent the man tumbling off his horse, screaming with pain as Gar savaged his sword arm. A heartbeat later a deep, fierce battle cry rent the air. Edina had no idea whose battle cry it was, but she did not hesitate to take advantage of this further distraction. She grabbed Malcolm by the back of his gown and ran toward Dunmor.

Out of the corner of her eye she saw three familiar figures race from the trees straight toward Simon and his men. The moment they were between her and Simon she paused, sheathed her sword, and pulled a crying Malcolm into her arms. She rubbed his back, calming him as she waited for Gar to trot up to her. Lucais, Ian, Andrew, and three other men from Dunmor were pressing Simon and his men hard. It was tempting to stay and see how the battle went, but she had to think of Malcolm's safety. At least now she was certain who the enemy was. After giving Gar a rewarding pat for his bravery, she trotted back toward Dunmor, praying every step of the way that Lucais would win, that he would kill Simon and put an end to the threat to Malcolm's life.

"Curse it a thousand times," yelled Lucais as he stopped, bent over slightly, and tried to catch his breath. "We will never catch the bastard."

After a moment, Lucais straightened and looked at his men collapsed around him. Somehow Simon and one of his men had escaped. Desperate to get the man, he and his men had tried to chase him down, but they were no match for men on horseback. This time he would have to be satisfied that only Simon and his men suffered in the attack. Malcolm and Edina were undoubtedly safely behind the walls of Dunmor now, and none of his men had suffered any more than a few cuts and bruises.

"Weel, we had best get back to Dunmor," he finally said, smiling slightly when he saw that three of the men had already begun to walk back, leaving him and his cousins behind.

Andrew stood up from where he had collapsed on the ground and brushed himself off. " 'Tis a great pity that the coward still lives, but at least we ken one thing now that we werenae sure of before."

"Aye? And what is that?" Lucais asked as he and his cousins started back to Dunmor.

"Edina is exactly what she claims to be. She has no

part in Simon's murderous plots. She found Malcolm, saved him from dying in the wood, and believes it her duty to stay at his side until that danger is gone."

"Aye, from what little I heard, Simon didnae ken who she was or understand what she was doing there." Although this proof of Edina's innocence elated him, Lucais found that it left him a little confused as well. "I have to admit that I share Simon's confusion. Aye, she has it in her head that it is her duty to stay at Malcolm's side until she is sure he is safe, but why would she have that idea? Why not just be satisfied that he is with his kinsmen? She must ken by now that we willnae hurt the child, yet she stays."

"There is something behind her determination, but I cannae say what it is. I just sense that she does this for more reasons than the child's safety." Andrew smiled crookedly and shrugged. "I make no sense, I ken it. I just ken that there is some reason we cannae guess at. Mayhap something that happened in her past that makes her so determined. She doesnae just speak of Malcolm's safety. She mixes it all up with his comfort and care."

Ian nodded as they approached the high gates of Dunmor. "I think I ken what Andrew is trying to say. The only way to ken what is in her head is to ask her though, dinnae ye think?"

"Aye," agreed Lucais, espying Edina waiting just in-side the bailey and walking straight toward her. "How is Malcolm?" he asked even as he looked her over care-fully for any wounds, relieved to find none.

"Weel, he was a wee bit upset o'er the rough way I picked him up and ran with him, but he has recovered." Edina inwardly breathed a sigh of relief when she saw that he was no more than bruised and scratched. "Is Simon dead?"

"Nay. We lost him."

"Then it is not over yet."

"Not yet. He was mounted and, when he managed to break free of the battle, there was no hope of catching him, although we did run after him for a ways."

"I still dinnae understand how anyone could kill two people and try to kill a bairn, but I saw what pushes him to such cruelties. He is filled with anger. He nearly stinks of it."

"And, sadly, he has decided to unleash it upon my family."

"After a fortnight where nothing happened, I had hoped that he would not seek out Malcolm, that whatever had made him kill your sister and her husband had been sated and he would leave the bairn alone. He will never cease trying to kill the child. The brief moment of humanity that stopped him from taking a sword to Malcolm before has gone."

"We will watch. Now I must clean this dirt off and I want to give Gar a verra large bone."

Edina smiled as she followed him inside of the keep. "I didnae ken who was attacking at first, only that it allowed me to flee. But ye used Gar's attack to signal your own, didnae ye?"

"Aye. He drew all eyes his way. Before that we risked your life and Malcolm's." At the bottom of the stairs he paused to look her over again. "Are ye sure ye are unhurt?"

"Aye, I am fine."

"There will be no more walks outside of these walls unless ye take armed men with ye."

"None, not until that mon is dead."

"Good. Now go and let Mary see to your scratches."

She nodded, a little surprised that she had any, then recalled that she had paid little heed to rocks, brambles, or anything else in her way as she had run back to the safety of Dunmor. As she climbed up the stairs to her bedchamber, she watched Lucais disappear into the great hall. When he had walked up to her she had felt shy, at a loss for words. The proof of his innocence still filled her mind and heart, and she had feared she would say something about it. It was not something she should speak of, for it would reveal to him that she had suspected him of being the sort of coward who would murder a child. Even though her suspicions had been weak and wavering, and he had known that she did not fully trust him speaking of such things aloud would only cause hurt and insult.

As she stepped into her bedchamber, she saw Mary tucking Malcolm into his crib and asked, "Is he unhurt?"

"Aye, mistress. Ye and the laird saved him from Simon, did ye not?"

"Aye, I suppose. I was just a little worried that I might have bruised the poor lad, as I was rough with him when I tried to rush him out of harm's way." She stepped over to the crib and looked down at the sleeping child, relieved to see no obvious signs of her rough handling.

"Better a few wee bruises than a cut throat."

Edina shivered at the thought and moved to the washbowl to clean the dirt from her hands and face. She was glad that Lucais was the good man everyone said he was, that her instincts and her heart were right in their judgments. However, that left her with a man who wanted to kill a child simply because he was twisted with jealousy and anger. Such a thing was beyond her understanding, and, if she did not understand it, how could she fight it?

Chapter 5

A soft curse escaped Edina as she slipped out of the keep and started to walk around the bailey. It had been a week since the confrontation with Simon, and in that short time her life had been turned upside down. Lucais had changed. He had been a little flirtatious before, stolen a kiss or two, but now he seemed to be doggedly pursuing her. At every corner he was there, smiling, flattering, touching. What really frightened her was how much she was enjoying it. She needed to get away from him so that she could think clearly.

Clutching her cloak more tightly around her to ward off the chill in the late August night air, she scowled at the ground as she walked and struggled to sort out her confused mind and heart. One thing she was sure of was that no one was suspicious of her any longer. Just as the battle had shown her that Lucais was innocent, so it had shown the people of Dunmor that she was equally innocent. Since she had nursed a few suspicions about them, she did not feel insulted that they had nursed a few about her. A child's life was at stake. One had to be very careful about whom one trusted.

The trouble with knowing that Lucais was innocent was that the knowledge had taken away the one restraint she had used to hold back the feelings she had for him. The possibility that he was a threat to Malcolm had been enough to make her hesitate. Now each time he smiled at her, all her feelings flooded through her, making her weak, causing her to melt in his arms. She could no longer ignore it. She loved him. It should make her happy, but there was no indication that he returned her feelings. He was also too high a reach for her. Men like him did not take a poor, landless, orphaned girl for a wife.

She had to fight the urge to flee Dunmor. Malcolm was still in danger, and although she now knew that Lucais and the people of Dunmor could protect him, she had made a vow to stay with the child until the danger had passed. She also knew that she would not be able to sleep at night if she did not stay until she was absolutely sure that the child was safe. Fleeing was no answer.

"Slow down, woman," said a familiar voice from directly behind her a moment before Lucais caught her by the arm and halted her blind march around the keep.

Edina looked up at him and her heart sank. She wanted him. The desire he stirred in her haunted her dreams. It was so much a part of her that she was sure he was aware of it. Her only comfort was that he could not know it was born of love. He had not asked for that, and no matter what else happened she wanted to be able to cling to at least some tiny shred of pride. It would devastate her to offer him her love, only to have him reject it, and she had the feeling she was going to be suffering enough pain very soon.

"I have a question I have been meaning to ask," he began a little hesitantly, threading his fingers through his thick hair as he frowned down at her.

"Weel? Ask it, then," she said. "I will either answer it or tell ye to go away."

Lucais smiled faintly, then grew serious again. "Why have ye taken on this duty of being Malcolm's protector? Aye, at first I could understand. Ye didnae ken what was going on, or who ye could trust. But now? Why? He is no kin of yours."

Edina only briefly considered telling him it was none of his business or making up some grand tale of vows and honor. She did not want to bring up all the old, painful memories of her childhood, but decided he was owed the truth. He had tolerated a great deal from her, allowing her into his home, and even respecting her claim of being his own nephew's protector, a role that was his by birth.

"I fear some of what makes me act as I do is that I, too, was left in the forest." She smiled faintly when his eyes widened, and he slipped his arms around her in a silent gesture of comfort. "My mother told my uncle that she was going riding and took me with her to make the tale seem the truth. When we got into the forest to the south of my uncle's lands, my mother met with her lover. She set me down on the ground, turned, and rode away with the mon, never looking back."

"How old were you?"

"Five. I waited, ne'er moving from the spot, but she ne'er returned. I waited the whole night and much of the next day, and then my uncle found me."

Lucais could not believe what he was hearing. Such cruelty was beyond his understanding. He felt a need to soothe that hurt, but knew he could not. It did explain her strange, fierce determination to stay with Malcolm until she was sure he was safe and loved, however. The urge he had to find the woman and punish her for her cruelty also told him that his feelings for Edina went a lot deeper than lust.

He inwardly smiled, amused at his own vagaries. He wanted her even then, and that did not surprise him. The desire he felt for her had been there from the beginning, growing stronger every day. At the moment, however, he was also feeling things like outrage over what had been done to her, fury at the ones who had done it, and an overwhelming tenderness. Very soon he was going to have to sort out his own heart and mind, decide just what he was going to do about Edina Mac-Adam, because the moment the threat Simon presented was eradicated, Edina would leave. Now, he decided, was not the time, and he turned his full attention back to her tragic story.

"Did ye e'er see her again?" he asked.

"Nay." Edina sighed and leaned against him. This was the first time anyone had ever offered her sympathy concerning her mother's desertion, and she decided it did not hurt to enjoy it for a little while. "When I was twelve my uncle called me to him and told me that my mother had died, stabbed by a jealous wife. He said she had lived like a whore and that it was justice that she had died like one. We ne'er spoke of her again."

"What of your father?" he asked in a slightly hoarse voice, not sure whom he detested the most, her mother or her uncle, who was obviously a cold man.

"He died but months after I was born. I ne'er

kenned the mon. From the way Maida the cook spoke of him from time to time, I dinnae think he would have been much better than my mother." She leaned back and smiled at him. "Dinnae look so sad. I was kept weel enough. I was clothed, fed, and housed. Many a bairn left orphaned doesnae get e'en that. Howbeit, when I saw wee Malcolm lying alone in the wood—" She shook her head.

"I understand. I am almost sorry I asked," he murmured, and shook his head. "Ye have had an unhappy life, havenae ye?"

"It wasnae so bad that ye need to pity me," she said, starting to tug away from him only to have him hold her a little tighter.

"Dinnae confuse sympathy with pity, bonnie Edina." He touched a kiss to her forehead. "I might pity ye if all that had happened had turned ye into some terrified wee lass who cowers when she sees her own shadow, but ye arenae that."

"I am afraid of the forest," she whispered.

"Most people are, even if only at night. I am eight and twenty and I wouldnae be eager to spend a whole night alone in the forest. Ye were no more than a bairn and, if your lack of size now is any indication, little more than a bite or two for any beastie that might have found ye." He met her scowl with a brief smile. "Nay, I am but passing sorry that ye had to grow to womanhood among such an uncaring lot. The way your uncle told ye of your mother's death tells me that he is a cold mon. Ye couldnae have found much comfort there."

"He is a good mon, truly," she said as she eased out of his hold, finding such tender proximity dangerously arousing. "He ne'er beat me and he gave me all that was needed to stay alive. I think he just doesnae ken how to be, weel, happy or kindly. Dinnae forget, he was the one who came searching for me, took me home, and raised me."

"True. Mayhap he just didnae ken that there is a wee bit more needed to raise a bairn than food, clothes, and a roof," he said as he took her by the hand and started to lead her back to the keep. "Mayhap that was all he e'er got, and he was ne'er shown another way."

"Ye have decided that I have walked enough, have ye?" she asked, but she made no attempt to break free of his light grip.

"Aye. The summer fades quickly and there is a bite to the air."

"I am stronger than I look. A wee chill in the air will-nae cause me to fall ill."

"Ye have also not had any food this night."

When he passed the door to the great hall and led her up the stairs, she frowned. "Have they cleared the tables, then?"

"Nay, I have had the cook prepare us something that is just for us."

Her suspicion grew in one large bound when he opened the door to his bedchamber. She tensed as he tugged her inside. This was far too intimate and far too close to a bed. It was undoubtedly just how he wanted it, and a large part of her did as well, but Edina knew she had to fight that reckless part of her.

"I dinnae think this is a good idea," she said, and turned back to the door.

Lucais grabbed her by the hands and tugged her over to a small table set in front of the huge stone fire-place that warmed his room. "I swear to ye, loving, that I will do naught that ye cannae agree to," he vowed as he gently pushed her down into a chair.

And that was the real problem, Edina mused as she watched him sit down across from her and pour each of them some wine. She could easily be persuaded to agree to most anything Lucais asked of her. Smiling faintly, she touched her silver goblet to his when he raised it in a silent toast. It had been difficult enough for her to turn from his gentle seduction when they had been surrounded by people as in the great hall or the bailey. Now they were enclosed in privacy, warmed by the glow of a low-burning fire, and facing each other over a fine meal. Edina was not confident that she had the strength to resist his wiles. She could try to flee to her room, but, as he smiled at her over the savory roast lamb they dined on, the door through which she could escape suddenly looked miles away.

Lucais saw the soft look in Edina's eyes and inwardly smiled. He easily pushed aside the small twinge of guilt he felt over his attempts to seduce a wellborn maid. Edina wanted him; he was certain of it. The desire was there to see in the way she looked at him, and it was clear to feel every time they kissed. He had no intention of forcing her to his bed, but he was going to do his best to make her give in to that desire and come into his arms willingly.

Chapter 6

"I have spent most of the evening speaking of old battles," Lucais murmured as he moved the table out of the way and sat down on the sheepskin rug by the fireplace. "Come, our bellies are full and 'tis time to take our ease." He patted the rug by his side. "Now 'tis your turn to tell me of your adventures."

Edina eyed the spot where he wanted her to sit. The unease she had felt when he had first tugged her into his room had been lulled by conversation and good food, but now it returned in force. There was a warmth in his gray eyes that told her talk was not all he wanted from her. The moment she sat down beside him she was silently offering him the opportunity to gain what he really sought.

She glanced at the door and thought about leaving, claiming a need to seek her own bed and a good night's sleep. It almost made her smile when she realized that she could not do it, she could not retreat again. He offered no more than passion, but she ached for it. Soon

Simon would be defeated and there would be no reason for her to linger at Dunmor. She would return to Glenfair and all its coldness. Here was a beautiful man offering her warmth, no matter how fleeting, and Edina decided she wanted some. Even if it were for only one night, she wanted to be held in his arms, to taste the fullness of the passion promised in his kisses. She also wanted love, marriage, and babies, but had little hope of being offered that. Edina knew that if she tried to gain it all, she would end up with nothing, not even a sweet memory. Inwardly taking a deep breath to steady herself, she sat down beside him.

"I fear I have no great adventures to tell ye about," she said, silently cursing the tremor in her voice that revealed her nervousness and desire.

"Have ye led such a calm, peaceful life, then?" Lucais reached out to undo the strip of deer hide she had tied her hair back with, smiling gently at her when her eyes widened.

"Aye." She swallowed hard when he began to comb his fingers through her hair, plainly enjoying the feel of it. "The most exciting thing I have e'er done is a wee bit of poaching, but I have ne'er been caught at it."

"That is what ye were doing when we found you." He refilled her goblet and draped his arm around her shoulders, lightly tugging her closer.

"Aye. My uncle's lands are verra small, and sometimes there isnae any game to be found on them."

"Ye will get yourself hanged."

"Aye, I have feared that at times, but then the fear passes and I do it again."

"Weel, try to cling to the fear a little harder in the future. Hanging is the gentlest of punishments visited upon poachers, and I dinnae think your beauty and sex will save ye. Not every time anyway."

She nodded and shivered when he touched a kiss to the hollow by her ear. Her heart was pounding so hard and fast, she wondered that he did not hear it. Fear and anticipation raced through her veins alongside her increasing desire. Edina almost smiled when she realized that now that she had made her decision to be his lover, she was a little annoyed that he was moving so slowly. She lifted her gaze to his, saw the warm, steady way he was watching her, and briefly feared that he could read her thoughts.

"Lass, I fear I dinnae have the wits left to keep on talking, and ye arenae helping to keep the conversation alive."

"I think my wits are a wee bit scattered just now as weel," she whispered, her breathing growing heavy as he inched his mouth closer to hers.

Lucais threaded his fingers through her hair on either side of her head and looked deep into her eyes. He could read a desire in their clear depths that he was sure matched his. As he brushed his lips across hers and felt her tremble, he decided the game of seduction had grown very tiresome.

"Ye ken what I seek, dinnae ye, dearling?" he asked in a soft voice as he covered her upturned face with soft, warm kisses. "I dinnae think I have kept it a verra close secret. Nay, especially not during this last week we have been together."

"Not since ye were certain that I was innocent, that I wasnae working with Simon."

"Aye, though it shames me to admit that I held such suspicions about you."

"Dinnae be shamed. I held them about ye from time to time too."

Lucais laughed even as he moved his kisses to the pulse point in her long, graceful throat. "I want ye, Edina MacAdam. God's tears, I want ye so badly that I wake in the night all asweat with the need. I think ye want me too."

"I should say nay and leave just to dim that arrogance."

He lifted his head to look at her, smiling faintly when he saw the amusement in her expression, but then he grew serious. "But ye willnae say nay, will ye?" He stroked her cheek, a little surprised to see that his hand was shaking.

"Nay, I willnae say nay. It may be unwise, reckless, e'en stupid, but I willnae say nay to you, Lucais. I fear I havenae got the strength to do as I should."

"Thank God for that," he said as he stood up, and scooped her up into his arms. "Although," he added as he walked to the bed and gently set her down on it, "I should prefer to think that ye arenae weak, that this isnae happening because of weakness. I should prefer to think that ye just have the strength to reach out and take what ye want."

"That is a much better way to think on it," she murmured as she welcomed him into her arms.

A soft groan rose from the very depths of her body as he kissed her. There was such passion in his kiss, such sweet tenderness, she was lost in it, so lost that she paid no heed to the removal of her clothes. With each touch of his hands on her body, with each heated kiss, he kept her blinded until they were both naked. It was not until he took off his braies and slowly lowered his body onto hers, the feel of his flesh meeting hers for the first time searing away the haze his kisses had encased her mind in. She shuddered and blushed beneath his gaze as he looked over every exposed inch of her.

"Ye are lovely, sweet Edina, all black silk and white linen."

"Ye arenae such a poor sight yourself, Lucais MacRae," she said, smoothing her hand down his side, the feel of his warm, hard skin sending her reeling.

He touched a kiss to her breast and she gasped, the warmth of his lips flaring through her body. She could feel a faint tremor rippling through him and knew he was caught as tightly in the grip of desire as she was. The way he touched her, caressed her skin with his lips, told her that he was struggling to go slowly. When he enclosed the hard tip of her breast in his mouth and drew on it, she decided she did not have the will or the strength to go slowly. She slid her hands down his back to cup his taut backside and laughed huskily when he came alive in her arms, all hesitation gone.

A heedless passion took control of her. She met his every kiss and touch with one of her own, equaling the ferocity of his lovemaking in every way. There was a wildness to their need for each other, and she reveled in it. It was not until she felt him press to enter her that a hint of sanity broke through. She wrapped her body around his, gasping with a strange mix of pleasure and pain as he joined their bodies. When he broke through the barrier of her innocence, the sharp pain of that loss made her cry out, but it became of little importance very quickly.

Edina held him close, smoothing her hands over his broad back as she savored every sensation caused by the unification of their bodies. It was as if her body had been sleeping for twenty years and had suddenly been brought to life. When she shifted, drawing him deeper within herself, she heard him groan and felt him shudder. It was only then that she realized he was so taut that she could feel the veins standing out on his arms.

"Arenae ye supposed to do a wee bit more?" she asked with a mixture of curiosity and amusement.

Lucais looked into her eyes, saw the faint glitter of laughter, and grinned. "Aye, just a wee bit more." He quickly grew serious and brushed a kiss over her mouth. "Is the pain gone?"

"What pain?" she whispered against his mouth.

When he moved, the last of Edina's amusement was swept away. She clung to him as he moved, greedily meeting his every thrust. A brief spasm of confusion and fear broke through the desire that so completely possessed her when her need grew almost painful, her body tightening with an anticipation she did not understand. Then something inside her broke free and she was lost. Edina was only faintly aware of crying out Lucais's name, and of the way he suddenly held her still, pushing deep within her as he shuddered and called out her name. Her inability to think clearly, to even know what was happening around her, did not really fade until Lucais had cleaned them both off and returned to the bed.

Edina cautiously opened her eyes as Lucais gently brushed the tangled hair from her face. He did not look disgusted or surprised, only gently amused, so she began to think that what had just happened to her was normal. She slowly reached up to touch his cheek and realized she was making sure that this was no dream, that he was real. That made her smile at her own foolishness.

"Does something amuse you?" he asked, brushing a kiss over her cheek.

"Only myself. I just realized that I touched you to be sure that ye arenae a dream."

He chuckled and briefly kissed her when she blushed. "And I have been touching ye so much for the verra same reason."

"Ah, I am disappointed."

"Why?"

"I thought ye were touching me for another reason."

"Ye must let a mon rest, dearling," he said, laughter shaking his voice as he turned onto his back and pulled her into his arms.

Edina looked at him and idly wondered how she could love him so deeply when he gave her no love in return. She smoothed her hand down his chest to his taut stomach, toying with the tight dark curls encircling his navel as she marveled at her own greed. Her body ached from her first taste of lovemaking, and yet she was hungry for more. She suspected some of that greed was born of the knowledge that this could not last for long, that her time with him was fleeting.

As she slid her hand around to his waist, she leaned down and touched a kiss to his rippled stomach. He shivered and she smiled against his warm skin. There might be weeks left in which they could be lovers, but there could also be only hours. Edina decided that she would give in to her greed and worry about the right or wrong of it later, when she was all alone at Glenfair.

"How long do ye need to rest?" she asked as she slipped her hand beneath the coverlet and curled her fingers around his staff, feeling her desire return as it hardened beneath her touch.

"I think I have rested enough," he replied in a hoarse voice as he pulled her back into his arms.

Edina laughed when he turned so that she was sprawled beneath him and greedily welcomed his kiss. "Aye," she said hoarsely when he tore his mouth from hers and began to kiss his way toward her breasts. "Your strength does appear to have returned."

"Lass, do ye mean to love me to exhaustion?"

"What a lovely idea."

"Weel, I challenge ye to try. We have time enough."

She threaded her fingers through his thick hair, arching toward his mouth as he lathed and sucked the aching tips of her breasts, and heartily prayed that he was right. Instinct told her, however, that their time together was rapidly slipping from their hands. Edina hoped that if all she would be given was this one night, that she had the strength to be satisfied with that.

Chapter 7

A cold draft brushed against Edina's back, and she muttered a curse as she tugged the blanket around herself. When she heard the sound of someone approaching the bed, she tensed and warily opened her eyes even as she pressed closer to Lucais. A blush heated her skin as she looked up into Andrew's face. She and Lucais had spent the whole night making love, and she was sure that was obvious to the young man. Even as she cursed herself for going to sleep and not slipping back into her own room, she noticed the somber expression he wore, and nudged Lucais.

"Andrew is here," she said as Lucais groaned softly and tried to pull her back into his arms.

Lucais came awake and sat up so quickly that she had to scramble to keep herself modestly covered by the blanket. Her heart was in her throat and she was not sure why. There were any number of reasons for Andrew to look so serious and to seek out his laird so early in the morning.

"Malcolm is gone," Andrew announced.

When Edina cried out in alarm and started to get up, Lucais grabbed her and held her still. "No need to go and look, dearling. If Andrew says he is gone, he is gone." He looked back at his cousin. "Tell me everything."

" 'Tis clear that Simon had someone here that he could use. Mary was knocked on the head and the bairn was taken from his wee bed. No one saw anyone go into the room or come out with the bairn. Mary thinks it happened but an hour or two ago. She cannae say for certain. She was rising to tend to him, for she was sure she had heard him cry out just before sunrise, and that is when she was struck down."

"No one saw anyone leave with the child?" Lucais demanded as he climbed out of the bed and began to dress.

"Nay, but if it was someone from here, he or she would have kenned how to slip away without being seen."

"Gar didnae stop them?" Edina asked.

"Nay, he was asleep." Andrew frowned. "In truth, he was just waking and was a wee bit unsteady. He should have done something, shouldnae he?"

"Aye," agreed Lucais. "He still stops even me from taking the child out of the room."

"Something else a person from Dunmor would ken, and they clearly did something to remove that threat. Something in the dog's food mayhap."

"Go, ready the horses. We may find a trail we can follow. And begin a search for who is missing. We must learn who the traitor is."

"I ken where he took the bairn," Edina said, her

voice softened by surprise that she could think so clearly when she was so afraid for Malcolm.

"How could ye ken where Simon will take him?" asked Lucais, waving to the departing Andrew to wait a moment.

"I think he told me that day by the brook. Truly," she insisted when he frowned. "He said, 'A bairn should be with his parents. I mean to take him there.' Where are your sister and her husband buried?"

"Are we there?" Edina whispered as Lucais reined in, slowing his mount from the furious gallop he had maintained for two hours to a walk.

"The burial site is just through those trees, in the yard of a wee chapel where Walter's kinsmen are always buried," Lucais answered in an equally quiet voice as he signaled to the ten men riding with him to move and encircle the area.

"Is he there?" She waited impatiently for an answer as Lucais exchanged a few signals with Andrew, who appeared a few yards ahead of them, then disappeared into the trees again.

"Andrew says he is."

"Is Malcolm still alive?"

"Aye."

She sensed the anger gripping Lucais so tightly and eased her hold on his waist. "I am sorry."

"Ye have naught to feel sorry for," he said as he dismounted and helped her down.

"I should have stayed close to Malcolm as I had vowed to do. Mayhap with two women in the room he wouldnae have been stolen away."

"Or ye would have been knocked on the head as weel." He gave her a brief hard kiss, then began to move toward the churchyard that was on the other side of a thick growth of trees. "Now, dinnae forget that ye are here only to care for the bairn. Not to try and save him or to fight, just to care for him when we get him away from that madmon."

Following close behind him, Edina nodded and idly patted Gar's head as the dog finally caught up to her. As they crept toward the churchyard, she prayed that little Malcolm was unhurt. Despite Lucais's assertions that she had nothing to feel guilty about, she could not stop blaming herself for the danger the child was in. If anything happened to Malcolm, she was not sure she could forgive herself.

When Lucais stopped and crouched down, she silently edged up next to him. It took all her willpower not to race out into the churchyard they looked out on. Simon stood before two graves, Malcolm crying at his feet. He held a sword in his hand and six mounted men watched the wood that surrounded them. At any moment Simon could cease talking to the grave and kill the child, and there would be nothing they could do but watch.

"Ye cannae reach him," she whispered.

Lucais cursed softly, for it did look bad. He suddenly turned and looked at Gar. The dog had worked to divert the men before, but he was not sure it would work a second time. Simon was a lot closer to Malcolm than he had been to Edina and the child that day at the brook.

Edina saw the direction of his stare and also looked

at her dog. "If he is seen, Simon can kill Malcolm ere any of us can reach him."

"I ken it. Do ye think he can get near one of the men without being seen?"

"Simon has himself weel encircled with watchful eyes this time. I cannae be sure."

She looked at the men in the churchyard, then back at her dog. The idea forming in her mind could easily mean Gar's death. Edina patted his big shaggy head and felt like weeping. It was a horrible choice to make, but the child's life was more important. She briefly hugged the dog, then looked at Lucais.

"There is something he can do that might at least give ye the chance to save Malcolm. Gar can put himself between Simon and the bairn."

Lucais clasped her hand, squeezing it in sympathy, for he knew how much she loved her dog and she could be sending the animal to its death. "How?"

"I will tell him to go and fetch Malcolm. I will get him to race into the churchyard and try to grab the child and run with him."

"Would it be better to tell him to attack Simon?"

"Nay, for all Simon needs to do is cut him down as he runs at him. One of those men will see him. If Gar runs for the child instead, it might confuse them, giving ye that brief opening needed to pull Simon away from the bairn so that poor wee Malcolm can be pulled out of harm's reach. Simon may still kill Gar, but my dog's body will then be between Simon's sword and Malcolm for one brief moment."

"Tell Gar what he needs to do and I will pass along the word to my men."

Lucais disappeared into the underbrush for a mo-

ment and Edina hugged her dog again. Softly she told
him what he had to do, finding his eagerness painful.
He trusted her completely and could not know that she
was asking him to risk death. Even as Lucais reap-
peared, he nodded, and she sent Gar on his way.

Her heart pounding, Edina clasped her hands tightly
together as she watched. It surprised her a little when
Gar approached slowly, as if stalking an animal. When
one of Simon's men cried out a warning and everyone
looked toward Gar, the dog lunged. He ran straight for
Simon, who readied himself to cut the dog down as
soon as he was in sword's reach. For one brief moment
Edina thought Gar had misunderstood her command,
then he veered. She gaped in wonder even as Lucais
cursed when Gar darted around a screaming Simon,
grabbed Malcolm by his little nightshirt, and kept on
running. Simon and his men moved frantically to catch
the dog, and that was when Lucais and his men attacked.

When Simon and his men turned to protect their
own lives, Gar trotted back to her, little Malcolm swing-
ing from his mouth. Edina quickly took the baby in her
arms and hugged her dog. Following Lucais's orders to
go to the horses and wait if she got Malcolm back safely,
Edina rose to her feet. She paused only long enough to
look at the men fighting in the churchyard. Already
three of Simon's men had been cut down, and Lucais
was facing Simon sword to sword. Edina realized that
she did not fear Lucais losing this battle and turned to
go to the horse, soothing a frightened Malcolm as she
walked.

She had just finished changing Malcolm, and was
feeding him some goat's milk when the men from Dun-

mor returned. A quick look at the men revealed no serious injuries, and she turned all her attention to Lucais. He came to stand in front of her, bending slightly
to pat Gar.

"This dog may be the ugliest animal I have e'er set
eyes upon, but he is surely the smartest. Ye shall have to
breed him. 'Twould be a true shame if he was the only
one." He reached out to ruffle his nephew's curls. "Is
he unhurt?"

"Aye. He was just hungry, wet, and frightened. Is
Simon dead?"

"Aye. It is over."

It was over, she thought, fighting to hide the sudden
sadness that nearly overwhelmed her as she secured
Malcolm in his sling and mounted Lucais's horse behind him. She was glad that Simon would no longer
threaten Malcolm, that the child was now safe. But the
end of Simon also meant the end of her time with Lucais.

Once back at Dunmor, she used the excuse of caring
for Malcolm to slip away from Lucais. She took the
child up to her bedchamber, murmuring her good-byes
to him every step of the way. The moment she entered
the room she handed Malcolm to Mary and used the
woman's distraction with the child to collect up her
meager belongings and slip away.

Everyone at Dunmor was caught up in the joy of Malcolm's safe return and the death of Simon. No one paid
her much heed as she crept down the stairs, hurried
through the wide doors of the keep, and dashed across
the bailey. As soon as she got outside of the gates, she
ran, determined to put as much distance between her
and Dunmor as she could. There was no outcry from

the walls, for they had been emptied upon Lucais's return. Edina knew that there had never been a better time to make her escape, and she pushed aside all pain and regret and took full advantage of it. Later, when she could stop running, she would think about what she was doing.

"Where is Edina?" demanded Lucais as he marched to the head table in the great hall and faced his two young cousins. "Have any of you seen her?"

"Nay, not since we rode in through the gates," replied Andrew.

"We thought she was with you or with Malcolm," said Ian.

"She is nowhere to be found." Lucais poured himself a tankard of ale and took a deep drink to steady himself. "I have spent this last hour trying to find her."

"Do ye think she has left?" asked Andrew.

"Aye, I do. She isnae at Dunmor, that is certain." He ran his hands through his already badly tousled hair. "I dinnae understand."

"Weel, she did say that she would stay until the child was safe and she was sure that he would be weel cared for. She kens all that now. Still, ye would have thought she would say fareweel." Andrew frowned and looked at Lucais. "Unless she feared someone might make her stay for all the wrong reasons."

"Ye mean me. Do ye think I am a *wrong reason*?"

"Aye, if all ye wanted was a lass to warm your bed."

"That is not all I wanted, and she kens it."

"Ah, ye talked to her about that last night, did ye?"

"We didnae do much talking last night." Lucais began to feel uneasy. "I had thought that there would be time to think about this and to talk. I ne'er thought she would just run away."

"She probably saw that it was the perfect time to get away without any awkward good-byes or ye trying to make her stay just to warm your bed."

"Will ye stop saying that?" Lucais snapped, but Andrew just shrugged, unmoved by his cousin's temper.

"If ye want more than that, then ye have to tell her so."

"Mayhap she doesnae want any more." The mere thought that Edina had wanted no more from him than a brief moment of passion was uncomfortably painful, and Lucais tried to shrug the thought away.

Andrew made a derisive sound that was echoed by Ian. "She will take whate'er ye want to give her, or would, save that she has a lot of pride for a wee lass. Ye are probably the only one that hasnae seen how she looked at you. There was more than passion shining in those bonnie eyes. And she was a weelborn maid, an innocent no doubt. That kind of lass doesnae leap into a mon's bed just because he has a pretty smile. Of course, since she isnae here, ye cannae ken what she thought or felt."

"Ye think I ought to chase the lass," Lucais said even as he decided that he would do just that, right to the gates of Glenfair if he had to.

"I think ye ought to. I would. I would run her down and tell her all that is in my heart, for that is what she needs. 'Tis your decision. Of course, she is poor and landless and ye willnae gain anything but her if ye wed her."

"I think that will be more than enough," Lucais said as he started toward the door.

"Talk to the lass," called Andrew.

"Aye," agreed Ian. "She hasnae had a verra happy life and she needs to ken that ye are offering her more than a warm bed and, mayhap, honor and duty."

As he strode to the stables to get his horse, Lucais idly wondered how his cousins had come to know Edina so well. The moment his horse was ready, he swung up into the saddle and galloped out of Dunmor. If Edina needed sweet words, he would do his best to give her some, but he would get her back to Dunmor even if he had to drag her back. The moment he had realized that she was gone, he had known that he needed her and that the sweet passion they shared was only a small part of that. Lucais just prayed that she felt the same.

Chapter 8

With her hand shading her eyes, Edina looked toward the hills in the distance and sighed. There was still a long way to go. She was not afraid of the journey. The weather could be harsh in early September, but she knew how to find or build a shelter. Late in the summer the land teemed with food if one knew where to look, and she did. She had Gar, her weapons, and was a skilled hunter, so she did not fear hunger. What twisted her insides into painful knots and made her head ache with the urge to weep was the fact that she was walking away from everything she wanted and needed. At the end of her journey was Glenfair, her cold, dour uncle, and his equally cold, dour people. She had always been alone, but now she knew she would suffer deeply from it. Now she knew that the love, friendship, happiness, and caring she had often dreamed of could really exist. It was going to be torture to live without it.

"Do ye think I have made a mistake, Gar?" she asked the dog sitting at her feet.

"Aye, but I begin to wonder if ye have the wit to ken it."

Edina was both frightened and elated by the sound of Lucais's deep voice right behind her. It also surprised her that she had not heard his approach and that Gar had given her no sign that they were no longer alone. She had not thought that she was that deeply sunk into her own musings. When she slowly turned to face Lucais and saw that he was on foot, his horse nowhere in sight, she felt a little less upset about how he had managed to sneak up on her.

"Ye didnae follow me all this way on foot, did ye?" she asked, curiosity briefly overwhelming her unease.

"Nay, I left my horse back among the trees. He will be safe enough. These are still my lands." He crossed his arms over his chest and looked down at her, one dark brow raised in an expression of slight derision. "Ye havenae gone verra far."

"Weel, I have been walking only for two, mayhap three, hours."

"And ye intended to walk all the way back to Glenfair?"

The bite to his words began to annoy her, and she put her hands on her hips, staring at him belligerently. "Aye. Mayhap ye failed to notice that I dinnae own a horse. The only way I can get back to Glenfair is to walk there."

"Ye didnae think ye should tell me that ye were leaving? One usually pauses to thank one's host before fleeing his home."

"I said faretheeweel to Malcolm," she replied, some of her belligerence fading as she fought a sense of guilt over the way she had crept away from Dunmor.

"Oh, aye, ye spoke to the only one who couldnae understand and certainly couldnae tell anyone that ye were leaving."

"I came to Dunmor to be certain that Malcolm was safe and that he would be weel cared for. That has all come to pass, so there is nae any reason for me to stay another day."

"Not even to say a proper faretheeweel to your lover?"

Edina cursed the blush that immediately warmed her cheeks. "One night of madness doesnae make ye my lover."

"Weel, then let us make it two so that ye can reconsider your decision to creep away like some thief."

Before Edina fully understood what he was saying, Lucais grabbed her and tossed her over his shoulder. That abrupt move and her own surprise kept her breathless for a moment as he started to walk back in the direction of his keep. She was not sure why he was acting so offended or even why he had come after her, but as she regained her senses, she decided that she did not like the way he was toting her about like an old blanket.

"Put me down, ye great oaf," she snapped, and punched his broad back, cursing when he did not even flinch. "Gar," she called, and frowned when she looked around and did not see her dog. "Where is that foolish beastie?"

"He trotted off into the wood, nose to the ground." Lucais lightly slapped her on the backside when she wriggled violently in his hold. "Enough, or ye shall tumble to the ground and break your bonnie, empty head."

"Empty head?" She hit him again, then watched in growing suspicion as he took a blanket roll from the back of his saddle and tossed it on the ground, spreading it out with a few nudges from his feet. "Just what are ye planning?"

A soft screech that was a mixture of alarm and annoyance escaped her as he picked her off his shoulder and gently tossed her onto the blanket. Before she could get away from him, he pinned her there by sprawling on top of her. Her attempts to hit him were stopped with an embarrassing ease when he lightly grasped her by the wrists and held her arms down on the blanket. Edina glared at him, struggling to cling to her sense of outrage and ill use and not be distracted by how good it felt to have his big, strong body pressed so close to hers.

Lucais saw her beautiful eyes darken slightly, the hint of passion in their clear depths contradicting the anger on her delicate face, and he inwardly smiled. That small sign that she wanted him still was enough to restore his battered confidence and soothe some of the pain she had inflicted by leaving so abruptly. His cousins might be right. He just needed to tell her how he felt and offer her more than passion.

At the moment, however, the feel of her soft, lithe body had him eager to do something other than talk. Mayhap, he told himself, it would not hurt to remind her of the sweet fire she was walking away from. And, when lying in his arms, sated from the fierce passion they shared, she might also be more inclined to listen to what he had to say. If nothing else, he decided as he lowered his mouth to hers, he craved one last time in her arms before she walked out of his life forever.

Edina gasped when his mouth covered hers, unwittingly giving him the chance to deepen his kiss immediately. A part of her was outraged. That little voice spoke of sin, warned her about allowing herself to give in to passion without love, and urged her to say no. As Lucais released her wrists and smoothed his big hands down her body, a louder, stronger voice told her cautious self to be quiet. Edina groaned softly as desire rushed through her veins, silencing the argument in her head. She wrapped her arms around Lucais's neck and returned his impassioned kiss.

It was not until they were lying flesh to flesh, their clothing scattered over the ground, that she grasped a fragment of clear thought. She briefly wondered how they had gotten undressed so fast, then struggled to think about what she was doing and not about how much she wanted to do it. The night she and Lucais had spent together had been beautiful. In a strange way, the need to go and save Malcolm had enhanced the sweetness of it. There had been no morning regrets, no wrong things said or done to spoil everything, even the memory. This time they were alone with no chance of interruption, and this time she could not use Malcolm as a reason to stay close, hoping for more than passion.

Lucais slowly kissed his way to her breasts, and Edina shuddered. There had been no promises, no words of love. Lucais could have sought her out because he hungered for another taste of the passion they shared, and for no other reason. As he drew the hard tip of her breast deep into his mouth, she decided that she did not care why he was there. Another taste of the passion they shared would just add to the memories she could cherish when she was alone again. She wrapped her body around his and let passion rule her.

Lucais held Edina close as he regained his senses. Never had lovemaking been so sweet or so fulfilling. He could not understand how she could walk away from that. When he felt her start to tense and shift slightly in his hold, he knew he had to start talking, demanding a few answers from her, and being painfully honest himself.

"Edina," he said, touching a kiss to her forehead as he gently but firmly held her still when she tried to move out of his arms. "We must talk. Since we first set eyes on each other we have suspected each other and desired each other. We have protected my sister's child, beaten my enemy together, and talked about little parts of our lives. Now we must swallow our pride and our doubts and talk about what is to happen between us."

She peered at him through the tangled curtain of her hair, not sure what he meant. A little knot of fear formed in her stomach. If he was planning to ask her to be his lover, to stay with him as his leman, she was not sure she had the strength to refuse.

"What about us?" she asked, her voice little more than a whisper.

"This might be a wee bit easier for me if ye didnae look so frightened," he said, and smiled crookedly.

"Uncertainty makes me frightened."

"Edina, do ye think I ran after ye just for this, sweet as it is?"

"I am not sure why ye are here." She took a deep breath and decided to be completely honest. "I cannae stay if all I am to be is your leman. 'Tis best if I leave now."

"I wouldnae chase my leman down if she left me. I would just go and find another." He brushed a kiss over her mouth when her eyes widened slightly. "Aye, I want ye in my bed, but I also just want ye." He grimaced. "I have ne'er spoken of such things with a lass before, so I ken that I may not say it weel, or prettily."

"Say it badly or any way ye choose," she whispered. "Just say it."

He laughed and pulled her into his arms. "I was nae really sure until I found ye gone, but I love ye, Edina MacAdam. I want ye to stay with me as my wife."

"Are ye sure? I have no dowry." She was not surprised that she found it hard to speak, her voice choked with tears, for she was elated, stunned, and afraid that she had not heard him right.

"Ye are all I need. I have lands and I am wealthy enough to satisfy all my needs." He looked at her, frowning a little when he saw a tear roll down her cheek. "I was hoping that ye would answer in kind."

She hugged him with her whole body. "Idiot. I love ye. Aye, I will marry ye. I have just dreamed of hearing ye say such things so often that I feared I had imagined them." As she got her emotions under control, she looked at him and smiled slightly. "Actually, I do have a small dowry." She glanced at Gar as he trotted up to sit beside them. "A big, furry one."

Lucais laughed and reached out to pat the dog. "A prize any mon would welcome. We shall have to find him a fine bitch to breed with."

"And then we shall have puppies tumbling underfoot. Puppies, and Malcolm, and mayhap a bairn or two of our own?"

"As many as ye want." He gently kissed her. "And they will ne'er be left alone, nor will their mother."

Edina did not think she could ever love him more than she did at that moment. "I do so love you, Lucais."

"And I you, my wee forest maid."

She smiled and looked around at the trees encircling them. The forest was where her mother had cast her aside. The forest was where she had found Malcolm and where she had met Lucais. And now it was in the forest that they pledged their love. Perhaps, she thought with an inner laugh of pure joy as she gave herself over to his kisses, there is something good to be found in the forest.

The Magic Garden

Chapter 1

Scotland
Summer, 1390

"He willnae hang me. He only wants some food."

Rose Keith repeated those words again as she took the apple tarts she had made out of the stone oven. It had to be the hundreth time she had said those words, but she was not feeling any calmer. She said them again as she dribbled honey over the top of the tarts, but noticed that her hands still shook a little. If she did not calm herself down, she would never make it to the keep. Someone would find her sprawled on the road in a swoon, crushed tarts all around her.

"Why would the laird wish to see me?" she asked the black-and-white cat sprawled on her kitchen table, but he simply opened one eye a little, yawned, and turned onto his back. "A fat lot of good ye are, Sweetling."

She took off her apron and hung it on the hook by the back door of her cottage. The day had dawned so bright and warm, she had been certain it would be a good day. Then little Peter had arrived with word from the castle that the new laird wished her to bring him some of her fine apple tarts in time for his evening meal. Rose had felt her heart plummet into her feet and it had not returned to its proper place yet, no matter how many comforting things she told herself.

Visiting the old laird had never troubled her so. She had skipped up to the keep several times a week since she had been a small child to deliver food to the old laird. He had been very kind to her, had even grieved with her when her mother had died three years ago. In fact, she was sure it was the old laird who had left the basket of kittens at her door in an attempt to cheer her. But the old laird was dead now, his son now home to take his place.

As she braided her hair, she tried to recall the boy she had once known. Dark, she thought, and smiled faintly. Dark hair, dark gray eyes, and dark skin. He had been so surprisingly tolerant of and kind to the child she had been. It had saddened her when he had left to fight in France almost ten years ago. His visits home had been rare and brief and she had not seen him, so her last clear image of him was as a young man of barely nineteen years. Now he was nearing thirty, his youth given to battle and the last of his family dead. It was no wonder he was dark-humored she thought, then scolded herself for heeding rumor and gossip.

Men grew up. Kind, smiling young men were changed into stern, solemn lairds. It was a sad fact of life that the sweet joy of youth faded. She had been a happy child, sheltered and blissfully innocent. Time and understanding had stolen that cheerful ignorance. Her mother had not been able to mute all the ugly whispers about the Keith women or halt every outbreak of fear and anger. Rose could understand people's fears, for she had felt the touch of them herself from time to time, but she was not sure she would ever understand why their fear made them cruel.

Gently setting the tarts in her basket, she prayed the laird was one of those rare people who felt nothing when eating her food. Or, that he accepted the soothing or lifting of his spirits as simply the result of eating something delicious. Rose had enough trouble in her life without having the new laird cocking a suspicious, fearful eye her way.

"Weel, lads, wish me luck," she said as she donned her cloak.

Rose shook her head when only two of the four cats sprawled around the kitchen deigned to glance at her. It was very sad, she decided as she picked up her basket and headed out the door, when a woman of only one and twenty was reduced to talking to her cats. Even sadder was the fact that, since her mother's death, she rarely had anyone else to talk to.

"Pssst! Rose!"

Then again, she mused, there were times when talking to cats was preferable to talking to some people. She hastily scolded herself for being unkind and smiled at the young girl who stumbled out from amid the tangled shrubbery she had been hidng behind. Meg was at that awkward age of not quite a child, but not quite a woman. Even harder, Meg had a lively mind that was not being kept fed. Unfortunately, that lively mind had become fixed upon Rose, her family, and her garden.

"I fear I cannae visit now, Meg," Rose said, almost smiling at the way the young girl had to brush her thick dark hair off her face. "I must hie to the castle."

"I ken it," Meg said as she fell into step beside Rose. "The laird wants to see ye and test your food for himself."

Rose frowned slightly. "How did ye hear about that?"

" 'Tis being whispered all about the village."

"Oh, dear."

"Aye. Seems the old laird kept a journal. 'Tis said he thought it might help his son settle in as laird if he kept clear records of all that was said and done at the castle, in the village, and all about the lands of Duncairn."

"And the old laird wrote about Rose Cottage, the Keith women, and the garden."

"He did. He praised your apple tarts, 'tis said."

"Weel, that is kind, but I rather wish he hadnae done so."

"Why? The young laird lived here nearly a score of his years. I suspicion he heard all about it."

"True." Rose sighed. "He may have forgotten it, though."

"Wheesht, even if he had, he would soon have been told about it all." Meg shook her head, then had to brush the hair off her thin face again. "S'truth, Mistress Kerr has nay doubt complained, as is her wont."

"She has already been to see the new laird?"

"Fast as she could. He *has* been home a fortnight, ye ken. She was dragging poor Anne up there 'ere the dust had settled behind his horse. The laird has no wife, has he?"

Worse and worse, Rose mused, eyeing the stout walls of Duncairn warily as they appeared before her. Joan Kerr hated her, had hated her mother, and was the most vicious and consistent voice speaking out against the Keith women. She had married a Kerr but returned home once widowed. Rose's mother had often jested that the Kerrs had probably had a grand celebration when the woman had left. Joan was a distant cousin of the old laird and made far more of that connection than it was worth, considering how many of the clan could claim the same. For some reason Joan had always disliked the Keith women. Rose had a feeling her mother had known the reason for that animosity, but she had never shared that information.

"It would be a good match," she murmured, wondering why the thought of the new laird with Anne should irritate her. "Despite her mother, Anne is a sweet woman."

"Too sweet. I think the laird terrified her. That seemed to be what Mistress Kerr was scolding her about as they walked home. Timid, wee mousie, her mother called her. Anne stayed to the shadows and the few times she spoke to the laird, 'twas in a tiny, shaky whisper."

"Ye listened for quite a while, didnae ye?"

Meg nodded, revealing not a glimmer of remorse. "Thought they might catch me at it a time or two."

"Did the laird do something in particular to frighten Anne?"

"Not anything they mentioned." Meg frowned and scratched her slightly pointed chin. "All Anne would say, or could say with her mother moaning on and on about ungrateful bairns, was that he was too big, too dark, and too fierce."

"Too fierce?" Rose's steps slowed even more as she neared the towering gates of Duncairn.

"Och, weel, I wouldnae pay much heed to that. Anne is sweet, as ye say, but she is also a coward. A wee brown rabbit shows his teeth and she is all aswoon."

Rose looked away as she swallowed a laugh. It was not well done of her to listen to Meg's gossip, but she was unable to resist the allure. It was also, sadly, often the only news about those she lived among that came her way.

"I begin to understand poor Anne," she muttered, pausing in front of the gates.

"Nay, ye are far braver than her," Meg assured her. "Anne could ne'er live alone, although I suspicion she oftimes dreams of it."

This time Rose could not fully restrain a giggle. "Naughty Meg." She quickly grew serious again and sighed as she stared through the gates at the thick walls of the keep. "I dinnae feel verra brave at the moment." She looked at the basket of tarts she held. "I keep wondering why the mon wants my apple tarts? Is he but wishing to see if he finds them as delicious as his father did? Or is he seeking proof that I am a witch, that I am an evil thing that must be cast out of Duncairn?"

"Wheesht, ye have been thinking on this too long." Meg got behind Rose and gently pushed her along until she was inside the gates. "If naught else, ye cannae run away and hide, can ye? Best to get this o'er with. And, doesnae your food make people happy and at ease, scowls turning into bonnie smiles? A calm, smiling laird isnae apt to be hanging ye from the battlements."

"Thank ye." Rose nimbly eluded Meg's pushing and turned to frown at her. "I was recovering weel until ye said that."

"Ah, good, there ye are, Rose," called a lanky young man named Donald as he hurried over to her.

"Aye, *here* she be," said Meg. "Ye are *so* clever to track her down right here in the bailey."

Donald glared at Meg. "This rat's nest of hair on a stick wasnae invited. Hie along home, bairn."

When Meg returned that insult with an impressive one of her own, Rose sighed. Only four years separated Donald and Meg, yet Rose could not think of many times when the two were not arguing or insulting each other. Her mother had found the pair a source of great amusement, even called what the two did a mating dance. Flora Keith had always revealed a great skill at judging such matches, but Rose sometimes wondered if the two would survive it.

Taking a deep breath, Rose squared her shoulders and walked into the keep. Donald and Meg needed no audience to their strange courtship. Meg was right in saying it was best to get this confrontation over with. Anticipating it, thinking of all that could go wrong, was only agitating her. Rose was almost tempted to eat one of her own apple tarts. Her agitated state might be uncomfortable, but it kept her wary. She felt that was more important than greeting the new laird with a calm heart and a pleasing smile.

She paused in the doorway to the great hall to study the two men seated at the laird's table. With his long gray hair, Robert the steward was easy to recognize. Rose cautiously turned her full attention upon the new laird, Sir Adair Dundas.

The long black hair, the dark gray eyes, and the dark skin told her the man next to Robert had to be the new laird. A closer look revealed the shadows of the old laird in the strong line of Adair's jaw and his long, elegant nose. Fighting for France had added the muscle the boy of nineteen had lacked, although the lean, almost graceful lines of the tall body were still clear. Little else of the boy she had once known remained, however. There was no hint of a smile upon that well-shaped mouth, no sign of softness at all in his finely hewn features. France and its wars had taken the boy she had once known and sent back a stranger.

"Mistress Keith," exclaimed Robert when he finally noticed her. "Come, sit down," he said as he stood up, along with Adair. "Do ye recall Sir Adair?"

"I do. My laird," she murmured and curtsied.

"Where is Donald?" asked Sir Adair. "I sent him to meet ye at the gates."

"Meg was with me, laird."

"Oh, dear." Robert frowned toward the door even as they all took their seats, obviously wondering if he should go and rescue his son.

"Meg?" Sir Adair frowned for a moment. "Lame Jamie's lass?"

"Aye," replied Robert. "She and my son seem to forget all else when they meet and begin to trade insults." He smiled crookedly at Rose. "I ken that your mother said they would be mates, but I oftimes wonder if they will survive each other long enough to see that truth."

"I, too, wonder. Indeed, I pondered that riddle e'en as I left them hurling insults at each other." She set her basket upon the table. "It does seem more of a battle than a courtship."

As Robert and Rose talked, Adair studied the woman he had last seen as a too thin, slightly untidy child. High full breasts, a tiny waist, and gently rounded hips declared her a woman grown, but he could still see that sweet, beguiling child in her delicate heart-shaped face. Her bright hair had darkened to a rich copper and hung down past her waist in thick, tempting waves. Most of the freckles had faded from her skin, leaving no more than a scattered trail across her small straight nose and soft cheeks. Thick, dark lashes and gently arched brows enhanced her wide, beautiful, sea green eyes. Her full mouth was curved in a smile as she and Robert wondered at the odd behavior of the two young people she had left behind in the bailey. He felt a slight tightening in his body and was not surprised that he would desire her.

There was something missing, however, and it took him a moment to decide what was gone. The child he had known had been a cheerful sprite of a girl, ready with a smile or a laugh. That joy had been dimmed. It pained him to see that, but he was not sure why. He had no time or interest in such foolishness. In truth, such joy and laughter as Rose had once possessed belonged cast aside with her childhood. It was born of the ignorance of blind innocence. At some time during the years he had been away, Rose had finally seen the world as it truly was, a place full of misery, grief, and pain.

He inwardly cursed when he realized that dose of good sense had not completely banished his disappointment. Adair feared he had hoped Rose still had the gift to make him smile as she had so often as a child. Whenever he had thought of Duncairn, he had thought of her, smiling and laughing. It was past time to bury that foolish memory.

"I was sorry to hear about your mother's death," he said when Rose looked his way, then inwardly grimaced over that appalling attempt at conversation.

"Thank ye, laird," she said. "I still miss her sorely."

"Aye. Father wrote of her death with great sorrow."

"He was always verra kind to us and will be sorely missed as weel."

Adair nodded and touched her basket. "He spoke often of the cooking skills of ye and your mother. Father was verra fond of the apple tarts."

Rose reached for the goblet of wine Robert had poured for her, realized her hands shook, and quickly clasped them tightly together in her lap. Adair had a beautiful voice, deep and slightly rough. Her all-too-vivid imagination could hear it condemning her as a witch and she felt cold. She tried to find comfort in the fact that Robert was so at ease. He certainly did not act as if she was, more or less, on trial.

"When he had them in the dead of winter, he often called them a touch of spring," she said.

"Father also said he found them most comforting, that eating one was sure to pull him free of a dark mood. He talked so often of them, I felt compelled to try some myself. I hope my request didnae inconvenience you."

She managed a smile. "Nay, laird."

When he tugged her basket closer, she tried to remain at least outwardly calm. The boy she had known would have never been a threat to her, but that boy was gone. Rose was a little surprised that she felt so strongly attracted to this dark man but knew that did not mean he was safe. Her mother had taught her that desire, even love, could cloud one's thinking, dull one's instincts. As he chose a tart and moved it toward his mouth, she prayed that, if the food did anything to him, it simply stirred to life the spirit of that kind young man she had once known.

Chapter 2

Sweet, yet tart, Adair mused as he chewed. The blend was perfect. Even the texture of the food was perfect. It seemed strange that such a simple food could be such a delight to the tongue. Adair reached for another one.

Slowly, he relaxed in his chair. A gentle warmth seeped through him, easing the tense readiness of his muscles that seemed to afflict him even in his sleep. Although he had always thought of Duncairn as home, for the first time in far too long, he felt its welcome reach out and touch him. He looked at Rose, noticed she was looking a little pale and was clenching her hands in her lap, and felt an urge to take her into his arms. Adair realized he wanted to kiss and stroke away the fear from which she was suffering.

Adair reached for his tankard and had a deep drink of ale. It did not banish the feelings. Comforting, his father had called the food of the Keith women, and that was exactly what Adair felt. He felt just as he once did when his late mother used to stroke his brow and kiss his cheek. Adair felt he ought to be alarmed by that, but he was not. If it was due to sorcery, as Mistress Kerr suspected, it was certainly a very benign sort.

Then again, he mused, if little Rose could make food that gave comfort to a man who had not known it for far too long, what other trickery could she produce? He studied her lovely face and felt guilty for that suspicion. There was no evil in Rose, no darkness. At worst, she was misguided.

"They are verra good," he said at last, resisting the urge to have another. "I shall save the rest for later, I think."

"As ye wish, m'laird," she murmured.

"Ye grow the apples yourself?"

"Aye. Rose Cottage has a lovely garden."

She inwardly cursed. The last thing she wished for was for his attention to turn to her garden. When people turned a fearful, superstitious eye on Rose Cottage it was mostly set upon the Keith women. Only rarely was it turned upon the garden itself. Rose preferred it that way. The garden was not only her heritage, but it was far more vulnerable than she was. If nothing else, it could not flee the anger and fear of the people.

"Mistress Kerr spoke of your garden when she was here."

"Did she?" This time Rose was grateful for the anger she always felt toward that woman, for it dimmed the fear she could not conquer on her own. "I believe she has intruded upon it once or twice." With torch in hand, Rose added silently.

Adair heard the hint of anger in her voice and noted that her hand no longer trembled when she took up her goblet and had a drink of wine. Mistress Kerr had managed to slip out several disparaging remarks about Rose Keith during her visits. There had even been a few less-than-subtle accusations. His father had written of the long-standing animosity the Widow Kerr had for the Keith women of Rose Cottage, but not the cause of it. It was clear from Rose's reaction to the woman's name that the animosity was still alive and strong.

"Come, I will escort ye home," he said as he stood up.

"That isnae necessary, laird," she said.

The moment he grasped her hand in his to help her to her feet, Rose decided that Sir Adair walking her home was not only unnecessary, it would prove disastrous. That tickle of attraction she had felt while looking at the man was increased tenfold at the touch of his hand. A little stunned by the feelings rampaging through her, Rose somewhat meekly allowed Adair to lead her away.

Her mother had warned her about such feelings. Flora Keith had not believed it wise to keep maidens ignorant of such things as desire. Rose knew she desired Sir Adair, that her affection for the youthful Adair had somehow lingered in her heart and might well be struggling to become something more. She could not allow that. Sir Adair was her laird, a man so beyond her touch it was laughable.

"The Keith women have held Rose Cottage for a long time, aye?" asked Sir Adair, telling himself there was nothing wrong with being so intensely curious about Rose, for she was living on his lands, one of those he was sworn to protect.

"Aye," she replied, "for nearly as long as the laird has been a Dundas." She knew she ought to tug her hand free of his but told herself it was a small, harmless indulgence. "The tale is that the first Keith woman was fleeing a mon and sought shelter in a small copse. The Laird of Duncairn was moved by her troubles and offered her shelter, told her she could make her home upon his lands. She built Rose Cottage with the help of some of the laird's men and started the garden. Keith women have been there ever since. They always keep the name Keith as weel, e'en if they wed. That was done mostly in the beginning. The family grew enough after that, so that if a Keith woman was to marry, another Keith woman would come to tend the garden."

"Your mother remained a Keith."

"Aye, she wed one. My father died when I was a wee bairn, though, and I dinnae recall him."

"And when did the women become so famous for their food?"

"I think it was from the first time the garden gave us enough food to cook with." She sighed. "My mother ne'er told me the why of it all. She may have intended to, but the fever came upon her swiftly. She was ill and then she died, too quickly to settle any of her affairs or tend to matters left undone. I have yet to get through all of her writings. The tale may be in there."

"Do ye read and write as weel?"

"Aye. The Keith women have long been healers. 'Twas thought wise to keep careful notes of herbs and cures. If something new was tried, it was quickly noted, and its success or failure as weel." As they neared her cottage, she tugged her hand free of his. "I thank ye, laird. 'Twas most kind of ye to walk me home."

Adair fought to ignore the sense of loss he felt when she pulled her hand away. "I suppose 'tis too dark to see the garden now."

"Oh, aye. 'Twould appear as no more than shadows." She opened the door to her cottage and grimaced when all four of her cats hurried out to twine themselves around her legs.

"Four cats?"

"Shortly after my mother died someone left a basket of four kittens on my threshold. Your father denied it, but I am sure it was he. Oddly enough, there are three toms and one female."

"Why are ye nay o'erwhelmed with the beasts?" He bent to scratch behind the ears of a large ginger tom and almost smiled at the deep, loud purr that erupted from the animal.

"I have a wee but verra comfortable cage I lock the female in when she is in season." She picked up a sleek gray cat. "Lady accepts her occasional banishment. She has had but one litter, quickly dispersed among the villagers." Rose frowned down at her biggest cat. "Sweetling broke through the door. 'Tis thicker now." Looking back at Adair, she caught the faintest hint of a smile curving his lips.

"Sweetling? Ye named that monster Sweetling?"

"Weel, he was but a wee thing when I got him. The ginger tom is Growler, for he did a lot of that, and the gray-striped tom is Lazy, which he still is."

"All alone as ye are, ye ought to have something more protective than cats."

"Weel, Geordie the blacksmith's son found them a fierce obstacle when he was creeping about here one night. Of course, he couldnae tell people he was sent to heel by four cats, and the tale he told caused me a wee bit of trouble for a while."

Her familiars, the Widow Kerr had called Rose's cats, demons in disguise. Adair suspected Geordie's lies fed that nonsense. Many people feared cats. Even those who kept them to control vermin were often uneasy around the animals. He was sure the rumors about Rose only enhanced the tales whispered about her pets.

Adair was not exactly sure what he felt about magic. Most of the time he did not believe in it. On the rare occasion when he found himself wondering if it did exist, he disliked the idea. Rose had made no mention of it, and he hoped that was because she did not believe in it either.

He told himself it would be necessary for him to spend some time with Rose to search out the truth, ignoring the inner voice that scorned his thin excuse. In his writings, his father had talked of magic and the trouble it often caused the Keith women. Rose's trouble was being brewed by the Widow Kerr, as her mother's had been, and by others like Geordie the blacksmith's son, who wished to turn critical eyes away from his own shameful attempt to attack Rose. He would not allow this superstitious nonsense to exist upon his lands.

When he fixed his attention back on Rose, he found her and her cats staring at him, their heads all cocked at the same angle. Adair could easily imagine how such things could stir superstition in the ignorant. He found it both charming and a little amusing. At the moment, it was not hard to see the beguiling child he had once known. He reached out to brush his knuckles over her soft cheek.

"Mayhap ye havenae changed as much as I thought," he murmured. "Good sleep, Rose."

Rose watched him walk away. With a faintly trembling hand she touched the still warm place upon her cheek. Such a light caress he had given her, yet she had felt it right down to her toes. The man was definitely a threat.

* * *

"Robert, has someone been eating my tarts?" Adair asked his steward.

Once back in his great hall, Adair had made himself comfortable in his chair and poured himself some ale. He had set Rose's basket in front of him, intending to indulge himself. Although he had been greatly distracted by Rose, he was sure that eight tarts had remained when he left to escort her home. There were only six now. He counted them a second time to be certain, then eyed a blushing Robert.

"I had one, laird," Robert confessed. "Your father always allowed me to have one, and I fear I helped myself out of habit."

"Ah, and then it tempted ye to have a second. I understand. They are indeed verra tempting."

"Aye, they are, but I only had one. My son had the other 'ere I could stop him. He was agitated after his confrontation with Meg and, as he ranted and raved, he snatched one up and ate it. I reprimanded him severely, m'laird, and he was verra sorry. Although it did ease his temper."

"Of course it did. No harm done," Adair murmured, then he frowned at the tart he held in his hand. "They are verra good. Rose is an excellent cook."

"As was her mother, laird."

"Do ye think there is magic in her food or in her garden?"

Robert grimaced. "I dinnae wish to use the word *magic*. 'Tis a word that can stir up trouble and talk of evil. I believe the Keith women have a true skill at cooking food that pleases both the mouth and the heart. I think they chose wisely when they chose their land,

picking a place with rich soil and ample water that en-
hances the flavor of all they grow."

Adair smiled faintly. "Weel said. I believe I will still
have a close look at that garden."

"Do ye suspect magic, or, weel, witchcraft?" Robert
whispered the last word as if merely speaking it stirred
his fear.

"Most days I dinnae believe in either. Howbeit, many
others do, and the Widow Kerr seems most intent upon
stirring up that fear. If I have a good look at that garden,
I shall be able to turn aside such fear and superstition
with clear, cold fact. I would prefer to tell the widow to
close her mouth and cease with her lies, but—"

" 'Twould be easier to make the wind cease to blow
or stop the river's flow," muttered Robert.

"Quite probably," replied Adair, faintly amused by
this sudden show of temper in the usually sweet-natured
Robert. "The game she plays is dangerous, however.
She could get that poor lass hurt or killed. I will try to
weaken the power of her poison, but if I cannae, I will
make her cease. I willnae have that idiocy at Duncairn."

Brave words, he thought later as he lay in his bed and
savored the last of Rose's apple tarts. Superstition and
fear were difficult enemies to fight. Especially when
Rose made food such as these apple tarts, he mused, as
he savored the sense of peace and well-being that
flowed through him. Any fool knew food, no matter
how delicious, should not have such an effect upon
one's humors. Adair still resisted calling it magic, but
he had to admit it was unusual. If he was not feeling so
pleasant, such a reaction to eating an apple tart might
even make him uneasy.

Crossing his arms beneath his head, he closed his
eyes and was not surprised when visions of Rose Keith

filled his mind. She had grown into an enchantingly beautiful woman. He had wanted her immediately and knew a long celibacy had nothing to do with it. Something about Rose stirred him in more ways than he could count. He wanted to ravish her even as he wanted to shelter her from every harsh word. He wanted her to soundly disavow any taint of magic yet found the mystery surrounding her and her garden intriguing. Just thinking about her made him feel like smiling, yet it had been a very long time since he had seen or felt anything worth smiling about.

Despite his confusion, seeing Rose in his dreams would be far preferable to what usually haunted him. Adair had a suspicion he would not be suffering any of those dark dreams this night. The painful memories and grief that had kept such a tight grip on him for so long were still there, but not so insistent, so overwhelming. He had lost so many friends, bold young men who had gone to France to find glory and riches only to find pain and death. Although he had gained some wealth, it could never buy him back the time he had lost with his family, now all dead and gone.

The grief inside his heart stirred a little, but only a little. It was as if some unseen hand had restrained that demon. He thought for the thousandth time that it was his own pride, his own arrogance, that had kept him in France, that he should have seen more clearly how time was slipping away. A soft voice in his head told him true arrogance was thinking he could foresee God's will. Guilt, yet another demon with which he had long wrestled, raised its head before it, too, was subdued.

Dark, bloody memories of battle and capture were still there. He could see their nightmarish shadows lurking in the back of his mind, eager to scar his dreams and disturb his sleep, but they did not surge forward as they always had before. They were in the past, a voice soothed, one that sounded very much like his late mother's.

That was a little alarming, he thought, yet he did not *feel* alarmed. He felt comforted. Adair could almost feel his mother's touch, her soft kiss, and hear her say, *Aye, my braw, wee laddie, 'twas a sad time, weighted with grief and pain, but 'tis past. Ye are alive, ye are home, and ye have met a bonnie wee lass. Let those truths fill your heart and mind and sleep, my laddie, sleep.*

A bonnie lass who fed him apple tarts that made him hear his mother's voice in his head, he mused, but could not gather the strength or will to be troubled by that. He would court Rose, he decided. It was time he was wed and set about the business of breeding an heir. Rose was the first woman he had met who had stirred such a thought in his head.

For one brief moment he feared that, too, was caused by her apple tarts, but only for a moment. Adair knew the feelings Rose stirred within him were caused by Rose and Rose alone. The seed had probably been planted years ago by the endearing child she had been. He would have her for his own, but first he would get her to cast aside all this dangerous foolishness about magic.

As sleep crept over him, Adair thought he heard his mother's voice again. She was scolding him for thinking he could take only a piece when true happiness and the prize he sought would only come to him when he could accept the whole. Adair decided he was too tired to understand what that meant.

Chapter 3

"Ye willnae get away with using your witch's tricks on the laird."

Rose sighed, then took several deep breaths to try to smother her anger. Mistress Kerr's voice was enough to stir her anger now. After years of enduring the woman's poison, she simply had no patience left. She knew she had to be careful, however. Every word she said to the woman had to be carefully weighed or it could come back to haunt her. It was not fair, but Rose knew she had to remain calm and courteous. It was her own fault she was going to have to endure this confrontation. She had been so caught up in her thoughts about Sir Adair that she had undoubtedly missed several opportunities to elude the woman.

"Pardon, Mistress?" she asked in a sweet voice as she turned to face the woman.

Mistress Kerr crossed her arms and glared at Rose. "Ye heard me. The mon has barely warmed the laird's seat and ye are trotting up there with some of that cursed food. Aye, and then ye bewitched the lad so that he followed ye home."

"Ye make our laird sound like some stray pup. And might I ask how ye ken he walked me home?"

"Geordie saw the two of ye walking along hand in hand. Ye have probably already lured him into your bed."

"Ye insult the laird *and* me. Our laird is a gallant knight and didnae like the idea of my walking home alone. Since Geordie was obviously lurking in the wood again, it appears the laird's protection was needed."

"If ye hadnae bewitched the poor lad, he wouldnae be such a trouble to ye."

"Mither," whispered Anne, shock and a tentative condemnation in her voice.

Rose glanced at Anne, who stood just behind her mother. She was a little embarrassed to realize she had not even noticed the young woman, then told herself she had nothing to feel guilty about. Anne had developed a true skill at hiding whenever her mother was near. The fact that Anne could do so when only a few paces away from the woman was astonishing. It was also, Rose decided, a little sad.

"Geordie is nay bewitched," Rose said, surprised at how calm and reasonable she sounded, for she was furious. "He is a rutting swine who sees a lass alone as easy game. I would think he deserves far more watching than I do."

"Oh, aye, ye would like it if I ceased to watch you," snapped Mistress Kerr. "That would leave ye free to ensnare the laird."

"The mon has survived ten years of fighting in France. I dinnae think he can be brought to his knees by a wee, red-haired lass."

"Heed me, Rose Keith: I mean for my Anne to become the laird's wife."

"I dinnae want to be," protested Anne, even as she retreated a few steps from her mother.

"Hush, ye stupid lass," snapped Mistress Kerr. "Ye will do as ye are told. And ye can begin by ceasing to fawn o'er that fool Lame Jamie."

"The laird doesnae want to wed me, either."

Mistress Kerr ignored her daughter and returned her glare to Rose. "I mean what I say, Rose Keith. I have plans for the laird and I will be verra angry if ye interfere with them."

Rose watched Mistress Kerr stride away, Anne a few steps behind her. Since Mistress Kerr was always angry with her, Rose idly wondered how much would change if she did interfere. Then she sighed and started to walk home from the village. Even if she fled to a nunnery on the morrow, if Mistress Kerr did not get her daughter wed to the laird, Rose knew the woman would still blame her. She also knew she should take the woman's threats very seriously, but it was a warm, sunny day and she would not spoil it with dark, chilling thoughts of what might happen.

Instead, she fixed her thoughts on what Mistress Kerr had let slip about Anne. Anne wanted Lame Jamie, Meg's father. Rose grimaced, not fond of the name Meg's father had been stuck with. The man had only a slight hesitation to his walk due to a broken leg that had not healed exactly right. Unfortunately, there were half a dozen men named Jamie around Duncairn, and people felt compelled to mark each one with some extra, identifying name, and Meg's father did not seem to mind.

She frowned as she wondered exactly what Mistress

Kerr's objections were to Lame Jamie. The man was barely thirty, was a widower, had a fine cottage and only one child. He was not rich, but he was far from poor. And, unlike Mistress Kerr's thin claim of kinship to the old laird, Lame Jamie was second cousin to Sir Adair. Of course he was not the laird, she thought, and felt sorry for poor Anne. Even though Anne was two years older than she, free to choose her own husband, Rose knew the woman lacked the courage to break free of her mother's tight grip.

"Wheesht, if I was a witch, I would brew up a potion to give poor Anne some backbone," she muttered as she started up the path to her cottage.

Suddenly Rose stopped and carefully put down her basket. It took her a moment to understand what had so firmly caught her attention. Her front door was slightly open. That was not an immediate cause for concern, for Sweetling was capable of opening the door. He only did so, however, when something outside strongly caught his attention. She told herself that there was still no need for alarm—a cat's interest could be firmly caught by a falling leaf—but she still looked around very carefully. Geordie was still after her, always lurking in wait.

Her heart skipped with fear when she saw that the gate to her garden was open. Sweetling could not do that. Only human hands could manage to open the heavy, iron-banded gate. Picking up one of the stout cudgels she kept in several strategic places, Rose crept into her garden. It was not until she reached her apple orchard that she saw the intruder.

The laird was strolling through her garden. In some ways, he had the right, as she was on Duncairn land despite the hereditary rights granted the Keith women. Nevertheless, she was irritated that he had not waited for a personal invitation. It was that irritation that subdued the urge to laugh at the way her cats trailed behind him, stopping when he stopped and even studying what he studied. It was impossible to completely restrain a brief grin, however, when he crouched to pick up a handful of dirt and her cats joined him in poking and sniffing at the ground.

Sir Adair's years as a warrior were revealed by how quickly he heard her approach, and the speed with which his body tensed and his hand went to his sword. He stood up, brushed the dirt from his hands, and bowed slightly in greeting. When he glanced down at her hand and faintly smiled, she blushed, realizing she still carried the cudgel.

"A stout weapon," he murmured. "Ye hold it as if ye ken how to use it."

"I do." She leaned the cudgel up against the trunk of an apple tree, idly stroking the trunk as she often did, for it was the tree her mother had planted when she was born.

"Did ye have one near at hand when Geordie attacked ye?"

"Aye, but my cats got to him first."

He looked down at the cats flanking him. "I didnae let them out."

"I ken it. Sweetling can open the door." She smiled faintly. "He does so when something catches his interest. I kenned he couldnae open the garden gate, however."

"Ah. I came hoping ye could show me the garden so many talk about, but when ye didnae appear after near half an hour, I decided to meander through it on my own. 'Tis weel laid out, and the wall that encircles it is a fine tall and stout one."

She nodded and started to follow him as he resumed walking. "It took many years. Some was done by the Keith women, some by their husbands, and some in return for food when harvests were poor or destroyed."

"And your harvests have ne'er been poor or your crop destroyed?" He paused by some blackberries growing near the wall and plucked a few ripe ones.

"My harvests have been hurt at times, but my garden is weel planned, the wall shields it from damaging winds as weel as from intruders, and I have plenty of water close at hand. We dinnae have large fields to protect, and o'er the years we have done all we can to protect what grows here. Some of the people have accepted our ways, if their own gardens are small or in one small area of the larger fields they plow and plant. At times, the fact that our garden still grows whilst others falter and fail has caused us trouble. 'Tis mostly good planning, its size, and ample water within these walls that makes it flourish."

"And what makes it so, weel, comforting?" Adair moved so that Rose was standing between him and the trunk of an apple tree. "I should like to scorn its effect upon people, but I cannae. Nor can any others. 'Tis the one thing they all agree upon."

That was a question Rose heartily wished he had not asked. She knew the food from her gardens did something other food did not, most people calling it a comforting, a soothing, even saying it gave them a sense of peace. Her mother had never truly explained that. Flora Keith had spoken of a blessing by the fairies and that, some day soon, she would tell Rose the whole tale.

Sadly, death had stolen her mother's chance to speak. Sir Adair was not a man who would accept talk of fairies, however.

" 'Tis just good food, the fruit plump and sweet, the vegetables and grains hearty and strong. Nay more," she said.

"I think ye believe there is more than that. I think ye believe there is magic in this garden, just as so many others do."

"Ye think a great deal," she muttered. "Mayhap ye need more work to do."

Adair popped a blackberry into his mouth to halt the smile forming on his lips. He savored the softening that happened within, that continued blunting of the sharp edges of his dark memories. It was impossible to deny what food from Rose's garden made him feel, but he did not want to attribute it to magic. Something in the water or even in the soil was causing it. That was his preferred explanation. Adair knew he would not cease to eat anything she allowed him to, for he ached for the calm the food gifted him with, the growing ability to look at the past with more understanding and acceptance.

"For now, my work is to discover why the food from this garden affects what people feel," he said, stepping a little closer and placing his hands on the trunk of the tree to either side of her head.

"Why is that so important? It is what it is. It does what it does. It harms no one."

"It harms you."

"Nay, it—"

"It harms you. It causes talk, dangerous talk. Dark whispers of magic and witchcraft."

"Not everyone thinks such things."

"Not now, but we both ken that, at times, such whispers have gained strength, roused the people, and put the Keith women in danger. I want the whispers stopped. I dislike the thought that I might be dragged from my bed some night because some fools have gotten themselves all asweat with fear and are determined to root out the evil at Rose Cottage. I mostly dislike the thought that the chances of getting here too late are verra good."

Rose took a deep breath to steady herself only to feel her breasts brush against Adair's broad chest. She knew he had drawn close to her, but not that close. That nearness made it difficult for her to think clearly. She was far too aware of his strength, his size, and her own deep attraction to the man. Rose knew she should move, that he probably would not try to restrain her, but she lacked the will.

"If they come hunting me, I will do my best to nay let it wake you," she said.

"This isnae a game, Rose."

"Do ye think I dinnae ken that? Mayhap better than ye do?" She thought it odd that she could be both tense with unease and tremble with pleasure when he stroked her cheek. "I cannae stop the whispers. I cannae hold back fear and superstition. I am but a wee lass who tries to make a living with what she grows in her garden and, occasionally, with what she can cook. I harm no one and, in truth, have helped many. There is nay more I can do."

"Ah, lass, that isnae good enough and weel ye ken it. Ye must openly deny there is magic here. Ye must show people there are reasons why your food tastes better, why your garden stays healthy nay matter what afflicts the others."

Adair closely watched her face. It was evident she was trying to neither deny nor admit that there was any magic at Rose Cottage. He wanted denial, but he began to suspect he would not get it. That troubled him, for he also wanted Rose.

He fixed his gaze upon her mouth. For now he would help himself to a little of what he wanted. All the other complications could be dealt with later. Adair almost smiled when her eyes slowly widened as he lowered his mouth to hers. Since she made no attempt to move, push him away, or speak a denial, he deemed that a silent acquiescence and kissed her.

Rose felt his warm, surprisingly soft lips touch hers and felt trapped by her own desire. Heat flowed through her body, softening her, rousing a heady welcome. A tiny part of her was shocked when she wrapped her arms around his neck, but it died when she parted her lips and he began to stroke the inside of her mouth with his tongue. Her whole body shivered with the strength of the delight she felt. This was what she wanted, needed, despite every instinct that warned her against reaching so high. Or for a man who was determined to make her deny the magic that was her heritage.

That thought gave her the strength to pull away when he began to kiss her neck. She met his gaze, saw how passion had darkened and warmed his eyes, and nearly threw herself back into his arms. Taking a deep breath in a vain attempt to calm herself, she stiffened her spine and faced him squarely. Despite her own confusion about magic, whether it even existed and, if it did, where it came from, it was all tangled up with her heritage, with who she was. She had to be wary of a man who scorned it, disliked it, and wished her to do the same.

"That was unwise," she said, silently cursing the huskiness of her voice.

"Aye?" He stroked her cheek and felt her tremble slightly even as she pressed herself back against the tree, away from him. "Ye didnae cry me nay."

"I should have—verra loudly."

"Ah, lass, 'twas but a kiss. The sweetest I have e'er had, and I ken I shall be longing for another taste, but, when all is said and done, 'twas just a kiss. 'Twas no great stain upon your honor."

"I ken it, yet I am a lass who lives alone. I must guard my honor with greater vigilance than some other maid. Since I have no guardian here, if anyone learned ye had kissed me, many would quickly assume there was far more between us. I cannae afford that sort of talk."

He reluctantly let her move away. " 'Tis strange that ye so firmly guard your reputation for virtue yet allow the far more dangerous talk of magic to continue."

"Do ye expect me to stand in the middle of the village and vow I have none of this magic, ne'er deal in it, and dinnae believe in it? And why would anyone heed me? They will believe what they wish."

"But ye feed these beliefs. All the Keith women have. Ye dinnae seem as bad as the others were—"

Rose put her hands on her hips and glared at him. "There have been Keith women here since the first Dundas laird claimed these lands. Did ye ne'er think that alone is enough to stir tales? Few women hold land, and we nay only hold some but have done so for more years than most can count."

"Your mother did naught to still the whispers. In truth, she often spoke or acted as if it was all true."

"Aye, she did, and I willnae dishonor her memory by spitting on all she believed just to make my life easier." She started toward the cottage. "And I am nay sure I dinnae believe it, too. Some days I do; some days I dinnae." She reached her door and turned to glare at him again. "Ye are my laird, but ye dinnae have the right to tell me what I can and cannae think, feel, or believe. Good day," she said as she stepped inside and firmly shut the door behind her.

Chapter 4

Adair stared at the door that had been shut in his face. He was not accustomed to such things, especially not when he was in the middle of a conversation. Rose might think it was done, but he did not. Even as he considered the wisdom of following her into the house, he watched Sweetling stretch up, cleverly work the latch, and open the door. The cat then pushed the door open and walked inside, the other three cats right behind him. Adair shrugged and followed the cats inside. He smiled when Rose turned to stare at him in surprise.

"Your cat let me in," Adair said as he followed her cats right into her kitchen.

Rose scowled at Sweetling as the cat sprawled on the hearth and began to clean himself. "Traitor."

"I wasnae through talking with ye, Rosebud." Adair sprawled in a chair at the table and started to look around.

It annoyed Rose that his use of the name he had given her as a little girl should cause a softening within her. "I was done. Just because I hadnae said what ye wished to hear didnae mean I wasnae done discussing the matter."

"Ye are a stubborn lass. 'Tis a verra fine cottage ye have here. There are nay too many who have such fine fireplaces, yet ye have two. Or more? Upstairs as weel?" Rose nodded. "And good stone floors. More than one room and the same in the loft, I suspect."

"And glass in the windows," she drawled as she began to chop up some leeks for the stew she was making. "Some years have been verra profitable and we could afford such gentling touches to our home. Some things were done by those helped by the Keith women. We ne'er asked for anything, but people have their pride. I also think that, although a mon might be verra glad there is someone ready to help him feed his family, he needs to pay for that in some way. The fact that it was a woman who did so only makes that need greater. And so we find ourselves living in a verra fine cottage indeed."

"Aye, a mon would need to dull the bite of failure e'en if he kenned it was nay his fault."

She nodded. "A few things were done in trade. The mon who put a fireplace in my mother's bedchamber jested that his wife was pinching at him for one. The right stone wasnae easy for him to find, nay on his land. My mother kenned where there was a good supply— right where she wanted to enlarge the garden at the rear of the cottage. The two of us would have needed years to clear that land, but the mon and his sons wouldnae. E'en better, he had the sort of rock that makes a good wall. So we got our garden, a goodly start to the wall, and his wife got a fine fireplace."

"And everyone was satisfied."

"Exactly. And no magic was used."

Adair gave her a narrow-eyed look and helped himself to an apple from a large, elaborately carved wooden bowl on the table. "Lass, ye ken 'tis verra dangerous to let talk of magic continue." He took a bite of the apple and was no longer startled by how it made him feel. "The way the food makes a person feel—"

"I ne'er feel anything different or unusual," she said, staring down at the carrot she had begun to chop, for she found she was unable to directly meet his gaze while telling such a big lie.

"Ye ne'er were a verra good liar, Rosebud."

She scowled at him, annoyed when that only made him smile faintly. "I feel something, but nay so verra much. My mother said that is because I am mostly content, with myself and with my life, and I have few scars upon my heart. When my mother was sad because she so badly missed my father, she said she was comforted by the food, could feel the spirit of the love he had for her. Since my mother died, I have often felt the same, only 'tis her I feel."

He nodded. "I felt as if my mother soothed me. I e'en thought I heard her voice in my head."

"Ah, ye are a troubled soul, so ye feel it more strongly. Most people feel, weel, soothed." After her outburst in the garden, she decided it was foolish to continue speaking as if there was nothing odd about her garden.

"And why should it do that?"

"I told ye, I dinnae ken. In truth, I am nay sure I would have fully believed whate'er tale my mother may have told me if she had lived long enough." She shook her head. "Mayhap 'tis just the water," she muttered as she tossed the chopped vegetables into the stew pot hung over the kitchen fire. "No matter what I do or dinnae believe, it doesnae change things. Again, as I have said, it is what it is and does what it does. I am but the farmer and the harvester."

"Weel, I dinnae think it is so verra simple."

"Ye are welcome to your opinion."

"Kind of ye." He sniffed the air as she stirred the stew. "Smells good."

"I am sure your cook has begun to prepare a verra fine meal for ye," she said sweetly as she sat down and poured them each a tankard of sweet, cool cider.

"I wouldnae be so sure. Did ye ken that Old Helga died?"

"Oh, aye. So who cooks for ye?"

"Meghan, Old Helga's niece." He almost laughed at the grimace she could not fully suppress. "The lass was taught by Old Helga for near to ten years, but 'tis verra clear she ne'er heard a word."

"I have heard that said about her." Rose felt sorry for the people at Duncairn, for Meghan was said to be able to ruin a raw carrot. "Ye cannae keep her as the cook. I ken 'tis an important position, but mayhap ye can find one for her that is nearly as important. Then ye might watch to see which men rarely come to the meals. 'Twould mean they are being fed elsewhere. Ye might find a new cook there."

"A good plan." He smiled faintly. "And ye arenae going to invite me to eat with ye, are ye?"

"I cannae. By the time the food is ready and ye have eaten your fill 'twill be verra late and ye will have been here, with me, for a verra long time. 'Twill start whispers ye may find as upsetting as the ones about the magic of the garden."

Adair finished off his cider and stood up. "I would nay be too sure of that," he murmured and started out of the kitchen.

Rose followed him and inwardly cursed herself for a soft fool even as she said, "Send Donald here in an hour. I will send ye enough stew and a few other things to make ye, Robert, and Donald a meal. Just be sure to watch the food carefully around Donald. The lad's stomach doesnae seem to have any bottom."

"Roused your pity, did I?" he drawled as he paused in the doorway and looked at her.

"Weel, aye. And now I ken why Donald wanders by here more often than he e'er did before, and always near to the time I might be sitting down to a meal."

"Clever lad." He grasped her by the chin and held her face steady as she leaned down. "A fareweel kiss, lass."

"Someone might be watching," she whispered just before he brushed his lips over hers.

"Ye worry too much for a bonnie wee lass."

He pulled her into his arms and gave her a kiss that left her weak in the knees. Rose slumped against her door and watched him stride away as she fought to regain both her wits and her breath. It annoyed her a little that he did not seem to be equally affected, if that confident stride was any indication.

"Weel, that looked heated."

Rose clasped her hand to her chest as her heart briefly leapt into her throat, then glared at Meg, who now stood directly in front of her. "Where did ye pop up from?"

"Weel, I was just about to rap on your door when the laird stepped out," replied Meg. "So I slipped into the shadows just off to the side here."

"Couldnae ye have just said a cheerful greeting and joined us?"

"I could have, but then I wondered why he was here. Then I remembered that ye were a wee bit scared when ye went to the keep. That started me thinking ye might have been right to be afraid and that matters had grown verra dire indeed. Thought ye might need rescuing."

"Weel, as ye could see, I didnae."

"I am nay so sure of that," murmured Meg.

"And might I ask why ye are out at such a late hour?"

"Ah, weel, my father has gone off to a fairing to sell his bowls and the like. He will be gone two days, mayhap a little longer if the weather doesnae hold fine. I told him I could stay with you."

Rose shook her head and almost laughed. "Ye are a wretched brat, but come on in. In truth, I shall be glad of the company. Something Mistress Kerr said today revealed that that cursed Geordie is lurking about again."

Meg cursed as she stepped inside and set her bag down on a chair. "Someone should do something about that swine."

"They should, but it willnae be you."

"Weel, I might be able—"

"Nay. If the fool grabs me again, weel, much as I hate to do it, I will speak to the laird."

"Good idea," Meg said as she followed Rose into the kitchen and sat down at the table. "He certainly wouldnae like anyone mucking about with his woman."

Rose sighed, collected a good-sized basket, and started to fill it with things that Adair and the others might like for their dinner. "I am nay the laird's woman."

"He was kissing you."

"I ken it. That doesnae have to mean much at all, Meg. Men like to kiss women. To be honest, I rather liked kissing him. That is all it was, though—a kiss. E'en if I felt like it was more, it wouldnae matter. He is the laird and I am nay much more than a crofter on his lands."

Meg snorted and shook her head. "The laird doesnae go about kissing just any lass. Fact is, he has been home a fortnight and hasnae e'en bedded a lass despite all the offers. Nay, ye can think what ye will and I willnae be telling anyone about all of this, but I think 'tis more than *just a kiss.*"

"Mayhap he has decided he needs a leman to pass the time whilst he looks for a wife," she said, hating to even speak the sudden suspicion infecting her heart.

"And I think the smell of those leeks ye put in the stew have addled your brain. The Keith women may not be lairds' daughters, but they have all been better born than some crofter's lass. The laird wouldnae choose ye for a leman. Ye can claim kinship with enough of the high-born Keiths to make ye a dangerous choice. But I am just a wee, skinny lass. I suspect ye will need someone older and wiser to talk sense into ye."

"Do ye think 'tis the food that makes him want to kiss me?"

"If your food made people feel amorous, we would be tripping o'er rutting fools in the road."

"Meg!" Rose tried to look shocked and stern but quickly gave in to the urge to laugh. "Ah, weel, I am just confused. Save for that fool Geordie who keeps trying to grab me, no mon has shown much interest in me. For the laird himself to be the first seems most strange."

"Most of the men at Duncairn ken ye are a wee bit above their touch, and I think ye scare them a little. Nay because of the magic, but because ye can read and write and ye have these fine lands. I think the laird is a mon who cannae or willnae believe in anything he cannae see, touch, or feel, and he, more or less, owns these fine lands. What makes the other lads timid just isnae important to him."

"Aye, that could be it."

"Why are ye packing that basket with food?"

"Oh, it seems the cook at Duncairn is Old Helga's niece Meghan."

Meg grimaced. "I am surprised any of them are still alive up there."

Rose grinned. "I ken it. I was moved to pity for the laird and told him to send Donald here to collect enough food for him, Robert, and Donald to have a fine meal. Dinnae frown; there will be enough for the two of us to eat as weel."

"I wasnae frowning about that. I was frowning because that rutting boy is coming here."

"Rutting boy?"

"He has been tumbling about in the hay with Grizel the alewife's daughter."

That explained some of the intensity that had lately been behind Meg's insults, Rose mused. The girl was jealous, although Rose doubted Meg knew it or would admit to it if she did. It had to be hard for Meg, as she was too old to ignore it and too young to understand why it troubled her so. And if she did understand, she was too young to challenge Grizel in any way for Donald's lusty attentions.

"Weel, all lads feel the need to test themselves in that way. I believe Grizel has been the testing ground for quite a few." She grinned when Meg laughed. " 'Tis unfair, but I doubt many men come to their marriage bed as innocent as they demand their wives to. I sometimes wonder if they feel the need more. And the first time for them doesnae hurt, though I suspect it may be embarrassing now and then."

"And they dinnae need to fret that they may get with bairn."

"Verra true. Grizel willnae. She takes a potion, ye ken. 'Tis nay one of mine. I dinnae like to deal in such things except when asked by some wedded woman who needs a wee rest from the birthing bed. But I have studied what Grizel takes and I cannae like it. Told her so, but she wouldnae heed me. I fear she may ne'er have a child; probably doesnae need to take the potion at all now."

"Oh. She has hurt herself."

"Aye." Rose spooned out a large quantity of her stew into a pail and then covered it. "So, if Donald has reached the age to test his monly wings, so to speak, at least he willnae leave a trail of bastards behind him. And mayhap 'tis nay such a bad thing that the lads put themselves to the test a few times 'ere they wed. It cannae hurt to have at least one of the newly wedded couple kenning what to do." She shared a giggle with Meg, pleased to see that the shadow of hurt had left the girl's eyes.

"That must be Donald," Meg said when there was a rap at the door.

"Ye stay here. I dinnae wish an argument to start between the two of ye, for the food will get cold." As she hurried to the door with the food she had packed, Rose admitted that it really was going to be nice to have Meg visit for a few days.

It was late by the time Rose sought her bed. She closed her eyes and cursed when her mind filled with thoughts of Adair. Just thinking of his kisses had her lips aching for a return of his. It had helped a little to speak of her fears with Meg, but the girl was right—she really needed someone older to discuss it all with. There was no one, however, so she was doomed to try and sort out her confusion all by herself. Rose found herself very afraid that she might allow her heart to lead her into a great deal of trouble.

Chapter 5

"Rose? Where are ye?"

Rose was tempted not to answer, but curiosity got a hard grip on her when she realized it was Anne Kerr who was looking for her. She suspected she had not immediately recognized the woman's voice because she had never heard Anne speak much above a whisper. Anne actually had a pleasant, clear voice when she chose to use it.

"O'er here, Anne," she called. "I am sitting under an apple tree."

Enjoying a moment of peace, she mused, then scolded herself for being selfish. Not too long ago she had bemoaned the lack of company or someone to talk to. It was foolish to complain now that she had some simply because it did not appear at her convenience. Anne rarely spoke to her, or to anyone, for that matter. The woman had never come to visit, although Rose suspected that was not an intentional avoidance. In truth,

Rose could not recall ever seeing Anne unless her mother was there.

"Ah, there ye are." Anne hurried over. "God's mercy, 'tis rather warm."

"Sit in the shade, Anne, and have a drink of cider." When Anne sat down, Rose handed her the wineskin she had filled with cider. "Ye will feel cooler in a moment or two."

After she had a drink of cider, Anne stared at the wineskin. "Oh, dear. I just had some of your food."

"Dinnae fret. Ye willnae turn into a newt." It was difficult to hide her astonishment when Anne giggled.

"I ne'er thought it would do that. Nay, I just feared it would change my humor enough so that my mother might notice the change."

"Nay, that willnae happen."

" 'Tis so pleasant here. So cool and shaded. And 'tis surprising when the walls are so high, but there is also a pleasing breeze."

Rose prayed Anne would not ask why that was, for she really had no explanation.

Anne clasped her hands in her lap and looked straight into Rose's eyes. "I had meant to be here earlier so that I wasnae just asking ye for something and then hurrying away, but I had to wait for Meg to leave. I would like a love potion."

"A what?" Rose sat up straighter.

"A love potion."

"Ah. Anne, I am nay sure there is such a thing." She briefly wished she could brew one right up when she saw the way Anne slumped with disappointment.

"I had heard that all the Keith women left behind writings and receipt books. I thought one of them might have known of such a thing." Anne took another drink of cider and appeared to relax a little. "Are ye verra sure there are no such things?"

"Anne, I can make ye a potion to ease the pain of your woman's time. I can e'en make ones to loosen tight bowels and tighten loose ones. I cannae make a potion to make someone fall in love with ye or ye with him. And 'twould be a false love, too, wouldnae it?"

"Oh, I hadnae considered that. But I am sure they sell love potions at some of the fairings."

"False brews, naught but trickery and lies, and some could even be dangerous. At best they might give ye something to make ye or the mon feel amorous for a wee while. Love must come from the heart, Anne, or it willnae last."

"Ye havenae asked who I want it for," Anne said quietly.

" 'Tis for Lame Jamie. I heard your mother scold ye about it two days ago." She smiled faintly when Anne blushed. "Ye are three and twenty, Anne. Ye dinnae need your mother's approval to wed."

"I ken it. I need to ken if he wants me, however. I have loved the mon for years. Yet I am ne'er without my mother close at hand, and as soon as she kenned where my heart lay, she made her disapproval verra clear."

"How did ye get free of her today?"

"She thinks I am with the priest."

"Oh, dear." Rose fought the urge to look around for an enraged Joan Kerr.

"I ken it: I am a selfish woman, for I may have caused ye a great deal of trouble. Yet I am desperate. As ye say, I am three and twenty. I have wanted Jamie for near as long as I can recall. Yet year after year passes and naught changes. I am stuck at Mother's side and cannae

e'en speak to the mon." She shook her head. "I sometimes wake in the night all asweat with the fear that I
shall live and die in the shadow of my mother. Or, mayhap worse, I shall see the mon I love wed another."

"Anne, only ye can stop that fate. Ye are the one who
must break free. Many can tell ye to do so, but only ye
can actually do it."

"I ken it. I sometimes weep o'er what a wretched coward I am. When my mother's scold told ye my deep secret, I wanted to come here immediately to see if ye
could help, but it still took me two days to work up the
courage." She frowned at the wineskin. "I was feeling almost sick with fear."

Rose smiled faintly. "Cool cider can be verra calming."

"Of course," Anne murmured, but gave Rose a look
that told her that she did not believe a word of that explanation. "I am certain that, if I could get some sign
from Jamie that my love is returned, I could walk away
from my mother. To do so 'ere I have that is what holds
me where I am. After all, if I take the chance and he
doesnae care for me, I shudder to think of the scorn
and ridicule my mother will pile upon my shoulders
when I must return to her."

"Ah, aye. I think that would make me hesitant as
weel. Start small."

"What?"

"Start small. When ye are verra sure your mother
isnae watching and ye see Jamie, give him a smile."

Anne looked both horrified and intrigued. "That
would be so brazen."

"Nay, 'tis just a smile. 'Tis just enough to tell him ye
find him pleasant to look upon. How he responds to
that smile can tell ye a little about how he might feel

about you. Dinnae take it to heart if he acts confused or e'en startled. Just try again. A smile doesnae cost ye anything and 'tis nay enough to make ye look some lovesick fool." When she saw how Anne still hesitated, she said, "Ye must do something, Anne, or ye will fulfill those chilling dreams ye spoke of."

Anne nodded. "Ye are right. I must take the first step, tiny though it is. And I think I must also try to take a small step away from my mother from time to time."

"Slowly ease the choking hold of her apron strings?"

"Aye." Anne sighed as she started to twist her hands together, and hastily took another drink of cider. "My mother is a verra strong woman and, I fear, nay verra kind. I have spent my whole life enduring that until I am nay sure I ken how to stop. But I will be four and twenty all too soon, and I suddenly realized I might ne'er be free. She talks of me wedding the laird, but that willnae happen. Aye, I might be coward enough to march to the altar despite loving another, but the laird has no interest in me, thank ye God."

"At least that worry is off your shoulders."

"True. I want bairns, Rose. I want a family. I want to love and be loved. I ken that I must find the courage to reach for it, but I am nay sure I have it."

Rose reached out to pat Anne's hand. "Just keep your eye on what ye want. Ask yourself from time to time if Jamie isnae worth it all. He is a good mon, a kind mon. If he can return your love, I think ye would be verra happy, e'en if your mother continued to disapprove. Try to let the love ye feel for him give ye the courage ye seek."

"That might work." Anne suddenly turned pale and leapt to her feet. "Oh, nay."

The look of horror on Anne's face told Rose who was

walking her way. She sighed and looked in the direction Anne was. Mistress Kerr looked as angry as Rose had ever seen her.

"How dare ye lure my child into this garden of sin," Mistress Kerr snapped as she grabbed Anne's hand and yanked her daughter behind her.

Rose did not even bother to rise. "Anne sought a moment of respite from the heat."

"She didnae need to come here for that." She glared at her daughter. "And ye lied to me. Ye ne'er went to the priest." She looked back at Rose. "Ye have already begun to poison her heart and mind, teaching her the sin of disobedience." She looked at the wineskin and gasped. "And ye have been feeding her that witch's brew!"

"Och, 'tis far too hot to deal with your nonsense today," Rose said, her voice still calm but her temper beyond her control. "Ye have found your daughter; now go. Anne was welcome here. Ye are not."

"Ye heard her," snapped Meg as she appeared from behind the apple tree and sat down next to Rose.

"Ye heed me, Rose Keith," hissed Joan. "I willnae forget or forgive this. Ye have tried to steal my child from me. That cannae be tolerated."

"Mither," Anne protested.

"Silence," Joan snapped. "Ye and I will talk on this when we are safe at home."

Rose watched the woman drag poor Anne away, sighed, and closed her eyes. She wished she could do something for Anne, but the strength to change her life had to come from within Anne. She had to break her mother's tight grip herself or she would never be completely free. She opened her eyes a little and looked at Meg.

"Where did ye come from?"

"I saw that vicious crone march into your garden and slipped 'round her, staying in the shadows. She wasnae hard to elude, for her eyes were set on ye and Anne. What was Anne doing here?"

"Seeking answers."

"Such as what sort of poison might silence that fool of a mother she is cursed with?"

Rose laughed softly, then grew serious. "Anne is a verra unhappy woman, Meg. She is a coward and she kens it weel, but her mother made her one, has shaped her into what she is from the day she came into this world. It willnae be easy for her to change. Yet she lied to her mother and came here. A small step, but a step away, nonetheless."

"But what did she think ye could do?"

For a moment she studied Meg, then decided the girl could be trusted with a confidence. "I will tell ye, but only if ye swear ye will say nothing to anyone."

"I swear."

"Anne is in love." She frowned when that news appeared to worry Meg.

"With who?"

"She loves your father, Meg."

Meg breathed a hearty sigh of relief and helped herself to a drink of cider. "I was worried for a moment."

"Ye dinnae mind?"

"Och, nay. I have begun to think my father might have a soft place in his heart for Anne. He always mentions seeing her, e'en talks of how bonnie she looked. I doubt they have passed two words between them because of the tight guard Mistress Kerr keeps on Anne, and my father is a shy mon."

"Then there is hope."

"How can there be if she willnae leave her mother and my father is too shy to brave approaching Anne?"

"If Anne does as I say, she will soon be giving your father a wee hint that she favors him. I told her to slip him a smile whene'er she can do so without her mother seeing. Anne needs some hope to give her strength. If your father smiles back, weel, mayhap she can find some."

Meg nodded. "I will try to stay close to him when he returns."

"I dinnae think ye should interfere too much."

"Och, nay. I willnae. I will, however, make sure he is looking the right way when Anne gets a chance to smile, and mayhap pinch him into responding. I ken he likes her and, weel, he is lonely. He is but thirty and I think he needs a wife."

Rose was surprised at Meg's wisdom. "I am sure he values your company."

"Oh, aye, but 'tis nay the same, is it? And he would sore like to have more children, but he needs a wife for that. I ken there are one or two other things he would like a wife for, too, though one doesnae always like to think of one's father doing such things. Has to, to beget children, though, and I wouldnae mind a few brothers and sisters."

"Ye are a good-hearted lass, Meg."

"I just want him to be happy, and he always seems so when he speaks of Anne. I think I might take a few of your apples, if ye dinnae mind. Mayhap I can slip one to Anne now and then. They might help her. If she feels softened, she might ease the grip of some of that fear that keeps her tied to her mother."

"Just dinnae get caught." Rose closed her eyes. "I believe I need a wee rest. Solving troubles and battling crones can make a body verra weary."

Meg giggled. "I will go and see if any of the garden are sprouting a weed."

Rose murmured her thanks and listened to Meg move away. She hoped Anne and Jamie could find their way to each other. They would be good for each other. Rose suspected her mother would have approved the match. Mistress Kerr was a formidable obstacle, however.

And pure trouble, she mused. The warnings were gaining in number and force. If Anne and Jamie wed, Rose knew Mistress Kerr would blame her. It was something she had best be prepared for. If Meg had decided her father and Anne should be wed, Rose suspected it would happen. Meg was almost dangerously clever at times.

There was really nothing she could do to stop the trouble coming her way, she realized. There was no reasoning with a woman like Joan Kerr. The woman looked at things with a twisted heart. It seemed beyond comprehending that she could not see where her child's happiness lay, or, if she did, simply did not care.

Thinking on the things Anne had said, Rose realized that Anne felt her mother had no real love for her. Anne had said that she wanted to love and *be loved*. That rather strongly implied that she had never felt loved. Mistress Kerr was in danger of losing her only child and did not seem to see it.

And I will be blamed for that as well, she thought with a sigh. She put her hand on the trunk of the apple tree she sat under, the one that had been planted when her mother had been born. It was at times like these that she sorely missed her mother. Flora Keith had understood these things far better than she could.

A part of her wished Anne had never come to see her, pulling her into the midst of her troubles, but she told herself not to be selfish. It would make at least three people happy if Anne and Jamie were wed. That was a gain worth any trouble Mistress Kerr wished to hurl at her.

Chapter 6

"Weel met, Iain, ye handsome fool."

Iain stared at the woman who greeted him with a smile. "Mary? Mary Keith?"

"Aye." Mary winked. "Come, I havenae changed so verra much, have I?"

"Och, nay." He stepped closer to the fence that enclosed this part of his fields and wiped his face on the sleeve of his shirt. "What are ye doing here?"

"Weel, I felt the need to come. Is someone courting my niece?"

"Ah, weel, there are a few rumors that the laird may be interested in her."

" 'Tis that, then. I woke in the middle of the night a fortnight ago and kenned it was time to get myself to Rose Cottage. I couldnae head right out, for my son was to be wed in a few days. But as soon as he was wed and I recovered from the grand celebration, I packed my wee pony and set out."

"Your husband?"

"Dead for near to six years. Your wife?"

"Dead for near to eight."

"Ah, a shame; Fiona was a good woman. Cannae say the same for the fool I wed, but he did give me three fine lads."

"No lasses?"

"Nay." Mary sighed and leaned against Iain's fence. "I have been set a quest as weel. There have been few Keith women born in the last generation or two, and e'en fewer left. Me, Rose, and one other, a cousin. I fear I cannae find the cousin."

"But why should ye need to?"

"I am nay sure yet, but it must be done. 'Twill come to me." She smiled at Iain. "Ye havenae changed all that much, ye great hairy brute."

Iain laughed. "Older. Nearing five and forty years. Got me five sons, though, and they help their old mon. I was surprised when ye didnae come after Flora died."

"Nothing called to me. Why? Has there been trouble for Rose?"

Iain nodded at the woman marching down the road. "There is the trouble."

"Curse it, is that that wretched Joan Kerr?"

" 'Tis, and she is still a vile-tongued wretch. Since Flora died Mistress Kerr has turned her attention to young Rose."

"Who is that poor girl she is dragging along behind her?"

"Her daughter Anne. And, since they are coming from Rose Cottage way, I have the ill feeling that the girl slipped away to visit Rose. That could cause a storm or two. The woman keeps a verra tight grip on that lass and intends her to be the laird's bride." He shook his head. "She has seen ye."

"What are ye doing here?" demanded Joan Kerr as she stopped in front of Mary. Her eyes widened when she noticed the full packs on the pony. "Sweet Jesu, ye arenae moving into Rose Cottage, are ye?"

"Aye, I am," replied Mary, and then she smiled at Anne. "And ye must be Anne. I am Mary Keith, Rose's aunt."

"And more trouble for Duncairn," snapped Joan before Anne could do more than nod in greeting. "Weel, I willnae stand for it."

"Then sit." Mary winked at Anne when the young woman started to smile, but quickly banished the expression when her mother glanced her way.

"Ye were always the worst of the Keith women," said Joan. "Enjoy your wee visit with your niece."

" 'Tis nay a visit. I intend to stay."

"What ye intend and what ye will be allowed to do are two verra different things. I wouldnae become too friendly with this woman, Master Iain. She willnae be here long."

Mary shook her head as she watched Joan stride away, still dragging her daughter along. "Wheesht, that woman still has a thistle stuck up her boney arse, doesnae she?" She grinned at Iain when he laughed.

"Just be wary, Mary. She managed to stir up a fair crowd against poor Flora once. The old laird stopped it, but it was unpleasant. She could stir them up again."

"I ken it." She bent closer and gave him a kiss on the cheek. "Dinnae be a stranger, Iain."

"Ne'er that, Mary." He watched her walk off toward Rose Cottage for a while, then straightened up only to find himself surrounded by his five sons. "Nay any work to do?"

"Who was that woman?" asked Nairn, his eldest.

"Weel, ye ken that I loved your mother and was ne'er false to her." All his sons nodded. "If I had met that woman e'en a day or two 'ere I wed Fiona, there is a verra good chance ye would be calling her mother."

"Ah. A fine-looking woman. Ye still havenae said who she is."

"Mary Keith, Rose Keith's aunt."

"Wheesht, no wonder Mistress Kerr left here with fire in her eyes." Nairn grinned and nudged his father. "So, are ye going courting?"

"Ye dinnae mind?"

"Nay," Nairn said and his brothers all mumbled in agreement. "I think she was giving ye the invite to do so, too."

"Then, aye, your old father is going courting, and all of us are going to keep a verra close eye on the Keith women."

"Trouble is brewing?"

"It is, and I dinnae want it to disturb my courting." He grinned when his sons laughed and, after one last glance toward Rose Cottage, he returned to work.

"That bitch wore ye out, did she?"

Rose frowned, certain she recognized that sweet, husky voice. "Aunt Mary?" she asked even as she slowly opened her eyes.

"Aye. I have come to stay." Mary laughed when Rose leapt to her feet and fiercely embraced her. "Ye have grown into a bonnie woman, lass," she said as she held Rose a little away from her; then she noticed Meg moving to stand at Rose's side. "And who is this?"

Rose introduced her aunt to Meg and took a moment to steady herself. Her aunt looked so much like her mother, with her sea green eyes and bright red hair, that it was both a pain and a pleasure to see her. The woman's arrival seemed a little too much like the answer to her prayers, as well.

With Meg's help she got her aunt settled in her mother's old bedchamber, moving Meg in with herself. As Mary enjoyed her bath, Rose and Meg prepared a meal. Rose was looking forward to talking with her aunt. Perhaps Mary could give her the answers to a few questions.

It was late before Rose found herself alone with her aunt. She suddenly was both eager to talk and yet unsure of what to say. Although she had a lot of questions, she was not sure how much she wanted to tell Mary.

"Come, child, let us go for a walk in the garden," said Mary, taking Rose by the hand and leading her outside. "I will start by saying I am sorry I didnae come to visit after coming for your mother's burial. I fear I have no real excuse, except that all three of my sons found their loves and got wed one after the other. 'Ere I kenned it, three years were gone."

"No need to apologize, Aunt Mary," Rose said. "Ye had a family and your own home." She looked around the garden as they began to walk through it. "Believe me, I can weel understand how fast the days go by."

"Weel, I am here now. I was called, ye might say. Had a dream that told me to get that last boy wed and settled and get myself to Rose Cottage."

"Why would ye be, er, called?"

"Because ye are soon to mate."

"Pardon?" Rose asked in a choked voice as she stopped and stared at her aunt.

"Ye heard me. Ye will soon be wed. I spoke to an old

friend on the road here, and he told me the laird has been sniffing about your skirts. 'Tis true?"

"Aunt, he is the laird. Far and above my touch."

"Pah. Ye have good blood in your veins, lass. Near as good as his. Ye are clever, learned, and beautiful. Ye would make him a fine wife and I suspect ye would like it just fine."

Rose sighed. "I would, but I am nay sure why he seems to seek me out. I fear that somehow the food has made him—"

"Nay," Mary said firmly. "I refuse to believe that."

"He doesnae like the talk of magic, doesnae believe in magic, and doesnae want me to."

"Now that is a real problem. Lass, did poor Flora e'er tell ye about the garden?"

"Nay. She said a few things, hints and pieces of the truth, but ne'er actually sat me down and told me the tale."

"This garden is fairy blessed, lass. The first Keith woman to come here saved the lives of several fairies, hiding them from some mortal fools. In return they asked her if she wished for anything. She told them she wanted a garden, a garden that gave people peace, that would soothe them in times of trouble and ease their heart's wounds. I think she was just asking for a pretty garden and one that would produce weel. They took her at her word. After they had her walk the borders of the land the laird had given her, they put their blessing on it all. She still had no real idea of what they had given her, but she invited them to make their home on her lands. She promised that, as long as a Keith woman was able, one would be here to guard this place, to tend it and keep it from harm."

"And, again, they took her at her word?"

"They did. Have ye ne'er seen them?"

Rose sighed and crossed her arms over her chest. "Aye," she reluctantly admitted. "I have seen them. Some nights more clearly than others. I can see some now, their glow all 'round the apple trees."

"Aye, your mother said they seem to love the trees most of all. Ye cannae deny that heritage, lass. E'en if ye tried, the truth would come out. The magic is in ye, as weel as in this land and all that grows from it. 'Tis in all the Keith women descended from that first one. The fairies need the guardians of the garden to remain aware of them, to believe in them, so each guardian is kissed with magic. 'Tis nay always an easy gift, or a pleasant burden, but 'tis our fate and we must accept it."

"I ken it," she muttered and went to stroke the trunk of her mother's tree. "Do we linger here, Aunt? At times I swear I can feel my mother's presence in this place."

"Oh, aye, all of them are here in a small way, e'en the first one. 'Tis why a tree is always planted when a Keith woman is born. That is your mother's"—Mary touched the one opposite it—"and this is mine. Yours is o'er there, aye."

"Aye." She touched the tree on the other side of her mother's. "And this belonged to a Margaret Keith. Mother was afraid she had died, for she seemed to disappear. I am nay sure who this young one belongs to." She touched the tree her mother had planted thirteen years ago. "Mother simply said she had to plant it. Something told her to plant this tree. Ye dinnae look surprised."

"Nay. I am nay only here to be guardian after ye wed, but to find the one who must follow me."

"Oh. I willnae have a daughter?"

"I forsee a lot of braw laddies for ye, and only one lass, but she will have a different destiny. Nay, this tree is the one belonging to the guardian who will follow me. I just hope I am nay forced to search too far and wide. Most Keith women ken when it is time to come here, but this could be a lass left untold about her heritage, ignorant of what her dreams might try to tell her."

Rose sat down on a stone bench within a group of trees and smiled faintly when her aunt sat beside her. "'Tis not such a bad place to linger."

"Och, nay. Ye have been having trouble with Joan Kerr?"

"Oh, aye. Her daughter slipped her leash and came to visit me. Wanted a love potion." She smiled when her aunt laughed. "She loves a mon her mother willnae let her marry. Her mother wants her to be the laird's wife. Anne wants Meg's father. Anne is old enough to do as she pleases, but—" Rose shrugged.

"She has been too long under Joan's boot heel."

"Exactly." She told her aunt what she had advised Anne to do and what Meg planned to do.

"Good advice, lass. Aye, and the wee lass Meg will do her part weel. She is a canny one. And though she has a tongue as sharp as mine, she has a soft, loving heart. All that is good, but nay for ye."

"Och, nay. With the laird showing me what Mistress Kerr sees as interest and now Anne easing free of her grip, I have become the verra worst of enemies. I wish I kenned exactly what the laird is about, besides stealing kisses and trying to prove there is no magic here. Most times I dinnae think the food has stirred his interest in me, and I am almost always sure he isnae after naught more than a quick rutting, but I just dinnae ken."

Mary put her arm around her niece and kissed her

on the cheek. "When 'tis a mon's feelings ye must judge the worth of, it can take a while to get to the truth. I offer ye but one piece of advice: Dinnae let him make ye deny what ye are. That road leads to misery. He must accept ye as all ye are or leave ye be."

"I ken it. I didnae want to, but I do ken it. I may nay be sure of anything else, but of that I am. I realized it during one of our arguments. I felt that, if naught else, 'twould be like spitting upon my mother's memory, e'en on that of all the ones before her, if I denied magic. I can still waver in my belief, or mayhap 'tis more a waver in my wanting to believe. Life would be so much easier without such complications."

"Ah, but nay so interesting."

Rose laughed. "True. Do ye have any thoughts on how to deal with Mistress Kerr?"

"Aside from sewing her mouth shut, nay." She grinned when Rose giggled. "We must prepare ourselves. She will try to hurt us in some way. Her daughter will have that mon she seeks and that will cause her to fair foam at the mouth."

"So, Anne will be with Jamie?"

"I believe so." Mary frowned. " 'Tis a little hard for me to say it with certainty, for I got such a sense of conflict and fear from the girl when I met her on the road here. But Meg is right. Her father is a shy mon, and if Anne is brave enough to give him a hint of interest, it would be best if someone is there to be sure he responds."

Rose nodded, then quickly placed her hand over her mouth to hide a wide yawn. "I didnae do a great deal today, yet I feel verra tired."

"Ye suffered through a lot of turmoil and were afflicted by Joan's bitterness and anger. Emotions can weary a person as easily as hard work." She stood up, took Rose by the hand, and led her back to the house. "I hope your young lad comes round soon, for I am eager to have a good look at him."

"Oh, dear."

Mary laughed. "It willnae be so bad. Mayhap I will charm the fool."

"Oh, ye can be verra charming when ye wish to be, but ye are also verra open about, weel, magic. That is why I said, 'Oh, dear.'"

"He has to face it, lass. No one is asking him to become a believer, just to cease refusing ye the right to believe."

"He is verra concerned about the trouble it could bring me."

"A good sign. Yet the trouble coming our way has a verra clear source—Joan Kerr. In truth, most of the occasional trouble visited upon the Keith women has come from but one person. Sad to say, 'tis most often a jealous woman. We Keith women are simply too beautiful and charming for some women to accept."

Rose laughed and kissed her aunt's cheek. "I am glad ye have come. Meg is clever and good company, but just lately I seem to have been besieged by problems I wished to speak to another woman about."

"I understand. Ye ken that ye can talk to me about anything."

"Och, aye. Even Mother used to laugh and say ye were a blunt-tongued wretch who ne'er seemed to be embarrassed by anything."

"Aye, she was verra fond of me." Once they were inside the cottage, Mary secured the door as Rose moved to bank the fire. " 'Tis a verra fine place," Mary said as she looked around. " 'Twill be easy to call it home. Weel, I am to bed. See ye in the morning, lass."

Rose wished her aunt a good sleep and, after securing the house, made her way to her own bed. Her aunt was lively, loving, and sometimes far too outspoken, but it was good to have her at Rose Cottage. Although a part of her was delighted by her aunt's prediction that she and Adair would be wed, Rose forced herself not to put too much faith in that. There was a lot she was yet unsure of, and there was also his aversion to magic. Neither obstacle was a small one.

Chapter 7

Adair dismounted in front of Rose Cottage. He felt embarrassingly eager to see Rose. It had been a full week since he had last seen her. Even though the week had been full of hard work, his mind had often been filled with thoughts of her. Once he had often awakened in the night asweat with fears caused by nightmares. Now he often woke all asweat with desire for Rose. She had faithfully sent an evening meal to him, Robert, and Donald for the whole week. Even though he was not sure he wanted to give them up, he had taken her advice, followed the men who had consistently missed the meal in the great hall, and found himself a new cook. He knew it was only right to tell Rose she no longer needed to do all that extra cooking. It also provided an excellent reason to visit her.

Just as he was ready to rap on her door, he noticed her four cats arranged in various indecent positions on the top of the sun-drenched garden wall. A neatly stacked collection of kegs and barrels revealed how they had gotten up so high. He had known some men who treated their hunting dogs better than they did their children, but Rose took the spoiling of her animals to new lengths. The woman had far too soft a heart.

Then he heard a soft familiar voice drifting up from behind the wall. Strolling over to the garden gate, he found Rose in the middle of one of her raised plots just beneath the wall the cats were sprawled on. He grinned as he entered the garden and moved up behind her. Her skirts were tucked up, exposing a fine pair of slender legs to just above the knee. When he realized what she was saying he had to bite back the urge to laugh.

"This is your last warning, Sweetling," Rose muttered as she used her small garden spade, a hand-sized one the annoying Geordie's father had once made for her, to remove a clump of dirt from the garden. "Ye are to cease using my garden as a privy. Aye, 'tis fine, soft dirt and ye ne'er hurt the plants, but I dinnae like finding it. Have I nay set ye aside a fine, large plot of dirt in the garden behind the cottage? Use that, ye wretch." She tipped fresh dirt into the small hole she had made.

"I dinnae think he is listening to ye," Adair said.

Rose gave a soft screech and stumbled as she tried to turn. Adair moved quickly to catch her around the waist and lift her out of the garden. He set her down on her feet, keeping his hands on her waist, and grinned. Rose's face was smudged with dirt. Long strands of hair had escaped the loose braid she had forced it into to tangle around her face. There was even the faint gleam of sweat upon her face and neck.

"I didnae mean to startle ye," he said.

"Ye shouldnae creep up on people that way."

"I didnae try to be stealthy. Ye didnae hear me because ye were too busy scolding your cat."

It was not easy, but Rose suppressed the urge to curse. She had a very good idea of how poorly she looked, dirty and disheveled. That was embarrassing enough. To realize he had heard her talking to her cat was almost more than she could bear. She tugged free of his grasp and went to the well in the heart of the garden. If she cleaned herself up a bit, she might be able to regain some small scrap of dignity.

"Just why are ye here?" she asked as she pulled a soft rag from a pocket in her skirts and used the water from the well's bucket to wash her face.

"Would ye believe me if I said I missed ye?" He smiled at the way she rolled her eyes. "I did. Howbeit, I also felt ye should ken that Duncairn has a new cook. Ye were right. When I took the time to notice who didnae eat in the great hall, then followed them, I found a cook. 'Tis Sorcha, Colin the shepherd's eldest daughter. She and her family consider it quite an honor I have given her."

"Oh, aye, it is." Leaning against the side of the well, Rose idly wiped her hands and neck with the wet cloth.

"Her sister will help." He stepped closer, placing a hand on the rim of the well to either side of her and lightly caging her. "I offered Meghan several other places, but she didnae want them. Didnae seem to care that she had been replaced, either."

"Does she think she can just live at Duncairn and nay work at all?"

"Nay. She has gone to work at the alehouse." He slowly smiled at her shock. "It seems Meghan does have one skill. As Sorcha told me, the lass spends more time on her back than a dead beetle." He grinned when she laughed. "Sorcha feels Meghan intends to gain a few coins now for what she oft gave away for little or naught."

"Oh, dear. Grizel willnae be pleased. So, ye came to tell me my plan worked and that I dinnae need to cook your meals again." Her last word ended on a gasp as he moved closer until their bodies touched and began to kiss her throat. "Adair."

" 'Tis but a wee kiss I seek. One to show ye how verra grateful I am that ye didnae let me starve."

Even as she opened her mouth to inform him that a simple thank ye would do, he kissed her. Rose rapidly lost the will to object, as well as the ability to think of any of the very many reasons why she should push him away. She wrapped her arms around his neck and returned his kiss.

"Weel, this must be the new laird then."

The sound of her aunt's cheerful voice startled Rose so much that she suspected she would have tumbled back into the well if Adair had not kept such a tight grip on her. She quickly eluded his grasp to stand beside him. As she lowered her skirts and brushed them off, she introduced Adair to her aunt.

" 'Tis good that Rose is nay longer alone in the cottage," Adair said, idly deciding that the Keith women aged well, for Mary Keith was still a fine figure of a woman.

"Oh, Rose was ne'er really alone here," murmured Mary.

Adair decided to ignore that and looked at Meg, who stood next to Mary. "I met your father in the village, lass, and since I was coming here, he asked me to tell ye to come along home now. He is sorry he was away longer than he had planned, but he is weel." He smiled faintly as Meg babbled out her gratitude for everything to the two Keith women, then raced off.

"She was beginning to fret o'er him," said Rose.

"He feared she might have. He also wished me to convey his deep thanks for watching o'er her whilst he was gone."

"She was far more help than hindrance."

Mary nodded. "She has a true feeling for the garden."

" 'Tis one of the best gardens I have e'er seen," Adair said. "Holding both beauty and purpose."

"And ever so much more. Cannae ye feel none of it, laddie?"

Rose sighed, realizing that her aunt intended to bludgeon Adair with all manner of talk about magic. It was, perhaps, not such a bad thing to be blunt, to speak the truth as one saw it, be it good or bad. She just wished her aunt had warned her that she was going for the throat. Since she was still reeling from the effects of Adair's kiss, Rose did not particularly feel like getting into an argument. She was not sure her aunt ought to be calling the laird *laddie,* either.

" 'Tis a verra peaceful place to visit." Adair began to suspect that Rose's aunt was about to make Rose look like a complete nonbeliever.

"Stubborn, stubborn lad. Your fither ne'er cared one way or t'other. But, ye do, dinnae ye?"

"My father wasnae so verra fond of the trouble it all caused."

"He kenned full weel that the trouble didnae come from Rose Cottage."

Adair glanced at Rose and caught her watching him

with the glint of sadness in her fine eyes. If he had made any progress at all with Rose in getting her to cast aside all this foolishness about magic, Mary Keith would steal it all away. That made him angry. He decided he should leave, but not before he got this stubborn woman to see the risks she was taking, that she was endangering herself and her niece.

"Where the trouble has started doesnae make a great deal of difference when it kicks in your door," he snapped.

" 'Tis good that ye worry on the lass's weel-being."

Rose's aunt was one of those women who could make a man crave the oblivion of drunkenness, Adair decided. "Ye refuse to see reason."

"Oh, I often see reason." Mary smiled faintly. "Too often, 'tis said. The trouble here is that ye refuse to accept that there are some things that defy reason, things that one cannae always explain. I dare ye to tell me that ye dinnae feel the wonder of this place or taste it in the food. 'Tis a magic place, my braw laddie, and ye can scowl, mutter, curse, and growl all ye like, it willnae change that fact."

"To speak of magic and fact together is foolishness. 'Tis also foolish to speak of magic at all. It stirs fears, Mistress Keith. Dark, violent fears. If ye continue to spit in the eye of that truth, it could cost ye verra dearly."

"The Keith women of Rose Cottage have faced trouble before and won."

"Weel enough, then. Ye keep talking and bring that trouble down upon your heads. Just dinnae expect me to put out the fire after they set the kindling about your wee feet."

As she watched Adair stride out of the garden, his

anger clearly visible in every lean line of his body, Rose
had to bite her tongue to stop herself from calling him
back. She realized how dangerously close she was to giving up her heritage, a large part of herself, just to make
him happy. It was not good or wise to want a man so
much that she was willing to consider changing all she
was. When she caught her aunt watching her with concern and sympathy, Rose suspected she looked as if she
was about to burst into tears at any moment. She certainly felt inclined to do so.

"Weel, that rather settles that, doesnae it?" she murmured.

"Nay, child, that was just an argument," said Mary.

"He was verra angry, Aunt."

"Aye, and I suspect he will get angry a few more
times 'ere he comes to his senses. That is a stubborn
mon. He kens the food from this garden has helped
heal his heart and loosen the grip of the dark memories
he brought back from France, but he willnae call it
magic."

"How did ye ken about his troubled soul?"

"The scars are still there to see, lass. 'Twill be a while
'ere he is completely free, but he can sleep now, I suspect. And he can do that because of the food from this
garden and he kens it weel."

"But doesnae wish it to be magic."

"He will, lass. He will."

"Mayhap. As ye say, he is a verra stubborn mon." She
sighed. "I think I will go for a walk."

"A walk can be verra good for hard thinking. Where
do ye go?"

"Down to the river that marks the eastern boundary.
I think I might e'en walk into it."

"What?"

Rose smiled faintly and shook her head. "Nay for any dark reasons, but because 'tis a hot day and I am dirty."

"Ah, of course." Mary followed her out of the garden. "Dinnae be gone too long or I shall worry."

"Duncairn is a peaceful place, Aunt. I shall be safe."

Mary shrugged. "E'en peaceful places have their dangers."

It was not until she had been walking for a few moments that Rose began to wonder if her aunt had sensed something to prompt that subtle warning. She shook her head and continued on. It might not be something her aunt had ever done at her home, but Rose had often walked alone throughout Duncairn and had never come to harm. Duncairn was, she suddenly realized, unusually peaceful. Mayhap the fairies had something to do with that, too, she mused with a smile.

She grimaced when she had to admit that she truly did believe in all the magic of Rose Cottage. Despite her moments of trying to ignore it all because she so badly wished to be just like everyone else, she had always believed. As a child she had even danced in the garden with the fairy lights.

Of course, she had had few children to play with, Rose thought. The mothers of Duncairn were reluctant to let their children get too close to the ladies of Rose Cottage. She inwardly cursed. That thought tasted of resentment, and she had to admit that such feelings had gained strength in her over the years. It was true that the garden was a burden at times, a weighty responsibility, but it was also a blessing, and one the Keith women had willingly shared with the people of Duncairn. If she was going to resent anything, she decided, it should be the ignorance and ungratefulness of those in Duncairn.

It felt better to have faced that truth about herself, but Rose doubted anything could make her feel better about the problems between herself and Adair. Even if she tossed aside all other doubts about their relationship, there was still the magic to contend with. Adair's angry response to her aunt's talk of the garden and its wonders told Rose that Adair's uneasiness about that magic went deeper than a simple concern for her safety.

Once at the river, she sat down to take off her shoes. Rose stood up, tucked up her skirts, and cautiously dipped her toes into the water. It was a lot colder than she had anticipated, but she decided a little wade would probably feel very nice.

She had barely gotten her feet wet when someone grabbed her braid and yanked her back so forcefully, she felt as if she was about to be snatched bald. Her first reaction was to reach for the braid to try and free it or, at least, grab enough of it to try and ease the pain in her scalp. As she stumbled around, she came face-to-face with her attacker.

Rose decided that, in a strange way, being found alone by Geordic was almost to be expected. The day had begun badly and was about to end very badly indeed. Despite the tears slipping from her eyes due to the pain he had caused her, she glared at him.

"Do ye ne'er stay at home to help your poor father?" she snapped, and almost smiled at his shock, for he could not have expected her to simply scold him for sloth.

"I kenned that, if I waited long enough, I would find ye alone," he said.

"How verra clever ye are. Tell me, my clever brute,

just how do ye intend to explain rape? Dinnae think I willnae cry this crime to the verra rooftops."

"Wheesht, do ye think that will gain ye anything? I will just say that ye bewitched me, that I was caught in some spell. Mistress Kerr will hasten to support me."

There was a chilling truth to that, but Rose fought to ignore it. It could make her lose some of her strength. She kicked out at him and nearly caught him square in the groin. He yowled and then cursed her as he tossed her to the ground. Rose managed to get out of his way when he tried to pin her down with his brawny body, but she did not escape completely.

As she wrestled with Geordie, Rose found herself thinking of Adair. She did wish he would ride to the rescue, like some gallant knight in a minstrel's tale, but knew the chances of that were very slim. Rose also thought of how, if Geordie got what he was after, she would have only a horror to recall concerning her first time with a man and not the loving interlude she might have enjoyed with Adair.

Chapter 8

Reining in several yards before the gates of Duncairn, Adair sighed. His anger had faded. He had not handled himself well in the confrontation with Rose's aunt. The woman had believed in the tales of the garden her whole life, as had Rose. It was not reasonable of him to expect such long-held beliefs, wrongheaded as they were, to be cast aside just because he said they should be. Weaning Rose away from the grip of those tales and fancies was going to take time and patience. He had shown very little of the latter in the garden.

Adair decided an apology was in order. He turned his mount and started to ride back to Rose Cottage. If nothing else, he had intended to spend some time with Rose, and he would not let an argument with her stubborn aunt rob him of that.

As he rode up to the cottage, he was surprised to find Iain of Syke Farm standing by the garden gate talking to Mary. "Greetings, Iain. I hadnae expected to find ye here."

"Came to fetch some herbs," the man replied.

"Ah." Adair bowed slightly to Mary. "I apologize for my earlier display of anger."

"Nay need, laddie," Mary said. "I have been kenned to stir up a temper or two."

Although he was sure Iain was suppressing a laugh, Adair was more interested in seeing Rose than trying to discern what was or was not going on between her aunt and Iain. "I was hoping to speak to Rose."

"She went for a walk down to the river."

"Alone?"

"Aye. She told me she often does it and that 'tis safe."

"No place is that safe," muttered Adair as he turned his mount and rode off to the river.

"That lad is verra concerned about my Rose," murmured Mary as she watched Adair ride away.

"Aye," agreed Iain. "He may nay ken it, but I am thinking there will be a wedding atween those two. "

"There will be. And why did ye tell him ye were here for some herbs? Ye arenae ashamed of kenning me, are ye?"

"Nay. I just had me the sudden thought that, for a wee while, it might serve us weel if people dinnae ken that ye have an ally here and there."

"Ah, ye may be right." She took one last look in the direction Adair had gone, then shrugged. "They will be fine. I must try nay to poke my nose in there too much. He has to sort out his concerns on his own."

"Aye. 'Tis always best to let a mon think he got to the place ye wanted him to be all on his own." Iain grinned when Mary just laughed.

* * *

Adair heard the trouble before he saw it. A feminine screech of fury and fear firmly caught his attention. What roused his concern and fear was that it had come from the river, where Rose had gone. He kicked his mount into a slightly faster speed, searching the area as he rode. There was no sign of any other people than the two he could now hear, so that meant that this was a private squabble.

When he cleared a line of trees and saw what was happening, he drew to a halt. Shock and a rapidly building rage held him still for the barest moment as he struggled to bring both feelings under control. Then Geordie got Rose pinned firmly beneath him, and Adair decided he would be showing more than enough control by not drawing his sword and killing the man on the spot.

He dismounted, walked over to the pair, and grabbed Geordie under the arms. He had a brief glimpse of Rose's eyes, looking huge in her pale face, as he tossed Geordie to the side. Even as he reached out a hand to Rose, she was already scrambling to her feet.

"Ye are unhurt?" he asked Rose.

She nodded, annoyed at her sudden attack of mute shock. There was such fury evident in Adair's face, however, she was not surprised at the tickle of fear she felt. When Geordie groaned, Adair turned and moved toward the man. Rose took several long, deep breaths, fighting to gain control over her confused emotions. There was a good chance she would need all her wits about her to stop a killing.

"Ye dare to attack a woman on my lands?" Adair asked as a white-faced Geordie struggled to his feet.

"She bewitched me!" Geordie said, his voice cracking with fear. "I couldnae help myself, laird."

Adair felt Rose move nearer and knew he had to restrain himself. Taking a deep breath, he punched Geordie in the mouth, sending the burly man back to the ground. He really wanted to beat the man within an inch of his life but had never believed in such violence. Now, however, he had a better understanding of the feelings that might cause a man to act so brutally.

"Take yourself home. I will deal with ye later. 'Tis best if I dinnae do so now. I dinnae think it for the best if I go about killing my own people, nay matter how much one or two of them might deserve it," he added in a calm voice and watched Geordie stumble off toward the village.

"I wouldnae have thought Geordie could move so fast," Rose murmured, then tensed when Adair turned to face her. He still looked angry.

"Do ye have no sense at all?" he snapped. "Ye shouldnae walk about all alone. Nay, especially not when ye have suffered an attack by that swine once already. Duncairn is a lot safer than many another place, but nowhere is truly safe for a lass wandering about on her own."

The whole time he scolded her, he gently moved her closer to the stream. He knelt, tugged her down beside him, and tugging off his shirt, used it to bathe her face and hands. Rose suspected she ought to protest being spoken to and treated like a terrified child, but she was finding it a little difficult to think straight. She could not tear her eyes from that broad, dark chest. Adair was all smooth skin and taut muscle.

She gave in to the urge to touch him and, reaching out, ran her fingers over a jagged scar on his right side. "Ye didnae come home from France completely untouched, did ye?"

"Nay." He felt himself tremble beneath her touch and grabbed her hand. "I gained several scars. Nay all of them are from battle. I was caught once by the enemy. They were nay kind. Lost two friends there to torture 'ere I and three others escaped."

"How sad. 'Tis sad enough to have young men die in battle, but to have a precious life lost to men whom ye are nay e'en able to fight is verra sad indeed."

Adair was astonished that he had told her all of that. He had been forced to relate a few tales about his years in France, but the time he and five others had spent eight months in a dark hole, their days filled with pain and humiliation, was one tale he had not told anyone. Yet, suddenly, he blurted it out to Rose. It was odd behavior on his part and he was not comfortable with it.

"Are ye certain he didnae hurt ye?" he asked.

"Aye. There will be a few bruises, and I feared he was going to pull all my hair out, but naught else," she replied.

"I must think of how to deal with the fool, but I think I need to wait a wee while 'ere I do. I am still of a mind to just kill him."

"For a few moments there, if I had had a knife, I would have done it myself." She leaned forward and kissed his chest.

"Rosebud?"

She smiled against his skin, for he had come perilously close to squeaking. "Do ye ken what I thought when I realized that I could nay win a fight with the fool?"

He pulled her into his arms. "Nay. What did ye think?"

"That he was going to make my first time with a mon

something out of a nightmare, and I dearly wished I had done it with ye first."

"Oh, hell."

Rose found herself on her back on the ground again, but this time the position pleased her. In that moment of fearing that Geordie would succeed in raping her, she had come to a decision. She might not fully trust the passion Adair felt for her, occasionally questioning its cause, but she knew he wanted her. And she wanted him. Now that she knew how easily she could become the victim of a man, could have lust forced upon her, she chose to take control. There was no doubt in her mind that making love with Adair would pleasure her.

When he kissed her, she wrapped her arms around his neck and fully returned his kiss. Heat pulsed through her body. Hunger for his touch made her shift beneath his weight. Rose blushed as he removed her clothes but did nothing to stop him.

"Ah, Rosebud, ye are so cursed beautiful," he muttered as he tossed aside the last of her clothes and looked her over from head to toe.

"I am a wee lass," she whispered, her eyes widening as he began to tear off his clothes. There was an awful lot of Adair Dundas.

"Wee but perfect."

She gasped with pleasure when he returned to her arms, their flesh touching. That delight was quickly surpassed by the feel of his hands and lips against her skin. Rose lost all concern about Adair's size. She tried to return as many of his caresses as she could and soon had only one clear thought. She wanted him, needed him.

"I will try nay to hurt ye," he rasped as he shifted his body and prepared to possess her.

"I ken it must hurt some the first time. Ah, but the ache I feel now must be nearly as bad."

"There will be nay turning back, my love."

"Hush." She kissed him. "I am yours. Here. Now. Do ye really wish to pause and discuss the rights and wrongs of it all?"

"Nay."

Rose bit back a cry when he joined their bodies. The pain was sharp but fleeting. For a little while she allowed Adair to soothe her with soft words and stirring caresses, but then her need grew too strong for play. She wrapped her legs around his slim hips and arched her body, shuddering with delight as he went deeper within her. Then he began to move, each graceful thrust of his body enflaming her, but she quickly decided she did not want grace and gentleness.

Adair groaned as Rose moved her slim, long-fingered hands over his body. He was fighting to go slowly, to not frighten her with the ferocity of his desire and need. Then she caressed his backside, grasped it in her tiny hands, and made it very clear that she was feeling no less fierce than he was. He released his control, giving in to the wild passion thrumming through his veins. When Rose cried out in release, her movements becoming somewhat wild, he held her close and let her take him with her.

It was a long time before Adair found the strength or will to move out of Rose's arms. He wet his shirt in the river and cleaned them both off. Her blushes amused him even as her silence began to worry him.

His own silence was probably not helping to ease the awkwardness of the situation. There was so much he wanted to say, yet there was still a lot standing between

them. He wanted her as his wife, at his side night and
day. He needed that. Yet he did not want magic at Duncairn, and Rose showed no sign of giving it up. Adair
feared that, if he spoke of their future now, before they
had settled that problem, he was telling her that it was
already settled. The last thing he wanted was misunder-
standings following them to the altar.

"Rosebud . . ." he began as she stood up and finished
dressing.

"Ye dinnae need to give me sweet lies and promises,
Adair," she murmured.

When he had not spoken of love or a future for them
after the haze of passion faded, Rose had decided she
would offer no hint of her feelings either. Since she had
felt so profoundly moved by their lovemaking, knew
that he was the mate of her body, heart, and soul, it was
painful not to hear or see that he felt the same. It was,
however, a sad fact of life that men did not have to feel
much emotion at all to indulge in lovemaking. She had
her pride and she would not chance humbling herself
before a man who saw it all as little more than a moment of delight on a fine summer's day.

He stood up and went to put his shirt away in his saddle pack. "I have ne'er been good with sweet words,
lass," he admitted as he walked back to her side, leading
his horse.

"I begin to think many a mon isnae."

"Weel, ye need nay worry about sweet words from
any other mon," he grumbled as she started to walk toward Rose Cottage and he fell into step at her side.

"Nay, I suppose not. I have reached the age of one
and twenty and ne'er heard one. I doubt there will be a
sudden swarming of men ready and eager to whisper
flatteries in my ears in the next few weeks."

"Rose, ye are mine."

"Am I? Is that how ye see it?"

"Aye."

This was going all wrong, he thought. Yet even hearing her speak of unknown and yet unseen men wooing her stirred his jealousy until it was difficult to think. One thing he was sure of, and that was that Rose was his. When she gave herself to him by the river, that merely sealed the bond between them. It annoyed him that she did not seem to feel that way.

"I see. And are ye mine?"

"Aye." That much, at least, he could confess to. Whatever else passed between them, he was hers, did not want any other woman, and, he suspected, never would.

"Fair enough." Rose took him by the hand. "We seem to have trouble agreeing on so many things, 'tis nice to ken we think alike in this matter."

"I would like to think we could agree on many another thing if we but set our minds to it."

"Mayhap. It shall depend upon how much of the matter concerned is one of reason or one of emotion." She frowned as she realized Meg had returned and was standing in front of the cottage talking excitedly to Mary and Master Iain. "I hope naught has happened to Lame Jamie." She had barely finished speaking when she had to nearly run, for Adair had begun to trot toward her home.

"Oh, Rose," Meg cried as she ran forward to hug her. "Ye will ne'er guess what has happened. I ran home to see my father and Anne was standing at the door."

"Anne was?"

"Aye, I think her mother may have said one thing too many when she was scolding her. Weel, she looked at me and I looked at her, and I gave her some of the blackberries I had brought home for my father. Then I told her to cease standing there like a post and do something 'ere her mother chased her down."

Rose heard Iain and Adair choke back a laugh. "That is what ye think is helpful?"

"It worked. So did the blackberries. She ceased to tremble, looked me in the eye, and said I needed a mother's guidance. I said that might be true, and was I looking at one who thought she could do the job? Then she got a wee bit cowardly again." Meg shook her head.

"But ye set her aright, did ye?" asked Adair.

"I did, laird. Told her the best thing to do was just say what she had to say, because this was the second time she had slipped her mother's noose and it was sure to be tightened after this until she couldnae say a word. Almost had to rap on the door for her."

"Anne did finally rap on the door, did she?" asked Rose.

"Aye, after a few more blackberries," replied Meg. "Then she stared at my father and my father stared at her, and I was getting sorely bored. So I told Anne that if she didnae have the wit to speak, why didnae she just kiss him? Thought she might swoon right there, but my father had more wit. He kissed her. I left them alone for a wee while."

"Verra wise," murmured Adair, but everyone except a grinning Iain ignored him.

"Weel, they eventually recalled that there was a child standing about outside. I think the singing told them." She grinned when Iain and Adair laughed aloud. "So 'tis settled. Ye are all invited to a wedding. 'Twill be in two days' time. My father feels that is about as long as he will be able to deal with Mistress Kerr trying to get her daughter back."

"Anne didnae go home?" asked Rose.

"Nay. She didnae want to, and I think my father is verra happy that she is staying away from her mother." Meg winked at Rose. "Especially since there is only my bed and his bed, and Anne isnae sleeping with me. So, will ye come?"

"Aye," said Mary and kissed Meg's cheek. "And we shall bring as much food as we can carry."

"And some of our mead for the bride and groom," said Rose.

"Tell your father me and my lads will be there," said Iain.

"And I shall be certain to tell everyone at Duncairn. I will contribute the ale." Adair covertly patted Rose on the backside, then mounted his horse and held out his hand to Meg. "Come with me, lass. I will take ye home."

"I have ne'er ridden a horse before," said Meg as she nimbly swung up behind him. "I will see ye at the wedding," she called as Adair nudged his horse into a slow trot.

By the time Rose got over the shock of Adair's rather intimate touch and turned to face her aunt, Iain was already gone. "I ne'er thought Anne would act so quickly."

"I think Meg has the right of it. That fool Joan said one nasty thing too many. Since the thought of leaving was already in the lass's head, the poison didnae pass o'er her as it used to. I wouldnae be surprised if it was something unkind about Meg's father." Meg suddenly looked closely at her niece. "Ye are looking a bit rough, lass."

As she and her aunt went into the cottage, Rose told her about Geordie's attack. A part of her ached to share the news that she and Adair had become lovers. It would be good to be able to discuss it with an older woman, one who had known a man.

For the moment, however, Rose realized she wished to hold the secret close. When she did finally talk about it, all the doubts and questions she had would undoubtedly come out. For a little while she wanted to remember that moment on the soft grass by the river through the haze of desire and love, untarnished by reality. The time to face the consequences of it all would come soon enough.

Chapter 9

"A fine wedding," Mary said as she and Rose stepped into the cottage.

"I cannae believe Mistress Kerr would be so cruel as to refuse to attend her own daughter's wedding," muttered Rose as she moved to light the fire. "Ye would think she would be happy for Anne. 'Tis nay as if Jamie is some poor, ragged stable lad."

"He isnae the laird." Mary poured each of them a goblet of sweet cider and, after handing Rose hers, sat down in a chair in front of the fire. "But Joan wasnae far away. Nay, nor was that fool Geordie. He is verra lucky his punishment was so light."

Rose grimaced as she sat down in the other chair set before the fire. Geordie had gotten fifteen lashes, and the whip had been readily wielded by his enraged father. Considering the rage Adair had been in, it was a merciful punishment. She had just never liked whippings.

"Where was Mistress Kerr?" asked Rose.

"Near."

"Aunt?"

"Have it your way. She was but 'round the corner, sitting in front of the alehouse with Geordie. In truth, by the time we left there was near a dozen people with them."

"Oh, dear. She has blamed all of this on me, hasnae she?"

"Loudly and repeatedly. 'Tis why I decided we should leave sooner than I might have wished to."

"I noticed ye were having a fine time with Master Iain." Rose almost laughed when her aunt blushed.

"He is a fine figure of a mon and I am nay in my grave yet."

"Far from it, I pray." Rose frowned, felt the tickle of fear, and took a long drink of cider to quell it. "Do ye think there may be trouble?"

"I cannae be sure, lass. This cursed gift of mine can be an uncertain thing. I feel as if there will be, but mixed in those feelings of warnings are ones of happiness. All I can think is that mayhap there will be trouble, but it willnae cost us so verra much. And somewhere in the mess, a few problems will be solved or hurts eased."

"I think it might be wise to prepare for trouble. Ye heard Mistress Kerr spouting her poison and saw a fair crowd gathering to listen. 'Tis a strong warning right there. I would rather be ready for trouble and have the threat fade away than nay be ready and have the threat catch us unprepared."

Mary nodded. "Wise. As soon as we have finished our cider, we will go out and set the water buckets around."

"Aye." Rose shook her head. "Someone should sew that woman's lips together." She managed a tired smile when her aunt laughed. "Anne did look bonnie, didnae she?"

"Aye, and Jamie looked verra happy, too. Meg is happy because her father is, and I think she likes Anne. It will be fine. She will soon have all the brothers and sisters she could want."

"I ken how Meg feels. I often wished for brothers or sisters. My mother wanted no other mon after my father died, however."

"Some people love only the once. Like ye. Like that stubborn lad Adair."

"Ye do ken he is the laird, dinnae ye?" Rose drawled.

Mary grinned and winked as she stood up. "I ken it. I tease the lad, 'tis all, and I ken he really doesnae mind. Nay sure he e'en realizes I do it." She took Rose by the hand and tugged her to her feet. "Come. We will set the buckets around and then we can get some sleep. It has been a long busy day."

Rose set the last of her buckets, brimming with water, next to her mother's apple tree. She grimaced as she stood up and tried to rub away a pinch of pain in her back. It was more work than she had wanted to do after tiring herself out at the wedding, and with all the cooking she had done in the days before it. She tried to ease her temper by telling herself that, if no trouble came their way this night, watering the garden in the morning would be a great deal easier, as the water had already been drawn from the well. Then she tensed, a sound she dreaded cutting through the quiet of the night.

"Ah, me, here the fools come," muttered Mary as she joined Rose. "Let us meet them at the gate."

Following her aunt, Rose winced at the sound of the angry voices. She stood beside her aunt just inside the gate and sadly watched two dozen people stride up. Mistress Kerr marched at the fore like some conquering hero. Rose idly wished she was a more violent person, for there was a woman she would sorely like to beat into the mud. Then she caught sight of Geordie at her cottage door.

"Ye get away from my house, ye bastard," she yelled.

"Aye, lass, there be the way. Keep a firm grip on your temper," drawled Mary, but she grinned when Rose sent her a look of apology. "In truth, say and do as ye please, lass. 'Twill make no difference to this lot of fools. Most of them are weel soaked in ale and wouldnae ken reason if it fell on them."

"Witch!" screamed Joan Kerr. "Ye ensorcelled my only child and turned her against me."

"Do ye really think one needs magic to turn anyone against ye, ye nasty old woman?" snapped Mary.

"Verra calm, Aunt," murmured Rose, but she fixed her gaze on Mistress Kerr. "Ye wouldnae let her choose the mon she wanted. If Anne has left ye, 'tis nay anyone's fault but your own."

"She should heed what I say, nay ye, nay him, and nay her," Joan said, pointing at Mary. "And I ken weel that ye poisoned her mind and heart against me with the food ye grow in there. Weel, we have let the tools of the devil sit secure inside those walls for far too long."

Even as several men came forward to pound at her gates, Rose saw three of her cats come racing out of her house. Fear for her pets distracted her enough that the gates were pushed open, nearly knocking her to the ground. Her aunt pounded on the two men who tried to get inside the garden with a thick cudgel, but one boy holding a torch slipped by her.

Cursing, Rose hurried after the boy, catching him

just as he tried to set her mother's tree alight. She used the bucket of water there to dampen down both him and the tree. Grabbing him by the ear, she dragged him back to the gates, where her aunt stood, cudgel in hand. Rose pushed the boy back outside, wondering how long it would take Mistress Kerr's drunken followers to realize that, even though she and her aunt could give a lot of them some hard bruises, they could not stop them from pushing their way in.

"Oh, dear," murmured Mary. "Some of them look like they might actually be trying to think."

"Now that could cause us trouble," agreed Rose, then frowned as three of her cats ran into the garden and under her and her aunt's skirts.

"If they do rush us and get by, just set your mind to putting out any fires they may start. Me and the others will take care of pounding some sense into these heads."

Before Rose could ask what others, Joan Kerr glared at her. "That witch stole my child as surely as if she had dragged her to an altar to sacrifice her. Are ye all going to just leave her safe here until she comes after your children?"

"I fear that may have been a good prod on that bitch's part," grumbled Mary.

"Are ye saying I should prepare for the real fight?"

Mary took Rose's hand in hers and held her cudgel more firmly in the other. "Aye. Ye might try your hand at a wee bit of praying as weel."

"Laird!"

Adair looked toward Donald as the youth stumbled into the hall, yelling for him. He had come home from

Jamie's wedding feeling a little sorry for himself. There was a woman he had chosen for his wife, but fate and nonsense seemed to want to keep them apart. All he asked was that she cease all this talk of magic. He did not see that that was so very much to ask. Since his mind could not seem to cease chewing over the problem until his head ached, Adair almost welcomed this alarum of Donald's. It might keep him too busy to think, at least for a while.

"Wheesht, are we being raided, lad?" he asked as Donald's father, Robert, halted the youth before he stumbled right into Adair.

"Och, nay. I dinnae think that would worry me as much as this does."

"What has happened?"

"Mistress Kerr spent her daughter's wedding stirring people into a frenzy. She kept saying the Keith women had ensorcelled her daughter, stolen her away with their magic."

"The woman got married. Most all the village was there. Are there really any fools who would heed her?"

"With their heads clouded with ale fumes, aye," Robert replied.

"Mayhap ye should have let the Keith women bring the ale as weel as the food," said Donald.

"And what good would that have done?" demanded Adair.

"Weel, their ale mixed together with their food, and there wouldnae have been anyone Mistress Kerr could stir up with her talk. I mean, their food makes people happy, aye?"

"Aye," Adair agreed a little reluctantly. "So, I suppose I best hie to the village and try to beat some sense into a few fools."

"They are nay there."

Adair felt a chill seep over him. "Be quick about it, lad. Where are they?"

"Headed to Rose Cottage. I tried to stop them, e'en gave away a few tarts I had saved for later, but that only stopped a few. So I felt I best come here and tell ye about it. They were carrying torches, and Mistress Kerr was saying it was time to be rid of that witch's source of power. I just dinnae understand it. The women and their food dinnae hurt anyone. If 'tis magic, 'tis a verra peaceful sort."

"I should have done something sooner to shut that bitch's mouth," snapped Adair as he stood up and marched out of the hall. "I will be taking six men with me, Robert. Ye and Donald must see to their replacement at their posts."

"Aye, laird," said Robert.

"I will get your horse," Donald said, even as he raced toward the stables.

"Though it would be more pleasant about Duncairn, I think it wouldnae be wise to kill Mistress Kerr," drawled Robert after Adair bellowed orders to the six men he had chosen to go with him.

It surprised Adair that he could do so, but he laughed briefly, and was sure that was what Robert had intended. That moment of lightness had eased the murderous strength of his fury. The very fact that, even for a brief instance, he had considered killing a woman, made him even angrier with Joan Kerr, for she drove him to such dark thoughts. If there was any evil in Duncairn, it rested in Joan Kerr's heart and mind.

"I willnae kill the woman," Adair said. "It was but a brief, pleasing thought. Nay more. I would like to banish her from my lands, but that might hurt Anne, and she is a good lass. Howbeit, I think I do have a way to steal the sting from that adder's tongue."

"Ye do?"

"I do. It, too, will hurt Anne, so I may nay use the weapon. 'Twill depend upon how hard that woman pushes me."

"She will probably push ye verra hard." Robert held out an apple. " 'Tis one from the garden that fool woman seeks to destroy. I doubt it will still your anger for 'tis a righteous one, but it may help ye gain some control o'er it."

Adair took the apple and stared at it. It would help. He could not deny that truth. The food from the garden had eased his nightmares, soothed his pain, and taken away his guilt. It had even roused the spirit of his gentle mother in his mind and heart. What grew in the garden at Rose Cottage was not just unusual, not simply a product of rich soil and good water; it was magic. He had fought that truth because he did not understand it, and that troubled him, made him uneasy. Well, he mused, Mary Keith was right—sometimes there were things that could not be explained and one just had to accept that.

He took a bite of the apple even as he mounted the horse Donald brought him and felt a sense of calm seep through his veins. It did not banish his fury, but it gave him the strength to think clearly despite it. That only confirmed his growing conviction that he had been wrong, that, in a small way, he, too, had given in to the fear of the unknown. The food did not change him in any way. Something in it simply reached out to soothe a person's pain or sorrow, to calm agitation and fear. Strange as that was, there was no harm or evil bewitchment in it.

Seeing that his men were ready, Adair rode out of Duncairn. He had to reach Rose before she could be hurt or her cherished garden destroyed. The fear he felt over her safety brought him to yet another realization. He loved her, loved her with all his heart, soul, and mind. Now he understood what his mother's voice had whispered in his mind the night he had decided he would have Rose. As long as he decried the magic at Rose Cottage and demanded she turn her back on it, he would never really have her. He was asking her to give up something that was a very large part of her, something that had helped to make her the woman he loved.

Suddenly he did not care about what the magic was or where it had come from. He did not even care if Rose brought it into the heart of Duncairn, so long as she came to him. Spurring his horse to a greater speed, he prayed he would find her unharmed so that he could tell her of the changes in his heart and mind.

The moment Rose Cottage came into view, Adair signaled his men to halt and dismount. It was tempting to just ride into the midst of the torch-bearing crowd and scatter them like rats, but he knew that would not really solve the problem. A confrontation was long overdue. As he strode toward the garden gate, he saw the crowd begin to move forward, and hoped he could control his temper long enough to make the fools see sense.

Chapter 10

"Hold!"

Rose clasped her aunt's hand and thanked God as the tall form of Adair pushed through the crowd. Half a dozen of his men followed, turned, and stood between their laird and the crowd, their hands resting on their swords. She gave Adair a weak smile as he stepped close and looked her over.

"Ye are weel? Unhurt?" he asked, briefly glancing at her aunt. "Both of ye?"

"Aye, Adair," Rose replied. "They were trying to burn the garden. I ken Aunt and I wouldnae have been able to stop them. Nay alone."

Adair looked over the crowd. He was pleased to see that several people already looked uneasy, even embarrassed. Even as he prepared to speak, he saw Lame Jamie, Anne, and young Meg hurry up, cudgels in hand, to push their way through the crowd.

"Nay alone, my bonnie Rose," Adair said.

"Are ye hurt?" demanded Meg, running over to Rose

and then turning to glare at the crowd. "Fither, ye can start knocking heads now," she said to Lame Jamie, who lingered near the battered gate to the garden, Anne at his side.

Reaching out to give Meg's tousled hair a light tug, Adair said, "I will deal with this, brat." He bowed to Lame Jamie. "I commend your father for the speed with which he came to the aid of the women, however. 'Tis good to ken that nay everyone has had all their wits addled by the rattling tongue of a bitter woman." He did not need the way everyone looked at Joan Kerr to tell him she was the one behind this madness. She stood to the fore of the crowd, as stiff and fierce as any commander, unaware that the loyalty of her troops was already beginning to fade.

"Those women bewitched my daughter, setting her against me," Joan Kerr snapped. "Anne has ne'er disobeyed me, yet one visit to this accursed cottage and Anne thwarts all my wishes."

"How old is Anne?" asked Adair.

"Three and twenty."

"Far past the age for her to cut free of your apron strings."

"She married against my will! She walked out of my house and went to that man!" Joan Kerr pointed at Lame Jamie.

"I should think that, when the lass is three and twenty, ye would be glad she has found herself a husband. Lame Jamie has a fine cottage, a good living, and is my second cousin. Most mothers would be dancing with joy o'er such a fine match." He lightly poked Meg when she stuck out her tongue at Joan Kerr, but the soft chuckles the girl's impertinence stirred told Adair he had muted that accusation.

An eerie howl drew everyone's attention. Geordie was walking toward the crowd holding a writhing, hissing Sweetling by the scruff of the neck. Rose moved to help her cat, but Adair grasped her by the arm and held her back. Lame Jamie was already striding over to the youth, cudgel in hand.

"I got one of the witch's familiars," Geordie said, then cursed and dropped the cat when Jamie rapped him on the back of the head with the cudgel. "The beastie got away! Didnae ye hear the evil noises he made and how fierce he was?"

"Ye were near to strangling the poor animal, ye half-wit," snapped Jamie. "He was fighting for his life. Where did he go?" Jamie looked around. "Is he hurt?"

"He is weel, Jamie," Rose replied, feeling her cat trembling against her leg.

Adair looked down and saw Sweetling's rump and tail sticking out from beneath Rose's skirts. "Wheesht, such a fierce demon." He heard a ripple of laughter go through the crowd and quickly looked up to grin at them, drawing their attention and hoping no one else saw that yellow paw slip out from beneath Rose's skirts to nudge Sweetling's backside underneath.

"How do ye explain this garden?" demanded Joan Kerr, her voice shrill as she realized her allies were rapidly deserting her.

"Rich soil and plenty of water," Adair replied.

"It takes more than that to make it grow e'en when others fail."

"Iain," Adair called to a burly, hirsute man he strongly suspected was an ally of Mary's, and the man quickly stepped forward. "Ye are considered a skilled farmer, aye?"

"I believe so, m'laird," the man replied.

"Rose, get a handful of earth to show the mon," Adair said and frowned when she shook her head.

"I cannae move," she said. "Sweetling and Growler are wrapped about my ankles. Lady and Lazy cower under Aunt's skirts."

"I will get it, m'laird," offered Meg.

"Take some from the bed where the peas grow," instructed Rose as Meg hurried off.

A moment later Meg held out a handful of dirt for Iain. The man took it into his own hand, inspecting it closely, even sniffing it. Adair was not sure what some of the things the man did tell him, but Iain's eyes grew wider and wider.

"Wheesht, ye could grow anything with ease in dirt this fine." He looked at Rose. "Do ye add things to it? I think I can smell fish."

"Come round in the morn, Master Iain," said Mary, "and we shall be verra glad to tell ye what little we ken."

"The water," began Joan Kerr.

"Here ye are, Master Iain," said Meg, who had already fetched the man a small bowl of water.

Iain sipped the water, swished it about in his mouth, then spat it out. He sniffed it, swirled it in the bowl, and stared at it as he trickled a little over his fingers. Finally, he drank the whole bowl full.

"Sweet, clear, and I dinnae feel any change coming o'er me," said Iain. "I am nay growing a tail, am I?" he asked and winked at Rose.

That brought a few crude jests from the others. Iain strode back to his laughing sons and gently clapped each of them offside the head. Joan Kerr stared at the crowd and clenched her fists. No one stood near her now.

"Fools! Cannae ye see how she has bewitched your laird?" she shrieked.

"Mither," protested Anne, but words failed her, and she shook her head.

Adair saw a few people waver in their retreat and frown at him. They had come here to root out evil at the behest of a distraught woman. It was obvious they hoped for some hint that they had not been made complete fools of.

"Ah, weel, mayhap there is some truth in that," he said, and winked at the men before taking Rose's chin in his hand and turning her face up to his. "How could any mon look upon this bonnie face and nay feel a wee bit bewitched. Eyes the color of the sea and skin like rich, sweet cream." He grabbed a handful of her hair, held it up, and slowly released the strands. "And I challenge any mon here to tell me this bounty isnae enough to steal a mon's wits. I willnae praise all her beauty, for I dinnae wish all ye fools leering at my bride." He put his arm around Rose's slim shoulders and kissed her cheek before returning his gaze to the crowd.

"Aye, mayhap there is a wee touch of magic here, mayhap the land is blessed in some way. 'Twas certainly blessed to fall into the tender care of the Keith women. I challenge any of ye here to tell me of someone hurt by a Keith woman. They have been here for as long as a Dundas has been laird, yet ye cannae tell me of any evil done by any one of them, can ye?" He nodded when many of the people shook their heads. "But ye can tell me of a hand always extended to help, of no one being allowed to ken the cramp of hunger as long as there was e'en one leek left in this garden ye sought to destroy.

"Go home and I will try to forget that ye endangered the lives of the lass I love and her kinswoman." He felt

Rose start beneath his arm but kept his gaze upon the crowd. "I will also try to forget that ye let the poisonous lies of a bitter woman turn ye against women who have been naught but kind and generous."

"Lies? I but tried to—" protected Joan Kerr.

Adair knew he was not concealing the cold fury he felt at the woman very well, for she paled when he fixed his gaze upon her. "Nay more, woman. Ye almost succeeded this night in destroying one of the few almost continuous sources of food at Duncairn, and ye didnae care if two innocent women were hurt or killed in the doing of it. 'Tis past time the truth was told. I was curious about your enduring animosity toward Rose and her late mother, so I went searching for answers.

"What I discovered was that 'tis nay righteousness that stirs your poisonous whispers and accusations but jealousy, mayhap e'en envy. Ye wed a strutting vain cock, a faithless swine, and he turned his lecherous eye upon Flora Keith. 'Tis nay such a surprise. She was a beautiful woman. She would have naught to do with the fool, scorned him openly, but ye had to blame someone for his wandering eye. So ye blamed Flora Keith. And mayhap ye were a wee bit angry that she could so clearly see what the mon was and ye didnae.

"Ye e'en held on to that anger and let it brew after ye left Duncairn with him. When ye returned ye started to spew it out, e'en carrying it on to the daughter when Flora was nay longer in your reach. I suggest ye take yourself to a priest, Mistress Kerr. Mayhap a little confession and penance will release some of that bile." When the woman stormed away, Adair looked at Anne. "Sorry, lass. She wouldnae relent, and I needed to take some of the sting out of her words."

"No need to beg my pardon, laird," Anne said.

" 'Twas a truth that should have been told long ago."

After watching Anne leave with Lame Jamie's strong arm wrapped comfortingly around her slender shoulders, Rose realized that most everyone else was gone as well, and she looked at Adair. "Did ye mean it? I will understand if ye just said such things to—"

Adair silenced her with a brief, hard kiss. "I meant it all. I want ye as my bride, I love ye, and, whether 'tis magic, fairies, God's blessing, or just skilled farming, I dinnae care."

"Are ye sure 'tis nay the food that has made ye feel this way?" she asked, unable to completely still that fear.

"Nay, 'tis nae the food. In truth, I decided I wanted ye 'ere I had taken my first bite of anything from this garden."

"Oh, Adair."

"When I heard that ye were in danger, I realized none of it mattered save that I love ye. That first night ye gave me those apple tarts, I swear I could hear my mother's soothing voice helping me to still my nightmares. As I went to sleep, I decided I would have ye for my bride, but that I would get ye to deny all this magic first. In my head I heard my mother scold me for a fool, telling me that I would ne'er hold the prize I sought unless I accepted the whole. I didnae understand until now. I love ye for *all* that ye are. All I ask is that, if ye decide to dance naked under a full moon, ye let me watch." He grinned when she scowled at him even as she blushed. "So, lass, will ye have me?"

"Oh, aye, Adair." She brushed her fingers over his cheek. "I do love ye so. I think I have since I was a wee child."

He held her tightly, briefly overcome with emotion. "Ye willnae be sorry, lass." He stepped back and held both her hands in his. "And I willnae keep ye from your garden. I ken how much a part of ye all this is."

Rose looked around and felt a brief sadness. For every day of her life the garden had been the center of her world, and she would miss that in many ways. It would not be a complete loss, for she could visit the garden whenever she wished to, and renew her ties to this land that had nurtured generations of Keith women whenever she felt the need. She smiled at Adair.

" 'Tis a part of me and I shall always need to come here, but only for a visit," she said. "My time here is o'er. 'Tis my aunt's turn now. She kenned this time was near and that is why she came," she added in a soft voice, so that his men did not hear. Adair and others might be able to accept the magic of the garden, but her aunt's *feelings* were another matter entirely.

"Ah, I see. Then come, lass. We will go to Duncairn and"—he winked at her—"talk on our future."

A blush stinging her cheeks, Rose looked at her aunt. "I think I best stay here. We are nay wed yet, ye ken."

"Go, lass," said Mary, smiling widely. "The lad told near all the village that ye are his bride and that he loves ye. Go, and I will come to see you on the morrow to help ye plan the wedding. I think it should be a grand celebration."

"Aye, verra grand," agreed Adair, but when he tugged on Rose's hand, she did not follow him. "Rosebud?"

Releasing his hand, Rose lifted her skirts a little to reveal two of her cats. "I am still shackled by Sweetling and Growler."

Adair rolled his eyes and, ignoring the laughter of his men, coaxed the two cats out. The amusement of his men was increased when the other two cats stuck their heads out from beneath Mary's skirts and cautiously looked around before emerging. That laughter was good, however. These men would never be able to see these animals as *familiars,* as evil lurking in disguise. He picked up Sweetling, who quickly draped himself over his shoulder. Rose picked up Growler and cradled him in her arms.

"Come, love, we will take these wretched, spoiled beasties back to Duncairn," he said as he wrapped his arm around her shoulders.

Rose went only a few steps before glancing behind her, stopping when she realized her other cats were not following. "Lady? Lazy?" She looked at her aunt when the cats did not move. "They willnae leave?"

"Not yet, lass." Mary smiled at the two cats and then winked at Rose. "Nay until Lady has her litter and she and the proud fither are sure their bairns are weaned, strong, and hale. Then they will come to you, leaving the young to take their place here."

"Lazy is the father?"

" 'Tis clear he can bestir himself now and then," murmured Adair. He kissed Rose's cheek and whispered, "Come, my love. I am eager to show ye how verra much I love ye."

"I suddenly find I am most eager to show *ye* how much I love *ye* as weel."

Mary watched the two lovers walk away. Her eyes widened when Sweetling lifted his head from Adair's broad shoulder and winked at her. She giggled and winked back, before stepping out of the garden and shutting the battered gate. Leaning her arms on the gate, she stared into the garden that would now be her responsibility.

" 'Twas close this time, Mary," said Iain as he moved to stand beside her. "Thought I might have to knock open a few heads."

She smiled at the man she would soon marry. "Aye, but good came of it. Few will heed Joan Kerr's poison now, and it made the laird open his eyes and see what was truly important."

"And ye put on a fine show, Master Iain," said Meg as she moved to stand next to Mary.

"Dinnae trouble yourself, Iain," Mary said when the man attempted to stutter out some denial of trickery. "Our Meg is a canny one." She looked at the girl. "I thought ye went home."

"Nay. Anne was sad and hurt and my father will need to soothe her. Felt they should be alone for a while. Thought to visit Rose, but she and the laird will be busy saying all they were too timid or foolish to say before. So ye get me."

"And ye are most welcome to stay for a while. In a wee while we can all go in and have some blackberry tarts."

"So, ye now take o'er here," Iain said, "holding it for Rose's lass."

"Oh, Rose will have a lass along with her eight sons, but that lass's destiny lies elsewhere," said Mary.

"But if ye have no daughters and Rose's lass willnae take guardianship, is it to be an end to the Keith women of Rose Cottage?"

"Nay, one will appear. I feel it, though I cannae say from where or when."

"Oh, Mistress Mary, look at all the dancing lights," cried Meg. "Do ye think the garden is happy for our Rose?"

After exchanging a wide-eyed look with Iain, Mary stared at Meg. "Ye see dancing lights?"

"Aye," replied Meg. "Cannae ye?"

"*I* can and *Rose* can." Mary gently grasped Meg by the chin and turned her face up to hers. When she found herself staring into a distinctive pair of sea green eyes, she inwardly cursed her own stupidity for not seeing it sooner. "Did ye ken your mother, lass?"

"Nay; she died when I was born near thirteen years ago."

"Always a sad thing, but I meant do ye ken her name?"

"Oh, aye. She was a Margaret, too. Margaret Keith. I always like to think I might be a cousin to Rose."

Mary laughed, gave a grinning Iain an exuberant embrace, then grasped Meg by the shoulders. "Ye *are* her cousin. Your mother was my first cousin. I cannae believe I ne'er thought to look for her here when she disappeared so long ago."

"Ye mean I am a Keith woman?"

"Aye, lass, ye are, and ye will be the next to take o'er guardianship of this garden. Ye already have an apple tree planted for ye, planted by Flora on the day ye were born, though she wasnae sure who she was planting it for at the time."

"But, Rose—"

"Believe me, lass, ye willnae be stealing another's place. 'Tis ye I have been looking for. Now, tell me what ye see in the garden, and dinnae fear to speak before Master Iain. He kens all."

Meg stared into the garden, and slowly her eyes grew very wide. "The lights! They are more than lights!" She looked at Mary. " 'Tis true, then, all true. The garden is fairy blessed. 'Tis really magic here."

Wrapping an arm around Meg's thin shoulders, Mary nodded. "Aye, it is, and I will soon tell ye the tale of how that came to be. I will also teach ye what is needed to keep the magic alive."

"I think I ken what it is. 'Tis love, isnae it?"

"Aye, my canny brat, 'tis love, for love is a strange, sweet magic, too. Love is the strongest magic there is. Ye will do weel, lass. Verra weel indeed."

Isbel

Chapter 1

Scottish Borders, Fall, 1362

He lay deep in the wood, blood seeping from his wounds and darkening the leaves he had collapsed upon. The late October frost was already creeping over the ground he was sprawled on, glistening, shimmering in the moonlight. His horse stood nervously by, its eyes white with fear, loyalty its only tether and that fraying rapidly as the night deepened. The man murmured in helplessness, and the threats that lurked in the night shadows crept even closer.

"Nay!" Isbel cried out, sitting up. Her rope-strung bed creaked its protest at her abrupt movement.

Isbel shivered and wiped the sweat from her face with the corner of her white linen sheet. She could still see the man clearly, easy prey for the unseen enemy that inched toward him. It was a bad night for a man to be helpless and alone in the dark wood. It was a bad night for anyone to be out. She wanted to ignore her dream, but the man called to her, silently but with a power she could not fight. A soft curse escaped her lips as she got up and began to tug on her clothes.

"And what are ye about, lassie?" snapped a gruff voice from the doorway.

As she yanked on her hose, struggling to do so without revealing too much of her legs, Isbel cast the little brown man in the doorway a cross look. A brownie, being barely three feet tall, was not much of a protector, but Pullhair had assumed that role with a vengeance. He stood firm in her bedchamber doorway, stiff and narrow-eyed. She was certain that even his shaggy brown beard was bristling. It was not going to be easy to get around him.

"I have had a dream," Isbel replied.

"And it told ye to rise and get dressed, did it?"

"It told me that there is a mon who is in sore need of my help."

"A mon, eh?" Pullhair further narrowed his eyes until they nearly disappeared beneath his bushy brown eyebrows. "So, now ye are creeping off into the night to meet a mon. Dreaming about a mon too," he muttered and shook his head.

"The mon is wounded, alone, and in the woods." She patted her cat, Slayer, and started toward the door.

For one long moment she and Pullhair stared at each other. Isbel knew that, if he pushed her to it, she would physically move the little man out of her way. That could be risky, for brownies were easily offended and even more easily angered. Not only could Pullhair stop coming to her tower house and working all the night long, making her lonely life not only tolerable but a great deal easier, but he could well do some great mischief before he stormed away. Isbel knew she would take that risk, however. The call to go to the man was too strong. Pullhair suddenly stepped aside, and as she passed through the door, Isbel wondered if he had seen in her eyes the determination she felt.

"Ye cannae go out there," Pullhair snapped as he followed her to the great hall.

Isbel turned her back to the little man and rolled her eyes. He was fretting over her like some old woman. His agitation was affecting the spirits that roamed the halls of her tower house. She had left the family lands of Loch Fyne in the vain hope of escaping her gifts only to discover that they had grown stronger in her new home. In fact, she was sure the shadows of Loch Fyne were not half as populated as the ones around Bandal, her tower house. She often thought it a good thing that her husband had not lived long enough to realize the full extent of her gifts or just how magical his lands were.

She cursed softly as she had to wrestle her thick woolen cloak free of a ghostly hand. "Your fretting has stirred the ghosties, Pullhair," she complained. "Now even they try to hinder me." She tugged on her cloak and reached for her walking stick standing next to the heavy oak doors of the great hall.

"I ne'er thought I would side with those spirits, but I now wish them more power," Pullhair grumbled, crossing his arms over his narrow chest. "You should think on your own safety. If that mortal mon was fool enough to get himself wounded and lost in the woods, then let him rot."

"Such a hard heart ye do have. I fear I dinnae have that blessing."

"What ye dinnae have is the wit to ken what ye should fear."

"Oh, I fear. I am terrified to go out into the forest at night, but I must go. The dream has ended but its strength lingers. The mon calls to me, Pullhair. 'Tis as if he has a firm grip upon my arm. Nay, upon my heart and mind, upon the verra soul of me. I cannae ignore his need, his cries for help. I must go to him."

"Do ye think he has gifts, as ye do?" Pullhair asked, revealing a tiny hint of interest.

"I dinnae ken. At this moment, he has power o'er me. I sense that he doesnae ken the full peril of his position. He only fears for his weel-being, for the dangers represented by untended wounds and the cold."

"Then go. Fetch your lordling. But dinnae go blindly into the night. The Sluagh ride tonight."

Isbel shivered. The Sluagh were the most formidable of the faerie folk. It was said that they were the unforgiven dead. They battled each other throughout the long, clear, frosty nights, staining the rocks below them with their blood. Tonight was clear and frosty. If the Sluagh found the man in the forest, they would take him up and command him to follow them, making him slay and maim people for them. If such enslavement was not torture enough, the Sluagh were said to be pitiless masters; Isbel wondered if that was the danger she sensed approaching the man. She had to try and save him from that living hell. Even the Unseelie Court, the malignant faeries, could not torture a man as unceasingly as the Host of the Unforgiven Dead.

"I dinnae go unprotected, my friend," she assured the brownie. "I have my cross hammered out of iron hung about my neck. I have bread and salt in the pocket of my gown and a flask of holy water to sprinkle about if need be. I also carry my walking stick carved from the branch of a rowan tree and banded with iron. And just this morning I said prayers for protection beneath a holly tree."

"Mayhap ye forsaw this."

"Mayhap." She started for the door, inwardly shoring up her flagging courage. "Howbeit, I believe I have enough gifts. I dinnae think I wish to add the one that curses me with the ability to ken what is to be."

"It can be a help as weel as a curse."

Isbel frowned when she realized that Pullhair was following her out into the bailey. "I dinnae need an escort to the gates. I believe I can find them on my own."

"I have decided to go with you."

Isbel stopped and stared at him. Even in the depths of her surprise she found herself musing that he was probably the only person, save for other denizens of the netherworld, that a tiny woman like her could tower over. The runt of the litter was what she had always been called. She occasionally wondered if the opportunity to be of a superior height was why she was so tolerant of so many of the creatures of the spirit world.

"Ye ken that ye dinnae wish to do that, Pullhair," she said in a very gentle tone, hesitant to cause him any offense. "I ken that ye have no love of the faeries, the good and the bad, and there are a great many things lurking out in the dark that hold no great love for brownies either."

"That is all true. Let us go. The sooner gone, the sooner back." The little man took a deep breath and stepped out through the heavy, iron-studded oak gates. "Why are ye hesitating?" he demanded when Isbel did not immediately follow him.

"I just wait for the spirit of my late husband's nursemaid to leave go of my cloak," muttered Isbel, stumbling a little as she finally yanked free of the unseen hand trying to pull her back inside the tower house.

"Ye should try harder to send those ghosties on their

way," Pullhair complained as he and Isbel began to walk toward the surrounding forest. "That is why there are so many of those spirits gathered here. They seek your help."

"And I give it when I can."

"There are far too many of them gathered here."

"I agree, but I cannae do much to solve that problem."

"Ye have the gift to send them away, to show them the path they need to walk. Ye just have to use it."

"And I do, whenever I can. Aye, the spirits do seem to gather here, but not all are ready to leave this earth. They seem to be drawn here, but many are uncertain. Mayhap the path they must take is clearest in this place. Howbeit, sometimes I can help them, sometimes they help themselves, sometimes they dinnae even ken why they are here, and sometimes they still dinnae wish to leave."

"Why should they wish to stay here? Why wouldnae they wish to finish their journey?"

"Because they are afraid," she replied quietly as she held her lantern forward a little to light their way through the thickly growing trees.

"Ye arenae afraid."

"Oh, aye, I am, Pullhair. I am. All mortals are afraid of what lies beyond death. I see more than most mortals do, am privy to more of the secrets of this world, yet I, too, fear that final journey. And dinnae roll your eyes in that manner," she said when she glanced at him and caught a glimpse of his expression. "Ye cannae judge we poor mortals on this fear for 'tis not one that ye must face. Ye arenae mortal. And e'en ye and yours fear something. Every creature upon God's earth fears something, from the tiniest bug to the most fearsome of giants."

Pullhair nimbly jumped over a fallen tree. "But ye shouldnae be plagued by such mortal weaknesses. Your blood—"

Isbel made a soft, sharp noise indicating her annoyance. "Please, dinnae plague me with talk of my bloodlines. I have heard it all. The laird and the faerie, the cursed brother, the secret room, and all the rest. I sometimes wonder if one reason I left Loch Fyne was that I grew weary of being told, over and over again, that I carried the look of the wondrous Lily."

"Ye do," Pullhair said quietly. "Ye have the same delicate beauty, the same wide, beautiful blue eyes, and hair the warm golden brown of sweet honey. Aye, Lily is who I see too."

"Ye kenned who she was," Isbel said, eyeing him suspiciously.

"I have served the MacLachlan family for many years. Ye arenae the first I have blessed with my skills."

"So? What did ye ken about her?"

"Nay much. I but saw her a few times. 'Twas many a year ago. 'Ware of those brambles, lassie."

She inwardly cursed. The way Pullhair had answered her told her that he would reveal nothing. He clung to the secrecy all of his kind treasured. The faerie blood in her veins made no difference to him. There might come a time or two when he would let slip a tiny piece of information, but mostly, he would hold fast to his knowledge. After so long, the truth about her ancestors, Duncan and Lily, had faded into fanciful tales told to children in the nursery. It was annoying to know that Pullhair held the truth but would not share it.

A sudden chill rippled down Isbel's spine and she tensed, trying to peer into the deep shadows surrounding them. She could sense malevolence all around her yet could not determine its source. Something in the shadows hated them yet was held at bay by all the protections she carried. She looked at Pullhair, saw how deeply he scowled into the darkness, and knew that he sensed it too.

"I can sense the evil but not whence it comes," she said, her voice little more than a whisper.

"An Unseelie, an evil faerie," Pullhair replied, waving Isbel on. "Many of the Unseelie Court dinnae like your kind, lass. They hold a special anger for mortals who hold faerie blood. They ne'er forgive a faerie for casting them and their ways aside to embrace a mortal. 'Tis a miracle, and the result of careful guarding by ones such as I, that has saved ye all from a curse."

"Not all of us were saved. Duncan's brother was cursed."

"Aye, but that was mostly of his own choosing. He wanted to try and save the soul of his lover."

"Ah, so that much of the tale is true." She met his cross look with a sweet smile as she started to scramble up the side of a hill.

"Ye try to trick me into telling ye things ye shouldnae hear."

"I but wish to ken the truth about my past."

" 'Tis not just your truth, and the others concerned prefer secrecy." Panting a little as he followed her up the steep hill, he grumbled, "Ye didnae tell me that the fool was so many miles away."

Isbel smiled faintly as she took the last few steps to the top of the hill. " 'Tis nay miles. And the mon lies at the base of the hill, in amongst the trees."

"Did ye dream a map too?"

She ignored his ill-temper, responding to his testy words as if they were a simple question. "I told you that he pulls me to him. He has guided me here."

"He isnae dead yet?"

"Nay," she replied as she started down the hill. "And ye may as weel cast aside the disapproval I can see in your every glance and hear in your voice. It willnae turn me back. I may not understand the how or the why of how I came to be here, but I am verra sure that I walk fate's path now."

"Are ye truly certain that 'tis fate guiding ye?"

"Such suspicion ye hold." She smiled briefly. "I may twist the truth from time to time, but I have ne'er lied to you, Pullhair. Aye, 'tis fate. It would be kind if fate told me why I must see this mon, but she is a mischievous mistress. Howbeit, every drop of blood in my veins tells me that my destiny lies but four yards ahead inside that group of trees. Are ye prepared to meet it at my side?"

"Aye, I have naught else to do this night."

Chapter 2

A faint crackle of leaves caused Sir Kenneth Davidson to tense. He dragged himself free of the heavy stupor caused by the cold and loss of blood. Groping along the ground at his side he finally found his sword, clutched the hilt tightly, and prayed that he had enough strength to strike at least one telling blow before he died. A little afraid of what he was about to see, he slowly opened his eyes and gaped.

It took Kenneth a full moment to accept what he saw. Crouched at his side was a beautiful young woman and a glowering little man. A strange thought wafted through his mind as he studied the little man from his shaggy brown hair to his tiny brown boots, but Kenneth quickly pushed it aside, blaming it on the pain and loss of blood. Brownies did not exist. They were but fanciful creatures who populated the tales nurses told children.

"Who are ye?" he demanded, startled by the weak unsteady sound of his own voice. " 'Ware, I am armed."

"Sir, ye may be a great warrior," said Isbel, "but I doubt

ye could cut a weel-stewed rabbit just now. I am Isbel MacLachlan Graeme, lady of Bandal, and this is my friend Pullhair."

"Pullhair? 'Tis an odd name. Of what clan?"

"Mine. We have come to help you." She cautiously edged closer to him and began to examine his wounds, wincing in sympathy when she tried to lift his jupon and he groaned in pain.

The pain caused by her gentle attempt to administer to his wounds caused Kenneth to sweat. He then began to shiver so fiercely that his teeth clattered together as the cold air dried the sweat on his body. Harsh words flooded his mouth, but before he could spit them out, the girl and the little brown man suddenly tensed and peered into the shadows that encircled them. He looked too, but could see nothing. Despite the lack of any visible threat, however, he felt the tight grip of fear.

Suddenly, the girl stood up, took a leather flask from inside her voluminous black cloak, and sprinkled water in a wide circle around them. Kenneth glanced at the little brown man and caught a look of horror and anger on his small unattractive face. When the girl sat back down, Pullhair glared at her.

"Is there something out there?" Kenneth asked her.

"There are many things lurking in the dark and the shadows, sir," she replied. "'Tis best if ye dinnae see them. I have protected us for now."

"Aye," snapped Pullhair. "Ye and this fool are protected, but I am trapped. None of the evil out there can cross the line ye just dribbled o'er the ground, but I cannae either."

"I will get you out," Isbel assured him. "Now, sir, may I ken who ye are?"

"Sir Kenneth Davidson of Glenmal, just this side of

Edinburgh," Kenneth replied, struggling to speak clearly yet not use up too much of his waning strength. "My clan was on a border raid. I was chosen to guard the rear. A few Sassanachs were reluctant to allow us a share of their goods. A few miles back I fought them and won, but I suffered a few wounds."

"And your people just left ye behind?"

"The rear guard is chosen to take that risk for the sake of the others."

"For the sake of the loot they scramble home with, ye mean."

"Could ye argue with the mon later?" said Pullhair. "Ye said ye came here to save him. 'Tis advisable that ye get about the business of doing so. All ye came here to rescue him from is still out there and the others draw ever nearer."

"I need a litter," Isbel muttered, reluctantly accepting the wisdom of Pullhair's words.

"Ye will need to step outside the circle and I cannae help you this time."

"I have ample protection."

Isbel grabbed the length of rope curled around Sir Kenneth's saddle horn, took a deep breath, and stepped out of the protective circle. She felt the malevolence all around them edge closer but clung to her faith in her protection against it. Nevertheless, she moved quickly as she gathered what was needed to make a littler for the wounded Sir Kenneth. She smiled to herself as she removed a small hatchet from her belt, for she did not even recall looping it onto the wide piece of leather around her waist. The fates were certainly using a strong hand in directing her. They not only had forced her to meet Sir Kenneth, but had done all possible to make sure that she could help him when she found him.

As she worked to lash together saplings and branches with Sir Kenneth's rope, she thought about the man she had rushed into the night to save. He was pale, dirty, and helpless, but she found him breathtakingly handsome. He was tall, lean, and strong. Although it was a little hard to see clearly in the poor light of her small lantern, Isbel was sure that he was dark-haired and dark-eyed. Such particulars did not really matter, however. Isbel knew that she would like them no matter what their true color proved to be.

She grimaced as she tugged the completed litter back to Kenneth and Pullhair. She did not think she was going to be allowed to be too particular. The moment she had set eyes on Sir Kenneth, she had known why she had been drawn to his side, pushed and pulled by him and the fates that ruled them all. This man was her mate. It was a startling realization, but in her heart, mind, and soul, she knew it. Instinct told her that even her brief marriage to the ill-fated Patrick Graeme had been no more than one step in her journey to Kenneth Davidson. It had brought her to Bandal so that she could be close enough to aid him now. The next step was the hardest, and it depended almost solely upon her. Somehow she had to make Sir Kenneth understand and want to be her mate.

And the fates had decided to make that very difficult indeed, she mused as, with Pullhair's help, she settled Kenneth on the litter and hitched it to his horse. Everyone told her that she was lovely so she supposed it must be true. However, she was not fulsome and men liked fulsome women. Her own husband had made a number of less than flattering remarks about the lack of meat on her delicate bones and had often tried to force her to eat more. She did not have the sort of purse a man of any standing looked for in a mate, having both a very modest wealth and equally modest land holdings. Sir Kenneth's fine attire and equally fine mount told her that he was probably a few rungs above modest or came from a clan that was. Knights from a wealthy clan were expected to marry lasses who could add to that wealth and the power it brought.

She inwardly cursed as she did what little she could in the dark to temporarily bind Kenneth's wounds and make him comfortable and warm. As if her looks and near poverty were not enough to turn him away, there were her many gifts. "Gifts," she decided, was an odd word for her strange skills as they often felt more like curses to her, especially when someone turned from her in fear. Even though her husband had thought that he could use her skills for gain, he had still feared them, even hated them at times. She often thanked God that Patrick had not had the time to realize the full extent of her skills. Her own family had occasionally found her a little intimidating, despite their own history and acceptance of such things, and her gifts had strengthened since she had left them. She dreaded seeing Sir Kenneth's reaction when he began to understand and see the truth of her many gifts. Fate could at least have picked a man who understood, perhaps even shared, her peculiarities, she thought crossly.

"I cannae cross that circle, lassie," Pullhair said, his gruff voice interrupting her thoughts.

"Aye, ye can," she replied as she grabbed the horse's reins. "Get on top of Sir Kenneth, but please be careful of his wounds."

"Ye want me to get on that fool?"

"Aye. His body will be your shield. 'Tis but a swift crossing and it should serve to protect you."

"Are ye certain?"

"Weel, *I feel* it will work."

"I dinnae suppose anyone means to ask me if I want this wee mon lying atop me," Kenneth said, his deep voice little more than a raspy whisper.

"If it puts ye at ease, I swear that it will be for no more than a heartbeat. He doesnae weigh verra much and I will be in sore need of his help to tend to you when we reach Bandal."

Kenneth stared at the little man when he sprawled his small, brown body on his chest. Pullhair flashed him a broad grin as Isbel started to urge the nervous horse forward. The little man had a set of very white, very pointed teeth, Kenneth mused. Although he continued to deny it, vehemently, everything about the tiny fellow bespoke a brownie, one of those creatures of whispered tales and dreams.

"Why couldnae ye just walk out of that circle?" Kenneth asked the man, a little nervous about the answer he might receive.

"Because of the holy water she sprinkled about, ye great fool," Pullhair replied, then he chuckled. "Ye ken what I am."

"I ken what ye remind me of and that ye are a little mon who, mayhap, carries too many superstitions in his head."

The moment they were outside of the circle, Pullhair scrambled off Kenneth but paused at the man's side to glare at him. "Just because ye dinnae choose to believe doesnae make them superstitions. I also ken the thought stuck in your head that ye cannae shake free. I am just what the wee voice in your mind keeps insisting I am. And since I am one of those wee creatures your wet nurse told ye tales of, ye might better spend your time asking yourself why ye can see me. Most of the rest of your kind cannae." He laughed at Kenneth's sour look and moved up to walk at Isbel's side.

"Are ye tormenting that poor mon, Pullhair?" Isbel asked, after a brief look back at Kenneth revealed the man's expression of mild annoyance.

"Me? I dinnae torment people," Pullhair protested, his air of insult too overdone.

"Aye, ye do and we both ken it weel. Ye often tormented Patrick."

"He deserved all ill that befell him."

Isbel inwardly grimaced at Pullhair's sharp response. The brownie had always detested Patrick and the feeling had been mutual. Patrick's biggest complaint about the little man was that he had never been able to catch him or really see him. Pullhair had plagued Patrick with small annoyances and curses, restrained in his actions against the man only because she was married to him. At times she wished she had paid closer heed to the way Pullhair, her spirits, and a myriad of denizens of the netherworld had reacted to Patrick. None of them had liked the man. If she had taken a minute to look beyond his handsome face and the sweet charm he had shown her before they were married, she might well have hesitated then ended the betrothal. Instead she had married the man and, within days, realized that she had made a serious error in judgment. The fine courtier she had been wooed by had quickly disappeared, leaving in its place an insulting, greedy, and often cruel man.

She finally gave in to temptation and softly asked Pullhair, "What do ye think of this mon?"

"That he is a fool."

"Why do ye call him a fool?"

"What else might one call a mon who nearly gets himself killed for the sake of a pack of thieves running back to their nest with a few skinny cattle?"

"Weel, 'tis true that I dinnae ken why men must steal from each other and certainly not why they must constantly fight and kill each other. Howbeit, if that makes him a fool, then most every land with men on it is full to overflowing with fools."

"Aye, it is." Pullhair bit back a smile when she cast him a disgusted look. "The mon can see me."

Isbel took a moment to fully understand the import of his words. When she did, she was so startled she nearly tripped. Few people saw brownies. Even fewer talked to them. Kenneth had done both.

"But he doesnae believe in such things, does he?"

"He doesnae want to, but the belief is there. He fights it as hard as he fought the Sassanachs."

Isbel felt her heart skip with hope. "Do ye think he has gifts akin to mine?"

"He has a sympathy, lassie. He feels, deep down he believes, and he isnae as afraid as he would like to be. I think he is also bonded with you in heart, soul, and mind so tightly that he precariously shares your gift."

"Oh, dear. That could make Bandal a most upsetting place for him. I had hoped for time with him, time for him to soften toward me ere he confronts the full truth of Bandal and me."

"Ye may still have it. This could be the only night that he has the skill to see me and mine. He has been weakened by his wounds and the veil that usually covers a mortal's eyes could have slipped a wee bit."

"And so it may fade as he grows stronger. I pray it does, that this sight he has is but a short-lived gift. Fate has chosen him for me, Pullhair. I was pulled here because that mon is my chosen mate. 'Twill be most difficult to make him see that if he learns too much about me too soon."

"Ye cannae hide what ye are forever, lassie."

"I ken it. I but ask for a little time, enough time to touch his heart ere his fears send him hieing for the hills."

Chapter 3

A low, steady rumble stirred Kenneth from his sleep. As he woke, memories of his rescue flooded his mind. He clearly saw the lovely young woman and her tiny brown companion and felt a lingering ache from the pain caused by their administrations. They had carried him up some narrow, winding stairs, placed him on a soft bed, sponged him down, and stitched his wounds. There was also a confused tangle of partial memories, but he shook them aside for he could make no sense of them. He slid his hand over the bandage on the right side of his waist and on his right leg. He was warm, comfortable, and despite the lingering pain, felt confident he would heal.

He opened his eyes and gave a soft cry of surprise. A huge gray cat was staring him in the face, its green eyes almost level with his. The source of the low rumble, he mused, as he cautiously lifted his hand and scratched the animal's ears. He smiled at the look of pleasure on the animal's face and at how the noise it made grew increasingly louder. It was unusual for a cat to be so friendly, so clean, and so well fed, and the animals were rarely allowed access to the bedchambers. Recalling the strange pair who had rescued him, he decided he should not be surprised that an animal most people scorned or feared would be made a pet.

"Slayer doesnae usually approve of people so quickly," said a soft, husky voice from the foot of the bed.

Kenneth started slightly, wondering how she could have entered the room so quietly. "Slayer?"

"Aye. Nary a mouse nor a rat dares poke its pointed wee nose onto my lands." She idly scratched the cat's ears when it moved to sit in front of her, rubbing its head against her stomach. "Ye are in the bed he has claimed as his own. Each morning the sun comes in that window to your right and shines o'er the bed. He warms himself in its light until it moves on."

"Ah, so that is why he was so friendly to me."

"Nay, not completely. He is most particular about the ones he chooses as his friends." She moved to the side of the bed and lightly felt his forehead and cheeks, relieved to find no hint of a fever. "How do ye feel?"

"I am still a wee bit weak, but I feel confident that I will heal. I do feel verra rested."

"Ye should. Ye have slept for nigh on three days." She smiled faintly at his shock. "I gave ye some herbal drinks to make ye rest. That is why ye slept for so long. I believe most strongly that sleep is the best cure for most illnesses and wounds."

"Aye. I believe so as weel. That does explain the pieces of memories I can make no sense of. A glimpse of a face or a few words, no more."

"Ye did rouse a bit now and again."

"I owe ye my life. Ye and that odd wee mon. Where is he?"

"He will be here as soon as the sun sets."

Isbel almost smiled when Sir Kenneth frowned, his expression telling her that he ached to ask a few questions and was fighting that urge. Pullhair was right. Kenneth knew what her little friend was, could see him clearly. The man either had a gift or two he was unaware of, or because they were so closely bonded, he had slipped beneath the cloak of her own.

Her delight over that faded abruptly. It was not really important why he could peek into the shadowed worlds. What mattered was that he could see all she had to deal with, and would quickly know exactly how magical Bandal was. That was not necessarily a good thing. The way he fought to deny the truth about Pullhair told Isbel that this was a new skill for him. Sir Kenneth Davidson was about to be privy to nearly everything most people were afraid of or, at best, simply preferred not to know about. That meant she would not have any time at all to win his heart before he discovered all of her secrets.

She inwardly battled with an almost overwhelming sense of defeat. Even if the fates were not using such a heavy hand in directing her, she knew she would have wanted Kenneth Davidson from the moment she set eyes upon him. He was breathtakingly handsome with his glossy, thick black hair and eyes of a deep rich brown. His smooth skin was a light shade of swarthy, as if he spent a great deal of time standing naked in the sun. He was long and lean, muscular in an attractive, subtle way. His features were cleanly cut, just sharp enough to be extraordinarily handsome, and unmarked by scars. The bottom lip of his well-shaped mouth was slightly fuller than the top. Several times as she had nursed him she had struggled against the strong urge to touch her lips to his. She was almost embarrassed by how badly she wanted him.

Cautiously, she reached out and covered his strong, long-fingered hand with hers. Patrick had bedded her only a few times before he had died, and she had found no pleasure in it. In truth, Patrick's manner of lovemaking had left her feeling bruised and ashamed. Every part of her told her that, if she and Kenneth became lovers, she would finally know what the poets and minstrels spoke so eloquently about, and she desperately wished to know. If nothing else went as the fates wanted, she prayed there would be at least one chance for her and Kenneth to make love. It was probably a shameful way to think, but she did not care.

"I shall fetch you some food if you wish it," she said quietly.

"I think I would yet I wouldnae trouble yourself too much. I am no stranger to wounds and healing and I suspect I willnae eat very much the first few times food is set before me."

"Nay, ye willnae. Ye are right about that. The trick is to eat a little as often as ye can. I will fetch ye a little hearty broth, some bread, cheese and wine. Will that do?"

"Aye, that is most kind."

The moment the woman left the room, Kenneth expelled a long, slow breath. He looked at his hand, still feeling the tingling warmth of her touch. He was not surprised that he wanted her for she was beautiful. Small and slender, she moved with the subtle invitation of a far more fulsome woman. Her thick, fair hair hung in long waves to her tiny waist. The most startling and alluring feature of her small face was a pair of wide, incredibly blue eyes rimmed by thick, long, pale brown lashes. Although her full mouth was sorely tempting, he always saw her eyes first. Each time she leaned close to him, he caught himself breathing deeply of her scent, the smell of clean skin touched with lavender.

Kenneth inwardly groaned as he felt his desire stir. Despite his pain and weakness, she could stir his blood with the slightest of touches or a brief, sweet smile. He would sternly remind himself that she had saved his life and that lusting after her was a poor way to thank her for that, but it did little to stem the longing. It made him feel ashamed of himself but he knew he was going to try and bed her before he left to return to his family's lands.

Isbel returned, smiling shyly as she sat on the edge of the bed and set a tray of food before him. Wincing, and silently waving aside her attempt to assist him, Kenneth sat up straighter against the pillows she had set behind him. In his current state of near arousal, the last thing he needed was to feel those soft, small hands on his body.

"You live here alone?" he asked before she filled his mouth with the warm, hearty broth.

She only hesitated a moment before nodding. In his weakened state he could do her no harm. Neither could Isbel believe that the fates had brought them together just so that he could hurt her. She had already endured one cruel, frightening mate. She could not believe fate would be so cruel and push her into the arms of another like Patrick.

"These are my husband's lands," she replied.

"Ye are married?" Kenneth could not believe how deeply disappointed he was.

"I was once, nearly a year ago. I am a MacLachlan from Loch Fyne and I married a Graeme and moved here. But months after Patrick brought me here, he drowned in the river just a mile north of here."

"Why did ye not return to your kinsmen?"

"I wished to remain here. These are my lands now, small though they might be. There were also things at Loch Fyne that I wished to run away from. I was not fully successful in evading my heritage, but I prefer the fact that I am alone now."

"I think I have heard of the MacLachlans of Loch Fyne." When she stuffed a large piece of bread in his mouth, stopping his words abruptly, Kenneth wondered if she was trying to veer him away from the subject of her family.

"They are not without power and wealth. I havenae heard of the Davidsons of Glenmal, however."

"And ye willnae hear much from me if ye keep stuffing food in my mouth." He tried to smile as he turned his head to the side, silently refusing another spoonful of broth.

"Ah, I see. It was not much, but 'twill do for a start."

Kenneth opened his mouth to thank her for her trouble, then tensed. In the far corner of the room he was certain he saw someone, an older woman in a stained gray gown. Even as he looked straight at her, however, what he had thought was a woman became no more than a glimmer of light.

"Now that was a wee bit odd," he murmured, meekly allowing Isbel to help him lie back down.

"What was odd, Sir Kenneth?" she asked, tucking the blankets over him and forcing herself to stop lingering over the chore.

"I thought I saw a woman over there in the corner, near the chest."

"There is no one at Bandal save myself, Pullhair, and Slayer."

"But I am sure—"

"'Twas just a flicker of the sun's light," she assured him as she stood up and collected together the remains of his small meal.

"I suppose."

Kenneth frowned as he watched Isbel scurry out of the room. Her leave-taking carried the strong scent of a hasty retreat. He looked all around the room but saw nothing. Sighing, he relaxed and closed his eyes. He wanted to believe her explanation but a small voice in his head told him there was a great deal Isbel MacLach-lan Graeme was hiding. Kenneth vowed that, as soon as he had regained his strength, he would search out a few answers.

"Curse that woman," Isbel muttered as she scrubbed out the bowl that had held Kenneth's broth.

"What woman?" Pullhair asked as he set a pile of wood by the kitchen fireplace.

"Mary, my late and little missed husband's nurse-maid."

"What has she done now?"

"Appeared to Sir Kenneth. He caught a glimpse of the woman in the corner of his bedchamber."

"I suspect she just wished to take a closer look at the mon ye intend to replace her sweet Patrick with." Pull-hair sat on the stool in front of the huge stone fireplace and looked at Isbel.

"Patrick Graeme ne'er had a sweet bone in his

wretched body," Isbel said as she sat on the sheepskin rug in front of the fire. "Mary was just too blind to see the evil in him. I think she saw the wee boy she nursed whene'er she looked at him and ne'er really saw the angry, bitter mon he had become."

Pullhair nodded and poked at the fire with a large stick. "He treated the old woman most unkindly in her latter years, but she ne'er ceased to care for him. Mayhap she feared that if she looked too closely, she might discover that she had had a hand in making him the wretched fool he was."

"Weel, next time I see her, I shall scold her soundly."

"I dinnae think that will do much good. The woman does as she pleases. What I find of interest is that Sir Kenneth saw her at all."

Isbel sighed and nodded. "He sees too clearly. Soon he may weel begin to believe in what he saw. Even if I twist my tongue into knots, I will not be able to change his mind about what he sees. I tried to be most clever in dismissing Mary as no more than a bit of sunlight dancing upon the wall."

"He will not long accept such explanations."

"I ken it." She stood up and moved to scrub the heavy wooden table set in the middle of the room, needing the hard work to try and ease her agitated state of mind. "I always thought it would be nice to have a mon who kenned the things I do, who saw at least some of what I did. It would mean I could cease to be so careful. Now, howbeit, I see the difficulty it could cause. If he had been born with such gifts, it could have served me weel, but he was not, or the gifts set in his heart and mind quietly, ne'er troubling him. For him to suddenly discover such things is no good at all, for he will fear these revelations and will certainly blame me for their arrival."

"Dinnae fret so, lassie. If ye are fated to be with this mon, then ye shall be."

She smiled at Pullhair. "Thank ye kindly for that attempt to cheer me, but we both ken the truth of the matter. The fates may have chosen Kenneth as my mate, but I am the one who must win him. I dinnae believe that showing him that all the frightening tales he was told as a child are not tales at all, but the truth will do that. All I can do is pray that the fates have not brought the mon to me just to snatch him away. For all I complain about my gifts, I have really hated having them. If they cause Kenneth Davidson to run from me, however, I may weel begin to loathe what I am."

"Nay, lassie. Ye have proud blood in your veins. Ye cannae think of turning against your own heritage."

"Pride and a great heritage willnae warm my bed or give me the bairns I crave, Pullhair."

"And ye would cast all that aside for that mon?"

"Aye, in a heartbeat."

Chapter 4

"What are ye doing out of bed? Are ye mad?"

Kenneth wiped the sweat from his brow with a trembling hand and, clinging tightly to the bedpost, glared at Isbel. She stood in the doorway of the bedchamber, her delicate hands on her shapely hips, and a chuckling Pullhair lurking behind her. Kenneth was not sure what annoyed him more, his own weakness, or the open delight the little man seemed to take in his helplessness.

"I am weary of lying in that bed with naught to look at but the ceiling and your twice-cursed cat," he snapped. "I have been stuck abed for a fortnight."

"And ye shall remain stuck in that bed for a few days more if ye have any wits at all," she scolded him as she helped him back into bed, Pullhair reluctantly moving to help her.

"What I should be doing is trying to regain my strength. If I dinnae use my leg, 'twill stiffen. I cannae be left a cripple."

"A wee bit of stiffness in your leg willnae make ye a

cripple. And using your leg too soon can be as harmful as not using it at all. Ye are healing weel but ye must nay rush things. Ye have been verra fortunate. Be pleased with that." She briefly checked his wound, knowing that there was little chance he had opened any of his injuries, yet unable to quell her concern for him.

"Ye dinnae need to fuss so o'er me," he muttered. "I hurt nothing save for my pride, just made myself so cursed weak that I couldnae take another step, neither to the door nor back to this wretched bed."

He scowled at Isbel as she soaked a cloth in a bowl of cool water. When she gently bathed his face, he reluctantly admitted to himself that it felt very good. The brief attempt at walking had left him so weak that he was shaking. Even as he felt stirred by her tender ministrations, he was infuriated by his own helplessness.

"I cannae abide this idleness."

"'Twill pass, sir. Endure this for but a wee while longer. The rewards are weel worth the price."

"Aye, mayhap."

"The fool accepts the truth with wondrous grace," Pullhair murmured as he sat on the end of the bed.

"My name is Kenneth," he said through gritted teeth, weary of the little man's constant insults.

"Weel, pride begins to pinch ye, does it? Fine then, *Kenneth,* ye had best heed the lassie. The art of healing is but one of her many skills."

Kenneth caught sight of the cross look Isbel sent the little brown man. She did that each time Pullhair referred to her skills or her gifts. She clearly did not want them speaking about such things. After so many days within the walls of Bandal, Kenneth knew the reason for her reluctance to talk. Bandal was a very strange place, filled to the parapets with a multitude of spirits and creatures he would prefer to remain ignorant of.

The moment Isbel hurried away to get him some food, Kenneth fixed his full attention upon Pullhair. Although he desperately wished to cling to his disbelief, he could no longer deny what the little brown man was. A brownie was not all that Bandal was cursed with either. He had fought hard to ignore it all, but that had proven to be impossible. Just because he could not see the spirits clearly did not mean that they were not there. At times he had overheard Isbel speaking to the ghosts who haunted her keep and at other times he had heard Isbel and Pullhair speaking of such things. It was far past time for someone to start telling him the truth, he decided.

"The two of ye hold tight to a great many secrets," he said, meeting Pullhair's steady gaze and not flinching.

"Now why would we be wishing to keep anything secret from such a brave knight of the realm?" asked Pullhair.

"Your tongue is nearly as sharp as your teeth." It pleased Kenneth a little when Pullhair scowled, revealing that the soft insult had struck home. "Let us cease to play these games. Aye, I have fought to deny what my wits and my eyes tell me so plainly, and ye make game of me because of it. Ye are a brownie. I dinnae understand why I should suddenly be able to see you, but that doesnae concern me just now. What troubles me is how much else I have been seeing. Either I have gone mad and dinnae ken it, or Bandal crawls with spirits of all shapes and sizes."

"And why should that concern you?"

"Because I am stuck in the midst of it. So is Isbel."

"Isbel is safe. She is weel protected."

Kenneth wisely bit back a smile of amusement over the way the tiny man puffed out his chest and tried to appear intimidating. He had never heard of a brownie taking on the role of a mortal's protector, but then he had ceased to heed the tales told of such creatures at a very young age. What little he could recall, however, told him that there were many things a brownie could not protect anyone from. His memories also warned him to be very careful not to anger or offend the tiny creature.

"Come, let us talk as men who share a concern over a tiny woman," he said gently. "Although I have ne'er glimpsed such things as brownies and ghosts before I met ye and Isbel, I cannae believe every place is as crowded with such beings as Bandal. Near to every corner of this tower house has something lurking in it. Why so many and are they a threat to Isbel?"

"I think Bandal is a place of passage," Pullhair said, glancing at the doorway to be sure Isbel had not come back and caught him being so forthright.

"Passage? To where?"

"To the land of the dead. Many mortals who have died find their way here. Most of them journey on, either right away or after but a short stay. And Bandal is a sacred place for my kind and others of the netherworld. There are several faerie mounds but a short walk from here."

"Faerie mounds?" Kenneth sat up straighter, tense and wary. "They could take Isbel away. That is what they do, is it not? They carry off mortals."

"Not as often as your kind would believe. They willnae touch Isbel, however. Oh, aye, there is a faerie or two who would love to do her ill, but she has too much protection, and I dinnae mean me or the things she carries about with her such as that cross pounded out of iron."

Kenneth winced slightly and rubbed his temples. "I begin to think I erred in beginning this talk. Ye are telling me more than I can fully understand."

"Foolish mon," Pullhair said in a gruff, faintly angry voice as he moved to stand at the side of the bed. "Ye weary what few wits ye have worrying o'er things that dinnae matter. Ye shouldnae concern yourself o'er why ye can suddenly see me and the ghosts that roam the halls. For some reason ye have suddenly been granted the gift of sight. 'Twould seem to me that ye are meant to do something with it. That is what ye should be trying to understand."

"If Isbel is in no danger, then there is no reason."

"There is always a reason for things that happen. There is also always some price to be paid for the gift ye now have."

"I must pay for something I didnae ask for and dinnae really want?"

"Aye. That is the way the game is played out, my pretty knight. Ye may just have the gift because ye are close to Isbel, bonded by a debt of blood. Howbeit, I repeat that ye may have been given it because ye are meant to do something."

Kenneth shook his head. "If I am meant to do something, I think I should have been given some hint of what that is when I was given these strange gifts."

Pullhair shrugged and started for the door. "That would be far too easy."

"Just tell me this then. I am not mad?"

"Nay, not in any way I have yet kenned."

"Then I am truly seeing ghosts and the like."

"Aye."

Before he could discuss the matter any more, Pullhair slipped away. Kenneth slumped against his pillows. He had not really found out much. In truth, he could not really depend upon Pullhair's assurances that he was not mad, that he was truly seeing what he thought he was seeing. After all, that brief talk to Pullhair could easily have been some delusion born of madness.

"Ye dinnae look to be very happy," Isbel said as she entered the room and shyly approached the bed. "Would ye like to play some chess?"

"Aye, that would pass the time nicely," he replied.

Isbel set the chessboard between them on the bed and carefully placed the small, hand-carved wooden pieces in position. It was going to be hard to keep her mind on the intricate game while sitting so close to Kenneth, but she knew she had to try and hide her deep attraction for the man. In all the time he had been at her keep, Kenneth had not revealed any hint of desire for her. Until he did, she intended to keep her longing for him as hidden as possible.

His agitation and ill temper had stirred her sympathies, however. She had occasionally been tied to her bed by illness or injury and knew well how maddening it could be. Although she could not spend that much time with him for she had chores to do, Isbel decided that she needed to make more of an effort to keep him occupied.

It did not take long before Isbel realized that she was outmatched. She had enough skill at the game to give him a reasonable challenge, but she doubted she would beat him, certainly not until she had had a great deal of practice. Reluctant to just give up, however, she struggled to do better than she ever had before. It did not really surprise her, however, to be checkmated by him.

"Ye need not look so proud," she murmured, smiling faintly as he set the pieces back in place, clearly intending to have another game. "One should try and win with a little more grace and humility than ye are showing."

"I shall endeavor to do so the next time I win."

"Of course. That would sound a more honest promise of improvement if your voice had not held the conviction that you will beat me this time too."

Kenneth laughed softly, then slowly grew serious as he studied her. She sat cross-legged on the bed and somehow managed to look both adorable and alluring. He scolded himself for even thinking of something as sly as the idea that flashed through his mind. but easily shook aside his brief attack of guilt. He fixed his gaze upon her full mouth and decided he was healed enough to try for a little more than her pleasant company.

"How about a wee wager on this game, Lady Isbel?" he asked even as he made his first move.

"How wee a wager?" She studied the board and prayed for a moment of inspiration.

"A kiss if I win."

Isbel was so startled that she dropped her chess piece. Kenneth glanced at her, then pretended that she had not made such a serious error. Her heart pounded so hard that she was sure he could hear it. Since she was certain she would lose again, she hesitated to accept his wager. It seemed a little scandalous. The temptation was too strong, however. She had ached to experience his kiss since the moment she had seen him. At least this way she could get her wish yet feign innocence.

"And what do I get when I beat you?" she asked.

"What would ye like?"

"One day where ye stay quietly in your bed and allow your poor battered body to heal."

"That is a high price indeed, but fair enough."

The whole time they played, Isbel forced herself to be calm. She ached for the game to be quick, for her defeat to come swiftly, but knew she would be deeply embarrassed if Kenneth guessed that. When, for one brief moment, it looked as if she would get checkmate, she nearly made a foolish move. It took all of her will-power to continue to play as if she wanted to win. She breathed an inner sigh of relief when Kenneth made his move and effectively cut off any chance she had of victory.

Even as he said the word "checkmate," he pushed aside the board and tugged her into his arms. Isbel could feel herself trembling faintly with anticipation and prayed that he would misread it as shyness or even a touch of fear. She tensed slightly as he framed her face with his hands. Suddenly she was afraid that his kiss could never match her expectations and the very last thing she wanted him to do was disappoint her.

" 'Tis but a wee kiss I mean to take, Isbel," he said in a soft, husky voice. "Ye need not look so frightened."

"I am but a wee bit nervous."

"Ye are a widow. Ye cannae be a stranger to a kiss." He began to brush soft, teasing kisses over her face.

"I am a stranger to yours," she whispered.

"That is something quickly and willingly changed," he murmured against her lips.

The moment his mouth touched hers, Isbel knew the kiss would be all she had imagined and much, much more. She slipped her arms around his neck and allowed him to pull her fully into his arms. Warmth flared through her body as his mouth moved over hers. He prodded at her lips with his tongue and she quickly parted them, welcoming the slow, intimate strokes inside her mouth. Her breath grew swift and uneven as he smoothed his hands over her body. His kiss began to grow fiercer, more demanding, and she shuddered with the strength of her need for him.

Suddenly the force of her own feelings for him terrified her. She broke free of his hold and stumbled off the bed. "I think ye have fully collected your wager," she said, her voice thick and hoarse.

"Isbel," he said, reaching out to her.

She stepped away, out of his reach, and then began to back toward the door. Every part of her cried out for her to return to his arms, and she decided that was a very good reason to get far away from him for a while. Isbel had known from the start that she desired Kenneth Davidson, but the feeling she had now could only be called a deep, almost overwhelming craving. She knew she had to remove herself from further temptation until she could gain some understanding of what she was feeling. She opened her mouth to say something, then gave in to cowardice and fled the room. As she ran to the safety of her own bedchamber, she prayed that Kenneth had no idea what had sent her running.

Chapter 5

It was a simple chore but Kenneth did not think he had enjoyed it more. He took a deep breath of the warm stable air as he rubbed down his mount. Wallace had not been ridden for days, did not really need a rubbing down, but it was one of the few things Kenneth could do. A lingering weakness, despite three long weeks of rest, made it almost impossible for him to do anything but the least strenuous of chores. It was highly irritating, for he felt well enough to do anything until he tried to really exert himself. Then his weakness revealed itself.

Knowing that it was only a matter of time until his strength returned, he decided to turn his mind to other things and was not surprised when his thoughts settled on Isbel. She had been in his thoughts almost constantly since they had shared a kiss. He had never experienced such a fierce and immediate passion. Since his youth, those days when he had just begun to learn the delights a man and a woman could share, he had never really ached for a woman, but he ached for Isbel. He could do nothing about it, however, for she had stayed well out of his reach all week.

That puzzled him, for he would never have guessed that Isbel was a coward yet she was acting very much like one. At first he had thought that her rapid retreat and obvious agitation was because he had moved too quickly or made his desire for her too obvious. That made no sense, however. She was a widow, no innocent maiden, and although he had not hidden the strength of his desire, he had not attempted to ravish her. Although he feared he could be thinking somewhat vainly, he could not stop wondering if her flight had been caused because she had experienced her first taste of passion. Her husband could well have been a poor lover, indifferent, unskilled, and hasty. If Isbel's passions had never been stirred by her husband yet had come to life in his arms, she could well have been startled, afraid, or even ashamed.

Kenneth cursed himself as a fool, even as he absently walked around the specter of a small ragged boy that had suddenly appeared by his horse's right flank. It did him no good to puzzle over Isbel's actions, for he had no facts or real knowledge to enable him to answer any of the many questions he had. The only things he knew about Isbel were that he desired her more than he had ever desired anyone, she was beautiful in an ethereal way, and she was odd. He simply did not know enough about her to understand why she did what she did.

There was something else to consider as well. All he could offer Isbel was a love affair. It would undoubtedly be fierce and sweet, but Isbel was not a woman a man married, certainly not a man in his position. His family was wealthy and powerful but he was a third son. His father had been more than generous, giving a small largesse to all of his children, but Kenneth knew he was expected to add to that wealth through an appropriate and advantageous marriage. Isbel not only had little money, but her land holdings were very modest and packed with all the things most people ran in terror from. He also knew that making Isbel a leman would hurt her, even insult her, and he realized he could not do that to her.

Enough musing and wondering, he said to himself as he started to walk out of the stable. Kenneth decided that the only way he could stop his mind from spinning in all directions yet solving nothing was to talk to Isbel. It could not hurt to ask why she had run from him and why she was staying away. The worst she could do was refuse to answer.

He found her near the chicken coop, blindly scattering seed to the birds. For a moment Kenneth stood a few feet away and just watched her. She looked as confused and as caught up in her own thoughts as he had been. He cautiously approached, not wanting to startle her too much, but needing to get close enough to grab her by the arm or the hand to stop her when she tried to elude him.

"Isbel," he called softly and prepared to catch her when she whirled around looking very much like a terrified rabbit. "We need to talk."

"I fear I am much too busy," she said, and gave a soft squeak of alarm when he gently but firmly grabbed her by the arm as she tried to walk away from him.

"Ye have been very busy for a full week. I ken that there are many things one must do before winter settles in, but I believe ye can spare me a moment or two without courting starvation."

Isbel inwardly grimaced and tried to still the tight nervousness that had gripped her. She knew they had to talk, had even planned out several conversations in her mind, but each time she caught sight of him, she gave in to her own cowardice. Even reminding herself that they were destined, that she had work to do if that destiny was to be fulfilled, did not help. It was not so much what he might say to her that she feared, but what she might say to him. She knew the feelings his kiss had stirred in her were born of far more than passion. Love had already found a place in her heart. That was not a secret she wished to reveal, however, not when he had showed no sign of even beginning to feel the same.

"What do ye wish to talk about?" she asked timidly as he tugged her over to a rough wooden bench set beneath a tree that was struggling to reach its full height.

"That kiss."

"It was very nice," she muttered as he sat down and tugged her down at his side.

"Such flattery."

"I suspect ye dinnae need pretty words and assurances from me, that ye hear plenty."

"I doubt I hear as many as ye obviously think I do. And I have not come to seek flattery or even sweet words. I seek some answers."

"About what?" She inwardly cursed, for her voice was tiny, little more than a timid whisper.

He sighed and ran the fingers of his free hand through his hair. "Ye fled from me that night as if I had just grown horns and a tail."

"Ye exaggerate."

"Nay. One moment we are sharing a verra fine kiss, a sweet and passionate embrace, and the next ye are leaping from my arms and scurrying out the door. What did I do wrong?"

She sighed and stared down at her feet. He had a right to a few answers. She had been enjoying the kiss, and revealed nothing but willingness, then had abruptly changed toward him and run away. The hint of confusion she could hear in his voice was probably heartfelt. Isbel was not sure what to say, however. She was not even sure why the passion he had roused in her had scared her so.

"Ye did nothing wrong," she finally said. "'Tis me. When ye wagered a kiss, I thought that would be nice. I confess that I had already thought of kissing you a time or two and was more than willing to satisfy my curiosity. What I had not expected was that it would be as, weel, as stirring as it was." She was not sure how she should read the brief, compulsive squeeze of her hand.

"I was stirred as weel," he said quietly. "Could ye not feel that I was?"

"Aye, and yet, to be honest, what ye were and were not feeling was not of any great concern to me at that moment." She finally gained the courage to look him in the eye. "My husband was not a particularly good man. He certainly never made me feel as ye did with but a kiss."

"Your husband has been dead for a year. Ye should feel no guilt that your passion didnae die with him."

"Oh, I dinnae. In truth, my passion wasnae stirred by him at all. For a while I suffered a deep guilt about that, but as I came to ken the mon he was, I realized that he did not notice that he was the only one gaining any pleasure from our coupling and that he probably wouldnae have cared had he kenned that I was cold to his touch. I thought I loved the mon, but soon realized that I had fooled myself as completely as he had fooled me, and he didnae marry me for love anyway." She shook her head. "Nay, I will say no more against him. 'Tis bad luck to speak ill of the dead."

He gently took both of her hands in his. "Did ye feel shamed that I made ye feel what he could not?"

"Nay. But can ye nay see? Aye, I am a widow, but in some things I am still a great innocent. The only mon I have e'er been touched by in my life left me cold. It sometimes puzzled me how the poets and minstrels could speak so eloquently of something so, weel, so cold. I decided that either something was wrong with me or they prettied up with soft words a necessary part of marriage." She caught a fleeting look in his fine dark eyes and smiled crookedly. "Nay, dinnae pity me."

" 'Twas not truly pity, more regret. Ye deserved better."

"Mayhap. And it was probably not all Patrick's fault. He found me too thin and I think, despite all his claims to the contrary, he feared my gifts."

"Ah, your gifts." She had been so truthful thus far, painfully so, and Kenneth briefly wondered if that would continue as he asked, "Ye and Pullhair oft mention your *gifts* but neither of you explains what ye mean."

Isbel stared at him. She knew that telling him the full truth about herself was not the way to make him love her. It could also end all hope of becoming his lover, even if for one brief night. Instinct told her, however, that she had to be truthful, that complete honesty was the only way she could deal with Kenneth Davidson and have any hope at all of a future with him. She knew now that her plan to hold fast to her secrets until she could find a place in his heart would never have worked. Kenneth would have seen that as a betrayal.

"Ye willnae like this," she warned him, wondering if she was also trying to remind herself of the consequences of telling him the whole truth.

"I believe I may have already guessed a great deal of it. I am not sure why but—shall we say?—my vision has become far more acute since meeting you and Pullhair."

"As I have told you, I was born into the clan MacLachlan of Loch Fyne." She took a deep breath and told him about Lily and Duncan. She was not encouraged by his widening eyes or his increasing frown.

"And so the MacLachlans of Loch Fyne believe they have faerie blood in their veins?" he asked gently.

"They do and the special gifts so many are born with seem to prove their claim. Every generation one is born who is said to look like Lily. This time it was me. And with those looks comes an added serving of skills. I can see all that lurks in the shadows, am privy to many of the secrets of the netherworld. I ken that ye have seen some of the ghosts who haunt Bandal's halls."

"I have seen something now and then," he reluctantly admitted, not wishing to elaborate, for that seemed like an admission of belief and he still clung to his need to deny it all.

Isbel smiled faintly. She knew that Mary had been his first sighting and that, after her, Kenneth had seen more and more. The ghosts had begun to appear to him with the same frequency and freedom that they appeared to her. He wished to deny that particular truth, however, and she decided she would not argue with him. What she was telling him was clearly upsetting him enough. She saw no gain in adding to that by insisting that he was just like her.

"Weel, ghosties like me, and when I came to Bandal, I discovered that 'tis a gathering place for them. I can help them step onto that final path, ye see, and one of those paths appears to be right here. At times I also have a wee touch of the sight, such as when I came to help you."

"I did wonder how ye had found me."

"A dream warned me of the danger ye were facing from your untended wounds and from, weel, other threats. I simply followed where I was led."

She could tell from the look on his handsome face that he did not like what he had heard. He had come to her wanting to speak of what they had shared, perhaps even to try and share a little more. Isbel could tell that each word she had said had killed his inclinations. He might yet be her lover for a little while, but she was certain he would never ask her to be his wife. If nothing else, most people would not wish to risk passing on such *gifts* to their children. Her only consolation was that he looked more uncertain and discomforted than afraid.

Kenneth slowly stood up. He did not know what to say or what to do. He had come to her to try and soothe any insult or ease her fears and, he admitted, to see what chance there was of gaining a fuller taste of the passion she had revealed in her kiss. Instead she had filled his head with truths he did not want to know. He did not know what to do next, what to say, or even what to think and believe. There was a shadow of pain in her brilliant blue eyes, and he deeply regretted it. At this moment in time, however, he knew he could not soothe it. Now he had to put some distance between them.

"I am not sure what to say," he murmured. "This was not the discussion I had planned to have. I do appreciate your honesty and I pray ye take no offense when I, too, speak the truth. I must consider this." He shook his head then bowed slightly as he started to back away. "I fear I no longer ken what I seek or what I am willing to accept."

"At least ye are not fleeing from me in terror," she said quietly.

"Nay, and yet my lack of fear only seems to add to my confusion." He lifted her hand to his lips and brushed a kiss over her knuckles then walked away.

Isbel fought the sudden strong urge to weep. She had not chosen to be what she was, had not willingly accepted the strange gifts that caused so many unease. It seemed most unkind of fate to give her skills that ensured she would always be alone.

A small flicker of hope came to life in her heart, but she forced it aside. While it was true that Kenneth had not shown the fear so many others did, that did not mean he would fully accept her gifts. He had said he needed to consider the matter. If she allowed herself to hope that, after some thought, he would come and take her in his arms, she would only end up hurt and disappointed. The saddest thing, she mused, was that she would now be denied the chance to know true passion and would have to keep her words of love locked away in her heart.

Chapter 6

"Why dinnae ye take the idiot his food?" grumbled Pullhair as Isbel set a heavily ladened tray in his arms.

"Because I believe he would rather I didnae," she replied, and sighed as she watched a grumbling Pullhair walk up the narrow steps to Kenneth's bedchamber.

For three long days she had seen little of the man. The few times they had inadvertently confronted each other, he had been polite but distant. Isbel found that not seeing him at all was easier to bear than that. It was beginning to look as if he had decided that he would simply stay away from her until he was well enough to return home. Fate, she decided, could be even crueler than she had imagined. She had the mate she was destined for within the walls of her home yet he may as well have been a hundred miles away.

"Here is your food, ye great, pretty fool," snapped Pullhair as he slammed the tray down on a small table near the arrow slit in the wall.

"I thought that we had agreed ye would call me Kenneth," Sir Kenneth said cautiously as he moved to sit at the table. The little man looked furious and he was well aware of how dangerous an angry brownie could be.

"Ye told me to call ye that. I dinnae recall that I agreed. And e'en if I had, I would still be calling ye a great fool now."

"I have offended you in some manner?"

"Nay and aye. Ye havenae insulted me, but ye have hurt the lass and that amounts to the same thing."

"I havenae touched the lass."

"Aye, and that be part of the problem."

Kenneth choked slightly on the wine he had been sipping. "Are ye saying that ye wish me to dishonor Isbel?"

Pullhair swore and stomped around the room for a moment before glaring at Kenneth. "I begin to think ye are worse than a fool. Ye are also stupid. Nay, I would ne'er ask that. But I see what has happened. The lassie tells ye the truth about herself, confides in ye things that she rarely tells others, and ye turn your back on her."

"She asks me to accept some verra odd things, things most people live in fear and trembling of."

"Ye believe in me."

"'Tis hard not to when ye are standing there yelling at me." He slathered butter on a warm slab of bread and was a little surprised when Pullhair laughed.

"And ye have seen the ghosts."

"I have seen something. It could be just the shadows flickering."

"Ye are verra good at lying to yourself considering what an honest mon ye are and all."

"Heed me, please. I like Isbel. Curse it, I lie abed at

night aching for her. I also owe her my life. Howbeit, she is a good woman, one who deserves a mon to wed her and give her children. After she told me the full truth about herself, I kenned that I could ne'er be that mon. The best thing to do, for both of us, was for me to step back ere we stirred more up between us than a fiery lusting."

"Did she ask ye for more?"

"Nay, but she isnae one that is meant to be naught but a leman."

"Laddie, I believe I have lived a few more years than ye." He lifted one shaggy brow when Kenneth laughed. "Isbel is what she is. In truth, her gifts have helped make her the woman she is now. True, she needs to be a wee bit stronger, a wee bit more certain of her own worth, but she is no innocent maid. What gives ye the right to decide what she will and willnae accept? Mayhap she has no interest in wedding you. E'er considered that? And how can ye listen to truth and immediately decide that ye cannae accept it? 'Tis almost cowardly. Ye heard something ye didnae like much or didnae understand and ye ran away and hid."

"That is an unfair accusation. I see no gain in opening my heart to a lass I can ne'er take as my wife. I certainly would consider it a great cruelty to try and win her love kenning that I will leave her."

"Then dinnae try and win her heart."

"I thought brownies were supposed to be such moral fellows."

Pullhair stood up straight, squaring his narrow shoulders. "We are. Ye arenae wed and neither is she. She is no sweet innocent ye are trying to seduce out of her maidenhead. Did ye not see the hand of fate in your meeting? I am nay one to argue with fate."

Kenneth shook his head. "I dinnae ken what game ye play."

"No game. I but see the lass all sad-eyed and mournful then come into this dark room and see ye acting the same. So mayhap what ye might do if ye allow yourselves some freedom would not be seen as moral by some and willnae lead to a marriage and bairns. Howbeit, for a wee while ye would both be a lot happier."

"Aye," Kenneth murmured, his thoughts going to Isbel as they had so often in the last three days. "Aye, we would be, but there could be a high price for it."

When Pullhair left, still grumbling about the idiocy of mortals, Kenneth concentrated on finishing his meal, but his mind refused to be stilled. After Isbel had told him the truth about herself, he had spent many an hour trying to call her mad, but it had not worked. If she was mad, then so was he, for he too saw the brownie and the ghosts. He had then tried to think of what would be if he gave in to his lusts, and slowly fell in love with her. The future looked to be a whirl of ghosts, brownies, faeries, and all that goes bump in the night and it would not stop with her. Any children they had would suffer from the same curse. No matter which way he looked at it, it still seemed that the safest and kindest way to go was to keep his distance until he was well enough to leave Bandal. He just wished that, once he had made that decision, he could have ceased to want her.

"Ye used to smile once or twice," murmured Pullhair as he watched Isbel scrub down the large table in her kitchen.

"Dinnae worry o'er me, Pullhair," she said, and gave

him a sad smile. "I will survive this. I but beg your pardon if, for a wee while, I suffer the occasional melancholy moment or regret."

"So ye stay here and sigh and he stays up there and sighs. It makes no sense to me."

"Sir Kenneth is sighing?" she asked, unable to hide her intent interest.

"As near to it as any mon allows himself."

"He kens where I am. If he wants for company, he can come and find me."

"Ye are as stubborn as he is. The fates have chosen him for ye yet ye avoid each other as if ye have some plague. How can ye win his heart if ye ne'er speak to or see him? How can ye make him want ye if ye stay far away from each other?"

"Pullhair, ye didnae see his face when I told him about me, about what I can do, and about the history of my family. I dinnae think there is anything I can do to make him wish to stay with me."

"But ye arenae sure, are ye?"

Isbel sighed and sat down on a stool near the huge kitchen fireplace. "Nay, I am not *sure*. Howbeit, the mon has turned away from me. Am I to chase after him?"

"Aye. Dinnae look so shocked, lassie. We are talking about fate and destiny, nay some base lusting. If he is fool enough to spit in the eye of fate, so be it. The consequences will fall on his head. Ye cannae be so foolish. Ye must do all ye can to fulfill the destiny chosen for you. If that means ye must swallow your pride, weel, take a hearty gulp, lass, and do it."

She lightly rubbed her temples in a vain attempt to ease the throbbing in her head. "I cannae even be sure he will let me near enough to try anything, not even to talk. He wasnae afraid, not truly, but I ken that I now make him very uneasy."

"Ye also make his blood warm." Pullhair grinned when Isabel blushed. "True enough, right now the mon thinks he will only dishonor you if he follows his desires for what ye told him makes him certain that he cannae wed you."

"Then why should I trouble myself with the fool?"

"Because, mayhap if ye lie with him, he will discover that ye stir far more than his lust. And consider this, mayhap the fates arenae concerned with love and marriage, just a bairn. They said he was your mate, but they ne'er said he would love you or stay with you."

"Oh." Isbel frowned as she thought that over and tried to decide if Pullhair was just trying to trick her into doing what he wanted her to. "If 'tis neither love nor marriage he is supposed to bring me, that leaves but one thing—a child. Do ye truly believe he may have been sent here to give me a bairn and no more?"

" 'Tis possible. Ye carry the strongest mark of Lily of any of the clan and I dinnae think any since her have had as many gifts as ye do. The fates may wish that to continue. 'Tis as if Lily has been reborn in you, and if ye die childless, then Lily dies again."

The thought of a child was temptation enough, Isbel mused. Pullhair did not really have to tug at her sense of family loyalty by mentioning Lily and the chance to continue her mark upon the MacLachlans. Patrick had failed to give her a child although he had certainly made an effort to do so in the short time he had been with her. What made her hesitate was the thought of the pain she would endure if she became Kenneth's lover and he still walked away. The day he would be strong enough to leave was swiftly approaching so she would not even have much time to persuade him to stay. And if he did leave her with child, she would be alone with a constant, living reminder of how she had failed to win his love. After a few moments of deep thought, she decided a child was worth the price.

"I suppose the only thing to do is to go to him, although I dinnae ken one tiny thing about how to seduce a mon." She smiled crookedly when Pullhair laughed.

"All ye need to do is wear your prettiest nightdress, close the door behind you when ye enter his bedchamber, and smile at him."

"That sounds a little too easy."

"Trust old Pullhair, lass. The mon wants ye. His desire is so strong I could almost smell it. He is just being honorable. Aye, 'tis most good of him and shows that he has great respect for ye, but ye dinnae need such things now. Ye need a mon."

Isbel stared at the heavy door, all that stood between her and Kenneth. She knew it could also be all that stood between her and complete humiliation. Just because Pullhair said the man wanted her did not make it so. The brownie also seemed to have little regard for the state of her heart. She felt sure Pullhair knew she was already in love with Kenneth and that sharing the man's bed would only deepen the emotion, yet he urged her to march into the man's arms and risk a pain no salve or magic could cure.

She took a deep breath to steady herself and smoothed her hands down her delicately embroidered, crisp white nightdress. She had not worn it since her wedding night, yet felt certain it was right to wear it now. Her long, thick hair was secured with a wide, blue silk ribbon, for when she had looked at herself with it hanging loose she had felt uneasy. It had looked far too wanton. As she lifted her hand and softly rapped on the door, she prayed it would take Kenneth at least a few moments to guess exactly why she had come. Isbel knew she would be sick with embarrassment if he knew immediately.

The door opened and Isbel felt her breath catch in her throat. Kenneth wore only his braies. She had tried hard to forget how good his body looked, but the memories of all she had seen as she had nursed his wounds had been impossible to discard. The sight of his tall, lean figure now brought all those memories back in a heady rush. The hint of brown to his skin made it appear warm and inviting. His thick, wavy black hair fell just past his shoulders and she was eager to thread her fingers through it. Her heart pounding, she briefly met his dark gaze, then stepped past him into the room and began to look around.

"Isbel," he said quietly as he shut the door, never taking his eyes from her, "why are ye here?"

Kenneth watched the thick swath of her hair sway to and fro as she moved, and he felt his insides twist with want. He also felt all of his grand intentions to be honorable seep away. He had been right to think that the only way to keep his hands off her was to stay away. Now she was in his bedchamber dressed in a sweet yet alluring nightdress. Everything about her invited him to reach for her, and if she did not leave in the next moment or two, he knew he would.

"I am looking for Slayer," she answered, not looking at him for fear he would see that she was lying. "There was a mouse in the kitchens. He should be down there hunting."

"He wasnae in here when I came in and I shut the door."

"And it has stayed shut?" She looked under the bed and idly noted that she needed to clean under there sometime soon.

He grimaced as he suddenly recalled a few incidents, ones caused by the ghosts he was still struggling to ignore and deny the existence of. "There was a brief time when it was difficult to keep the door shut."

"Oh. Sorry. I never have visitors, weel, living ones leastwise, and ye are of great interest." She stood up, brushed off her hands, and realized that he had moved closer. "I will speak to them but I cannae promise that they will heed me."

When he stepped even closer and reached out to trail his long fingers down the sleeve of her gown, she trembled. She clasped her hands behind her back, not wishing to let him see how they shook. There was a soft look in Kenneth's brown eyes that told her Pullhair was right. Kenneth did want her. Isbel prayed that she had tempted the man enough, that he would now push all of his fanciful thoughts of honor aside. A strong sense of honor would have him pushing her out the door soon and that was the last thing she wanted.

Kenneth gently grasped her by the shoulders and pulled her close, smiling faintly when he felt her trembling beneath his hands. "Isbel, did ye truly come to find your cat?"

"Do ye really wish to hear the truth?" she asked in a soft, unsteady voice.

"Aye, I have always favored the truth," he murmured and touched a kiss to her forehead.

"Nay, I didnae come to find the cat."

"What did ye come to find?" He cupped her face between his hands and brushed a kiss over her faintly parted lips.

"Another kiss," she whispered.

"Isbel, my sweet child of the faeries, if I kiss you, 'twill nae end there."

"I am nay an innocent. I ken what the kiss could lead to."

"There will be no *could* about it. It will lead to a bedding. Ye pulled away from the first kiss we shared and I let you. I cannae promise I will let ye free this time. Not unless ye put up a verra loud protest."

"I willnae put up a loud one." She curled her arms around his neck. "I dinnae think I will be inclined to even whisper one."

"Before we start to play this game, honor demands that I tell ye a few rules. I cannae promise ye I will stay—" He frowned when she stopped his words by touching her soft fingertips to his lips.

"I ken that there will be no promises made. I ask for none, save for a wee taste of the passion I felt when we kissed."

"Aye, that I can give ye easily enough. But are ye sure ye dinnae want more of me?"

"I didnae say I dinnae want more, just that I dinnae ask for it and accept that ye may ne'er wish to offer me more."

"Most lasses would want more."

She smiled and stood on her tiptoes, bringing her mouth close to kiss. "As ye may have guessed by now, I am nay like most women."

Kenneth laughed and picked her up then placed her gently on the bed. As he sprawled on top of her, he could not help but wonder if this was some dream. He had had enough of them about having Isbel in his bed, willing and eager. He could simply be having a particularly vivid one.

As he slowly pulled the ribbon from her hair and ran his fingers through the thick waves of soft hair, he decided he would ask no more questions. A dream as real as this was not one he wished to interrupt.

The moment Kenneth began to kiss her, Isbel knew she had made the right choice. If he did leave her, she would at least have sweet memories to ease her pain. Instinct told her that a passion as strong as this did not enter a person's life too often, and if she let him leave without fully tasting it at least once, she would regret it for the rest of her life. She wrapped her arms around him, met the ferocity of his kiss and equaled it, and let her desires rule.

Kenneth sighed with a mixture of satisfaction and regret as he finally eased away from the intimate embrace he and Isbel were locked in. He flopped onto his back, immediately reached for her, and pulled her into his arms. Although he was no profligate, he was not without experience and he knew he had never felt a desire so strong or found lovemaking so richly satisfying. Isbel was all any man could want in a woman. Unfortunately, she was also everything a man should not look for in a wife.

He smiled faintly when she snuggled up against him. He idly moved his hand up and down her side, testing the smallness of her waist, and exploring the gentle curve of her hip. Isbel was a woman of passion, had a quick wit, was beautiful and honest. She was poor in wealth and land, had a strange family history, had a brownie as her closest friend, and seemed to be surrounded by ghosts and all else that most people spoke of in fearful whispers. Kenneth delighted in the former and heartily cursed the rest.

"So, sweet Isbel, have ye found what ye sought?" he asked.

"Nay, ye were right, Slayer isnae here." She grinned when he laughed.

"Wench." He dragged her on top of him and gave her a quick kiss. "Ye could at least try to flatter a poor mon."

"Ah, ye need your vanity stroked."

"That and one or two other things."

"Beast. Aye, I found what I was looking for. And how fares your sense of honor?"

" 'Tis a wee bit bruised, but it will survive."

"Good, for I meant all I said."

"I believe you, and yet, 'tis odd but that makes me feel slightly guilty." He smiled crookedly when she giggled.

"Shall I leave you alone to wallow in it?"

"Try to move, my bonnie spirit, and I shall be forced to take swift and immediate—" He frowned when he suddenly noticed a faint shifting in the shadows. "I am nay admitting that I believe in ghosts, but are ye certain we have been private?"

Isbel sat up and glared at the specter lurking in the corner of the room. "Get out of here, Mary."

"Ye have betrayed Patrick." The old woman's voice echoed in her mind, and a quick glance at Kenneth assured Isbel that she was the only one who had heard Mary.

"Nay, I am a widow. Have been one for near to a year.

Now be away with you." The moment the woman disappeared, Isbel assured Kenneth, "I did look o'er the room 'ere ye kissed me and saw no one so I believe we had our privacy."

Even as she spoke, she realized Kenneth was not paying her any attention. His gaze was fixed firmly on her breasts. She blushed as she became aware of how much of herself she had exposed by sitting up.

When Kenneth reached out and covered her breasts with his hands, she murmured in pleasure. "I dinnae suppose ye are doing that to preserve my modesty."

"Nay, I dinnae suppose I am."

She laughed as he pulled her to him. Her happiness might be short-lived but she was determined to luxuriate in it while she could.

Chapter 7

"I wish ye could help instead of just watching," Kenneth grumbled at the faint image of the young boy that floated along at his side.

He picked up a piece of fallen tree branch and tossed it into the little cart he dragged along behind him. Collecting firewood was a menial task for a knight, but he had to admit that he enjoyed it. It was pleasant to walk through the sunlit forest on a crisp fall day.

It had been a fortnight since he and Isbel had become lovers, and he had almost immediately begun to help with the work around Bandal. At Glenmal he had done his share of the work but only that deemed worthy of a knight. At Bandal there were no servants to leave the less desirable chores to—only Pullhair, who arrived every day at sunset.

As he bent down to pick up another piece of wood, Kenneth suddenly found himself face-to-face with a very small creature. Not daring to even blink, he studied the thing floating just in front of his nose. It was a woman, a very small woman with wings. His mind told him it was a fairy, but he did not wish to hear that. The tiny woman suddenly grinned and Kenneth gaped. She looked exactly like Isbel. He gasped in shock and straightened up. For one brief moment the creature stayed right before him. Then she vanished.

He glanced at the ghost of the small boy, who smiled shyly, then back to the place where he had seen the tiny winged lady, and shuddered. What was happening to him? He was seeing things he should not be able to see. Worse, he realized with a start, he was accepting such things as if they were a normal part of life. He treated Pullhair as a friend, a man he could talk with about most anything. Ghosts flitted in and out of his sight and he did not even twitch, had even begun to talk to them. Yesterday, he was sure he had heard one of them answer. When Isbel had told him not to go outside two nights ago because the Sluagh were riding, he had accepted her words without question and stayed indoors. And now he had fairies popping up in front of him and grinning at him.

"Nay," he snapped as he threw the firewood into the cart. "I willnae be pulled into that pit of madness."

Kenneth was not really surprised to see that the boy had vanished. He was a very timid ghost. Dragging the little cart behind him, Kenneth started back to the tower house. His steps slowed a little as he neared the heavy gates of Bandal and he began to wonder what to do next.

While his anger had been hot, he had intended to march into Bandal, leave the firewood, and forcefully announce that he was leaving for Glenmal in the morning. He knew he could not do so, yet he also knew he had to leave. Each day he stayed with her, each day he breathed the air of Bandal, he became more deeply mired in its strangeness. If he did not get away very soon, he never would, because each day he also found himself becoming more and more willing to stay in Isbel's slender arms.

Isbel smiled at him as he entered the kitchen and he felt his heart sink. Leaving a lover had never been very hard for him. He would fill their ears with words of gratitude and sweet regret, give them some gift and ride away. For some reason he could not even consider treating Isbel that way. He knew he was going to have to be completely truthful, and for one brief moment he resented her for not allowing him to play the same game that he always had.

"I think I saw an elf," he announced, watching Isbel closely as he put the wood he had collected in a box by the fireplace.

There was a tone to his voice that made Isbel tense. She was not sure if it was anger she heard, but she was certain that he was far from pleased. A harsh curse echoed through her mind. He had accepted Pullhair and seemed at ease with the ghosts, but she knew he still did not want to believe in it all. Now he had seen one of the truly fabled creatures of the netherworld. It had to have recalled him to the fact that he was in a very strange place seeing things he did not want to see. The fates could have chosen a more willing recipient of such gifts, she thought crossly as she began to knead her bread with more force than was needed.

"A lass or a laddie?" she asked with hard-won calm.

"A lass. I bent down to pick up some wood and there she was right in front of me, so close she could have tweaked my nose."

"Ye must have startled her from her hiding place."

"Nay, she didnae look startled and I didnae flush her out of some bramble. She just appeared. Now that I think on it, she looked curious."

"Aye, faeries can be very curious."

"And she looked like you."

He said the words in a cool, flat voice. There was no compliment intended, but no insult either. Kenneth had just been strongly reminded of her unusual bloodline and he did not like it at all. Isbel struggled against a sudden urge to weep and flee the room. She knew what was coming next—the farewell. He was going to flee Bandal before he could see or learn any more.

For one brief moment she wondered if the faeries had sent one of their own to appear before him. They knew everything that happened at Bandal so they knew how badly she wanted Kenneth to stay with her and how uneasy he was about the magic of Bandal. It would not take much thought to realize that he only needed to see a few too many of the spirit world's secrets in quick succession to be sent running home.

Inwardly she shook her head. She could not blame the faeries or the ghosts or even Pullhair. Such things had always been hard for mortals to bear. It would have been wondrous if Kenneth had been different, but she should not condemn him because he was not, nor should she try and grasp some reason, some place or person to blame.

"I am sorry ye were given a fright," she said quietly.

"Nay, not a fright really." He stepped up beside her and idly stroked the thick braid hanging down her slender back. "I was but awakened to all I have been skillfully ignoring."

"Aye, I understand."

"Do ye? Ye were born to this. I was not. Ye have probably been taught that ghosts, faeries, and all such creatures are but a part of life. I was taught that they were the creatures of dreams, nay, nightmares. Ye were taught to understand them. I was taught to fear them."

She wiped the flour from her hands and turned to face him. "I could teach you to understand."

"Could ye? I am eight and twenty and was taught my fears as a child. 'Tisnae easy to banish the lessons set firmly in one's mind and heart whilst he was still young."

"And ye arenae sure ye really want to understand."

Kenneth could see the hurt in her wide blue eyes. He could even feel it and that disturbed him. It implied that he was truly and deeply bonded to Isbel and he did not think he wanted to be that close to her, to anyone. Such closeness left one's heart bared to sorrow and pain. That was something any reasonable man would shy away from. As he stared into her captivatingly beautiful eyes, he was not sure how reasonable he would remain if he stayed with her. The only thing he could be grateful for was that she had no idea of the power she had over him.

"Nay, I dinnae think I do. Lass, do ye ken how close ye stand to the secrets death holds? Ye are knee deep in the spirits of ones who have died and e'en ken where they journey to or at least the path they must take. That alone is enough to make a hardened warrior tremble."

"Ye didnae seem too troubled by the ghosts." She was not sure she understood why suddenly all he had accepted was now unacceptable.

"I wasnae, and that worries me." He dragged his fingers through his hair and scowled as he looked around the kitchen. " 'Tis as if this place has put a spell on me. Not only do I see things I never saw before but I am beginning to treat such sightings as but a part of life. Weel, it may be a part of life at Bandal, but it doesnae exist outside these lands."

"It does. 'Tis just that most people dinnae see it."

"Exactly. I want to be one of those blind, ignorant people again."

"Can ye just forget all ye saw and learned here?"

"I can try." He could see the glint of tears in her eyes and pulled her into his arms. "Lass, 'tisnae ye I run from. 'Tisnae ye I want to push from my mind."

After briefly hugging him, she stepped out of his light embrace. "But it is. I am Bandal. It is me. I believe I was fated to come here because this is where I truly belong. Patrick's kinsmen could have taken back the lands, for the marriage was a short one and there was no child, but they didnae. They gave it to me. Everything that has happened to me since I came here has only shown me more clearly that I belong here."

"Ye could leave. Ye could come with me," he said impulsively, then realized that he badly wanted her to. He wanted to leave Bandal and all its spirits behind but not her.

"Nay, I dinnae think I can."

"Why? Are ye trapped here?"

"In a way, for I am needed here, wanted and accepted. And this is all I own. Then, too, taking me from Bandal will change little." She smiled sadly. "My gifts werenae born here, merely strengthened."

"Ye mean to say that, wherever ye go, the same things will happen," he said quietly, disappointment sweeping over him.

"Aye, more or less. The magic is strong in Bandal, but 'tis everywhere. Faeries, brownies, ghosts, and all the rest, are everywhere. If ye must get away from such things, then ye must get away from me."

"I am sorry," he whispered and wondered if she would ever know how much he regretted leaving her.

"So the fool is running away, is he?"

Isbel looked up to see Pullhair standing beside her. She tossed aside the rag she held, suddenly realizing she had been rubbing that same spot on the table since Kenneth had walked out of the kitchen several hours ago. The pain she felt seemed to have become part of her blood, flowing through her constantly with every beat of her heart. She did not really want to discuss it but knew Pullhair would prod at her until she did.

"Aye, he is leaving in the morning. He saw a faerie today and she smiled at him. He has decided that he has had a bellyful of the magic of Bandal and cannae stomach any more."

"He is a coward."

"Nay, for he really doesnae flee out of fear. Aye, 'tis there, as it is in all of we poor timid mortals. Kenneth simply doesnae want to be a part of all this. He doesnae want to ken all the secrets this place holds. He doesnae want to see what few others ever will. He wants to return to what he was."

"And ye will just let him go."

She stood up so abruptly she knocked her stool over. "Aye. What would ye have me do? Tie him to the bed until he changes his mind? E'en if I could be so bold, it wouldnae work. As he says, this isnae his life, isnae what he was raised to accept or e'en like."

Pullhair shook his head. "I had thought him a better mon than that."

"Oh, I think he is." She smiled sadly. "He just doesnae think he wants to be. I can understand that. There are times when I heartily wish I wasnae what I am. I wish I could look into the shadows and see only shadows or walk through the forest and see naught but the trees. The blood I carry and the gifts I hold can sometimes be a great burden, Pullhair."

"That is only because your people willnae accept them."

"And what is wrong with wishing to be accepted, e'en liked, by your own kind? That is what Kenneth runs back to. He may ne'er say so, but if he accepts me, then he must accept near banishment by his own people. The choice is either me or the rest of the world. I was ne'er given that choice, but he has it and I cannae fault him for returning to all the others."

"But he hasnae e'en given ye a child yet," he grumbled.

A chill ran down Isbel's spine. One thing that had kept her from total despair was the thought that Kenneth had left her with child. Pullhair's cross words killed that hope.

"Are ye sure?" she asked, her voice tight with emotion.

"Aye. Here now," he cried in alarm when Isbel buried her face in her hands. "Dinnae start weeping. There is still hope."

"How can there be? The mon leaves in the morning." She righted her stool and sat down, knowing that Pullhair's presence was all that kept her from succumbing to her intense grief.

"There is still this night."

She gaped at him. "The mon is leaving me. Am I to go to his bed after he has said fare thee well? Surely that would mark me as little more than some hedgerow whore."

"Nay. Ye are letting your pride rule ye again. Ye became the mon's lover with no promises made nor love words spoken. In truth, ye entered his bed kenning that he might leave. I cannae see how it makes much difference now that ye ken for certain he will leave and when."

Isbel sighed and gently rubbed her forehead with her fingers. "Weel, it does. I am nay sure I can explain the why of it, but it does make a difference."

"Weel, ye had best swallow your pride again."

"Why? Why cannae he swallow his pride?"

"Because he willnae. 'Tis certain he willnae twixt now and sunrise. So, ye must be the one to do so."

"I begin to get a bellyache."

Pullhair reached out and yanked her braid, ignoring her sharp curse and easily avoiding the swat she aimed at him. "Ye want your belly filled, lassie, and ye cannae get that wish by sitting here weeping and moaning."

"I am *not* weeping and moaning. The mon might well be offended if he kenned we were using him for stud."

"Are ye planning to tell him?"

Her natural inclination to be honest welled up inside her, but she ruthlessly quelled it. "Nay, and I shall have to do a penance for that." She sighed and idly drummed her fingers on the table. "Are ye certain that, if I lie with that mon tonight, I will bear his child?"

"Now, lassie, ye ken that I shouldnae be telling ye such things."

"Pullhair," she snapped, then took a deep breath to ease her temper. "Ye are asking a lot of me and have your own purposes for doing so. I ken well that ye are my friend, but ye dinnae push me into the mon's arms solely for the sake of my happiness. For that, I think I deserve something. All I ask is some assurance that, if I go to Kenneth tonight, I will wake with child come morning."

"Aye, ye will."

"Thank ye," she whispered. "I am treating the mon most dishonestly and myself most dishonorably. Howbeit, I will do all that and more if it means I can hold a child in my arms."

Kenneth frowned when there sounded a soft rap at the door. He had just retired after a somber, quiet, and somewhat tense evening meal with Isbel and Pullhair. There was a good chance it was Pullhair at the door preparing to scold him or try to talk him into staying and Kenneth was certain that he did not wish to see the little man.

He opened the door and gaped. Isbel dressed in her fine linen nightgown with her hair loose and flowing over her slim shoulders was the last thing he had expected to see. For a moment he was afraid that he had not made himself clear.

"Isbel, did ye heed me at all this afternoon?" he asked uncertainly as she slipped past him into the room.

"Aye, ye are leaving when the sun rises," she replied as she sat down on the bed, clasping her hands in her lap to hide the way they trembled.

"Yet ye have come to me?"

"I do understand why ye must leave." She frowned when he shut the door but continued to just stare at her. "Why are ye looking at me like that?"

He smiled crookedly as he moved to stand in front of her. "I suppose I was feeling a wee bit unsettled because ye arenae upset o'er my leaving."

"I didnae say I wasnae upset. I said I understand. What I may have misunderstood was that ye were truly saying farewell this afternoon, setting yourself away from me right then and not in the morning."

When she stood up, he caught her in his arms, sat down on the bed, and settled her on his lap. "Nay, I am glad ye came to me tonight, more than words can say. I fear I am just confused as to why ye would do so after I have told ye I am leaving."

So ye can give me a child, she thought but bit her lip to keep from babbling out the truth. "Ye ken that I want you," she said, staring at their clasped hands to hide her blushes. "Ye saying fare thee well doesnae end that wanting. I like the way ye can make me feel and this is the last night I will e'er have the chance to savor that pleasure." She peeked up at him and felt the warmth of his gaze enter her blood. "I think no other mon will e'er make me feel as ye do and, let us face the cold, hard truth, there are none about to teach me otherwise."

The merc thought of another man touching Isbel both hurt and enraged Kenneth, but he fought to push such feelings aside. He had no right to feel them because he was walking away from her. He decided it might be wise not to think about who she might be with or what she might be doing once he was gone. The feelings raging through his body told him he could easily find himself returning to Bandal. That would be foolish since he would still be unable to stay, and also very unkind.

"I should be mortally ashamed of myself," he murmured.

"Why?"

"Ye have saved my life and ye have given me a sort of pleasure I have ne'er tasted before, yet I turn my back on you."

"I couldnae leave ye to die or be taken up by the Sluagh and I chose to come to your bed. The pleasure was also shared. Mayhaps I should be ashamed."

He fell back onto the bed and pulled her on top of him. "Then let us wallow in our shame together."

She smiled, clinging to him as he squirmed around until they were in a better position on the bed. " 'Tis always best to share such things."

Isbel cried out in amused surprise as he hastily removed his braies and her nightgown. When their flesh met, she shuddered. Their passion was so strong and so well matched. She could not understand how he could not see that, could not see as clearly as she did that they were meant to be together.

She slid her hand down his side, savoring the feel of his smooth, taut skin. Isbel knew she would not get much sleep, and if she had her way, neither would Kenneth. A greed born of desperation gnawed at her. As she touched her lips to his, she knew this would be the very last night of lovemaking for her. Kenneth might well find another. A man in his position was expected to marry and sire children. She could not do the same, could not seek out a new lover. After he walked away, she would be completely alone except for his child. As Kenneth began to make love to her, she prayed that Pullhair was right, that this was the night she would conceive a child. It could be the only thing that kept her from complete despair.

* * *

Kenneth silently dressed and donned his sword and padded jupon. For a long moment he stood at the side of the bed and stared at the sleeping Isbel. He wanted to crawl back in beside her, to hold her in his arms, despite a long night of lovemaking. He also knew that, if he gave in to that urge, he might never leave.

As quickly and as quietly as he could, he slipped out the door. Kenneth wished he did not feel quite so much like a thief in the night. He hurried to the stables, saddled Wallace, and let himself out of the bailey. The only clear thought in his mind was to get away before he changed his mind.

Isbel slipped out of bed, tugged on her night rail, and went to the window. It had probably been cowardly to feign sleep as Kenneth left the room, but she felt sure it was for the best. As she watched him ride away in the gray light of dawn, she placed her hand over her belly and prayed that Pullhair was right. If she could not have the man at least she could have some solace in bearing and loving his child.

Chapter 8

Isbel grimaced, straightened up, and rubbed at the ache in the small of her back. As soon as Kenneth had left, she had dressed and come to the stables to clean. It was hard, filthy work, and it almost succeeded in making her forget how alone she was. She just wished she could work through the night.

As she stepped outside to draw water from the well so that she could clean off the stench of the stables, she tensed. Something was wrong. Never before had she felt afraid or threatened within the surrounding walls of Bandal, but she did now. It was as if all the magic that had protected her had suddenly been yanked away.

She kept looking around as she washed up, anxious to get back into the tower house and bar the door. Even as she tossed the water into the dead garden near the stables, she knew it was too late. The gates of Bandal were pushed open and two men rushed in. She knew she had no chance of reaching the safety of the tower house but she ran for it anyway.

The thinner and taller of the two men charged her, caught her around the waist, and threw her to the ground. The bulkier man quickly joined them and helped his companion pin her down. An icy hand clutched at her heart. She knew what they planned to do and her only clear thought was that they would not damage the child she carried.

In her mind she screamed Kenneth's name but she knew it was hopeless. He had left over an hour ago. Even if she could somehow touch his mind with her pleas, he would never be able to reach her in time. Realizing that she was truly alone, that even her spirits had deserted her, she struggled even harder. The skinny man sitting astride her raised his fist and Isbel prepared for the blow. She felt almost grateful when his knuckles slammed into her for the blackness swiftly followed.

"Kenneth! Kenneth, help me!"

Kenneth abruptly reined in his horse to a stop and looked around. He saw nothing yet fear clutched at his insides and that plaintive cry for help still echoed in his mind. It was Isbel's voice, he was certain of it. What he could not understand was how he could hear her, for he was a full hour's ride from Bandal.

"Magic," he muttered. "She tried to use her magic to draw me back, Wallace."

Even as he spoke the words, he knew they were not true. Isbel would never trick him like that. The fear in her voice had also been too real. Something was wrong. The pull he felt, the silent demand that he race home to Bandal, was not one of greed or selfishness, but one of terror and need. She was not calling for his love or his passion, but his strength and protection.

He turned his horse back toward Bandal and spurred it to a gallop. Panic rose up in him but he forced it back down. It would not take him an hour to return to her for he was traveling much faster, but he was not sure he would be in time. Was the cry for help a premonition or was it torn from her own mind because she was already in danger? If it was the latter, he knew he could never reach her in time and he heartily cursed himself for leaving her at all.

The sight that greeted Kenneth's eyes as he rode through the gates of Bandal made him blind with rage. He screamed his battle cry as his horse reared to a halt, then he leapt from the saddle. The two men assaulting Isbel barely got to their feet before he was confronting them, sword in hand.

Kenneth cut down the bulkier of the two men quickly, but the tall, thin man had managed to draw his sword by the time Kenneth faced him. The battle was fierce but short. Kenneth knew he had the greater skill, and his confidence in himself was justified in but minutes as he ended the man's life with a clean thrust to the heart.

He hastily cleaned his sword blade off on the dead man's ragged jupon, sheathed his weapon, and rushed to Isbel's side. Some of his fear and rage seeped away when he saw that the braies Pullhair had demanded she wear were still securely in place. Her clothes were torn and there was a vivid bruise already forming on her chin, but he could not see any other signs of injury.

After hastily tending to his horse, all the while keeping a close eye on Isbel in case she began to wake, Kenneth picked her up in his arms. He carried her to the bedchamber he had used. The sight of Slayer basking in the light of the sun on the blankets was oddly comforting. The cat moved to sit at the end of the bed, watching as Kenneth tended to Isbel.

First he removed her torn clothes then gently bathed her. It troubled Kenneth a little that she still had not stirred by the time he had her dressed in her nightgown. He frowned down at her, absently stroking Slayer as the cat moved to curl up at her side. He reassured himself by noting that her breathing was steady and even and her color was good.

"Ye keep a close eye on your mistress, Slayer," Kenneth murmured. "I have to clear away that refuse I left bleeding in the bailey."

The moment Kenneth stepped out into the bailey, he knew something was wrong. It took him another moment to believe what he saw. The bodies were gone and the gates were closed. He stared down at the bloodstained dirt for a long while, needing to reassure himself that he had truly fought and killed two men.

"Ye do a fine job of cleaning up after the battle," he said aloud, glancing around and not surprised when he saw nothing, "but where were ye when the lass was in danger?"

He shook his head, no longer amazed at anything that happened at Bandal. A cry from within the tower house drew his attention and he raced back to the bedchamber. As he hurried to Isbel's side, he noticed that Slayer had had the wit to move out of the path of his thrashing mistress. Kenneth gently restrained Isbel and talked softly, trying to pull her free of her terror.

Isbel felt Kenneth's presence before she heard him. Slowly his soft words of reassurance reached her mind. She ceased fighting his hold, her breathing steadied, and her heartbeat slowed. When she opened her eyes to see him watching her with concern, she forced herself to smile.

"Ye came back," she whispered.

"Aye." He rose to pour her a goblet of wine from the jug by the bed. "I answered your call."

She frowned at him and took a long drink of the wine he handed her. "Well, aye, I did call out to you, but ye must be mistaken. Ye could never have gotten to me in time, for I called your name but moments ago, when those men attacked me."

"But I am certain I heard ye cry out. Ye said, 'Kenneth! Kenneth, help me!' "

"I did, but ye must have heard that an hour after ye left in order for ye to return here when ye did. I was not in danger then. In truth, I was mucking out the stables."

Kenneth just stared at her for several moments then cursed. She was right. Those men attacking her could not have arrived many moments before he did. Isbel had called for him only when she had been attacked, and he had heard her cry about an hour before that attack had happened.

"I have been made game of," he said as he poured himself some wine and drank it down swiftly in an attempt to cool his anger.

"I swear, Kenneth, I have done naught."

"Nay, bonnie Isbel." He sat on the side of the bed, took her hand, and kissed her palm. "I dinnae point the finger of accusation at you."

"Then who?"

"There are many possibilities. The faeries, Pullhair, e'en your cursed army of ghosts. They wished me to return, and they did what they had to to make that happen."

Isbel sipped at her wine as she thought over his accusation. She did not want to believe it, but could not refute it either. Too many things pointed to the truth of his charge.

"But I am certain those two men were real," she finally said.

"Aye, very real. The blood soaked the earth they fell upon and it wasnae cleared away although the bodies were."

"Someone took their bodies?"

"Aye, and closed the gates after them."

"Kenneth, did ye notice anything different about Bandal?"

"Nay, 'twas the same. Aye, there was e'en that moment as I rode up to it where I wasnae really sure it was there. 'Tis as if a haze clouds it from view, but then all was clear again.

"Yet when I stepped out of the stable, I felt something was wrong, something had changed. I recall thinking that it felt as if someone had yanked away all of Bandal's protection."

She cursed and thrust her empty goblet at him. As he refilled both their goblets, she struggled to think clearly. By the time he sprawled on the bed at her side, handed her her wine, and draped his arm around her shoulders, she had come to a decision.

"Ye are right, Kenneth," she said, her anger roughening her voice. "Someone has made game of you. Aye, more than you. Me and e'en those two men. We have been naught but pawns in someone's chess game." She looked at him, saw his grin, and nearly gaped. "Cannae ye see it? First, ye hear me call out to you an hour 'ere I do so. Second, the protection around Bandal that has kept me safe for so long vanishes. Third, suddenly two men rush in and attack me. Fourth, ye ride in to slay the two men and save me."

"A true hero," he drawled and laughed.

"Are ye not furious? They play with our lives."

"Mayhap they think we are too stupid to ken what is best for us."

She turned to face him squarely. The man should be furious but he was not. He was not even faintly annoyed. It made no sense to Isbel. He had fled Bandal because he could not abide the magic, yet when that magic tricked him into returning, he laughed.

"Kenneth, have ye suffered a blow to the head?" she asked, eyeing him warily when he just grinned.

"Nay, love." He tugged her closer and lightly kissed her. "Aye, when I first realized what had happened, I was angry, but that anger was mostly because of the danger they had put ye in. They allowed ye to be mauled and hurt just to get what they wanted. As I waited for ye to wake, however, I kenned I could forgive them their interference—this time."

"Weel, I am nay sure I can," she mumbled as she stared down at her nearly empty wine goblet. "Now I must bear hearing ye say farewell again."

"Nay, for I willnae say it."

Isbel tensed, but continued to stare at her wine. She was afraid to look at him, afraid she was just dreaming the words. When he gently grasped her chin, careful not to add to the pain of her bruise, she almost resisted his attempt to turn her face back toward him. Even though she now faced him, she could not look at him. Isbel was terrified he would see in her eyes the hope and the love she felt for him or, worse, not notice it at all.

"Look at me, Isbel," he commanded.

She slowly raised her gaze to meet his and felt her breath catch in her throat. There was a soft, tender expression upon his face, a warmth in his gaze, that she had never seen before. Although she told herself not to let her hopes get too high, Isbel felt taut and breathless with anticipation.

"Are ye planning to stay a wee while longer?" she asked, inwardly cursing the tremor in her voice that exposed her fierce emotions.

"Would ye like me to stay?"

For the first time since he was a gangly youth, Kenneth felt uncertain. There was an expression on Isbel's face that gave him hope, but he suspected it was easy to deceive oneself in such things. He knew what he had to do now, what he needed and wanted. Despite the passion she had revealed in his arms, he was just not certain she needed and wanted the same.

"Ye dinnae like the magic that is Bandal," she replied.

"Isbel, my sweet, overgrown faerie, ye didnae answer my question. Would ye like me to stay?"

"Only if ye wish to."

He laughed, amused by her vague responses and how they made him feel—more confident. The very fact that she could not bring herself to say a simple aye or nay told him that she was feeling as uncertain as he had been. Isbel was also afraid to expose her heart for fear such emotion was not returned. One of them needed to go first, to state clearly and plainly what they felt and what they wanted. Kenneth knew it should be him, if only because he had already left her once, but he was not sure he had the skill or the courage.

"I feel as if we do some strange dance," he said. "When I first heard you call to me, I fear my thoughts were unkind. For one brief moment, I thought ye tried to bring me back through some pretense, some trick."

"I would ne'er do that. And what purpose could it serve? Ye would surely discover what I had done and just leave again."

"It took but a heartbeat for me to ken ye would ne'er do that. Then I felt your fear. It became my fear. My only clear thought was to get to you as swiftly as I could and end the threat ye were under, end your fears. That need was so strong it was nearly a madness."

"Weel, I thank ye, but I think I will be safe now. The protection of Bandal has returned and I dinnae think they will play that trick again, whoever they are. The faeries are the ones I suspect."

"Isbel, I ken that ye will be safe, safer than e'en the king. That isnae what I am trying to say. The way I felt when I kenned ye were in danger told me that no matter how far I rode I could ne'er get away from ye. I am nay sure I could get away from the magic that surrounds ye and is within ye."

Her heart was pounding so hard and fast, Isbel was surprised Kenneth could not hear it. "Are ye saying that ye want to stay with me? That ye can now abide the spirits and all the rest?"

"Aye, I want to stay. I need to stay." He smiled when she clung to him for, although he ached to hear a few more words of love, the emotions she was revealing would suffice for now. "I kenned that ere I had passed through Bandal's gates."

"But ye kept riding." She pressed her ear to his broad chest and delighted in the steady beat of his heart.

"Aye. I am very skilled at deluding myself. I had said I had to leave and I was hard at work denying all my heart and mind told me. When I sensed the danger ye were in, I realized I played a fool's game, that I could deceive myself for a while, but only for a while. Soon the truth would come out and the truth was that I was making the greatest mistake of my life by leaving ye."

When he turned her face up to his, she readily accepted and returned his kiss. She offered no resistance when he gently pushed her down onto the bed, although she was astonished at how swiftly he removed their clothes. Their lovemaking was fiercely passionate, and she reveled in it despite the occasional twinge it gave her bruises. They lay entwined for a long time after their desires were sated, and when he finally eased the intimacy of their embrace, Isbel murmured her regret. She wanted to keep him close for fear he would change his mind again.

"Ah, Isbel," he said as he rolled onto his back and tucked her up against his side. "Such passion comes but once in a lifetime. I cannae believe I was such a fool as to try and leave it behind."

"Are ye certain ye wish to leave all else behind?" she asked, terrified that he had not really considered the consequences of staying at Bandal.

"I dinnae believe I need to turn my back on all I once knew." When she started to speak, he stopped her protest with a brief kiss. "Nay, hold your warnings. I ken that few people can bear the magic of Bandal and ye have often suffered the sting of that fear, the loneliness it forces upon ye. I think there may be a few of my people who are nay so timid, but if not, I willnae regret it. I will have ye and any bairns we are blessed with. And though they be spirits and creatures of the shadows, there are a lot of, er, people about."

"I pray ye are certain, that ye truly ken what ye may give up, for I dinnae think I could bear it if ye left again."

"Why?"

The words stuck in Isbel's throat for a moment as she stared at him. Then she decided it was her turn to be honest and bare her soul. Kenneth had not spoken of love yet, but he had certainly been forthright, and he was going to stay.

"Because I love ye," she whispered and gave a squeak of surprise and a little discomfort when he hugged her tightly.

"Sorry," he murmured, realizing how he was squeezing her. "Now I am sure we will survive, no matter how apart from the rest of the world we are, for we will have our love to keep us strong."

"*Our* love?"

Isbel knew she was trembling a little as she raised herself up on her elbows to stare at him. She was not sure which made her more unsteady, her anger or the fact that Kenneth truly cared about her. He could at least have the courtesy to say it clearly, she mused, and understood why she felt angry. Kenneth wanted the words from her but expressed his love in vague, sweeping statements.

"Ye dinnae look too loving just now, my bonnie elf," Kenneth said, eyeing her warily.

"I am nay sure I feel too loving. Ye pull the words from me, my fine knight, but I hear naught from ye."

"But I have told ye how I feel."

"Aye, I ken that ye think ye have and that is what is so annoying. Ye have spoken of staying, of needing and wanting me, and e'en of how glorious our passion is. Ye have not said how ye feel about me."

"Ah, Isbel, I love ye with all my heart and soul."

Her anger fled so quickly, replaced by such a strong surge of joy, that Isbel felt weak. She collapsed in his arms and fought the urge to weep. Kenneth would probably have a difficult time understanding that a woman could cry simply because she was so happy.

"Now I am certain we will abide well together," she said.

"Ye were concerned that this happiness wouldnae last?"

"Aye, for I didnae ken that ye loved me. I dinnae think we will skip merrily through the years ever smiling, but love is needed to hold two people together. Now I ken that we have that, that our bond is strong and will endure."

"We must be wed as soon as possible."

"There is a priest but a day's ride from here."

"Then we shall travel to him on the morrow."

"I dinnae suppose Pullhair can attend."

"Nay, and I am sorry for that. Howbeit, I believe our marriage will start more smoothly if we dinnae approach the priest with a brownie at our side." He smiled at her when she looked up at him. "Now kiss your husband and tell him how much ye love him."

"Are ye going to demand that of me a lot?"

"Oh, aye, most every day."

"And may I demand the same?"

"Ye will ne'er have the need to ask, for I will tell ye in every word and every act. Ye have won me, lass. Ye have woven your magic around me."

"Nay, love has," she said and kissed him.

Epilogue

Kenneth wrapped his arms around his wife and smoothed his hands over her swollen belly. It had been three years since he had raced back to Bandal and he knew he had made the right choice. For all of its strangeness, Bandal was home and Isbel was the mate of his heart and soul. If he had not returned to her, he knew he would have never felt whole again.

He looked around the bailey and smiled with pride. There were now others living and working at the tower house. After being duly warned, a few of his kinsmen and their families had joined him. It had been proven that all one had to do to learn the secrets was to live and love Bandal and care for its mistress. His people had needed some time to adjust but now they, too, accepted the magic all around them, even took pride in it.

"Young Robert has become very quick on his feet," Isbel said and pointed toward their son as the sturdy boy of two ran across the bailey, a nursemaid hurrying along behind.

"May it please God to make our next child as strong," Kenneth murmured, lightly kissing the top of her head.

"And as protected," she said as she turned in his arms and smiled up at him.

"Aye." Kenneth laughed and shook his head. "I think he draws the spirits to him even more than ye do."

"He does. At first Pullhair was disappointed. He thought I was to bear another Lily and how could that be when my child was a male. It did not take him long to see that Lily's spirit is very strong in the boy."

"Very strong."

"Ye sound proud of that."

"I am."

Isbel hugged him. "I dinnae think ye can ever ken how much I love ye."

"It cannae be any more than I love ye."

"Even after ye decided to stay, I still feared ye would ne'er fully accept the magic of this place, that it might still drive ye away from me."

"Never." He tilted her face up to his and brushed a kiss over her full lips. "I will ne'er leave again. I realized that there was one part of Bandal I could never live without, one of its magics that was no less than the very blood in my veins. That magic is ye, Isbel. Even if all the rest vanishes in the blink of an eye, Bandal will still be my home, for its mistress holds me firmly in her spell."

Isbel curled her arms around his neck and kissed him. Fate, she decided, could at times be extraordinarily perceptive.

Tatha

Chapter 1

Scotland, 1385

"Weel, there be another of the wretched lasses settled."

Tatha Preston halted as she reached for the latch on her father's chamber door. His deep voice penetrated even the thick oak of the door, but she did not fully comprehend what he was saying. The way he referred to her and her sisters as "wretched lasses" stung. It always did. Malcolm Preston, the laird of Prestonmoor, was always complaining about the fact that thirteen of his fifteen children were female. The way he said *settled* sounded ominous to her, and she pressed her small, slender body closer to the door, eager yet frightened to hear more.

"Are ye certain they will offer no complaint?" asked an even deeper, rougher voice Tatha recognized as that of her eldest brother, Iain. "All the lasses arenae as meek as Margaret and Elizabeth."

"Those two were settled at cradleside, as is natural," replied Malcolm. "It isnae that hard to settle one or two daughters. 'Tis nigh on impossible to manage when ye are cursed with thirteen of them."

Married? Tatha thought, and felt a cold knot of fear twist tightly in her stomach.

Marriage was something Tatha had given little thought to, despite being nineteen. From a young age she and most of her sisters had understood that there were no dowries for them, that the two eldest sisters had used up what little coin and land there had been for such things. Unlike her sisters Bega and Isabel, who, at three and twenty and one and twenty, were unhappy spinsters, Tatha had seen it as a good thing. Without the usual lands, alliances, and coin tainting a betrothal, she had thought she would have the luxury of choice, might even experience the miracle of marrying for love. It sounded very much as if her father intended to steal all that away.

"I just dinnae feel right about selling them," muttered her other brother, Douglas. "What sort of mon needs to buy himself a wife anyway?"

"I am sorry if this offends your delicate sensibilities, laddie," Malcolm said with a sneer. "God's bones, it isnae all that different from the way such matters are usually handled. Money and land exchanged hands when your first two sisters were wedded off. Aye, and most of it left our hands. Now at least we can get some benefit from the arrangement. And dinnae think the mon putting up the bride price goes away unhappy. He may get no dower, but he gets a healthy young lass of good blood to warm his bed, tend his hearth, and bear his bairns. 'Struth, I think the way I am doing this is by far the fairer way."

"And it certainly helps to fill our empty pockets," drawled Iain.

"Weel, aye, there is that sad truth," agreed Douglas. "I just wish the men werenae such sad specimens. It would seem that the lasses deserve better."

"They have naught now and no promise of anything," snapped Malcolm.

"Just dinnae expect them all to smile and thank ye. Bega and Isabel may not say too much, as they seem to be verra concerned about being spinsters, but Tatha willnae accept all of this so verra sweetly. Nay, not when she discovers the aging rogue who has bought her."

"Sir Ranald MacLean is wealthy, with some verra fine lands to the north."

A shudder went through Tatha. She knew Sir Ranald. He had been lurking about quite frequently of late. She still had bruises on her backside from his last visit, when she had been a little too slow to completely avoid his pinching fingers. The man had to be fifty if he was a day, had a sickly complexion, was lecherous, and was soft, like some pampered, overfed woman. He had also buried three wives with only one spindly legged, sneering son to show for their sacrifice. Marriage to him would be pure hell and nothing less.

Creeping away from the door, Tatha maintained her stealth until she felt she was far enough away not to be heard, then raced up the stairs to the weaving room where her sisters were gathered. She had to warn them of the plans being made for them. When she burst into the room she saw the way her sisters looked at her in surprise and then dismay, touched with a hint of disgust. Tatha was suddenly not sure they would see anything wrong with what their father was doing, and it saddened her. Although there was still hope that the six youngest girls, ages fifteen to nine, would display some pride and backbone, the others seemed to have accepted their father's oft-repeated opinion that they were little more than a burden upon him. Nevertheless, it was her duty to warn all of them.

"Ye really must learn some manners, Tatha," said Isabel, her voice heavy with disapproval.

For a moment, Tatha considered letting Isabel remain blissfully ignorant of her fate; then she shook aside her annoyance with her prim, self-righteous sister. "Father is selling us," she announced.

"What nonsense is this?"

"Ye are aware that there are no dowers for any of us?" Her sisters nodded, the older ones looking far more downcast by their circumstances than the younger ones. "Father has found an answer to that problem."

"He has found the means to dower us?"

"Nay, Isabel, he is allowing men to pay him to take us for their wives. He is selling us off to the highest bidders."

"And there are men who are ready to concede to this arrangement?"

Isabel actually looked delighted, and Tatha wondered if her sister truly understood all of the implications. "Our father is selling us off like cattle, Isabel."

"He is getting us husbands."

Tatha glanced at her other sisters and realized that they were going to allow Isabel to speak for all of them. "And what sort of mon needs to buy himself a wife? Have ye thought verra much on that?" She noticed a fleeting look of consternation on Bega's round face but, before her hopes could be raised too high over this hint of rebellion, it was gone.

"They will be husbands, something we have little or no hope of obtaining now," Isabel said firmly.

"Oh, aye, husbands. Useless, disgusting men like Sir

Ranald MacLean. That is the gift my father gained for me." Only her younger sisters showed any sign of sympathy for her. The ones of marriageable age revealed only relief that they were not going to be given to such a man. "Doesnae that make ye begin to worry o'er who may be buying you?"

"Nay," Isabel replied before anyone else could speak. "We are spinsters. Our fate, until now, was to grow old and barren in our father's house. Even a bad husband will be better than that. At least we will have our own households to lead and, God willing, bairns."

"Weel, I dinnae see it that way."

"Mayhap ye should. Ye too are a spinster, or near to. Aye, and ye are a too-thin lass with flame-colored hair. Red-haired and left-handed. Two curses in one wee lass. Ye also hold some verra odd ideas. Nearly blasphemous. Some have e'en whispered that ye are a witch, just as Aunt Mairi was. Aye, ye do have a verra fine pair of blue eyes, but they arenae so fine as to outshine all of your faults. If I were you, I should shut my mouth, bite down hard on my sharp tongue, and take what ye can get and be thanking God for it."

"Nay, I think not." Tatha fought down the pain caused by her sister's harsh words.

"And just what do ye think ye can do?"

" 'Tis none of your concern."

Tatha walked away, deeply saddened by this further proof of how different she was from her sisters. She had been her Aunt Mairi's favorite, spending most of her time in the old woman's tiny cottage. It was not only that Aunt Mairi had had nearly all of the raising of her that had separated her from her sisters, but the things Aunt Mairi had taught her. The woman had intended that Tatha would take her place as the healer for the clan. She had taught her niece all about herbs, medicines, and the arts of healing. She had also filled Tatha's greedy young mind with a myriad of old beliefs, beliefs the Church frowned upon. Such beliefs had been what had marked Mairi as a witch and threatened to mark Tatha with the same brand. In the year since Mairi had died, many people had sought Tatha out to make use of her indisputable skills at healing. Some people, however, also made the sign of the cross whenever they saw her.

As she slipped into the room she shared with her sisters Elspeth and Jean, Tatha wondered if her skill in the art of healing was one of the things Sir Ranald wanted her for. The man did not look very well at all, and Tatha now recalled Sir Ranald's deep interest in her knowledge of herbs. She dragged her saddle packs out from beneath her tiny bed and started to fill the panniers with her meager belongings even as she wondered if Sir Ranald suffered from some specifically male difficulty, for the herbs and medicines he had been the most interested in had been the ones pertaining to lust and one's performance in the marriage act. As she packed her herbs and small collection of stones, she decided that the man was probably just twisted in some sick, carnal way.

Elspeth entered their chamber just as Tatha finished packing. "Where are ye going?"

"To collect herbs," Tatha replied, hating to lie to her sister but feeling that it was best if no one knew of her plans.

"And ye need all ye own to do that, do ye?"

"Dinnae press me, Elspeth. 'Tis best if ye dinnae ken anything about this."

"Aye, probably. I am a verra poor liar, and eventually

ye will be missed. Did ye happen to hear who may have bought me?"

"Nay. I panicked when I heard who I had been sold off to. No one may have bid on ye yet."

"Ye should be more understanding of the others, Tatha," Elspeth said quietly. "We are nay all as brave as ye. And how is this so verra different from what was done with our eldest sisters?"

"Nay so much, I suppose. I had accepted that, without a dower, I would have no match arranged for me. Aye, in truth, I liked it that way. It meant that I might actually have some choice in the matter, might e'en have been able to marry a mon I loved. That has all been stolen away from me now."

"No lass has such a thing. Ye simply fooled yourself into thinking that ye did."

"Mayhap. And, aye, now that I think on it, this is different from what our sisters had arranged for them. This is nay the custom. At least when there is a dowry some care is taken in the choice of a husband, even if 'tis only an eye to alliances made and the land involved. There is no care at all taken in this. Our father may as weel stand us in the market square and let all and anyone toss out a bid on us."

" 'Tis nay that horrible. I am sure Father is choosing carefully."

"Aye? Ye think that drooling old lecher Sir Ranald shows careful choosing, do ye?" She nodded and picked up her saddle packs when Elspeth flushed and made no reply. "The mon has set three wives in the ground. I dinnae intend to be the fourth."

"Our father has made a bargain."

"I didnae agree to it, didnae put my mark on anything."

"Where will ye go?"

Remembering that she could not tell Elspeth the whole truth, Tatha murmured, "To the forests, as I always do."

Elspeth gave Tatha a brief hug and a kiss on the cheek. "Take care. The forest holds many a danger a wee sheltered lass doesnae ken much about and cannae defend herself against."

Tatha touched the cord with nine knots that was loosely tied around her waist. "I have protection."

A grimace briefly touched Elspeth's pretty face when she glanced at the rope. "Some of Aunt Mairi's witchery."

"She wasnae a witch. Aunt Mairi simply kenned a lot about the old ways. I dinnae believe they go against God and all His teachings, so I can see no harm in them."

"Then let us hope such charms work."

No one could hope that any more than Tatha herself as she went to the stables and saddled her stout Highland pony. As she rode away from her father's keep, no one tried to stop her. She often wandered away on her own, either to tend to someone's illness or injury, or to gather some herbs and wild plants.

What had Tatha's heart beating so fiercely it hurt was the knowledge that this time she could not return, might never be able to come home, at least not as long as the marriage to Sir Ranald was planned for her. Her family was not a very close or loving one, but it was all she had ever known, and it hurt to turn her back on them all.

And what lay ahead? she mused as she rode through the forest, impulsively stopping now and again to collect some herb or other useful plant. She could probably survive by practicing her healing art, she decided. If

nothing else, that skill would probably gain her a meal
and a bed as she needed them. She would have to be
careful about whom she met or spoke to, or she could
quickly find herself returned to her father and Sir
Ranald. Although some people might share her disgust
for what her father was doing, she was her father's chattel, and now probably Sir Ranald's as well. If she met
with anyone who knew of either man and had heard of
her escape, that person could well feel it was his duty to
take her back home.

By the time Tatha stopped to make camp for the
night, she was exhausted and afraid. The only thing
that stopped her from racing back to the safety and
comfort of her home was the knowledge that Sir Ranald
would be waiting for her. The fear gnawing at her while
she sat alone before a small fire was a tiny one com-
pared to that which was stirred by the thought of becoming Sir Ranald's wife. She prayed that her father
would soon see the error of his ways when he realized
that she had run away, but she did not really hold much
hope of that happening. Sir Malcolm was a very stubborn man. He was about to discover, however, that his
seventh-born child could be just as stubborn.

The dawn mists woke her with their chill. Tatha
winced as she stood up and discovered that sleeping on
the cold, damp ground made a person very stiff. It was
not until she had seen to her personal needs, washed
up, and dined on cold oatcakes that her stiffness had
eased enough for her to saddle and mount her pony.
She hoped she did not have to spend too many nights
outside, especially not with summer rapidly coming to
an end.

"Ah, me, Stoutheart," she murmured to her little pony after several hours of riding. "Is this madness?"

Her little pony snorted, and she smiled faintly. As she glanced around she saw little save the occasional crofter's hut and cattle. It appeared as if she had inadvertently picked a very isolated trail. It was going to be very hard to make a living if she never saw a village or a keep. Tatha decided that she would give it one more day, and then she would turn east. If she rode in a straight line she would eventually reach the coast, and there would be more than enough people there, from small fishing villages to larger port cities.

It was just as she was thinking that she should find someplace to camp for the night that Tatha saw the keep. For hours she had been feeling an increased reluctance to turn east as had been her plan, even though it was a good one. Despite the emptiness of the land, her heart urged her onward, north toward the Highlands. Now, suddenly, as she looked at the dark hilltop fortress ahead, that urge made sense, yet she would be hard-pressed to explain why.

As her pony cautiously picked its way through the bogs and the marshes that protected the approach to the keep, she noticed the river that bordered it on the north side. An admirable protection against raiders, she mused. In fact, everything about the keep promised one safety from the dangers of the world. And yet, she thought, frowning, that did not fully explain why she continued to ride toward its high, iron-studded gates.

Tatha suddenly smiled as she realized what pulled her ever forward. It was the call of the old ways, as Mairi had loved to refer to it. There was something or someone at that dark tower house, behind that high, dark

curtain wall, that called to her knowledge, to her understanding of the old ways. Nudging her pony forward
and keeping a close watch for the dangers all marshes
held, Tatha prayed the holder of the tower house would
allow her the chance to answer that call.

Chapter 2

Sir David Ruthven scowled down at the small figure riding toward his keep. He did not really have to see the long flame red hair swirling around the tiny rider to know that a female trotted toward his gates. In the five years since his mother's death it had become a somewhat common sight. If he had known how many women would seek refuge at Cnocanduin, he would never have made the vow he had to his dying mother. The last thing he wished to do right now was give refuge to another troubled woman, but, he thought with a sigh as he moved down off his walls, he knew he would yet again accede to his mother's wishes. He wondered crossly if some herald had been sent out to tell the world about the vow he had made.

"There is a—" began the tall, lanky young man who met David at the base of the curtain wall.

"I ken it, Leith. I saw the lass," David replied as he strode toward the tall gates, his cousin Leith quickly falling into step behind him.

"Mayhap this one isnae fleeing a husband."

Wincing as he recalled the trouble caused by the last woman to seek refuge at Cnocanduin, her evil-tempered husband hot on her heels, David nodded. "I cannae believe my mother intended Cnocanduin to become a refuge for wayward wives."

"Weel, mayhap ye ought to just ask the lass if she has a husband first, ere she even asks for refuge and ye are forced by your vow to bid her welcome."

"Aye, mayhap. 'Twould save us a lot of grief, but I would probably suffer a bellyful of guilt o'er it."

Although he felt the first pinch of guilt even as he stood blocking the way through the gates with his body, David decided to try Leith's suggestion. The last woman had nearly set him in the middle of a bloody clan war. He simply could not believe that had been his mother's intention when she had wrested that vow from him. Then again, he would have sworn to almost anything she had asked as he had stood by her deathbed, watching her life's blood slowly flow out of her broken and battered body.

The woman reined her pony in but a foot from him and, to his astonishment, frowned at him. There was no fear or sadness on her small heart-shaped face, no look of helplessness in her beautiful blue eyes. David wondered if she was simply a traveler who sought no more than food and shelter, or even was simply lost. If she was not running from something, it seemed odd that such a slight, delicately built lass would be riding over the dangerous countryside unescorted. What was puzzling at the moment, however, was the way she was looking at him as if he annoyed her. He had not even spoken to her yet.

Tatha started to order the man to get out of her way,

but a flicker of good sense kept the words back. The closer she had drawn to the keep, the stronger the pull of the place had grown. Once past the danger of the bogs she had urged her little pony into a faster gait. If the man had not suddenly appeared directly in her path, she suspected she would have heedlessly galloped right through the huge, imposing gates. Tatha forced herself to calm down. She could move with a little more caution and still find out what was drawing her to this place.

She studied the man blocking her path and wondered if it was him. He was certainly handsome enough in a dark, somber way. Thick, black hair fell to just below his broad shoulders. He was tall and leanly muscular. Rough deer-hide boots were laced around a pair of well-shaped calves. The plaid he wore swirled gently in the breeze, giving her brief glimpses of smooth, muscular thighs. His white shirt was unlaced, revealing a broad, dark chest. His form was fine enough to cause her heart to beat a little faster, but it was his face that truly held her fascinated when she finally took a good look at it. It was a beautiful face. The lines sharp but not too sharp, lean but not too lean. High cheekbones, a long, straight nose, a firm jaw, and a nicely shaped mouth, the lips holding just a hint of fullness. His eyes, set beneath faintly arched brows, were dark, appearing almost black, and were thickly lashed. One of those dark brows was suddenly quirked upward, telling Tatha that she had been staring at the man for just a little too long.

"I am—" she began.

"Are ye wed?" he demanded.

Slowly, Tatha blinked, confused by his abrupt question and somewhat bemused by his deep, rich voice.

She started to wonder why he should wish to know that, then quickly stopped herself. There were simply too many possibilities.

"Nay," she replied cautiously. "Ye dinnae wish wedded lasses behind your walls?"

"I dinnae wish the trouble wedded lasses fleeing their lawful husbands bring along behind them."

Tatha wondered if that would include lasses fleeing a betrothal. Although she felt a pinch of guilt, she decided that, since he had not asked, she did not need to tell him. She dismounted, marched up to him, and held out her hand, trying to ignore the fact that she reached only to his chest.

"I am Tatha Preston. I was wondering if I might seek refuge here for a wee while."

David stared down at her small, long-fingered hand, sighed with resignation, and shook it. "Aye, come along." As she grabbed hold of her pony's reins and followed him through the gates, he said, "I am Sir David Ruthven, laird of Cnocanduin. As long as ye feel a need to, ye may shelter here."

"That is verra kind of ye."

"I promised my mother on her deathbed to always shelter troubled lasses."

The tone of his voice told Tatha that it was a promise he was beginning to heartily regret. "I shall say a prayer for her."

"That would be kind. Aye, and needed. There were some dark lies muttered about her ere she died."

"I am sorry. I shall say several prayers."

He waved a stable hand over to take her pony. "Your mount's name?"

"Stoutheart." She shrugged when he looked at the

pony, then at her, amusement lightening his dark eyes. "He got me through the bogs," she said as she took her bags off the pony's back.

"True. Ye are from the north?" he asked as he took her by the arm and led her to the tower house.

"Nay, from south of here. The pony was a gift from an uncle when I was just a lass." When Tatha caught him looking down at her, the hint of a smile on his lips, she briefly thought about trying to stand taller, then inwardly shrugged. The only way to do that would be to stand on tiptoe, and that would look silly. "Six years ago, when I was but three and ten." She tried not to feel insulted when his beautiful eyes widened briefly with surprise, indicating that he found her not so great age of nineteen a shock.

"Jennet will show ye to a bedchamber," he said as he stopped near the foot of a steep, narrow flight of stone steps and waved over a young, dark-haired maid. "She can get ye all ye may need. We will be gathering in the great hall for a meal in but two hours."

David watched the woman follow Jennet up the stairs. Tatha Preston was a tiny, delicate woman. She was almost too slender, but, recalling how her small, high breasts shaped the front of her deep green gown, and watching the feminine sway of her slim hips as she climbed the stairs, he decided she had curves enough to tempt a man. With each step she took, her thick, flame red hair brushed against her hips, and David found himself wondering how it would feel in his hands or how it would look spread out beneath her body. That taste of lust struck him as odd, for she could not really be called beautiful. Her wide, bright blue eyes, heavily trimmed with long brown lashes and set beneath delicately arched brows, were her best feature, were in truth incomparable. Her nose was small and straight with a faint smattering of freckles, and it pointed to a slightly wide, full-lipped mouth that was very tempting indeed. There was a lot of stubbornness in her gently pointed chin. Her skin was a soft white with the blush of good health, and, David had to admit, it begged to be touched.

"She is a bonnie wee lass," murmured Leith.

Startled, for he had not realized that his cousin had followed them inside, David turned to look at Leith. "I was just thinking that, and yet, at first glance, I would ne'er have said so."

"Aye, she takes looking at, but 'tis often those lasses who wear weel. At least she isnae a wedded lass."

"Nay, and yet I think she may be trouble."

"What kind of trouble?"

"I dinnae ken, Leith. I just dinnae ken. 'Tis nay more than a feeling in my innards. If naught else, one must wonder what such a bonnie wee lass is doing riding o'er the countryside all alone, and I dinnae think the answer to that question is one that will please us."

Tatha watched the door shut behind the little maid, then flopped down on the huge bed with a heavy sigh of relief. She was inside the walls of Cnocanduin and, by what the laird had said, she could be staying until she chose to leave. Sir David had, in many ways, offered her sanctuary. The deathbed oath to his mother was a vow he would be loath to break.

She felt a twinge of guilt. He had asked her if she was married and she had been able to reply with a truthful no. But it was not the whole truth, and she knew it. Her father had sold her into a betrothal, promised her hand in marriage to Sir Ranald, and most people would consider that as binding as a marriage. Tatha doubted she would have an easy time finding someone to agree with her opinion that her consent was needed, or even that she should at least have been consulted.

Suddenly aware of how dusty she was and the strong smell of horse on her clothes, Tatha scrambled off the bed and began to undress. Even as she stood in her shift and started to unpack her bags, Jennet arrived with fresh, heated water and a tub, other maids quickly following with enough water to fill it. Tatha was barely able to wait until they had all left the room before she flung off her shift and climbed into the tub. With a sigh of pure enjoyment she sank down into the warm water, took a deep breath of the lavender-scented soap, and began to scrub away the scent of travel.

It was as she slipped on her clean shift and began to brush her hair dry that her guilt returned. She was accepting all of this grand hospitality under false pretenses. Tatha tried to soothe her unease by promising to tell Sir David the whole truth if he asked, but that helped only a little. Finally, she vowed that, if there was any sign of trouble due to her fleeing a marriage to Sir Ranald, she would leave Cnocanduin immediately. That restored her confidence, and she began to dress for the meal in the great hall in a much improved mood.

Her newly restored confidence wavered a little when she stepped through the heavy doors leading to the great hall. It struck her quite forcibly that she did not know any of the people now looking at her. She knew only the name of the laird.

To her relief, Sir David stood up and waved her to a seat on his left. As she smiled her gratitude and sat down on the bench, she promised herself she would spend the next day getting to know some of the people of Cnocanduin. For that reason, she smiled brightly when he introduced her to his cousin Leith, who sat on his right, and hoped that the dark young man's very brief smile in return did not mean her welcome was already wearing thin. She needed to find a few companions aside from the laird. Sir David undoubtedly had better things to do than to become her sole source of entertainment and conversation.

Although, she mused, as he placed some tender roast beef on her trencher, he was welcome to spend as much time with her as he pleased. Tatha surprised herself a little with that thought, for, until now, she had found little about men to interest her. His beauty of face and form was unquestionable, but she did not know the man at all. Thus far, he had offered her little to really hold her interest, yet she felt herself wishing that he would try, and even worrying that she would never be able to hold his.

"I find it curious that ye are riding o'er such dangerous country all alone, m'lady," David murmured, glancing at her and deciding that Leith was right, that Tatha Preston was a lass who wore very well on the eyes.

"Do ye? Why?" Tatha decided there was nothing to gain in questioning his form of address. Although her father was a laird, she was not sure titles of any sort should be used for the seventh of fifteen children.

"Ye are weelborn, are ye not?"

"Weel enough."

"And yet your kinsmen allow ye to trot about Scotland unguarded?" David frowned, the flicker of unease he had felt upon her arrival returning and growing stronger. "Ye have run away from something, havenae ye?"

Tatha sighed and took a deep drink of wine from her wooden goblet to steady herself. "I am neither a murderer nor a thief, so what does it matter?"

"It matters because whatever or whomever ye have run from could weel come pounding upon my gates."

"I dinnae believe anyone will come looking for me. Howbeit, if someone does, I shall leave. Is that nay fair?"

"Aye, fair enough, but why dinnae ye just tell me what it is ye are running from?"

Her reprieve had been a very short one, she mused, and sighed. "My father, Sir Malcolm, laird of Prestonmoor, has fifteen children," she began, her reluctance to explain clear in her voice.

"The mon is blessed. Your mother?"

"Dead. She was the second of his wives. He has just wed his fourth wife who, thank God, appears to be barren." She winced. "Nay, that was most unkind. She may weel wish for a bairn of her own. 'Tis nay her fault that her kin wed her to a mon who needs no more."

"Why so many?" asked Leith. "Does the mon plan to breed his own army?"

"If so, he had best work harder, for, much to his oftannounced dismay, thirteen of those fifteen children are females." She smiled faintly at the brief looks of horror the men could not hide. "My two eldest sisters were easily settled, betrothed at cradleside, if nay whilst they were still in the womb. Howbeit, that took all the dower money and dower land. There are nay so many men who are eager to bind their family with ours when there is no dowry to be had with the bride. So, depleted of dowries and unable to gain any more, my father realized that he was still burdened with eleven daughters. He has thought up what he believes to be the perfect solution—he is selling us."

"Selling ye?" David was relieved that she had not lied about being unwed, but it was beginning to look as if she was not exactly free either.

"Aye. If there is a mon who feels in need of a wife, he can buy one from my father. I was being sold to a Sir Ranald MacLean." She was pleased to see the grimace of distaste on David's and Leith's faces, although disappointed when they quickly recovered their composure. Their swift attempt to hide their sympathy indicated that they did not want to give in to it. "I warned my sisters, but the two who are older than me are verra worried about becoming spinsters. They didnae care how a husband for them was found. They also held sway o'er the others, although only Elspeth, who is eighteen, and Jean, who is sixteen, are in any immediate peril."

"And, so, because ye didnae approve of your father's choice, ye left," David said, trying to sound disgusted even though he fully understood why a woman would flee Sir Ranald.

"I did and, unless my father changes his mind on this matter, I willnae return to Prestonmoor."

Tatha could tell he was displeased, but he said nothing more. It was courtesy alone that made him offer to walk her around his keep and the inner bailey. She knew it but she accepted anyway. Perhaps, if he came to know her better, Sir David would cease trying to smother the sympathy she knew he felt for her. Tatha also admitted, with a mixture of sadness and alarm, that she was strongly tempted to spend some time with him. That attraction was most unwise. Even if she were not toting a lot of trouble along with her, Sir David Ruthven was not a man who would look favorably upon a skinny, left-handed redhead.

An instant later all thoughts of Sir David were pushed from her mind as he pointed out the well where his people drew their water. It was in a sad condition, tempting complete ruin if it was not seen to soon, but Tatha saw its beauty through the dirt, rubble, and tangled undergrowth that nearly obstructed all paths to it. She tried to go to it, but Sir David impatiently pulled her along as if he was anxious to leave the place. She allowed him to lead her away, but swore that she would return at first light. Suddenly she knew exactly why she had been drawn to Cnocanduin. It was not the promise of refuge. It was not a tall, dark-eyed man who made her blood flow warm. It was a neglected well that called to her, and Tatha was determined to find out why.

Chapter 3

"Where is she?" muttered Sir David as he finished his morning meal and realized his new guest had yet to appear in the great hall.

"I dinnae ken," replied Leith before having a deep swallow of sweet cider. "Mayhap she went on her way."

"We have ne'er been so lucky," Sir David grumbled, annoyed when he realized he did not wholly mean his cross words. He spotted the maid he had assigned to their guest over by the buttery. "Jennet, have ye seen the lady Tatha this morning?"

"Nay," Jennet replied, blushing upon being noticed by her laird. "She was already up and away when I rapped on her door to tell her 'twas near time to break her fast."

"Do ye think she has left Cnocanduin, continued on her journey?"

"Nay. All of her things are still within the bedchamber."

"I saw her by the well o'er an hour ago," called out one of the serving maids.

"She was fetching her own water?" David was certain the woman had been telling the truth when she had said that her father was a laird, yet tending to herself was an odd thing for a wellborn woman to do.

"Nay, though she was drawing water," said the plump serving maid. "It looked as if she had been clearing away the rubble when I saw her."

David frowned and sipped at his cider. He suddenly recalled his guest's intense interest in the well. She had tried to make him stop by it, then plagued him with questions until she realized he would not answer them. His mother and his grandmother had both cherished that well, had felt that it was a place of magic. The spring that fed it was the reason Cnocanduin had been built. Although he kept it in enough repair to continue to supply the tower house with water, he had otherwise let it sink into ruin. He was sure that it was his mother's talk of the well's magic, her deep belief in its powers, that had led to her violent death. David began to feel uneasy, suddenly certain he had seen that same gleam in Tatha's rich blue eyes.

"I believe I will go and see what mischief our guest has gotten herself into," he mumbled as he rose and strode out of the great hall. If Tatha was another who spoke of magic and the old ways, he would soon put a stop to it.

Tatha felt a rising excitement as she pulled the last of the rubble and overgrowth away from the side of the well. She dampened a rag in the water and rubbed away at an area that appeared to have some carving on it.

Once she had the whole area cleaned off, she sat back
on her heels and studied the inscription. It was in the
old script, and, although her aunt had taught her the
words, she had not been the best of students.

Again and again she struggled with the words. Slowly,
word by word, she sorted out its meaning. Leaning forward, she traced each letter with an unsteady finger.
Her voice softened with awe, she read aloud: " 'Any
woman of pure heart who drinks from the well of Cnocanduin will find protection, strength, and happiness as
long as it holds water.' "

Although she thought it might be vain to think of
herself as a woman with a pure heart, Tatha stood up.
She drew some fresh water from the well, took the battered dipper from the hook on the side, and drank
deeply. Frowning slightly, she stared into the dipper,
then peered into the well. Tatha was sure she would not
experience any sudden overwhelming change in herself, yet she thought she ought to feel more than a simple easing of her thirst.

"Ye have been neglected for a long time, havenae
ye?" she murmured and patted the cool stone, its white-
ness dimmed by years of dirt.

She turned to the small bag she had brought with
her. Pulling out a thick cord, she visualized a shield
and, softly repeating the promise carved into the side of
the well, tied nine knots in it. Tatha then attached this
protective binding to the bottom of the bucket. She repeated the simple spell and hung the second cord from
the rowan tree that grew next to the well.

Next she took out one of her holed stones, painstak-
ingly gathered from the sea. She rubbed it between her
hands as she murmured, "Stone, evil ye will deny. Send
it to the earth and sky. Send it to the flame and sea.

Stone of power protect Cnocanduin and all who dwell within its walls."

Then, with a pinch of regret over giving up one of her precious stones, she dropped it into the well. It was a worthy sacrifice, for not only would it enhance the protection the well promised, but it would strengthen the healing power of the water. Aunt Mairi would approve, she mused, as she lowered the bucket and drew up some more water to take another drink.

"What are ye doing?"

That deep voice sounding so close behind her made Tatha start and gasp in surprise. Since she was taking a deep drink of water at the time, she began to choke, some of the water going the wrong way down her throat. The rest, what was in her mouth and in the dipper, soaked the front of her gown. Sir David began to slap her on the back with such force that she stumbled against the well and had to grip the edge to steady herself. As soon as she got herself under control, she wiped the tears from her cheeks, and turned to glare at the man.

David glared right back. He had watched her for several minutes before speaking and did not like what he had seen. She was doing the same sort of things that had led to his mother being feared, then murdered. That alone was enough to infuriate him, lashing him with dark, painful memories. What troubled him was the fear he felt. It was not a fear of what she did, but of what such beliefs could cost her. He did not even know this tiny, flame-haired woman, yet his blood ran cold at the thought that she could soon suffer as his mother had. His fear was for her, and that made no sense. Unless it directly affected his people, what happened to a stranger should not matter much to him, but it did, and that only made him angrier.

"Ye scared several years out of me," Tatha complained as she tried to dab the water from the front of her deep blue gown with a scrap of clean linen. "Do ye always creep up behind people?"

"Only when they are behaving in a strange manner," he snapped.

"Strange? I wasnae doing anything strange."

"Nay?" He stepped closer to the rowan tree and reached up toward the knotted cord she had draped in the branches. "And what is this then?"

Tatha quickly moved to his side and slapped his hand away. " 'Tis naught to concern ye."

"Ye dinnae think people will wonder why there is a knotted cord in this tree?"

"Nay. I doubt anyone will e'en see the thing. Ye wouldnae have seen it put there if ye hadnae been tiptoeing about."

"I ken what that is. 'Tis some spell of protection."

Her eyes widening, Tatha looked at Sir David in surprise and a deepening interest. "The old ways are practiced here?"

"Nay, that nonsense isnae done here. I willnae allow it."

"Nonsense? Nay here?" Tatha stepped back to the well and smoothed her hand over the stone. "Aye, that *nonsense* is here. I suspect that *nonsense* has been here since long before this keep was built. And ye ken what it is, for all ye call it *nonsense,* or ye wouldnae ken the meaning of that knotted cord. Someone has taught ye a thing or two."

"Aye," he said in a cold, flat voice, "my mother, who

learned such foolishness from her mother, and 'tis just such blasphemous games that got the woman beaten to death five years ago."

Although she felt a surge of sympathy for the man, Tatha smothered the emotion, knowing that he neither wanted it, nor would he appreciate it. He was trying to frighten her. He succeeded to some extent, but fear of the dangers of superstition was an old one to her. Tatha had been taught at a very young age how to face it, accept it, and then push it aside.

"I am sorry. Ignorance and fear can be dangerous, deadly things," she said quietly. "My aunt Mairi was -oftimes threatened and was the subject of many an evil whisper. 'Tis odd, for she did no one any harm. In truth, she was a great healer. She taught me all of her skills. I oft wonder if the skill to fix that which so afrightens people, sickness and injury, is what marks healers. We touch, study, and sometimes cure what others consider evil, terrifying. Mayhap, because they believe God inflicts diseases and such, they think that we go against His will when we try to cure such things. Odd, though, that they dinnae turn against physicians, isnae it? But mayhap that is because physicians, or leeches if ye prefer, are men."

David blinked, opened his mouth to reply, then clamped it shut. He needed to regain his calm and put some order into his thoughts. Her words stunned him with their truth. His mother had done little more than try to help people, to heal their ills and soothe their pains. Some people had come from far away to seek her aid, her fame as a healer having become quite widespread before she was killed. David had always assumed, though, that the danger had come from her talk of such things as the power of the water, the magic of the stones, and the occasional little charm, but he realized that he had never fully believed that. His mother had understood, though scorned, people's fears, and, on most occasions, had tried to be circumspect about her beliefs. He shook his head. He did not want to think that simply helping people had cost her her life.

"Those men dinnae speak of magic waters or babble blasphemous words over rocks," he snapped.

"Ye shouldnae have seen that," she muttered.

"Weel, I did."

"Only because ye crept up on me like some thief."

"One of the maids saw ye."

"Nay, all she saw was me drawing water from the well and trying to clear away this mess. I was most careful, for my aunt taught me about the fears so many people hold." She frowned at the well. "Your mother told people of the well's powers?"

"She told some. Aye. She was verra proud of the power she mistakenly believed it held."

Tatha decided she would gain little by trying to argue the truth of his mother's beliefs. "'Tis odd then that the ones who killed her didnae attempt to destroy this well, too. When people cry such as we witches or worse, then try to kill us, they also try to destroy all they believe we gained our power from."

"She wasnae killed here," he said, pained by the memories yet intrigued by what she said. "She had been called to a village a half day's ride from here, on Sir Ranald MacLean's lands." He noted the way her beautiful eyes widened and she paled, but did not remark upon it. "By the time we heard of the trouble it was too late to save her."

"Sir Ranald had her killed?"

"I did wonder if he was part of it, but there was no

proof of that. 'Twas his men, however, who stirred the people into a fury, and his men who beat her. They will beat no more women," he added in a cold, flat voice.

"Why was she called to that particular village?"

"What can that matter?"

"It may matter a great deal to me. Sir Ranald kens what I am, yet paid a goodly sum to my father to take me as his wife. Aye, to take me to a place where one healing woman has already been murdered."

David frowned, suddenly wondering if there was more behind his mother's death than he had suspected. He had not been able to gain any proof that Sir Ranald had been involved in the murder in any way, and the man had allowed David to kill the men directly involved, had simply ignored the reckoning taken. Yet, despite the obvious temptation of Tatha's youth and beauty to a man like Sir Ranald, it did seem strange that he would seek a wife he knew his clansmen would hate and fear. Despite the man's age and unappealing nature, David was sure Sir Ranald could have looked elsewhere for a young wife if that was all he sought, one with a dowry.

"I will see what I can find out," he finally said. "It may not be easy. It has been five years and I had thought that the matter was settled. I buried my mother, a reckoning was taken, and no feud ensued. I believed that was the end of it all. Howbeit, ye have stirred my curiosity anew, and ye are right to think it could be of importance to ye."

Tatha studied Sir David even as she reconsidered all she knew about Sir Ranald. "Was your mother bonnie?"

"Aye," David replied cautiously. "I think so. She was a small woman, much akin to ye in size, only . . . weel, fuller of figure. Her coloring was akin to mine save that she had green eyes. She was also only nine and thirty when she died, yet looked verra much younger."

"I see." Tatha began to think Lady Ruthven's healing gift and belief in the old ways had had very little to do with her death. "Did ye seek me out for any particular reason?" she asked, deciding there was nothing to be gained in continuing to talk about Sir David's mother, not until she had a few more facts.

Her abrupt change of subject confused David for a moment; then he recalled what he had seen as he had approached the well. "I had heard that ye were here and, after remembering your interest in this well last evening, decided I would come to see what game ye were playing."

" 'Tis no game." She rubbed her hand along the stone, eager to return to the work of cleaning it. "I believe this is why I was drawn to this place."

"The well called ye, did it?"

She ignored his sarcasm. "Aye, it did."

David cursed and dragged his fingers through his hair. "Ye willnae practice this foolishness."

"Are ye intending to forbid it?"

He opened his mouth to do just that, but the words would not come. This young woman believed in all the things his mother and grandmother had believed in. Somehow it seemed disloyal to their memory to keep her from practicing her healing. He cursed.

"Nay." He glared at the knotted cord that was actually very well concealed in the branches of the tree and then at her. "Ye will nay flaunt it, though. I willnae have all that trouble stirred up again."

"I will be verra careful. I have always been," she assured him quietly, understanding the anger in his voice.

"If I or my beliefs bring trouble to your gates, I will leave."

When David realized he was about to vehemently argue that plan, he cursed again, and strode away. She had been at Cnocanduin only one night, yet she had him so beset by conflicting emotions he could not think straight. If the well had drawn Tatha Preston to his keep, it was certainly not working in his favor, he thought crossly.

Tatha sighed as she watched him leave. It saddened her that her beliefs should anger him and push him away. She decided it might be for the best not to study too closely why that should be. There was far too much else she had to worry about.

As she returned to the work of restoring the well to its former beauty, she found herself puzzling over the chilling coincidence that the same man who tried to buy her for his wife was connected to Sir David's mother's brutal murder. Suddenly she knew she was at Cnocanduin to do more than restore the well, that perhaps fate or even the restless spirit of Lady Ruthven had dragged her here. The more she considered the matter, the more she was certain she had been led to Cnocanduin for several purposes. Sir David needed to believe again, needed to yet again appreciate the heritage of the women in his family. The beauty and the power of the well needed to be renewed. And, most important, the truth behind Lady Ruthven's death had to be revealed. If she was right, it was a heavy burden fate had thrust upon her. Tatha prayed Sir Ranald and her father would leave her be until she could accomplish it all.

Chapter 4

"Where is she?"

Leith groaned and would have banged his head on the heavy oak table if his trencher of food was not in the way. "Ye have fretted o'er where the lass is nearly every morning of the mere week she has been here."

"I dinnae trust her," David muttered and savagely ate a chunk of bread.

That was not really the truth, and he accepted Leith's mildly disgusted look as well earned. He found that he did trust Tatha, trusted her in ways he had not trusted a woman for a very long time. Since he had known her only a week, he had to wonder why. What he was not sure of was whether she truly had the skill and the understanding to keep her beliefs hidden, to comprehend and guard against the danger such beliefs could plunge her into. David worried about her, a lot, and he did not want to.

"Weel, I think she is one of the best to yet arrive at our gates," Leith said.

"Oh, aye? She doesnae act much like a guest. She has fair usurped all running of the keep."

"She but tries to help. The lass is a skilled healer." Leith flushed and glanced warily at David. "I think she may be as good as, or better than, your mother ever was."

"High praise. What prompts it?"

"Ye ken that I have e'er suffered from rashes and the itch of them."

"Aye. Mother gave ye many a salve for them."

"And they truly helped ease my torment, but naught she did cured it."

"And this lass has cured ye?" David frowned and studied his cousin, his eyes widening suddenly when he noticed that Leith's neck was no longer covered with red blotches.

"Aye, and 'twas nay with any magic or strange potions. I dinnae have some skin ailment. 'Tis the wool."

"The wool? What does wool have to do with your skin?"

"Weel, my skin cannae abide the touch of it. Aye, I thought it all madness too," he said when David stared at him in disbelief. "How can ye nay wear wool? Weel, she told me to just try nay letting it touch my skin for just a wee while and gave me a willow-herb ointment to soothe my rashes. It couldnae hurt, I thought. So I still wore my plaid but I put a linen shirt on, and . . ." He blushed, looked around to make sure no one was watching them, and lifted the skirt of his plaid to reveal that he also wore linen leggings. "It took only a day or two for me to see the change. Beneath all of this wrapping there isnae one red spot. For the first time in my life I am nay itching myself. I have asked the lasses if they can weave me a plaid that isnae of wool, for e'en touching it causes me a few troubles still. Aye, and 'twill cost me dear to have warm clothes made that arenae of wool, but e'en after only a few days of ease, I feel the cost will be worth it. If only for the ease in my nether regions."

"Weel. Who would have thought it."

"Seems the lass kens a lot about what can trouble your skin. Ye wouldnae believe how many questions she asked of me, and some put us both to the blush. I have noticed that she doesnae wear wool, either. And many of your people have already sought her out for help. Donald's wife Sorcha was one of the first, for she is with child again."

"I pray to God that she can carry this one to term." David scowled. "Tatha hasnae promised that, has she?"

"Nay. The lass says such things are in God's hands. But she also said that women must ken a few things to help God's work be accomplished. She told Sorcha to nay lift anything heavy, to rest with her feet raised several times a day, to avoid strong smells that can oftimes trouble one's belly, for the retching can be harmful. Then she gave her a verra long list of foods she cannae eat."

"Such as what?"

"Weel, all Donald and Sorcha could recall was thyme, parsley, and juniper berries, but there were many others. Sorcha says she will simply eat verra plain food, nay a spice or an herb. And the lass gave her a sage brew to drink, sparingly. If the bairn still rests in her belly come harvest time, Donald may be asking ye to let his wife stay out of the fields."

"I shall tell him today that he need not fret on it. If 'twill give them a bairn, Sorcha can crawl abed now and stay there until the birth. It appears the lass has cured you and, if her advice gives Donald and Sorcha a live bairn, we may ne'er see the lass leave." He sighed. "And I will confess that e'en in the short week she has been here, the keep is cleaner, e'en to the smell of it."

"We didnae have a great problem with vermin such as fleas, but what few were here are now gone." Leith grinned. "Donald complains that the stables smell like a fine lady's bath, but I notice he doesnae remove any of the herbs she has hung up in the place." His smile widened and held a hint of lechery. "She may have e'en helped old Robert with his back trouble. Ye ken it has been a month or longer since he hurt it and it hadnae eased at all. He spoke to the lass and she told him all of the usual things, nay any heavy lifting, rest, and gave him a salve to ease the ache. Then she discovered that he has himself a bonnie new wife and tried to tell him to leave her be until his back is better."

"And Robert wasnae going to heed that advice, was he?" David laughed softly.

"Nay, said so clear and loud. Then he said that, though the lass was blushing as red as her hair, she called him a randy old goat and since he wasnae going to be wise, then he could at least change his ways."

"Change his ways?"

"Aye." Leith's voice was choked with laughter. "She told him to let his wife ride." He collapsed into loud, helpless laughter at the look of utter shock on David's face.

David shook his head, then finally laughed. He was also relieved by what Leith had told him. Tatha was not dealing in charms and potions. In truth, her healing skills seemed to depend a great deal upon common sense and getting people to act with a bit more wisdom. That she spoke freely and often of God's will was also good. Although it caused him a pang, and he muttered a prayer for forgiveness for any unintentional hint of disrespect for his mother, David began to think Tatha revealed a bit more common sense than his mother ever had. At times his mother had shown little tolerance or understanding of people's fears. It was an arrogance she had learned from her mother, one she had not learned to temper completely, and one that had often made the women seem to spit in the eye of God and church. Tatha seemed blissfully free of that vanity.

"Ye still havenae said if ye ken where she is," David said when his cousin finally grew quiet.

"She could be working in your mother's herb room or she could be out looking for more herbs and plants. She said there was little time left to gather a goodly amount ere the fall comes."

Even as he stood up and started out of the hall, David wondered what he was doing. Ever since Tatha Preston had arrived at his gates he had been overly concerned about where she was and what she was doing. It was true that he worried about her, his mother's brutal death and the reasons for it ever clear in his mind. Ruefully, he admitted that he just liked to look at her, to talk to her.

It did not take him long to discover Tatha had ridden to the village, begged by a woman to come and look at her sick child. David had his horse saddled and set out after her. After all Leith had told him, David was intensely interested in seeing Tatha at work. He hoped it would ease some of his concern for her safety.

Softly praying that she had the skill needed to save the child, Tatha followed the plump woman into the tiny cottage attached to the blacksmith's shop. The one thing she had never been able to accept with ease, to wholeheartedly embrace as God's will, was the death of a child. One look at the feverish, thrashing boy on the tiny bed made her heart sink. He could be no more than five, and he looked dangerously ill.

All the while she looked over every inch of the little boy, Tatha questioned the mother. Finally, Tatha found what she felt was the cause of the child's dire condition. On one thin calf was a small wound. It was closed, had ceased to bleed, but the area around it was hot, red, and swollen.

"Where did he get this?" she asked the mother as she dampened a scrap of cloth in some heated water and gently washed the child's leg.

"That wee scratch?" The look in the woman's dark eyes clearly told Tatha that she could not see why such a meager injury would hold any interest. "He cut himself whilst playing with his father's tools. 'Tisnae bleeding. It closed up verra quickly."

"Aye, too quickly. It shut all the filth and bad humors inside. Ye are going to have to hold the wee lad steady so that I may reopen this wound." Tatha took her knife from its sheath at her side and washed off the blade.

"Open it? Why?"

"I will do it," said a deep voice that was already achingly familiar to Tatha. David curtly nodded to the flustered blacksmith's wife and stepped over to the child's bed. "What do I do?"

"Hold him as firmly as ye can so that I can make a neat, small cut." Tatha looked at the boy's mother. "I will need clean rags and verra hot water. Do ye have them at the ready?"

"Aye." The woman hurried away to get what Tatha needed.

After taking a deep breath to steady herself, and checking that David had the child held firmly, she quickly made a cross cut over the boy's wound, neatly reopening it. The child screamed, then lay still. Tatha wrinkled her nose in distaste at the odor of the muck that immediately began to seep out. She was only faintly aware of how David cursed and the child's mother gasped in horror. Quickly taking the bowl of steaming water and bundle of rags from the shocked woman before she dropped them, Tatha began the slow process of trying to drain all of the poison from the wound. Once she deemed the wound clean, she washed it once more with water from the well, put a poultice of woad leaves on it, and wrapped it in a strip of clean cloth.

As she straightened up, Tatha grimaced at the ache in her back and realized that she had been bent over the child for a long time. She forced some blackthorn bark tea down the child's throat to help reduce his fever, although he was already looking less flushed and troubled. If her instructions were followed she felt the child would survive.

"A wee scratch and it could have killed him," muttered the boy's mother as she sat down on the edge of the child's bed.

" 'Twas the dirt," said Tatha. "I dinnae ken the why of it, but clean wounds heal better than dirty ones. I have seen the truth of it too often to question it." She carefully set out some medicines on a stool next to the bed. "I will leave ye the leaves to make another poultice or two and some of the blackthorn bark to make a few more cups of tea to ease his fever. God willing ye will

need no more than that. If ye dinnae see him growing
better in a day or two, fetch me. I think I got all of the
poison from his wound, but I cannae be sure. Aye, and
keep him, his bedding, and his bandage verra clean."

"Ye didnae stitch it?"

"Nay, 'twas but a wee wound, e'en after I reopened it.
And, because it had become poisoned, I think 'tis best
left open. 'Twill leave but a wee scar. I could return
and—"

"Nay," the woman said, impulsively hugging Tatha.
"'Twill nay trouble the laddie to have a wee scar."

Sir David escorted her out of the tiny cottage, and
Tatha frowned up at him when he paused by his horse
and stared at her. "Ye dinnae intend to tell me to cease
helping people, do ye?"

"Nay." He mounted and held out his hand. "I will
take ye back to the keep."

Tatha warily eyed the huge black gelding and slowly
shook her head. "Nay, I dinnae think so."

David watched her cautiously back away from his
horse then start walking back toward the keep. He considered the look he had seen in her eyes when he had
offered to pull her up onto his saddle. Tatha did not
ride her pony simply because it was a gift. It was probably the only horse she was not afraid of. He quickly dismounted, grasped his horse's reins, and hurried to
catch up to her.

"So, ye are afraid of horses," he drawled, watching
her closely, and grinning when she scowled at him.

"I am nay afraid of them," she said, trying to sound
confident, even haughty. "Stoutheart is a horse, isnae
he?"

"He is a wee, runty pony."

"He gets me where I need to go." She frowned at

him. "Just why did ye search me out? Is someone ill or hurt?"

"Nay. I but wished to see how ye used your skills."

"I told ye I would be careful," she reassured him. "My aunt Mairi was most clear about the danger of raising people's fears or attracting the critical eye of some churchmon. And I am no heretic or witch."

"I ken it. I begin to think your aunt was a verra wise woman, that she taught ye the good sense and caution my grandmother ne'er really taught my mother."

"And ye still think your mother was killed because she was too brazen about her beliefs? Hold," she ordered him in a quiet but firm voice as she moved toward some lichen growing at the base of a tree. "This makes a good poultice."

David leaned against the tree and watched as she carefully gathered the plant, wrapped it in linen, and placed it in her sack. "I will confess that your questions and observations have made me begin to wonder. I have many people trying to recall all they can of that time. And if 'tis shown that Sir Ranald had a hand in my mother's murder, would your father end the betrothal?"

Tatha sank down to sit on the soft grass and sighed. "I dinnae ken. Nay long ago I would have stoutly cried aye, but that was before he sold me to that drooling old fool, before I realized that he saw me as no more than a means to fill his pockets."

When she lifted a large, stoppered jug from her bag, he frowned slightly. "What is that?"

" 'Tis what I carry water from the well in. 'Twas that water I used to wash the lad's wound the first and last time, and I use only this water in my medicines and teas. I felt 'twas the wisest use of its healing powers."

Her eyes widened when he dropped down beside her and grasped her by the shoulders.

" 'Tis just water. Clear, fresh, and sweet of taste, aye, but 'tis just water," he snapped.

Her expression slowly grew mutinous. Instead of her obstinacy adding to his anger, however, David found his increasingly errant lust creeping to the fore. The frown on her sweet face made him want to kiss the hard line of her lips into softness again. The way her small, firm breasts rose and fell as anger flooded through her had his blood running warm. He cursed softly and pulled her into his arms.

"Sir David," she began to protest, but felt her breath stolen away by the feel of his hard body pressed so close to hers.

"Hush. Ye can scold me later." He brushed his lips over hers. "I have been thinking of this all week."

That one squeaked call of his name was all the protest Tatha intended to make. It was flattering beyond words that he had been considering kissing her all week. She had been thinking the same with an increasing and embarrassing regularity. What lass would not want such a beautiful man to kiss her at least once? Her curiosity demanded satisfaction. How much could one brief stolen kiss hurt?

When she parted her lips in response to the prodding of his tongue and he began to stroke the inside of her mouth, Tatha became acutely aware of the danger of even one kiss. Everything inside of her was responding with a dizzying strength. Her heart pounded, her skin felt warm, the tips of her breasts hardened, and there was an exciting, heated sense of fullness between her thighs. Aunt Mairi had been a blunt, earthy woman who had believed that Tatha should know all about the ways of the flesh, so Tatha knew exactly what was happening to her. This was lust in all its heady, fierce glory. What frightened her was that instinct told her it was also a great deal more. The moment David paused, she scrambled away from him before he could tempt her with another kiss.

"We had best return to the keep," she said as she grabbed her bag, her voice so husky and unsteady she barely recognized it as her own.

David opened his mouth to protest but Tatha was already striding away. He quickly gathered his horse's reins and followed. He had felt the passion in her, seen it in her beautiful eyes. If she thought one brief kiss was the end of it, she was wrong. Tatha Preston definitely tasted like more.

Chapter 5

"Where is Sir David?" Tatha asked, intercepting Leith as he strode toward the stables and wondering why he looked as if he was fighting the urge to laugh.

"Out on a hunt," replied Leith, grinning widely. "I am about to ride out to join him. Do ye have a message for him?"

"Nay. Naught but a question or two about something we discussed earlier. It can wait."

Tatha cursed as she watched Leith disappear into the stables. She had wanted to ask Sir David if he had found out anything more concerning the day his mother had been murdered. Deep in her heart, however, she knew that was not the only reason she sought out the laird of Cnocanduin. It had been only two days since he had kissed her, but she had done little else but think about it. As she tossed and turned on her bed at night she struggled between a fear of what could happen if she returned to his arms and an eagerness to do just that. The knowledge her aunt Mairi had given her about men and women filled her thoughts with detailed images that made her sweat with longing.

She fetched some water from the well and hurried to the herb room she had restored to its former usefulness. Tatha already loved the place. At Prestonmoor she had never had such a wonderful place to work in. As she began to prepare some of her salves, she prayed she could lose herself in her work. She was sure she would see Sir David at the evening meal, and she did not want to meet him while her blood was still heated from some sensual daydream.

David cursed as his arrow missed its mark again. Robert stepped forward to neatly bring down the deer. David had hoped that a day of hunting would take his mind off a certain flame-haired woman, but she refused to be shaken from his thoughts. Tatha had sought shelter at his keep. He had offered her safety. It would not be honorable to seduce her, but the constant ache in his body was swiftly pushing aside honor. He wanted her more than he had ever wanted a woman before, and with her so constantly close at hand, temptation was becoming very hard to resist.

He had also tried to distract himself with the puzzle of his mother's death, but even that was not fully successful. As little pieces of memory came together, his own and those offered by others, he did begin to think that Tatha was right to wonder. He had readily accepted the tale that fear and superstition had brought about her death, and now thought that was because he had always anticipated such an end for his mother. It began to look as if that expectation had blinded him to the truth, had in fact been used against him to keep him from looking any closer. The men he had killed in retribution had deserved their deaths, but he began to think at least one other had his mother's blood on his hands.

"Nay need to look so fierce, laddie," said Robert as he rode up beside David. "There will be meat aplenty."

" 'Tis nay my failing aim I frown o'er," said David. "Of late I have been puzzling o'er my mother's murder."

Robert scratched his gray and brown beard and nodded." 'Twas an odd thing, but ye took a fine reckoning."

"Aye, but I now wonder if I truly found all who were guilty."

"Sir Ranald did seem verra willing to let ye hunt down and kill three of his clansmen." Robert eyed David warily as he added, "Especially when they claimed they had done naught but kill a witch."

"I ken it. E'en the Church would have praised them. Yet ye are right, Sir Ranald was verra amiable when I demanded my reckoning. Too amiable. One of the men was his own cousin."

"Wee Tatha may ken more about Sir Ranald than we do. I have heard a few rumors and I ken he has buried three wives, but I think the mon visited her father's keep from time to time. I think they may be allies or friends. She may have more fact than rumor. Ken the mon better and ye can more clearly judge what may have really happened that day."

" 'Twill certainly help me seek out the truth. Ah, here comes Leith." He smiled faintly at his cousin, who took the departing Robert's place at his side. "Mayhap ye will bring me luck. My aim has consistently fallen short this day."

"Mayhap your mind is on other things." Leith tried

and failed to bite back a smile. "She was asking after you."

For one brief moment David considered telling his cousin he was not interested and not to be such a smugly grinning fool, then decided not to bother. He was interested and suspected too many of his clansmen knew it. "Did she now?"

"Aye. Caught me as I was headed to the stable. She asked where ye were and, after ye asking me where she was nearly every morning since she arrived, I fear I nearly took to laughing. She probably thinks I am daft."

"Ye are. What did she say she wanted?"

"She said she just wished to ask ye a question or two about something ye had discussed earlier."

"Ah, my mother's murder."

"I suppose. She was blushing like fire though." He returned David's sudden grin. "Now, I willnae claim to ken much about the lasses, but it seems to me she wouldnae be so unsettled if that was truly the only reason she was looking for you."

"Nay, it seems that way to me too." David was unable to hide his satisfaction.

"Just what do ye plan to do with the lass?"

"Does it matter to ye?"

"Aye, there is the odd thing, but it does."

"I have a suspicion it matters to others too." David shook his head. "Aside from wishing to see her sprawled naked on my bed, I am nay sure. Dinnae frown. She is a weelborn lass under my protection. I ken what honor demands of me. I ken I'd best be prepared to offer her more than a tumble in the heather if I let my passions rule."

"And ye dinnae ken if ye want to do that?"

David muttered a curse and dragged his fingers through his hair, deciding that, if he had to reveal his confusion to anyone, Leith was the safest choice. "She believes as my mother did, although she shows more common sense about it all, and doesnae wave the pennant of the old ways in everyone's face and demand acceptance. She is also betrothed. Although her father sold her like cattle to that swine Sir Ranald, and Tatha makes it clear she doesnae want the marriage, it doesnae change the fact that she has already been promised to a mon. Those two things alone create quite a hedgerow to leap."

"I think ye worry too much o'er her beliefs. She seems to mix the Church's teachings with those of her aunt verra weel, yet only lets most people hear her speak of God's will. And aye, she has been weel taught to respect fear and superstition. As for the betrothal, weel, once ye prove Sir Ranald killed your mother, that will be at an end."

Staring at his cousin in surprise, David asked, "Do ye believe Sir Ranald was behind my mother's murder?"

"Aye, always have."

"Why?"

Leith blushed slightly, and there was a wary look in his dark gray eyes. "'Tis nay something a mon should tell another mon about his mother. She didnae do anything to encourage the fool, ne'er think that, but Sir Ranald wanted her. Aye, wanted her and had for years. My mother told me about it, for I was oftimes the one sent to ride guard on your mother, and she wanted me to keep a watch out for the mon. Several times he appeared where your mother was called to go and 'twas clear that he had tried to arrange it. I didnae go with her on the day she was beaten, but I ken it was another ploy by Sir Ranald."

"Ye ne'er told me of this."

"Your mother didnae want it told. It embarrassed her. I was made to swear myself to silence. Weel, she has been dead now for five long years and ye are finally questioning if ye have the whole truth, and"—he shrugged—"I think we are strong enough to fight the bastard now. We werenae then."

For a moment David struggled with his anger over such secrets being held from him. Then he let reason rule. Leith, and probably everyone else who had known, had been sworn to secrecy by his mother. He had to respect the fact that such an oath was kept. And at the time, the cold truth was that a battle against Sir Ranald would have resulted only in the complete decimation of his people. They had been weak, the keep nearly in ruins due to battles with the English and raiders, and time had been needed to recover from several years of battle, hardship, and poor harvests. He had also been firm in his opinion that his mother's beliefs had led to her death.

"I am nay sure I would have heeded the truth anyway," he admitted quietly.

"Nay, ye had your own at the time and werenae to be swayed."

"And for that blindness my mother's killer has escaped justice for five years."

"Weel, aye, but ye did quickly seek a reckoning from the ones who actually did the deed. Sir Ranald's guilty of bringing it all about, I am fair sure of that, but he didnae actually bloody his hands."

"He didnae actually strike my mother, but he is

guilty, as guilty as the ones who did, and I will now work to prove that."

A cry went up from the men who rode ahead of them. At first David thought it signaled the sighting of some game. The next cry, however, had him tense and drawing his sword. Even as he realized they were under attack, an arrow slammed into his shoulder, propelling him back off his horse. Leith was swiftly at his side, sword in hand and using both their mounts to help shelter him. Just as David gathered enough strength to reclaim his sword and stand up, he knew the brief, fierce attack had already come to an end. A groan of pain escaped him as he sat down on the hard ground.

Leith sheathed his sword and, breaking off the tip of the arrow that protruded out of David's back, yanked the shaft out of his body. Grimly, David clung to consciousness as Leith bathed and bound his wound. It was not only strange that they had been attacked, but that the battle would be so swiftly ended. He needed answers.

" 'Tisnae mortal," Robert said as he walked over and studied David, the rest of the Ruthven men gathered behind him. "The wee lass will soon mend it."

"Who was it?" demanded David, wondering which of the many treaties he had negotiated with the other clans had just been broken.

"Weel now, there is an odd thing. They obviously took pains to hide their clan identity. We killed two, but the wounded were taken away, so there is no one to question. Howbeit"—he held out an easily recognizable clan badge—"one of the dead clearly loved this sad bauble too much to leave it behind."

"MacLeans."

"Aye. Sir Ranald's men. Methinks your sudden inter-est in your mother's death isnae much appreciated."

"Was anyone hurt?"

"Only ye, and the moment ye flew out of your saddle, the MacLeans retreated. That speaks clear, doesnae it?"

David nodded as Leith helped him stand. "I was the target. Weel, we had best return to Cnocanduin. I need to get this wound seen to. The sooner I am healed, the sooner we can take a reckoning that I now believe has been long overdue."

Ignoring David's complaints, Leith mounted behind him and let someone else lead his horse home. It was not long before David was grateful for the support, the loss of blood weakening him. He smiled crookedly as they rode through the gates of his keep. Now he would see for himself if Tatha's growing reputation as a skilled healer was fully deserved.

Tatha stared down into the water of the well. With the sun high overhead it was one of the few times she could clearly see the water, even see her reflection in its cool depths. Aunt Mairi had once told her that gazing steadily into water could bring on visions, could show one the path one must take. She desperately needed some sign at the moment. The path she wished to run down led straight into Sir David Ruthven's strong arms, but Tatha was not sure that was the right one.

She grasped the edge of the well. After staring into the water for nearly half an hour and forcing her mind clear of all thought, she was beginning to feel a little un-steady. She was determined to give this water-gazing trick her best try, however, for she desperately needed answers. Was it the well that had drawn her to Cnocanduin or the need to find the truth behind the brutal murder of a healer? Or had fate done its best to lead her to her true mate?

It was just as she began to think it was all foolishness, and the sun had moved enough to begin placing the water back into the shadows, that Tatha noticed something. She could still see her reflection, but it began to slowly change. Soon the newly forming image grew clearer, and Tatha gasped softly when she saw Sir David's handsome face. She continued to stare, deaf and blind to all around her, as if by the sheer force of her will she could make the well show her more.

Another gasp escaped her when, a few moments later, she saw Leith's narrow face off to the side of David's. It was as if he was peering over David's shoulder. Leith's mouth moved and she leaned closer. Suddenly, a hand tightly grasped her by the shoulder and yanked her back, away from the edge of the well. Tatha stared at a scowling Leith, who stood by her side, and felt a little foolish. The only thing that kept her from thinking it was all a dream was that there was no sign of David.

"It looked as if ye were about to fall in," Leith said quickly taking his hand from her shoulder.

"Nay, I thought I saw something and was just trying to get a closer look." She suddenly noticed how grim the usually amiable Leith's expression was. "Is something wrong?"

"David has been wounded," he replied, watching with intent interest how her eyes widened in alarm and she grew very pale.

"How?" she demanded as she quickly filled a bucket with water from the well.

"An attack whilst we were hunting." He hurried to keep pace with her as she strode off toward the keep.

Tatha belabored him with questions all the way to the keep. She dragged him into her herb room and ladened him with all the salves, brews, and bandages she thought she would need to treat David. When she burst into David's bedchamber everyone moved out of her way as she hurried to the side of their laird's huge bed. Tatha gave him one slightly frantic but thorough looking-over, then set to work. Her mind told her that he would be all right, that the wound need not be a severely troubling one if it was taken good care of, but her heart remained twisted with fear and concern. By the time she had him stripped, bathed, stitched, and bandaged, everyone had wandered away, feeling sure that their laird was in good hands.

After forcing a weak David to drink an herbal potion, Tatha sat in a chair Leith had set by the bed, and asked bluntly, "Who tried to kill you?"

"MacLean," he replied, smiling grimly when she paled. "Do ye think your betrothed kens that ye are hiding here?"

"Nay. And if he learned I was here, he would either come and collect me, as is his right, or tell my father to do so."

"Aye, so I thought." Feeling too weak and sleepy to discuss the matter, he closed his eyes, using the last of his strength to issue a stern command. "Ye arenae to leave the keep, nay to step one wee foot outside these walls."

Even as she opened her mouth to argue, she realized it was useless. He had gone to sleep. She felt a little bit like some carrion bird as she sat there watching him sleep, waiting, hunting constantly for some sign of fever. The arrow could have been tainted, or just filthy. Tatha had cleaned the wound as best she could, but it had been over an hour between when the wound had been inflicted and when she had been able to tend to it. Fever was a possibility, and she wanted to be right there to fight it from the start.

Several hours later, Tatha felt herself falling asleep, her eyes stinging from staring at David for so long. She rose from her chair, stretched, and went to the washbowl to scrub her face. As she held a cloth against her eyes, trying to soothe them, she wondered if she should get someone else to sit with David for a while, then shook her head. Time would be lost while they decided whether he even had a fever and then as they came to get her. A fever was best fought from the very beginning, before it could get too high.

As she prepared to sit down again, she suddenly tensed and leaned over David. A soft curse hissed past her lips as she touched his face and felt the warmth on his skin. Her whispered prayers were to go unanswered. The fever was on him, and now the battle would truly begin.

Chapter 6

David winced as he opened his eyes. He felt weak; his thoughts were unclear. Partial memories of cool water against his burning flesh, of a sharp, scolding voice telling him to drink, and of the same husky voice, soft and coaxing, urging him to fight, crowded his mind. Slowly, he became aware of the fact that he was not alone in the bed. He wondered why, when he had been so ill, he would have taken some willing lass into his bed. Then he recalled that he never bedded the lasses at the keep, and at the moment, there was only one he was truly interested in.

Cautiously, he turned his head, fully aware now of the wound in his left shoulder and not wishing to move that arm much at all. His eyes widened when he saw Tatha curled up at his side. Only for a moment was he concerned that he had attacked her while delirious with fever. She was still dressed and lay on top of the covers. There were dark smudges under her eyes and her hair was a bright, tangled mass around her face, but he found her beautiful. He also knew exactly who had taken care of him during his illness. As more memories rushed into his mind, he faintly recalled that his fever had broken during the night. Leith had been there helping Tatha wash him down and change the bed linen.

Slowly, so as not to cause himself pain or wake Tatha, he wriggled himself up into a partially seated position. His mouth felt as if someone had stuffed a dirty woolen rag into it and left it there for a few days. Using some of the wine set at his bedside, he rinsed out his mouth, gently rubbed his teeth clean with a scrap of the linen rags piled neatly on the heavy table, and then had a drink to ease the dryness in his throat. Although he still felt a bath and a good hair washing would be most welcome, and were decidedly needed, he felt more presentable.

As he made himself comfortable by Tatha's side, she murmured and huddled closer. When she placed her small, long-fingered hand on his bare chest, he drew in a sharp breath. His body's response to that light touch was startling. Despite the weakness left by his illness, he grew hard and warm with desire. The kiss they had shared had told him that he desired her; he just had not allowed himself to consider how much. Now there was no ignoring the fact that she was a fever in his blood.

He gave in to the need to touch her and brushed his lips over her forehead. Tatha murmured and shifted closer to him. The feel of her soft breasts pressed against his side had his heart pounding so hard and fast he was surprised it did not wake her up. He touched a light kiss to each of her eyes and felt her lids flutter beneath his lips. Watching her eyes open as he brushed his lips over her cheeks, his breath caught in his throat at the soft warmth visible in their rich blue depths.

"What are ye doing?" she whispered, trapped by the heat in his dark gaze.

"Kissing ye." He touched his lips to hers.

"Your fever has truly passed, I see."

"Has it? I am nay sure, for I am feeling verra heated." Her husky giggle made him tremble. He thanked God that the woman seemed blissfully unaware of the power she held over him.

"This isnae good for your wound."

"It feels verra good to me."

"I think ye are a rogue."

"Nay, lass. Although there is something about ye that makes me feel like one."

Before Tatha could say anything he kissed her. She hesitated only a moment before slipping her arm around his waist and pressing closer to his hard body, eagerly parting her lips to welcome the invasion of his tongue. The way his hand pressed against her lower back, moving in small circles, warmed her, urging her even closer, until she was almost sprawled on top of him. She trembled and heard herself groan softly in delight when he slid his hand over her bottom, moving her groin gently against his leg. Tatha found herself aching to rip away the covers between them, almost frantic to get as close to him as possible.

"Ye shouldnae," she mumbled in a weak protest as he began to kiss her throat. "Your wound."

"I am barely moving that arm." He slowly ran his tongue over the pulse point in her throat. "Ah, lass, ye taste so sweet. I fair ache to lick every soft, pale inch of ye."

When she gasped softly in shock, he quickly kissed

her again. His whole body trembled with the force of his need for her. The signs that she returned his passion, her rapid pulse, the soft noises she made, the faint tremor in her lithe body, all enhanced his own desire. He cursed his wound, his lingering weakness, and all else that kept him from fully possessing her now while she was warm, willing, and in his arms.

"Weel, 'tis glad I am to see that ye have recovered, cousin," drawled Leith.

That highly amused voice acted on Tatha like a dousing of icy cold water. She squeaked in dismay and pulled away from David so fast she tumbled off the bed. Tatha sprawled there on the sheepskin rug, almost afraid to move. She did not think she could add to the embarrassment she felt now, but she was not sure she wanted to risk it. Through her lashes she saw David leaning over the side of the bed to look at her and heard Leith walk to her side. She silently cursed, almost able to feel their amusement.

"Are ye all right, lass?" asked David, his voice strained as he struggled against the urge to laugh.

"Aye," she replied. "I shall just keep my eyes shut for a wee while so that the two of ye are allowed the privacy to laugh."

"Oh, lass, ye need not do that."

"Nay?" She slowly opened her eyes to look at a widely grinning David.

"Nay, we dinnae mind having a good laugh right in front of ye."

When he and Leith burst into hearty laughter, Tatha cursed and scrambled to her feet. Complaining loudly about men who had no respect for a lass's sensitive feelings, she grabbed her shoes and marched out of the room. Even when she slammed the door behind her they did not stop laughing. Tatha cursed again and strode off to her bedchamber.

By the time she had washed, changed her clothes, and flopped down on her bed to rest for a while, her embarrassment and sense of ill usage had passed. Tatha then began to wonder what to do about Sir David and the fierce, blinding desire he stirred inside of her. He was pure temptation from his thick black hair to his long, muscular legs, and she was tired of fighting that.

And why should she fight it? she suddenly asked herself. She was nineteen, a spinster by many people's reckoning. She was free of all bonds and vows. Her own father had sold her into a betrothal to a man she loathed, a man who might well have ordered the murder of David's mother. She dared not hope that some miracle would free her of the obligation her father had thrust upon her. There was still the chance that she would be found and forced to honor the agreement he had made with Sir Ranald. Tatha knew she would never allow David to put himself at risk by placing himself between her and her father.

"And why should I cling to my maidenhead for that disgusting old mon?" she asked herself. "Why should I hold to something my father bartered away without a thought?"

The answer to both those questions came swiftly. She should do as she pleased. There would be consequences if she found herself back in her father's hold, a maiden no longer yet still bound to Sir Ranald, but she could not make herself be concerned about those. Marriage to Sir Ranald would be such hell, a little sinning now seemed perfectly acceptable.

And she loved, she thought with a sigh. There was no ignoring it, no denying it. Her heart and mind would no longer allow her the comfort of a lie. She loved Sir David. Tatha suspected she had probably started her ill-advised fall into love from the moment she had set eyes on him. The kiss they had shared had sealed her fate.

As she huddled beneath her blanket and tried to relax enough to sleep, she decided that seeing Sir David's face in the well had indeed been a sign. There were several reasons she had been drawn to Cnocanduin, but the well wanted her to see that one of those reasons was most assuredly to meet Sir David. There was also the fact that he could turn her brain to watery porridge with just one warm look from his sinfully dark eyes. As the urge to sleep crept over her, she decided that the next time Sir David took her into his arms she would do her best to stay there. The chance that she might have to leave still loomed like a black cloud overhead, and she was now determined to savor all the joy she could before that time came. And, she mused, a faint smile touching her lips, there was always the chance that Sir David's passion could grow into something deeper. Occasionally miracles did happen.

"She has been sold to Sir Ranald," Leith said quietly as he helped David sit up and put a tray of bread and cheese on his lap.

"I ken it." David slowly began to eat the plain fare. "To even think of that mon touching her is an abomination."

"Aye, but ye needed to be reminded. 'Twas a bargain made by her father, and the mon may yet find her and demand she hold to it."

"By then I hope to have proven the bastard a murderer."

"It has been five years. That may not be possible."

David frowned at his cousin. "Are ye purposely trying to depress my spirit?"

Leith smiled as he sat on the edge of the bed. "Aye and nay. I but try to make ye see all of the truth, nay just what ye wish to see. Aye, no lass that young and sweet should be given o'er to a mon like Sir Ranald. Howbeit, she is her father's chattel, and unless ye can prove Sir Ranald had a hand in your mother's death, there is naught save war to stop her father from taking her back and handing her o'er to that mon. Aye, and fighting him o'er that right could cause ye more trouble than ye may realize. We dinnae ken how powerful her father is. If he has the king's ear, ye risk outlawry. "

A soft curse escaped David and he chewed his bread rather savagely. "I cannae let Sir Ranald have her. Aye, proving he had a hand in my mother's murder may be impossible after five long years, but I now believe him guilty. That also makes me wonder why he wants another healer, and I do believe Tatha's healing skills are one reason the mon seeks her. Mayhap the only reason."

"Have ye learned much about the mon from Tatha?"

"Nay too much aside from the fact that she loathes him. I was seeking time to speak about him when I got wounded. I dinnae believe her aversion to the mon rests solely in his age and ill looks or e'en in simple reluctance to obey her father."

"Nay, I think there had to be more than that to make her ride away from her home, alone, and with no place to go. She is a high-spirited lass but she isnae a stupid one."

David considered that as he finished the meal of bread and cheese and drank the wine Leith poured for him. His cousin was right. There was a streak of stubbornness and defiance in Tatha, but that alone would not have driven her to leave her home and family, to travel alone over some very dangerous countryside. She would have stayed and argued the matter if it was simply a matter of not wanting an aging, unattractive husband. Even in the short time he had known her, David had seen how well Tatha could judge people, how easily she could see into their hearts. He strongly suspected she saw something in Sir Ranald that was terrifying enough to make her choose traveling alone, seeking a life elsewhere.

Then he worried that he might just be making excuses, trying to find some reason to hold her. She had said she would leave if her presence brought trouble to his gates, and he believed her. There was a chance his desire for her made him try to find reasons to convince her to stay no matter what happened, perhaps even to excuse his taking up arms to keep her.

After another moment's thought, he inwardly shook his head. Even if he could not get her in his bed, there was reason enough to defy her father's plans for her. In his heart he was sure Sir Ranald was a murderer. David knew he could never hand any lass over to the man.

"Ye are looking verra troubled, cousin," Leith said as he removed the tray and helped David lie down again.

"I but argued with myself. I wondered if lust clouded my reasoning."

"Weel, 'tis clear ye lust after the lass, but e'en if ye didnae, she doesnae deserve the hell of being wed to that bastard."

"True. I wish I had more proof. Then I would send word to her kinsmen. Her father may be a hard mon who thinks naught of selling his daughters like cattle, but I cannae believe he would sell them into a sure grave."

"One would hope not. Then again, I am nay sure how I would feel if I carried the weight of thirteen daughters."

David chuckled. "Aye, 'tis a mighty burden. I dinnae envy the mon. Howbeit, she seemed honestly hurt and e'en confused that he would do this to her, so one must assume that it all came as a surprise, that she ne'er saw him as cruel or completely unfeeling."

"True. And if ye do save her from Sir Ranald's clutches, what do ye mean to do with her?"

"Ah, weel, there is a puzzle. I am in a fever for the lass, a heat I have ne'er suffered from before."

"Then wed her."

"At the moment her father has betrothed her to another mon. The bride price may already have been paid. I could pull us all into the middle of a clan war. Or, as ye said, I could risk outlawry."

Leith cursed and ran a hand through his thick hair. "Since the mon was willing to sell her to one mon, mayhap he would accept a higher bid."

" 'Tis a thought, but we dinnae ken what was paid for her. Sir Ranald is far richer than we are. E'en if we offered more than he has, he could simply top my bid. There is also the matter of a bargain made. 'Tis nay too honorable to break a bargain."

"I dinnae think it too honorable to sell your daughters off to the highest bidder."

"Most people would see nay real wrong in it. Nay, especially when 'tis discovered just how many daughters the poor mon has. Most would probably think he was mighty clever."

Leith stood up and idly fixed the blankets over

David. "Then the only answer is to prove Sir Ranald is a killer or pray that he has given up on her because none can find her."

"Tatha is a skilled healer. Word has probably already begun to spread. It doesnae have to go verra far to reach Sir Ranald's ears." He curled his good hand into a fist and lightly pounded the mattress. " 'Tis a poor time for me to be trapped abed."

"Dinnae waste your strength fretting o'er that. I will work to find proof, at least enough to convince her kinsmen that they made a poor choice."

"Thank ye."

"I do it for her too."

"I ken it."

"And I still think ye would be wise to marry the lass."

David smiled sleepily. "Aye, ye may be right. I wasnae looking for a wife, but mayhap 'tis past time I took one. The fever she can put me in certainly makes her a good choice."

"And ye are no longer troubled by what she is?"

"Ye mean her beliefs? Her healing skills? Nay, not truly. She isnae as caught up in the old ways as my mother. As she says, she is no heathen. Aye, mayhap that is what I must do. Wed her." He closed his eyes. "It begins to look as if I will bed her if she gives me the chance, and honor will demand it anyway."

"If ye mention marriage to her, I think I would try to be a wee bit more romantic," Leith drawled as he started to leave.

David laughed softly, then sighed as he heard the door close behind Leith. The only thing he was sure of concerning Tatha Preston was that he wanted her in his bed, needed her there. If there was a romantic way to explain that, he was too weary to think of one.

He had known she was trouble the moment she had appeared at his gates. A part of him wished he had turned her away, but even if he had not been bound by his vow to his mother, he suspected he would never have done so. From the moment she had frowned at him he had been captivated. He had just tried very hard to fight it. Now he had to admit that he had lost the battle.

Sleep pulled at him and he let it. It was the surest way to regain his strength, and he knew he was going to need it. He had a little flame-haired woman to seduce and woo, a killer to capture, and a father to soothe.

Chapter 7

"What are ye doing out of bed?" Tatha demanded as she entered David's bedchamber and saw him standing by the window.

"Walking," he answered, and grinned at her look of disgust.

Tatha set the tray of food she had brought on the table by his bed, then placed her hands on her hips and tried to look stern. "Ye had the stitches taken out only yesterday. Ye should be resting."

"I cannae rest any more," he said as he walked to the bed and sat on the edge, reaching for the flagon of ale she had brought him. "I have rested for almost a fortnight. There is too much I must do."

"Ye can tell others what ye need done. Ye need not do it all yourself," she complained as she sat down on the chair facing him.

She tried not to stare at him as he ate. Ever since Leith had caught them kissing she had approached David cautiously or only when someone else was in the room. They were alone and he was looking very healthy. It made her nervous. Although she had decided not to fight her attraction for him anymore, the thought of letting her passion rule was a little frightening.

Then she frowned. Since that kiss he had not really tried to steal another. She might be ready to succumb to desire, but she suddenly wondered if his had faded. Tatha mused that it would be highly annoying if, now that she had decided to give up her innocence, David was no longer interested in taking it. It would also hurt, but she struggled not to think about how much.

"No need to look so cross, lass," he said. "I willnae do so much that I weaken myself. I ken the benefit of rest."

"Aye, I suppose ye do. Ye have been a verra good patient." She stood up and nervously smoothed down her skirts. "Weel, if ye promise nay to do too much, I will leave ye to your meal."

He caught her by the wrist as she started to move away. "Nay, lass, stay and keep me company." He smiled when she cautiously sat down again. "I have a few questions for ye and have put off the asking of them for far too long."

"What questions?" She clutched her hands together in her lap, afraid that he was about to try to convince her she should return to her father.

"About Sir Ranald."

"I willnae marry the mon."

"I cannae fault ye on that. Nay, I but realized that ye may have knowledge of the mon I dinnae have. He came often to your father's keep?"

"Often enough, although I did my best to avoid him."

"Why?"

"He is a pig. A lecherous dog. The last time he was at my father's keep, I didnae get out of his way fast enough and had bruises in far too many places. The mon feels a lass likes a hard pinch. He savaged a maid or two."

"And your father did naught?"

"They werenae virgins or weelborn lasses. If he kenned what happened, he didnae consider it important. Many a mon doesnae concern himself with what befalls a maid, especially one who is kenned to bed down with a mon or two as the fancy takes her. I am nay sure the lasses told my father what had been done. I had to treat the bruises and welts left, but I didnae say anything either. I dinnae ken why." She frowned. "Mayhap I thought they would or, in my heart, I didnae wish to hear my father actually admit that he didnae care what had happened to them."

"Mayhap if ye had told him, he wouldna have sold ye to the mon."

The way his long fingers almost idly caressed her wrist clouded her mind with desire. Tatha found it a little sad that she could be so deeply affected by a touch, yet he seemed completely at ease. It would have been fine indeed if he were as mindlessly affected by her as she was by him.

"I am nay sure it would have made a difference. My brothers have bedded those lasses, and I think my father has too. The ones Sir Ranald set upon are used by many a mon. I dinnae ken what I thought. I just mended them and tried to forget it all. Again, mayhap I feared it would make no difference. In truth, once I realized I had been sold to that mon, I thought of little else save getting away ere he could get me."

David nodded. "I think I can understand that. Did ye learn much aside from his lechery?"

"He was most interested in my knowledge of herbs." She grimaced. "E'en that interest was based in his lechery. He mostly asked about what I might have to enhance a mon's virility, if there was something I had that could make a mon a better lover. Such as that. I began to wonder if he had some, weel, some male difficulty. I probably should have asked the maids. Mayhap he didnae savage them whilst taking his pleasure, but because he couldnae gain any from them. I just didnae wish to ken much about the mon. Whene'er he was about, I just wished to hide."

Seeing her agitation, he took both her hands in his and kissed each palm. "Dinnae fret, dearling. Ye cannae be expected to have foreseen that it was knowledge ye may be in need of. 'Tis also understandable that ye should shy away from such truths. Then too, mayhap the lasses said naught for they ken such treatment is the cost of their whorish ways."

"No woman deserves such treatment, be she whore or nun."

"I ken, and none of my men would be allowed to behave so, but few would agree with us. Ye cannae change the world. Just your own wee corner of it. Ye also had your own fate to change. Did ye, weel, sense anything else about the mon?"

She tried to concentrate, but David was kissing her hands, her wrists, even the inside of her arms. Tatha knew she ought to yank her hands away and soundly reprimand him for being so bold, but she sat there and let him have his way. She wanted him so badly she could taste it, she thought with a sigh.

"I ne'er liked the mon and wondered why my father tolerated him. Sir Ranald is sly, sneaking, and I dinnae think he holds his honor too dear. I ne'er felt he could be trusted, but it appeared that my father trusted him, so I had to wonder if I was wrong in my judgment of the mon. Or mayhap my father didnae care what the character of the mon was because it didnae matter to what he sought to gain from him. I wish I could tell ye more, but I and my sisters were ne'er allowed to ken what games my father played. He felt it none of our concern who he sought as ally or friend and why."

David decided he had heard all she knew about Sir Ranald, and his thoughts quickly turned elsewhere. Her skin tasted sweet and warm against his mouth. Her eyes had darkened and her breath was uneven, occasionally catching in her throat. It was clear that, despite her attempt to avoid him since his fever broke, her desire for him was still easily stirred. Those hints of passion made his own needs leap to the fore. Cautiously, watching her closely for any hint of rejection, he tugged her out of her seat and into his arms.

There were many reasons why he should not do exactly what he was going to try to do. She was a wellborn lass, a virgin. Her father had betrothed her to another man. It was wrong to take advantage of her innocence and untutored passion. He brutally silenced all qualms as he cupped her face in his hands and gently kissed her. He might not know what he wanted of her or felt for her besides passion, but if he had to wed her to feed the hunger he felt, he would. At the moment it seemed a very small price to pay.

"I dinnae think this is particularly wise," Tatha managed to say as he fell back onto the bed, taking her with him.

"Nay, 'tis probably the greatest of follies. 'Tis madness, but a verra sweet one."

"Aye," she whispered in agreement, shuddering faintly when she saw the desire darkening his eyes.

"I have tried to argue myself out of this hunger time and time again," he said as he turned until she was sprawled beneath him. "It willnae go away."

" 'Tis a torment."

"Oh, aye, that it is."

"I should hit ye and push ye away."

"Aye, ye should." He began to unlace her gown.

Tatha sighed and eased her hands beneath the jupon he wore, shaking as her hands touched his skin. "Mayhap later."

"If ye are going to cry me nay, lass, do it now. I dinnae want ye coming to your senses later and berating me. If ye lie with me now, ken in your mind and heart that it is what ye truly wish to do."

It was the perfect chance to retreat. Tatha knew she should take it. Every rule she had been taught told her to do so. He still offered her only passion, not love or promises of marriage. But as she searched her heart and mind, the only answer she got was a resounding yes. She loved him, ached for him.

"If I suffer any guilt afterward, I promise to keep silent."

"Ah, Tatha, bonnie Tatha, I mean to burn away all thought of guilt."

As he moved to take off her shoes and stockings, his big hands caressing her legs, Tatha decided that was no idle promise. When modesty prompted her to object to the removal of her clothes, he kissed away her protests. She trembled beneath the almost casual touches of his hands as he stripped her. It was not just embarrassment that caused her to tremble, however, when she finally lay naked before him. The heated appreciation in his gaze made her passions soar, and she felt almost beautiful.

David crouched over her for a moment, studying her from her thick, bright hair to her delicate feet. He was breathing so hard, he almost felt dizzy. Her breasts were small, but high and firm, the tips a tempting rose. Her waist was slender, her belly taut, and her hips gently rounded. Her skin was a soft, gently blushed white, begging to be stroked. The light tangle of flame red curls that hid her womanhood promised a warmth his body ached to savor. Her long, slender legs shifted slightly, and he forced his gaze back to her face, smiling at the deep blush coloring her cheeks.

"Ah, lass, ye are bonnie. All soft cream and a tempting hint of fire," he said as he rapidly shed his clothes.

"I am too thin."

"Ye are lithe."

"I am too red."

"Nay, ne'er that. I like the hint of fire. It promises me a heat I ache to bury myself in."

She found speech impossible when he shed the last of his clothes. He was big, big and achingly beautiful. Broad shoulders, a smooth, hard chest, a trim waist, and narrow hips all tempted her. A narrow line of black hair started just below his navel, blossomed around his manhood, and lightened to a faint cover over his long, muscular legs. The only thing that caused her to hesitate as he lowered himself into her arms was that fully aroused manhood. She had seen naked men before, some even aroused, unable to control themselves in the depths of their illness, but she had to wonder if Sir David had been blessed with a little more than most men.

"Ye frown," he murmured as he gently trailed kisses over her face. "Am I nay pleasing to your eye?"

"Verra pleasing. Headily so. I am just nay sure ye will fit."

He bit back a laugh. "Oh, aye, I will. 'Twill hurt the first time."

"I ken it. My aunt told me all about such matters." She gave in to the urge to run her hands over his broad, smooth back and felt the hint of a tremor beneath her touch. "She didnae believe maids should be keep ignorant, and also wished me to ken enough nay to be shocked by what I might see as I treated men for illnesses or wounds."

"Weel, 'tis just that ye have caused it to be at its fullest."

"I have seen that too." She smiled at his dark frown, sensing the hint of angry possessiveness behind the look and pleased by it. "I learned that it has a mind of its own and oftimes cannac discern between a touch meant to help and one meant to tease."

"They can be disobedient fellows."

She laughed, but her laughter caught in her throat when he covered her breasts with his big hands. Tatha cried out softly, wrapping her arms around his neck, when he touched a kiss to the hardened tip of each breast. Pure fire shot through her, and she arched into his kisses. When he drew the aching tip of her breast deep into his mouth and began to suckle, she feared her passion bordered on insanity, it grew so fierce.

An almost painful ache grew low in her belly. She felt compelled to rub against him, but it was not enough to ease the demand of her body. Touching him, running her hands all over his lean, hard body, made him less gentle, but it still did not satisfy her. When he slid his

hand over her belly and tangled his fingers in the tight
curls at the juncture of her thighs, shock was but a brief
flare of resistance in her mind. He stroked her and she
pressed herself into his hand.

David felt the damp warmth of welcome as he
stroked her, watched her whole body shake, and knew
he would soon have to possess her. Her passion fed his
own, though it did not really need feeding; it was already glutted. He gently eased a finger inside of her,
and feared he would spill his seed then and there. She
was so hot, so tight. He took several deep breaths to try
to calm himself. It was important to bring her pleasure.
The more pleasure she was feeling when he did take
her, the less pain there might be.

He kissed her as he stroked her, his body trembling
as he fought to control his own raging need. The moment he felt her tense, then shudder with her impend-
ing release, he spread her legs wide and plunged into
her. He met her maidenhead, gritted his teeth, and
breached it.

Tatha cried out, but she was not sure if it was from
the strength of the pleasure raging through her or the
brief, sharp stab of pain that cut through it. She
wrapped her limbs around him, but was it to steady herself or to pull him closer? Tatha felt confused by the
feelings assaulting her.

"Lass, are ye all right?" he asked as he held himself
still, sweating from the effort, allowing her body to adjust to his invasion.

"I think so." She wrapped her legs more securely
around his hips and cautiously arched upward. " 'Tis
wondrous strange."

That slight movement drove him deeper inside of
her and he groaned, not sure he could put two coher-

ent words together. "I was hoping it would be a wee bit better than strange."

"Oh, it is." She placed her hands on either side of his face and touched a kiss to his lips. " 'Tis beyond words. 'Tis worth every penance I might be forced to pay."

David laughed shakily, then began to move. When Tatha gave a soft cry of pure delight and immediately met his thrust, he lost all ability to go slowly. He gave a shout of triumph and deep joy when he felt her body tighten around him. Slipping his hand between their bodies, he searched out that spot that could stir her passion to new heights and stroked her toward a second release. The way her lithe body moved almost frantically around him as she reached passion's heights was enough to pull him into that abyss along with her.

It was a long time before sanity returned and David realized he had collapsed on top of her. He suspected he ought to move, but he felt too wrung out to make the effort. The way she idly stroked his back with her small, soft hands implied that she had no objection to his position, so he took another moment or two to try to recover.

Slowly he eased the intimacy of their embrace, propped himself up on his elbows, and looked at her. The passion they had shared had gone far beyond his heated imaginings. He had suspected there was a fire in her, but had never suspected it would burn so brightly for him. The way she had made him feel was startling, even a little frightening. He took some comfort in the fact that she seemed to feel the same blinding hunger.

He smiled at her, and to his delight she smiled back. "Weel, do ye think it was worth a penance or two?" he asked, hoping a light tone would hide the uncertainty he suddenly felt.

Tatha fought to hide her disappointment. It was foolish to think he would suddenly spout love words and declare undying devotion just because his lust had been satisfied. The only thing that eased her disappointment was the certainty that he had been as swept away as she had. Innocent she might be, but instinct told her he had shared the ferocity of the passion that had swept her.

"Oh, aye, one or two," she drawled.

"Impertinent wench."

He rose from the bed and, ignoring her blushes, cleaned them both off. As he returned to the bed, she started to get up, and he pulled her back into his arms. "Where are ye going?"

"To my bedchamber," she replied even as she let him tuck her up against his side.

"Nay, ye will stay here."

"Are ye sure that is wise?"

"Nay, but I dinnae care. I have ached to have ye right here since ye first stormed my gates. I have ye now and ye willnae leave."

She cuddled up to him and bit her tongue against the words she wanted to say. Although she had no real objection to sharing his bed, she was a little concerned about becoming his leman. There was also the matter of her father and Sir Ranald. Those troubles still lurked and could easily pull her from his arms. She closed her eyes and forced herself not to think at all. Ignoring the problems and doubts would not make them go away, but, for a little while, she was determined not to let them steal any of the joy she now felt.

Chapter 8

Tatha gently tied the bandage around the warrior's now cleaned and stitched leg wound. She struggled to return his smile of gratitude as she put all of her things back into her small sack. This was the seventh man she had had to tend to in almost as many days. David might not wish to admit that he had been plunged into the midst of a war with Sir Ranald, but it was clear that was what had happened.

At the moment, no one had died. The war as yet consisted of small forays made by Sir Ranald's men that were quickly retaliated against by David and his men. In truth, Sir Ranald was faring far worse than Sir David, for his men were dying. That did not really make Tatha feel much better. It was simply a matter of time before David's men also began to die.

As she walked back to her herb room, she struggled to decide what was the best thing to do. Tatha did not think this was because of her. Even if Sir Ranald had guessed she was here, the fighting was because David was too interested in what had really happened to his mother. The fact that Sir Ranald would try to put an end to that curiosity rather proved his guilt. Nevertheless, she had been the one to stir David's curiosity, to make him want to take another look at his mother's murder. So whether Sir Ranald was after her or not, this was still her fault.

There was also the matter of what existed or did not exist between her and David. For a month now they had blithely indulged their passions despite the increasing turmoil around them. She had worried that the people of Cnocanduin would be disgusted by her, but they showed no sign of that at all. They actually seemed quite pleased that she was sharing their laird's bed. Tatha had the sinking feeling that they foresaw a marriage, believed that Sir David had finally chosen a lady to be his wife and bear him an heir. She wondered if she ought to remind them that she came from a family of thirteen daughters. Begetting a son off her might be nothing less than a miracle.

Cursing softly, she sat down on the stool next to her worktable. While it was true that the fighting, small as it was, was not because of her, she could not help but wonder if she could put an end to it. If nothing else she might be able to draw Sir Ranald away from Cnocanduin. She might even be able to distract the man long enough for David to get the proof he needed, proof that would allow him to come out against Sir Ranald in force. David would probably do that now, and be justified, if not for her. He was in danger of having his motives questioned as long as she was at Cnocanduin, and especially for as long as she shared his bed.

She moved to begin work on some salves, hoping that work would help her think more clearly. Instinct told her that her presence was tying David's hands, but she needed to be sure in her heart. There was always the chance that she was trying to find a reason to leave him. Although she loved him more than was wise and she found only pleasure and joy in his arms, her heart could not long endure being no more than his leman. Slowly but surely, his lack of love and promises of a future for them would steal away that pleasure and joy. However, if she walked away from him, she wanted it to be for a better reason than the fact that she was too much of a coward to stay and hope for more than passion from him.

"We should just attack the fool and wipe him off the face of the earth," snarled Leith as he sat down at the head table in the great hall.

David slouched in his chair, sharing Leith's frustration, but trying not to give in to it. "We cannae. I still hold Tatha here. If we attack and win, and that becomes known, all my reasons for fighting the mon become questionable."

"Why? He killed your mother. This sly war he fights with us is because ye went searching for the truth. It proves his guilt."

"I believe it does. Yet if I claim that as my reason, will I be believed when I have no hard proof, or will it be thought I but try to make excuses for why I keep his betrothed wife in my bed? And to claim that before all will only dredge up all the ill talk of my mother. All the whispers of witches and heresy will be renewed. Aye, and once those fears are revived, how long will it be before they threaten Tatha?"

Leith cursed and dragged his hands through his

hair. "Aye, I can see the danger of having people think of witches and Cnocanduin in the same breath whilst Tatha resides here." He frowned. "Ye dinnae think Sir Ranald kens she is here, do ye?"

"He may have guessed by now, but this battle was begun ere he could have e'en heard the first whispers about a new healer at Cnocanduin. If he has heard something, I wonder if he remains uncertain, for it would give him a perfect reason to attack us in force. Aye, he would be within his rights to have me killed and need not even do so honorably. No one would fault him, for I have given him a grave insult by bedding his bride."

"Since ye have already insulted him by bedding her, why have ye not wed her?"

"I must needs summon a priest for that, and if Sir Ranald is still in doubt, word of a marriage would quickly end it."

"So we must endure this constant harassment."

"For the moment." David frowned and sipped his ale. "I begin to think I should send word to Tatha's father, tell him of my suspicions of the mon."

"But then he will ken where she is, and if he doesnae care or doesnae believe you, he may weel join forces with Sir Ranald."

"I need not mention Tatha. If I send word of my suspicions to all who ken Sir Ranald, it will appear that I but try to get the truth out, to win my right to openly fight him."

"That may work."

"There is but one problem with that plan."

"What?"

"It will stir up the ill talk about my mother again unless I can give some reason, other than claims of witch-craft, for Sir Ranald wanting my mother dead."

"She refused his suit."

"Aye, that could be enough. Something Tatha said makes me think there was more, however. She thinks he may have some problem with his manhood." He quickly told Leith all Tatha had said about what potions and herbs Sir Ranald was most interested in and what the man had done to the maids. "I believe the mon may be impotent and somehow thinks a healer can cure him, either with her healing skills or even through the bed-ding of her."

"Aye, 'tis possible. Despite three wives, he has but the one son, and he was born of the first wife, shortly after the wedding. There were no other births, no other breedings. It may even explain how three of his wives died but nay in childbed, which is what steals the life of most wives."

"If that is the way of it, then one must wonder what would happen to Tatha if he gained hold of her and she couldnae cure him."

"Another dead wife."

David nodded, his hands clenching on his tankard so hard his knuckles whitened. He ached to simply kill Sir Ranald, but he had to think of more than the man's threat to Tatha. His people were now in danger as well. If he acted too rashly and brought condemnation upon himself, it could cost his people dearly, even to their lives. He could not allow himself to forget that Sir Ranald had more power than he did, a closer relation-ship to the king, more allies, and more coin. Sir Ranald was a man one had to have firm, incontrovertible proof against.

" 'Tis a shame he is too much the coward to join his men in these attacks," murmured David. "All our problems would be solved if he met his death whilst raiding my lands."

"Aye, 'twould free Tatha and end this war that isnae a war," agreed Leith. "Ah, weel, winter fast approaches and mayhap that will give us some respite. Time to come up with proof or a plan."

"Aye, although 'tis irritating beyond words to pray that weather will be your ally."

"And if Tatha is freed? Do ye mean to wed her or has the fire that drew ye to her already begun to wane?"

"Oh, I will wed her, and nay just because all of ye seem to think I should. Nay, the fire hasnae waned and I begin to think it ne'er will."

"Do ye love the lass?"

David shrugged. "I dinnae ken. I am nay sure love is much more than a troubadour's song. I like the lass and she warms my bed. Why fret myself to see what, if anything, that means?"

"Weel, when ye do get around to telling her, be a wee bit softer in your speech. There are times when pretty words will gain ye more than the cold truth."

As David sprawled on his bed and watched Tatha brush her damp hair dry before the fire in his room, he thought about what Leith had said. Pretty words. He was not very skilled in flatteries and soft words, but he decided it was past time he gave it a try. When he was finally able to ask Tatha to be his wife, and he refused to believe that time would not come, he wanted her to show no hesitation in accepting. Some soft words now might well ease the way. It had been arrogant to think that, because she shared his bed, she would simply fall in with whatever plans he made for their future. Passion could have made her as heedless of the future as it had him.

It troubled him a little that she did not speak of love, did not tell him anything of what might be in her heart. Although he offered her only mumbled words of passion, he wanted more from her, unfair as that might be. He wanted her bound to him, tied in a way that would always keep her at his side. His sense of possessiveness was strong, and he made no attempt to understand why that should be, just accepted it.

When Tatha walked to the bed, shed her robe, and hastily slid under the covers, the color of a lingering modesty tinting her cheeks, he smiled and pulled her into his arms. He would make her love him. The passion she felt for him was easy to see, and he felt no doubt about its strength. He wanted more. Marriage would tie her to him by the laws of the Church and the king, but he wanted her heart to be his. Instinct told him that, if Tatha gave her heart, it would be forever. He wanted that depth of commitment.

"Lass, ye are the bonniest, softest woman I have e'er held in my arms," he murmured as he warmed her slender throat with soft kisses.

"I am nay sure ye ought to be mentioning those other women just now," she drawled.

David considered his words and inwardly grimaced, but since he could not claim to have lived the life of a monk, he decided to fumble on. "Not e'en to say that ye put them all in the shade? That ye make them such dim memories I cannae recall their names or faces?"

"Weel"—she slid her hand down his stomach and tentatively curled her fingers around his erection, enjoying the tremor that shook his body—"tis flattering in a way. 'Tis a pity, is it not, that I cannae repay the compliment in kind." She grinned at his brief look of disgust. "I do think that ye may be the brawest laddie I have e'er seen."

"Aye, I am." He laughed softly, then murmured his pleasure over the way her soft stroking made him feel. "Ye are making me feel more braw by the moment."

Tatha smiled against his skin as she kissed his chest. She had finally come to a decision. She would leave Cnocanduin. It would not solve all of David's troubles, but it would free his hands to act as he must to protect his people. It would rip her heart out to leave him, but it had to be done. Tonight, however, she intended to soak herself in the pleasure he gave her so freely. She planned to crowd her mind with so many memories it would be years before they began to dim, if ever.

Cautiously, alert for any sign of shock or disgust, she kissed her way down to his taut stomach. She had every intention of leaving her memory firmly planted in David's mind. Her free-speaking aunt had told her of the things men liked, and she decided it was time to put some of that knowledge to the test. She touched a kiss to the inside of each of his strong thighs, then slowly ran her tongue along the thick, hot length of him. The way he groaned the word *aye* and curled his fingers in her hair to hold her where she was told her clearly that he liked that. Tatha grew even bolder.

David clutched the sheets in his fists and struggled to cling to his control. He wanted to savor what she was doing to him for as long as he could. When the moist heat of her mouth enclosed him, he arched up off the bed and knew his control would not last much longer.

Finally, his endurance broke. With a harsh cry he

pulled her up his body. When she straddled him, he slid his hand between her thighs and growled his pleasure when he found her already damp with welcome. He plunged into her and savored her gasp of pleasure. She quickly learned the art of riding her man and took them both to a shuddering climax.

After washing them both clean, he slipped back into bed and pulled her close. "Tatha, I mean no insult, but where did ye learn of that?"

"My aunt," she replied, idly smoothing her hand over his broad chest. She loved the feel of him, loved his scent and his taste. "She was an earthy woman and much enjoyed her time in her husband's bed, sadly short as it was. She was still a young woman when he died and, although she ne'er married again, I believe she took a lover or two."

"And she spoke freely of such things?"

"Aye. She ne'er saw the sense of keeping maidens so ignorant. Aunt Mairi felt knowledge protected a lass against seduction and would aid her in keeping her mon's bed warm."

"I seduced you," he said, feeling a pinch of guilt.

"We seduced each other."

He grinned and pushed her onto her back. "And did your aunt tell ye what a woman likes?"

"Some," she answered, blushing faintly. "I think she felt I would learn what I liked all by myself."

She shivered with pleasure as he trailed kisses over her breasts. Curling her fingers in his hair, she held him close as he lathed and suckled her breasts, restirring her passion. Tatha dared not even think about how much she was going to miss him.

"Ye like that," he murmured against her stomach.

"Oh, aye."

"Weel, let us see if ye like me tasting your secrets as much as ye seemed to like tasting mine."

It took but one stroke of his tongue to make Tatha cry out her pleasure over his intimate kiss. Modesty fled hand in hand with sanity. She offered herself freely to his mouth and let her passions rule. He took her to the heights of pleasure, then, barely allowing her to catch her breath, drove her close to the brink again. Even as she demanded he join her this time, he sat up, dragging her with him. He straddled her across his lap and plunged into her. Bending her back over his arm, he slowly drew the tip of her breast deep into his mouth. Tatha cried out as she lost all sense of where she was, knew only the pleasure raging through her. As her release shuddered through her, she was faintly aware of his cry signaling that she did not travel to that pinnacle alone.

Later, as she watched him sleep, she fought against the urge to weep. There would be time for tears, too much time. There were still several hours before dawn, and she decided she would let him rest for a short time, then draw him back into her arms for one last taste of the joy they could share. She would be exhausted come the dawn, but she could not bear to spend her last night with him only sleeping.

Dawn was but a hint of color on the horizon as Tatha led her pony out through the gates of Cnocanduin. Some of the men on the wall called to her, but seemed to accept her explanation that she was just going to collect some herbs. She thanked God that they were, perhaps, too sleepy to recall that David did not want her riding out alone. Leith would have remembered, but luck was with her and he was still abed.

She mounted her pony and rode toward the forest to the north. Although she felt as if she were slowly dying, she kept on riding. When she had first arrived she had sworn that, if her presence caused Sir David any trouble, she would leave, and it was time to hold to that vow. Her whole body ached with the excesses of the night, but she savored that discomfort. She had made some very warm memories, and she would force herself to be satisfied with that.

Chapter 9

"Where is Tatha?" asked Leith as he answered David's sharp command to enter his bedchamber and looked around.

"I think she has fled," David replied as he buckled on his sword.

"Fled? What did ye do?"

"Naught, curse it."

He sighed and ran his hand through his hair. When he had awakened to find his bed empty he had not given it much thought, but a swift search through the keep and a few questions had revealed that Tatha had left at dawn. Loudly berating the guards who had let her ride away alone had not eased the sudden fury and fear that had seized him. He had returned to his bedchamber to arm himself, thinking to ride out after her, but now he wondered if that was wise.

After the passionate night they had spent he had found it hard to believe she would leave him. Then he had begun to see that she had been saying good-bye.

The question was, Why? The only thing that lay beyond the walls for Tatha was danger. What would make her wish to risk discovery by Sir Ranald? He simply could not believe it was something he had done or said. No woman could make love to a man as thoroughly and as often as she had if there was no longer some feeling for him. That left him with no answers, however.

"I dinnae ken why she has left. She told me naught, gave me no hint that she considered leaving," David said. "She simply crawled out of my bed and rode away."

"Were ye going after her?" Leith asked, glancing at David's sword.

"That was my first thought, but now I wonder if that would be wise. Sir Ranald is trying to kill me. Riding o'er the countryside searching for some fool lass is a sure way to give him an easy target."

Leith frowned as he followed David out of the room. "Do ye think she has decided to go back and face her father?"

"Nay," David answered as he entered the great hall, not really hungry but knowing he needed to eat something to keep up his strength. It could prove to be a very long and exhausting day. "The fools who let her ride out say she headed toward the forest to the north of us."

"Toward Sir Ranald's lands?" Leith sat down and began to fill his trencher with food. "Nay, there is no reason for her to go to him. He is why she ran away from her family."

"I dinnae think she goes to him. She just goes." The food David ate tasted like ashes in his mouth, but he forced himself to keep eating.

"Mayhap she grew weary of being your leman with no hint that she would e'er be more than that."

David frowned as he considered that possibility for a moment, then shook his head. "Nay. I believe Tatha would have said something. She slipped away ere I woke because she intends to do something she did not think I would agree with. Yet I cannae believe she would willingly walk into Sir Ranald's grasp. She kens that her presence here isnae why he is tormenting us."

Leith stared at David for a moment, then said quietly, "Nay, but she may have wit enough to ken that she is the reason we dinnae strike back fast and hard."

After a moment of thought, David cursed, then took a deep drink of ale to soothe his agitation. "Aye, she has wit enough. That is it. She saw that she was tying our hands. God's beard, she may have e'en heard us say so. She has unbound us."

"Aye, but could be riding straight into trouble."

"I believe she may have a true skill for that. Weel, we shall gather a few men and see if we can find her."

"And then what?"

"And then I drag her back here and tie her to the bed."

Tatha winced and rubbed at the small of her back. After such a rigorous night, even a few hours of riding were proving to be more than she could bear. Riding north, so close to Sir Ranald's lands, was probably not the wisest route to take, but she had felt it was the one David would be least inclined to follow. Now, however, she wished to rest and did not dare to. She needed to get as far away from both men as she could as fast as she could.

As she prodded her little pony over the rocky trail, she frowned. It was very quiet, too quiet. She suddenly realized that none of the sounds one usually heard in the forest were there. It was as if someone had just thrown a smothering blanket over the area.

Her heart began to beat faster as fear crept over her. This was a warning, but of what? She touched her knotted cord, silently trying to pull forth the protection it promised, as she looked around. Just as she began to convince herself that she was succumbing to nerves, she saw a movement off to her right.

A man on a horse slowly became visible through the trees. Tatha turned her horse to the left, only to see another. Within moments she was surrounded.

"If ye mean to rob me," she said, struggling to remain at least outwardly calm, "ye will find some verra poor gain. I have little or naught that would be of profit for you."

"Nay, Lady Tatha, we dinnae mean to rob you," said a tall, thin man with a huge beak of a nose as he rode closer and tore her reins from her hands.

"How do ye ken who I am?" she demanded even as she frowned at the man, something about him striking her as faintly familiar.

"I oftimes visited your father's keep with your betrothed. I am Baird, one of Sir Ranald's men."

"How unfortunate for you."

Ice trickled through her veins, but she fought the urge to scream in terror. She had obviously ridden right into the midst of one of Sir Ranald's raiding parties. She was right back where she had started from when she had fled her father's keep. Her freedom had been short, glorious, but short. The only hope she had, and it was a very small one, was that she would have a chance to speak to her father before the wedding. She might be able to make him listen to the truth about Sir Ranald.

"Weel, I shallnae trouble ye," she said, trying and failing to tug her reins free of Baird's grasp. "I was just riding home to my father. Mayhap I will see ye again at the wedding."

"Clever lass, but ye cannae fool me. Ye fled your father's keep near to two months ago. Ye have no intention of returning there. So we shall just take ye to your betrothed and let him deal with you."

"Sir Ranald is nay my betrothed."

"He paid a handsome bride price for you."

"Then he can just get it back, for I havenae agreed to wed the bastard."

She scowled at the man as he laughed and began to lead her north toward Sir Ranald's keep. She knew most people would consider her opinion that the betrothal was void unless she agreed to it pure nonsense, but she did not appreciate being mocked. Then she felt the weakening touch of defeat. What did suffering a little mockery matter when she would undoubtedly soon be dead?

David stood beside Leith staring down at the tracks upon the ground and not wishing to believe what they told him. Tatha had ridden right into the hands of Sir Ranald's men. David felt sure she had not done it on purpose, but that mattered little. She had been taken out of his reach, and he did not think there was any way he could take her back.

Without a word he mounted and headed back to his keep. The tracks were old enough to tell him that there was no point in trying to run her or her captors down. She was gone, and he found that cold truth too difficult to deal with, especially with all of his men staring at him.

Once back at Cnocanduin, David went straight to his bedchamber and poured himself a large tankard of ale. By the time he had downed a second one he felt a bit more in control, was even able to greet Leith's entrance with some appearance of calm. Inside he felt as if some animal were tearing him apart. He wanted to rage, but knew that would gain him nothing.

"He will hurt her," Leith said, helping himself to some ale.

"I ken it," David whispered, shuddering a little as his raging emotions tried to break free of the restraints he had put upon them.

"Is there naught we can do?"

"I have already sent word to her father concerning Sir Ranald's part in my mother's murder. Mayhap he will bestir himself to change his mind about the marriage."

It was not enough. David wanted to go to Sir Ranald's keep and tear it apart stone by stone until he found Tatha. He wanted to tear Sir Ranald apart as well. Neither could be done, but the only alternatives were meek, paltry ones that gave him little hope and no ease.

Somehow she had burrowed herself into his heart, beneath his very skin, and he had not seen it. He had favored her passion and enjoyed her company, but had never allowed himself to look beyond that. In his mind all had been settled. He would marry the woman who so gloriously warmed his bed and made him smile, despite her lack of dowry, despite her red hair, despite the

fact that she was left-handed, and even despite the beliefs she had that caused him such unease. Not once
had he wondered why he would. Not once had he considered losing her. Now that he had, he felt a cold
emptiness he feared could prove permanent.

He loved her. He saw that now. Now that it might be
too late. David cursed himself and his blindness. He
should have simply wed her and spit in the eye of all the
possible consequences.

"Mayhap ye should send word to her father again,"
said Leith, watching his gray-faced cousin closely.

"Why? If claims that the mon he sold her to is a killer
willnae move him, what else may?"

"Mayhap ye should tell him that she was here, tell
him all she said about what Sir Ranald sought from her,
about the maids. Is it nay worth the gamble? It may be
all that is needed to make him recall his responsibilities
as a father, and we could use his support. Aye, if we had
it, we could go to Sir Ranald's keep and tear her out of
his grasp."

"It will also tell him that Sir Ranald may weel have
righteous grievance against the Ruthvens."

"I ken it. I dinnae think ye will find anyone here who
willnae be more than ready to take that chance. I would
be willing. Donald would be, for his Sorcha is still carrying her bairn, grows rounder and heavier with it every
day, and 'tis a lively one. He tells us all of its every kick.
Robert's back is better, and he has discovered a new way
to enjoy his bonnie wife. The blacksmith near to kisses
the ground your lady walks on, for his son is alive and
getting into trouble again as all wee lads should."

"So weel loved in such a short time?"

"Aye, by all of us, and I think mostly by you. She
saved your life as weel."

"Aye, she did. Ye had best be sure of this, Leith. If that fool father of hers has no caring for her at all, thinks naught of who she weds but only of the coin weighting his purse, we could be setting ourselves in the midst of a bloody feud with no hope of allies."

"I am sure. Send him word. If he proves to be such a heartless bastard that he cannae e'en come to judge the truth for himself, then once we are done with Sir Ranald, we will go to his keep and steal all her sisters."

David laughed, surprised he could do so. Then he realized that he had some hope now. Even if Tatha's father did not join him, he had the support of his people. Pulling them into the midst of a feud, something that could be long and bloody, for the sake of a lass who was not a Ruthven, was something he had been reluctant to do. He had feared that he would be leading his people to their deaths simply to keep a lass he wanted. It was clear that his clan wanted her as well.

"Weel, find the lad who took the last message to that fool Tatha must claim as her father," David ordered. "I will try once more to rouse the mon's conscience. We willnae wait long for him, however, so we had best begin to plan our attack as weel."

"Dinnae worry, David." Leith briefly clasped his cousin's shoulder in a gesture of sympathy. "We will get the lass back."

David prayed his cousin's confidence was trustworthy. He dared not think on all that could happen to Tatha while she was in Sir Ranald's hold, nor what the man might do to her when he discovered she was no longer a maiden. Or, if he had guessed correctly about what ailed the man, how he would treat her if she could not cure his problem. All he could do was plan, and pray she could keep herself safe until he could get to her.

"Where is my daughter?"

David stared at the huge scowling man standing in his bailey, only briefly glancing at the well-armed force he had brought with him. It had been four long days since he had sent the last message to Sir Malcolm Preston, and he had begun to lose hope. It was hard to believe this angry brute of a man was Tatha's father, but David was willing to accept any help he could get.

"As I wrote you, she is in Sir Ranald's hands," David answered. "I am preparing to go and take her back." His eyes widened slightly as a slender, dark-haired girl stepped up next to the man.

"One of my other daughters, Elspeth." Sir Malcolm scowled down at the girl. "She made me bring her."

David almost smiled. Perhaps, in his gruff way, Sir Malcolm was not as heartless as they had all thought. If such a tiny lass could not only defy the man but make him accede to her wishes, there might well be some softness beneath the scowl. He glanced at his cousin, thinking to silently share his humor, only to find himself fighting the urge to gape. Leith was staring at the slender girl as if some angel had just alighted and offered him the keys to God's kingdom. When he turned back to look at the girl, she was staring back at Leith and blushing.

"Pleased to meet ye, Lady Elspeth," he said as he took her hand in his and lightly kissed it, breaking her and Leith of the spell they seemed to be caught in. "Your concern for your sister can only be praised." He looked back at Sir Malcolm, who curtly introduced his son Douglas. "Let us go to the hall and have some ale and food whilst we discuss this matter. Not a long discussion, mind, for I am preparing to ride out after Tatha."

"Oh? And ye think ye have that right, do ye?" demanded Sir Malcolm as he, Douglas, and Elspeth followed David and Leith into the keep.

"I promised her my protection. Aye, and many here feel they owe her."

Sitting down and helping himself to a large tankard of wine, Malcolm grunted. "So she has been going about healing hurts, has she?"

As he too sat down and filled his tankard, David nodded. "She is truly skilled in the healing arts."

"Aye, her aunt taught her weel." Sir Malcolm's eyes narrowed. "Though some called the old crone a witch, and 'twas something whispered about Tatha from time to time."

"We are nay so foolish here."

"Nay? Wasnae that what got your mother killed?"

"Papa," Elspeth snapped. "I thought we came here to help Tatha. I dinnae think that will be easy if ye make the mon want to cut your throat."

"Ye are verra saucy for such a wee lass," he grumbled.

"I but speak the truth."

"Aye, ye do, and 'tis best ye recall who decried my mother as a witch and whose men killed her," David said coldly. "That same mon now holds your daughter."

"A lass who is betrothed to him." Sir Malcolm held up his hand when both Elspeth and David started to speak. "A mistake. I see that now. The mon was old and ugly, but he was wealthy, powerful, and would have given the lass a household to lead, mayhap e'en a bairn or two. Or so I thought. Your last message has me thinking the old bastard was hiding the truth about himself. I talked with the maids and they confirmed your suspicions. Told the fool lasses they should have come to me. E'en a whore doesnae deserve to be beaten near senseless just because some old goat cannae get his rod to stand up." He grinned when Elspeth groaned, blushed, and hid her face behind her hands. "Ye wanted to come along." He blithely ignored the glare she gave him and looked hard at David. "Of course ye ne'er touched my lass yourself."

"I mean to get her back and marry her," David said, his look almost daring Sir Malcolm to argue with him.

"Weel, there could be a cost," Sir Malcolm began.

"Nay, Father," Douglas said. "No more. Ye have set that poor lass in the midst of deadly trouble with your fine plan. 'Tis clear it isnae the way to do things."

"Ye were ne'er fond of it from the start. Isabel and Bega didnae mind."

"Isabel and Bega would have wed with the Devil himself and any one of his minions if it meant they wouldnae be spinsters any longer," snapped Elspeth.

"Aye, and the ones who bought them were nay old, useless men who may have blood on their hands," said Douglas. "I wonder now if all of his wives died of illness as he claimed or were set in their graves because he blamed them for his lack."

"Insolent lot," Sir Malcolm grumbled, but he nodded as he looked back at David. "All right. If ye want the fool lass ye may have her. Now, how do we get her back from that old bastard?"

Two hours later, as the combined forces of the Prestons and the Ruthvens rode out of Cnocanduin, David felt his hopes rise. He nudged Leith, pulling his cousin's gaze from the slender girl waving them farewell from the walls of the keep. David had caught Douglas grinning at both Leith and Elspeth, revealing that he too had noticed the bewitchment that had apparently seized the two. He was not sure it was something that ought to be revealed to Sir Malcolm just yet, however.

"What ails ye, cousin?" he demanded, biting back a grin when Leith blushed bright red.

"Tatha's sister is a bonnie lass," Leith muttered.

"Aye, she is, and she smiles quite freely at you."

"I have no coin."

"Dinnae fret on that. It appears the father isnae as fierce in his ways as we thought, and the brother has clearly ne'er approved of the business. When we get Tatha back we will turn our attentions to getting ye the wee, bonnie Elspeth."

"We will get the lass back," Leith said firmly.

David just smiled and prayed that his cousin was right to feel so confident. Tatha had been in Sir Ranald's grasp for four long days. She was a clever lass, resourceful and brave, but how long could she keep herself safe from the man? He had been tormented day and night with thoughts of all that could be happening to her, and he had to stop, for it was threatening to make him useless. David forced himself to fix his thoughts on the battle ahead and nothing else, a battle he must win.

Chapter 10

Tatha winced as the light the guard carried stung her eyes. When Baird had delivered her to Sir Ranald, that man had glared at her for several minutes, then had her tossed in the dungeon. There she had been left, alone and in the dark. If she was right and the meager offering of sour ale and stale bread that arrived was really only sent once a day, she had been kept in the dungeons for four days. That also meant that Sir Ranald's silent, glaring visits also came but once a day, for she had endured those long moments of glaring four times. She was being punished.

She sighed as the silent guard changed her privy pot, left her a bowl of scummy water to wash in, and set down her meager meal. It was maddening to sit there alone, shrouded in silence and darkness, but she tried to be hopeful. At least Sir Ranald was not trying to assert his husbandry rights before the wedding. And if he was waiting to marry her it had to be because her father was coming. Her father had to frown on this treatment.

The man had never even struck them when they were naughty, for all he roared and grumbled. Sir Malcolm could never be called a loving father, but he had never been cruel, and she prayed this would shock him into listening to her pleas.

She had barely choked down her unappetizing meal when another guard arrived with a large bucket of hot water, some of her clothes, and what looked to be soap and a drying cloth. He set them inside her cell, then turned his back. For a moment Tatha stared at the things he brought, then at his stiff back. Surely he did not expect her to bathe and change while he stood there? It quickly became clear that he expected exactly that. Praying that he had been ordered not to glance her way, she turned her back on him and began to wash. She even rinsed out her hair, then rubbed it dry with the cloth and combed her fingers through it. It was a tangled mess, but at least it was a little cleaner.

"Are ye done?" demanded the guard.

"Aye," she muttered as she tied off the last of her laces. "Now what?" she demanded when he grabbed her by the arm and started to drag her back up the stairs.

"Sir Ranald wishes to speak with you," the guard answered.

"I am overcome with joy."

"I dinnae ken why the old fool wants such a sharp-tongued lass."

"I am young?"

"Aye, that could be the way of it. Ye must have made your father verra angry if he was willing to sell ye to this old goat."

Tatha did not reply, for she had often thought the same thing. Unfortunately, she had been unable to think of one thing she had done that would make her father condemn her to marriage with Sir Ranald. She could only pray that her father simply did not know what the man was like and that he would listen when she tried to tell him, that she would at least be given the chance to speak to him.

When the guard did not lead her to the great hall as she had suspected he would, she tensed. If Sir Ranald's keep was much akin to the others she had been to then she was being dragged to the sleeping rooms. Feeling the first hint of panic she tried to pull free of the guard's hold, but he doggedly dragged her onward. When he reached a heavy, iron-studded door, he knocked once, opened it, and practically threw her inside. Before she could catch her balance he had shut it behind her.

"So, my wee bride, how do ye like your new bedchamber?" asked Sir Ranald as he stepped up behind her and shoved her toward the bed.

"We arenae married yet," she said, straightening herself up and trying to meet his cold gaze with calm.

"We will be."

"Is my father coming to the wedding?"

She wondered why that simple question should make him scowl so darkly. Then she studied him more closely. He looked furious, but she sensed the anger was not all due to her blatant aversion to him. Something had gone wrong, and she began to suspect that that something was why he was about to try to claim his husbandry rights before they were actually married.

"Oh, aye, your father is on his way, but he will be too late."

"What do ye mean?"

"Your fine Sir David has been verra busy, verra busy

indeed. He has been sending messengers all o'er the countryside, telling one and all that I killed his mother."

"And did you?"

"What does that matter?"

"It gives David a righteous grievance against you. 'Twill hobble what few allies ye have, for none will wish to put themselves in the midst of a weel-earned reckoning. And my father willnae make me marry a woman-killer." She edged away from the bed when he took a threatening step toward her. "Has my father learned the ugly truth about you, Sir Ranald? Is that why ye have brought me here? Ye mean to try to steal what is nay longer yours by right, dinnae you?" ·

He stalked her around the room. "Your father and I made a bargain. I gave him a hefty purse for your sweet hide. Ye are mine now."

"Nay, I am not and I ne'er will be."

When he lunged for her, she darted out of his reach. She raced for the door, but he grabbed her, dragged her to the bed, and tossed her on top of it. For a slim, aging man, he was surprisingly strong. Tatha also suspected that four days in the dungeons with little to eat or drink had severely depleted her strength. Despite the growing conviction that she could not win a fight against him, she struggled with all her might. It did not really surprise her when he got her firmly pinned down beneath him on the bed, but it was difficult not to weep over her defeat.

The too-wet kisses he pressed against her neck made her stomach roll. His bony fingers clawed at the laces of her gown, and she felt herself shrink away from even the promise of his touch. Her growing panic eased abruptly when she realized there was no hardness in his groin. He ground himself against her, but she felt only his hip bones and a faint soft shape that was probably his manhood. The man might maul her, might even beat her, but she began to think that he would never be able to rape her.

"Curse ye, ye are failing me too, just as they all do!" he screamed, and backhanded her across the mouth. "My wives, Lady Ruthven, all of them. Useless whores, the whole lot of you."

She cried out in pain when he shoved her off the bed and she hit the floor hard. "'Tis nay the women who fail ye, ye great fool." She scrambled out of his way when he leaped off the bed and tried to kick her. "Ye have gone and damaged yourself somehow."

"Then cure it. Ye are a healer. Heal me." He grabbed her by the hair, yanked her back toward him, and slapped her again. "Heal me, ye twice-cursed bitch!"

"Is that what ye demanded of Lady Ruthven?"

"Aye, and she failed me. Then she forced me to make sure she couldnae tell anyone my secret. Aye, just like my useless wives, she needed to be silenced."

"Ye killed them all just because ye are impotent?"

"Nay!" He punched her in the face, releasing her hair when she fell backward from the force of the blow." 'Tis their fault! They cursed me. Aye, that is what the bitches did, cursed me. And they didnae ken what I needed."

"Ye need a new pintle, ye old goat."

"Ye are no healer. Where are your potions and salves, eh? I cannae even get hard enough to seek the cure in your body. What good are ye, I ask ye? Eh? What cursed good are any of ye?"

"I dinnae think anyone can cure ye," she said, struggling to get to her feet so that she might evade his next attack. "'Twas a wound or a fever, wasnae it? There is no cure, and ye are slaughtering women for naught."

"Nay, they all deserve what I deal out to them. And my secret is safe. And so will it remain safe."

Tatha tried to elude him when he advanced on her, but she was weak and unsteady. The blows he had already dealt her, her hunger and thirst, had all stolen away her chance to escape him. She cursed in frustration when he grabbed her and watched him draw his fist back with a sense of cold acceptance. He was going to kill her as he had killed the others, and there was little she could do to stop him.

A cry of alarm rang through the halls, and Tatha felt a surge of hope. It might not be anyone coming to her rescue, but any diversion at the moment could only be a blessing. If Sir Ranald was taken from her side for a while, she might be able to regain some of her strength.

She bit back a whimper of pain as he twisted his hand in her hair and dragged her over to the window. She could not see out, but whatever he looked down at caused him to go red with fury. He glared at her, then slammed her head against the cold stone wall. Tatha blinked once, then sank into darkness.

David was astonished at how easily they had gained the inner bailey of Sir Ranald's keep. His guard had been lax and slow to respond when they had seen his army riding hard toward their walls. They had been able to ride right through the gates, easily cutting down the men frantically trying to close them.

With Leith guarding his back, he fought his way into the keep itself. He ached to confront Sir Ranald, his fear for Tatha so strong it nearly had a life of its own. As he cut down the last man standing between him and entrance into the keep, he looked up to see Sir Ranald himself rushing down the stairs, sword in hand.

"Where is she?" he demanded, a little surprised that the man actually meant to face him.

"Ye mean the little whore of a healer?" Sir Ranald's smile was pure viciousness. "She wasnae as sweet a ride as I thought she would be."

David struggled to keep his rage harnessed, knowing the man tried to goad him into acting foolishly. "Her father stands at my side. Your keep is falling into our hands. The whole of Scotland will soon ken that ye are naught but a cowardly slayer of women."

"Aye, and my tally of dead whores has just increased by one."

" 'Ware, David," whispered Leith from behind him. "He tries to madden ye so that he may actually have some chance of killing ye."

"I ken it."

That knowledge did little to dull the sharp fear he felt, however. There was a good chance the man was lying, but he could also be telling the chilling truth.

He had held Tatha captive for long enough to do anything he pleased with her. David dared not think that he had come so close yet had failed to save her. That way lay madness.

"Ye killed my mother, didnae ye?" David said as he and Sir Ranald circled each other.

"Another whore."

"Is that how ye explain your own lack, Sir Ranald? Do ye blame your poor limp monhood on the lasses? Calling them whores makes ye feel like the mon ye can ne'er be, does it?"

As David had hoped, Sir Ranald was unable to endure even the slightest taunt. The man roared his fury and attacked. The strength the man showed was a little surprising, for he looked like an ailing, too-thin old man, but his skill was rough, his sword swings ill-timed and badly executed. It would not be a long battle.

"Where is she?" he demanded again. "Where have ye put Tatha Preston? Tell me, and if she is hale and unharmed, I may let ye live."

"Live? For what? To hang? To be laughed at? Nay, I think not. Your wee whore is dead, her soft, pale flesh cold. Ye rode her, didnae ye? Aye, ye did, and I made her pay for that."

It was clear that the man would never tell him what he wanted to know, would just continue to try to torment him with tales of the horrors he had made Tatha endure. Cursing the man, David strengthened his attack. Sir Ranald quickly weakened. Although it was tempting to make the man sweat and linger in the knowledge that he would soon be dead, David quickly delivered the death stroke.

Even as he stared down at the man's body, praying that all Sir Ranald had said concerning Tatha's fate was no more than lies spat out by a vicious man, David heard Leith curse in surprise. A moment later one of Sir Ranald's men landed in a heap at his feet. David held his sword at the terrified man's throat and glanced over his shoulder. Sir Malcolm stood there glaring down at the man.

"I think this worm kens where the lass is," said Sir Malcolm.

"It would be wise to tell me," David said, his gaze fixed upon the trembling man-at-arms. "I have had a bellyful of lies and taunts and willnae tolerate another. If ye wish to keep your head on your shoulders ye had best speak the truth and do so quickly."

"Sir Ranald kept the lass in the dungeons for four days," the man replied, speaking so fast in a shaking voice that it was hard to understand him. "But moments before ye rode through the gates he had her taken to his bedchamber." He lifted one trembling hand and pointed up the stairs. "The door on the right at the head of the stairs."

David bounded up the stairs, faintly aware of the sound of a fist hitting a body. He guessed that Leith or Sir Malcolm had rendered the man unconcious rather than waste any time securing him. Even as he threw open the door the man had spoken of, he could hear the others pounding up the stairs.

A soft curse escaped him and his blood ran cold when he saw Tatha sprawled on the floor near the window. Sheathing his sword, he hurried to her side. As he knelt beside her, he saw her chest move and nearly wept with relief. She was alive. At the moment that was all that mattered.

Gently, he picked her up and carried her to the bed. Leith and Sir Malcolm stood by the bed as David checked Tatha for any severe injuries. She had clearly been knocked around, and there was a sizable lump on the back of her head, but David could find no other wounds. He sat down on the bed and took her hand in his, lightly rubbing it warm between his two hands.

"The fool said Sir Ranald had only just brought the lass up here," Sir Malcolm grumbled, scowling down at his daughter. "'Tis clear she managed to enrage him right quickly."

David stared at Sir Malcolm, torn between disbelief

and anger. "I dinnae believe Tatha asked for this beating."

"That wasnae what I said. Dinnae tell me ye are one of them sensitive lads. I just said that the fool had been quick to beat her, and if ye try to tell me my lass didnae whet her tongue on his wrinkled hide then ye dinnae ken her as weel as I thought ye did."

"My father oftimes sounds as if he is saying something most unkind when 'tis nay the way of it at all," said Douglas as he entered the room and walked to the side of the bed.

"I hope ye arenae saying that I am kind," snapped Sir Malcolm, glaring at his son.

"I would ne'er insult ye so." Douglas frowned down at Tatha. "'Tis a shame that the best healer we ken is the verra lass who needs tending."

"If she would wake, she would be quick to tell us what to do. I wouldnae be surprised to see her heal the dead one of these days."

David hid his surprise. Sir Malcolm's words were spoken in the same gruff, nearly angry tone he always used, but the pride he felt in Tatha's healing skills was evident. It was increasingly clear that he had wronged the man to think he cared nothing for his daughter.

"She will wake soon," David said. "Her breathing has already grown stronger and her eyes move beneath her lids."

"Are ye a healer too?" asked Sir Malcolm.

"Nay, but my mother was, and I learned a few things."

"The woman Sir Ranald called a whore and near confessed to murdering?"

"Aye, that woman."

"Why did ye let the mon live?"

"Why did ye betroth your daughter to him?"

"A lass needs a husband, a home, and bairns. I have eleven lasses with nay a dower between them. I took what I could get. Aye, the mon wasnae the best choice, but I didnae see the evil in him. Aye, and he was old." Malcolm shrugged. "I felt he would probably die soon and the lass wouldnae have to endure him long ere she was weel settled, a widow with lands and coin."

David stared at the man in bemusement for a moment. A quick glance at Douglas caught him hiding a grin. In his rough way Sir Malcolm had been trying to do what was best for his daughters, and if that best also filled his purse, so much the better. David did think that Tatha might have misjudged the man. If she had stayed to make her distaste clear, Malcolm might well have ended the bargain. Then again, he would never have met her. She had erred when she had run away in panic, but since that error had set her in his arms, David decided he would not chide her for it.

Tatha opened her eyes and David quickly grasped her by the shoulders, lightly pinning her to the bed. His touch seemed enough to swiftly still the panic that seized her a heartbeat after she woke. She stared up at him for a moment, then yanked on his arms, pulling him down into her hold. David cast a wary glance at her father, amazed to find him grinning.

"Ah, weel, my lass was ne'er a shy one," Sir Malcolm drawled.

David felt Tatha tense and met her wide gaze. "David," she whispered, "I didnae just hear my father, did I?"

"Aye," he replied. "He is standing by the bed."

Tatha squeaked in shock and gave David such a hard shove he slipped off the bed, barely stopping himself from sprawling on the floor. Douglas and Sir Malcolm both guffawed, and, as he straightened himself up, David caught Leith grinning at him. He turned his attention back to Tatha, who was staring at her father with a mixture of pleasure and wariness.

"Glad to see ye didnae take any harm, lass," Sir Malcolm said, awkwardly patting her on the shoulder. "Ye should be in fine fettle for your wedding."

"I willnae marry Sir Ranald," she snapped, then rubbed her forehead, just speaking having been enough to set it to aching.

"Of course ye willnae. The mon's dead."

"Oh." She frowned. "Then what wedding are ye talking about?"

"Ye are marrying Sir David."

Chapter 11

"It would be nice if, just once, someone would ask me if I wish to be married," Tatha grumbled to her sister Elspeth as the girl helped her dress in her finest dark blue gown.

All the way back to Cnocanduin, no more had been said of the marriage her father had so bluntly announced. David had made himself conspicuously unreachable and Tatha had ached too much to argue with her father. A part of her had not really wanted to argue anyway. She wanted David, loved him deeply. It simply troubled her that he might be being forced into a marriage he did not really want.

"This mon is a far better choice than Sir Ranald," said Elspeth as she pushed Tatha down into a chair and began to gently brush out her hair.

Although she had taken a potion to ease the ache in her head, Tatha still found having her hair brushed almost painful. "A far better choice. In truth, a mon who could do much better than a too-thin, left-handed red-head."

"He wants you."

"Are ye sure?" Tatha hated to reveal her uncertainty before anyone, but she needed someone to boost her courage, and Elspeth had always been one of the closest of her sisters, as well as highly practical.

"Oh, aye. He was readying himself and his men to go and try to rescue you when we arrived. Papa said he took a chance in sending for us because he confessed that ye had stayed with him. If no one believed his claims that Sir Ranald killed his mother then he was exposing himself to a great deal of trouble. After all, ye were another's betrothed wife."

"I ken all that. 'Tis why I left here. My presence so complicated matters that he could not fight Sir Ranald openly despite the raids upon his lands. Everything he tried to claim about Sir Ranald was put into question because I was here."

"He had clearly decided that that no longer mattered. He was going to war with Sir Ranald to get ye back."

"That does seem to indicate that he has some feeling for me."

"Aye, and he had already told Papa that he meant to wed with you as soon as he got ye out of that mon's grasp."

"Oh. I didnae ken that."

"Weel, there hasnae been much time for talking."

"I love the mon, Elspeth, and I just wish he felt the same."

Elspeth patted Tatha on the shoulder. "Trust me in this. He feels something for you. Leith said the mon was devastated to find ye gone and ken that ye were in Sir Ranald's grasp."

"Leith says, does he?"

Tatha gave her sister a considering glance. Even though she had been groggy from pain when they had finally ridden through the gates of Cnocanduin, she had seen how Elspeth had run out to greet, not her family, but a blushing Leith. She had also seen the way the two of them could not stop looking at each other and smiling.

"Tatha? Did ye feel something for Sir David the verra moment ye set eyes on him?"

Tatha smiled at her blushing sister. "Aye, I did. Leith is a verra fine mon. Nay rich, but weelborn and holding a high place here."

"Weel, aye, but he doesnae have a bride price."

"Father still plays that game, does he?"

"I am nay sure."

"Weel, if Leith wants ye, I think that, between him and David, they will talk our father 'round to liking the idea. Would ye be willing to marry a mon ye have but just met?"

"In a heartbeat."

That was said with such conviction, Tatha did not even consider arguing with Elspeth. She decided it made her own qualms seem foolish. David had never spoken of love, but he did desire her. He was young, handsome, and she loved him. It was foolish to bemoan what she did not have when she was about to be given so much. She reached out and took Elspeth's hand, squeezing it gently in a silent gesture of support and comfort. She turned her thoughts to hoping Elspeth would also get what she wanted.

* * *

"Just go and speak with the mon," David urged, trying to hide his amusement over Leith's agitation.

In a way, David was grateful for the distraction Leith's problem caused him. It was preferable to wondering where his bride was and if, now that she was beginning to recover from the knock on her head, she would think to flee him as she had Sir Ranald. Turning his thoughts to helping Leith get the lass he had taken such a sudden fierce liking to kept him from racing up to Tatha's bedchamber and making sure she was actually getting ready to marry him.

"He wants a bride price." Leith dragged his hand through his hair. "I have naught. I am but your second-in-command. The lass could do better than me."

"Ye have a lineage as fine as hers and, although ye may ne'er be rich, I dinnae think she will suffer any hardship living here with us."

"She may wish her own household to lead."

"Mayhap that can be arranged. I plan to claim Sir Ranald's lands as a price for the murder of my mother. I may not get all of them, but I think something will be gained there. E'en if ye stay here, we may get ye a household of your own, a small one, aye, but one of your own." He frowned at Leith. "Are ye now wondering if ye want her?"

"Nay. I ken ye may think it madness, but I took one look at that lass and I was sure. Sure she was all I could e'er want." He straightened up and took a deep breath to steady himself. "Weel, there can be no harm in trying."

"I will go with ye. I dinnae think the mon is that set on getting money for his daughters. His thinking may be odd, but he seems to just want them to get what he believes all lasses need—a mon, a home, and bairns."

* * *

"I ken what ye want, lad," said Sir Malcolm the moment Leith approached him. He sprawled a little more on the bench at the head table, sipped his ale, and studied Leith closely. "I dinnae suppose ye have any money."

"Nay, not for a bride price, sir," Leith replied solemnly, "but I am nay a pauper. I have enough that your daughter Elspeth willnae be clothed in rags or starve."

"It sounds fine to me, Father," Douglas said, smiling briefly at Leith, "if Elspeth agrees."

Scowling at his son, who sat on his right, Sir Malcolm grumbled, "Aye, it would. 'Tis nay your purse that will go empty."

"Your purse isnae that empty," David said. "Ye still have the bride price Sir Ranald gave ye for Tatha, and since he didnae deal honestly with ye, I believe ye get to keep it."

"Aye, which means I need nay ask one of ye, but it wasnae meant to pay for two of my lasses," Sir Malcolm said.

"Ye still have seven." David reached out to grasp his tankard off the table and slowly filled it with ale. "I also ken a lot of men, unwed men. Aye, they may not fatten your purse, but they have titles and lands. Allies can be important. I dinnae even mind if, now and again, a few of your lasses stay here, and mayhap they could meet a few of these fine, landed, unwed gentlemen. Fine, honorable men who are sometimes left alone, for they dinnae have quite enough to please those with weel-dowered lasses."

"Ye have a clever tongue, lad. Aye"—he waved his hand at Leith—"if the lass wants ye, take her. I may not get any coin for her, but it does mean I dinnae have to pay for her keep any longer." He looked at Leith when the young man enthusiastically shook his hand. "She is a spirited lass. Take care of her."

"Oh, I will, sir," Leith said even as he hurried out of the great hall.

"He means to pull her afore the priest today, eh?" Sir Malcolm grinned, then winked as he lifted his tankard. "Two more of the wretched lasses gone. My burden lessens by the hour."

"I dinnae think it weighs as heavily upon your shoulders as ye wish the world to believe," David murmured, then squarely met Sir Malcolm's gaze. "He will cherish her."

"Aye, ye could practically smell their besottedness." He grinned when David and Douglas laughed, but then quickly returned to scowling. "And ye?"

"Tatha was mine the moment she set foot within my gates. It just took me a wee while to understand that." He glanced toward the door, saw Tatha entering the great hall, and immediately moved to her side. "How are ye feeling, love?"

Tatha looked up at him as he took her hands in his. His gaze was warm and filled with concern. That look eased her nervousness. He could not look at her that way if he were feeling at all trapped.

"I am fine," she replied. "I but ache some. I am glad I was ready to come down, for although I wasnae tossed from the room when Leith arrived, it was a near thing. Elspeth can somehow manage to shove a person out of a room yet make it look so benign." She smiled when he laughed and began to lead her to a seat across the table from her father.

"The lad is eager to take advantage of the priest," Sir Malcolm said, scowling blackly as he studied her bruises.

"Ye have agreed to his wedding her?" asked Tatha.

"Aye. They are besotted. I am glad I brought the priest."

"Ah, I wondered where he had come from."

"Weel, 'twas clear from what your mon wrote me that ye had been his guest since ye fled Prestonmoor. Ye are both young and bonnie. Felt a priest might be needed." He cocked one dark brow but said nothing more when Tatha blushed.

"And how fare Isabel and Bega?" she asked cautiously.

"They are wed and gone. Isabel was already packing her things ere the words concerning her betrothal had left my mouth. Bega will do better on her own, nay longer under Isabel's thumb."

"They were nay unhappy, Tatha," Douglas added quietly. "Truly."

"And your mon is going to help me wed off some of the others," Sir Malcolm said.

Sitting in his chair at the head of the table, David reached out to take Tatha's hand. "I will introduce them to some fine unwed gentlemen. Ones who dinnae have one foot in the grave," he added with a sly glance at her father. " 'Twill be up to them after that."

For a while they talked of the battle with Sir Ranald. Tatha told them all the man had confessed to her. Then David and her father got into an amiable argument about which one of them had the most right to try to lay claim to Sir Ranald's lands. She realized that at some time during her rescue, David and her father had become almost friends. It even appeared that David had looked closely and understood that the gruff, blunt exterior of her father hid, if not a truly loving nature, at least kindness.

The arrival of Leith and Elspeth ended the discussion of lands. The couple held hands and blushed as they reached the table. Their blushes deepened when

Sir Malcolm grunted and awkwardly patted both young people on the shoulder.

"So there will be two weddings?" Sir Malcolm asked.

"Aye, Papa," replied Elspeth.

"Good. Good. Now ye will be his problem."

"Aye, I will, and I intend to be a verra big one."

"That's my lass. Always do your best. Douglas, move yourself and fetch the priest."

All of Tatha's doubts and concerns returned in full strength as she and David knelt before the priest. She tried to judge what David felt by the way he said his vows, then by the way he kissed her after they were made, but it only made her head hurt. Tatha was relieved when he led her away from the increasingly boisterous celebration early. She suspected the reticence the guests showed, their comments tempered, nearly polite, was because she had so obviously been through an ordeal. She hoped Leith and Elspeth did not have to suffer any extra tormenting because of it.

Once in their room, David helped her undress and slip on her night shift. They crawled into the bed and he held her close. His kisses and the way he gently stroked her told Tatha that he was not going to demand anything of her tonight.

" 'Tis our wedding night," she said as she caressed his chest.

"Aye, but I can wait. Nay long," he said teasingly, "but at least until ye dinnae ache so badly."

"I think the time in the dungeon made me too weak to fight the fool off," she murmured, touching a kiss to his chest and feeling him tremble.

"Ye should ne'er have left, Tatha."

"I had to. My being here was tying your hands. Ye couldnae act as ye had to because all would question it as long as I was in your bed. How did ye get my father here?"

"I told him the truth. He isnae as hard as I thought."

"Nay, he isnae a bad mon. I may have erred in thinking I couldnae talk him out of the wedding he had arranged, but I fear I could think of naught but running when I heard Sir Ranald's name."

"Weel, it was foolish, as I think your father would have listened. I believe he simply doesnae ken how to show what he feels. Mayhap he was ne'er shown. He also seems to have a wee bit of difficulty understanding how others may feel about what he does or says. Howbeit, the moment he truly suspected ye were in danger he was here, armed and ready to fetch ye back. And he could see that Leith and Elspeth were besotted and gave little argument to a wedding."

"Aye, the truth is in how he acts, nay in what he says. Did he force ye to wed me, David?" she asked softly.

"Nay, lass." He tilted her face up to his and brushed a kiss over her mouth. "I wanted ye. In truth, I had long ago decided to wed ye, but there were a few matters that needed tending to first."

"Ye ne'er said."

"I ken it, and I should have. In truth, there was many a thing I should have said, and when I thought ye may be lost to me the words burned a hole in my gullet." He touched a kiss to her small, straight nose. "Ye are mine, lass. That has been the way of it since the day ye rode up to my gates, but I was fool enough nay to see it. The thought that I might ne'er be able to hold ye again left me cold and empty."

"Oh, David," she whispered, and then hugged him. "I do love ye." She frowned when he tensed.

"Ye love me?"

"Aye, but I willnae trouble ye about it—" she began, then found herself being heartily kissed.

"Idiot. I was about to tell ye that I love you." He smiled when her eyes filled with tears, then lightly kissed away the one that trickled down her cheek. "That wasnae supposed to make ye cry."

"Happiness can bring a woman to tears." She slipped her hand down to his taut stomach. "Do ye ken, I really dinnae ache that badly. Perhaps, if ye werenae too vigorous—"

David laughed and tugged off her night shift. "That could prove a verra great challenge."

Later, as she lay contentedly curled up in his arms, she decided he had more than adequately met that challenge. His lovemaking had been gentle, yet so filled with love that she had cried. Tatha smiled and wiped the last of the tears from her cheeks. She felt the warmth of his lips brush over her forehead and looked up at him.

"There is one thing I should like to do, David, if ye will allow it?"

He smiled down at her. "What?"

"I wish to go to the well," she said, watching him warily.

"Tonight?"

"Aye. I ken such things make ye uneasy, but I wish to bless our marriage at the well. 'Tis what pulled me here. 'Tis what brought us together. And although I am ne'er sure how much of the old ways are to be believed, I just feel, weel, compelled to go to the well tonight."

"Then we shall," he said, and got up, glancing her

way as they both began to dress. "Just what are we going to do when we get there?"

After yanking on her shoes, Tatha went to the small chest that held her things. She pulled out a small, finely wrought silver wedding cup. "We will share a drink of the water."

"Dinnae look so wary, lass. Aye, I may ne'er believe there is anything special about the well, but it was important to all the women in my family and 'tis important to you." He held out his hand. "Come, let us go and do homage to it then. It will be, in a small way, as if I speak to my mother. 'Twould be verra fine if she could see how happy her son is."

They crept out of the tower house and, careful to avoid being seen by any of the guests or the servants, made their way to the well. David watched as Tatha smoothed her hands over the cool white stone, then filled the wedding cup with water from the well. He frowned slightly when she bent to touch the letters carved into the side of the well.

"The promise?" he murmured as he took the cup when she held it out to him.

"Aye. It promises protection, strength, and happiness." She smiled when he drank from the cup, and then she did the same. "In you, David Ruthven, I have found all three."

He pulled her into his arms and kissed her. "And I in you, my love." He smiled crookedly and glanced at the well, its white stone gleaming silver in the moonlight. "Mayhap the women of my family werenae so mad after all. There may indeed be magic in that well."

"I have no doubt about it. It gave me you."